MW00781002

G

is for

Gerrold

David Gerrold

"Pickled Mongoose" copyright © 1994 by David Gerrold
"With A Finger In My Eye" copyright © 1972 by David Gerrold
"The Patient Dragon" copyright © 2017 by David Gerrold
"Enterprise Fish" copyright © 2008 by David Gerrold
"The White Piano" copyright © 2015 by David Gerrold
"Endless City" copyright © 2018 by David Gerrold
"The Further Adventures of Mister Costello" copyright © 2016 by David Gerrold
"The Bag Lady" copyright © 2015 by David Gerrold
"Bubble And Squeak" copyright © 2018 by David Gerrold & ctein
"Burning Blue" copyright © 2022 by David Gerrold (First Publication Here)
"The Ones Who Walk Away" copyright © 2021 by David Gerrold
"The Firebringers" copyright © 1993 by David Gerrold

Introduction and collection copyright © 2022 by David Gerrold. All rights reserved.
Cover illustration and design by David Gerrold and Glenn Hauman
Interior design by ComicMix Pro Services
www.comicmix.com/pro-services

ISBN 978-1-958482-00-1 hardcover
ISBN 978-1-958482-01-8 tradepaper

All rights reserved. No part of this book may be used or reproduced in any
manner whatsoever without written permission except in the case of brief
quotations embodied in critical articles and reviews.

For information address
David Gerrold at his official website:
www.gerrold.com

First edition

For Karen Malcor-Chapman
with all my love.

CONTENTS

INTRODUCTION

We read stories to experience other lives. If we read ambitious stories, we get stretched. We learn things. Sometimes we laugh, sometimes we cry, and sometimes we get angry. Sometimes we just feel good that we've been someplace worth the trip. And sometimes — sometimes we grow. Sometimes we stumble into a disturbing bit of empathy that sticks with us for the rest of our lives. Those are the very best kinds of stories.

Those are the kinds of stories I aspire to write. I don't always get there, but the ambition is there every time I sit down at the keyboard. Here are some of those efforts.

With A Finger In My I was first published in Harlan Ellison's *Again, Dangerous Visions* anthology. It was one of my very first sales. In his introduction, Harlan mocked the story he rejected—but that story, *In The Deadlands* ended up on the Nebula ballot and Harlan later admitted that he should have bought it instead. This one, however, was a breakthrough story for me. What had started as bit of silliness, an image from an odd dream, soon turned into a descent into surreal weirdness. Consider it an appetizer for everything that follows—or perhaps a warning that I shouldn't be trusted near a keyboard.

The Firebringers was written for a Mike Resnick anthology, Alternate Warriors. I began it as a satirical exercise, but by the time I got to the end, a some serious thought had crept in. It worked for me when I wrote it, but it's possible that readers who don't love old movies might miss the resonance.

One night in 1993, after tucking my son into bed, I sat down at my keyboard and started writing about our adventures together and how much I had fallen in love with him. *The Martian Child* was the result. I didn't know if it worked—but Kristine Katherine Rusch took a chance on it for *The Magazine of Fantasy & Science Fiction*. It turned out to be a good move. The story won a Hugo, a Nebula, and a Locus award. Later, I was invited to expand it into a novel. The *Pickled* Mongoose sequence is a true story and it shares a moment of true transformation.

Back in the 50s, Theodore Sturgeon got angry at the political machinations of Senator Joseph McCarthy. H.L. Gold, then editor of Galaxy Science Fiction told him to write his anger in a story. The result was "Mister Costello, Hero." It's an unforgettable little gem, and it stuck in my mind indelibly. So when this idea occurred to me, I asked the Sturgeon estate if I could write it as a sequel. They said yes, and the result was *The Further Adventures Of Mister Costello*. It was a challenge to see if I could have all the different layers in the story work together.

One night, I had a dream that was almost scary—an image of a ghostly figure at the end of a long hallway. I hadn't been planning to write a ghost story, and for a little while, I had no idea where this was going. Sometimes I have to keep typing to find out. *The White Piano* let me explore an overlooked moment in history. It was an adventure in time and place.

Endless City was a stretch, an attempt to write a cyberpunk mystery. It was my first sale to *Analog Science Fiction* and came in second in the annual readers' poll. It demands a sequel. Maybe one day.

One of the greatest stories in the entire genre is Ursula K. Le Guin's astonishing *The Ones Who Walk Away From Omelas*. If you've read it, you know it. If you haven't read it, put this book down and go find a copy immediately. That story asks a question that is intended to disturb the reader — and it bothered me for years. I wanted closure. One day, something crystallized in my thinking. I realized what bothered me and I had to write *The Ones Who Walk Away From The Ones Who Walk Away*.

Several decades ago, George R.R. Martin invited me to participate in the *Wild Cards* anthology. I said I would write about a superhero called *The Bag Lady*. But I could never come up with the story—until decades later, flying home from a convention in Canada, I popped open my laptop and started typing. An hour later, the story was complete and finished. I closed the laptop, put it back in the case, and relaxed for the rest of the flight. It's not a feel-good story. Sometimes heroism has a price.

Yes, I am working on *The War Against The Chtorr*. I do intend to finish it, but I keep discovering new pices of the story, so I keep writing chapters ahead. Here's one of those chapters — *Enterprise Fish*.

I grew up with science fiction that had at least one foot firmly rooted in hard science. That has always been my favorite flavor of SF—especially where competent human beings demonstrate they will not be messed with. There are stories in that subgenre that I want to read, but nobody else is writing them, so I have to. *The Patient Dragon* is one of those.

One of my favorite people is a fellow named Ctein, an expert in digital photography and restoration—a few years ago, we got the idea of collaborating on a disaster novel, *Ripple Effect*. He wrote his sections and I polished them. I wrote my sections and he polished them, so it was a good collaboration. Two of the pieces I wrote were published in *Asimov's Science Fiction*. *Bubble And Squeak* won the readers' poll for that year. Parts of it are sweet, parts of it are harrowing. And this is why I live far inland.

And finally, *Burning Blue*. It's a short and fitting finale for this collection. There's not much I need to say about it. This story speaks for itself, as well as for the author.

As I said at the beginning, we read stories to experience other lives. If we read ambitious stories, we get stretched. But there's the rest of that thought — those stories don't just stretch the reader, they demand that the writer stretch as well.

Each of these stories was a stretch for me. I hope they stretch you too.

—David Gerrold
May 2022

WITH A FINGER IN MY I

When I looked in the mirror this morning, the pupil was gone from my left eye. Most of the iris had disappeared too. There was just a blank white area and a greasy smudge to indicate where the iris had previously been.

At first I thought it had something to do with the contact lenses, but then I realized that I don't wear lenses. I never have.

It looked kind of odd, that one blank eye staring back at me, but the unsettling thing about it was that I could still see out of it. When I put my hand over my good right eye, I found that the eyesight in my left was as good as ever, and it concerned me.

If I hadn't been able to see out of it, I wouldn't have worried. It would have meant only that during the night I had gone blind in that eye. But for the pupil of the eye to just fade away without affecting my sight at all—well, it bothered me. It could be a symptom of something serious.

Of course, I thought about calling the doctor, but I didn't know any doctors, and I felt a little bit embarrassed about troubling a perfect stranger with my problems. But there was that eye and it kept staring at me, so finally I went looking for the phone book.

Only, the phone book seemed to have disappeared during the night. I had been using it to prop up one end of the bookshelf, and now it was gone. So was the bookshelf—I began to wonder if perhaps I had been robbed.

First my eye, then the phone book, now my bookshelf had all disappeared. If it had not been that today was Tuesday, I should have been worried. In fact, I was already worried, but Tuesday is my day to ponder all the might-have-been that had become never-wases. Monday is my day to worry about personal effects (such as eyes and phone books) and Monday would not be back for six days. I was throwing myself off schedule by worrying on a Tuesday. When Monday returned, then I would worry about the phone book, if I didn't have something else of a more pressing nature to worry about first.

(I find that pigeonholing my worrying like that helps me to keep an orderly mind—by allotting only so much time to each problem I am able to keep the world in its proper perspective.) But there was still the matter of the eye, and that was upsetting me. Moreover, it was *distorting* my perspective.

I resolved to do something about it immediately I set out in search of the phone, but somewhere along the way that too had disappeared, so I was forced to abandon that exploration.

It was very frustrating—this distressing habit of disappearing that the inanimate objects had picked up. Every time I started to look for something, I found that it had vanished, as if daring me to find it. It was like playing hide-and-go-seek, and since I had long ago given up such childish pastimes, I resolved not to encourage them any further and refused to look for them any more. (Let them come to me.)

I decided that I would walk to the doctor. (I would have put on my cap, but that would have meant looking for it, and I was afraid that it too would have disappeared by the time I found it)

Once outside, I noticed that people were staring at me in a strange way as they passed. I realized that it must be my eye. I had forgotten about it, not realizing that it might look a bit strange to others.

I started to turn around to go back for my sunglasses, but I knew that if I started to look for them, they too would surely disappear. So I turned around and headed once again for the doctor's.

"Let them come to me," I muttered, thinking of the sunglasses. I must have startled the old lady I was passing at the time because she turned to stare at me in a most peculiar manner.

I shoved my hands into my coat pockets and pushed onward. Almost immediately I felt something hard and flat in my left-hand pocket. It was my sunglasses in their case. They had indeed come to me. It was rewarding to see that I was still the master of the inanimate objects in my life:

I took the glasses out and put them on, only to find that the left lens of the glasses had faded to a milky white. It matched my eye perfectly, but I found that, unlike my eye, I was quite unable to see through the opaqued lens. I would just have to ignore the stares of passersby and proceed directly on to the doctor's office.

After a bit, however, I realized that I did not know where I was going—as I noted earlier, I did not know any doctors. And I most certainly knew that if I started to search for the office of one, I would probably never find if at all. So I stood on the sidewalk and muttered to myself, "Let them come to me."

I must confess that I was a little bit leery of this procedure—remembering what had happened with the sunglasses—but in truth, I had no alternative. When I turned around I saw a sign on the building behind me. It said, "Medical Center." So I went in.

I walked up to the receptionist, and I looked at her. She looked at me. She looked me right in the eye (the left one) and said, "Yes, what can we do for you?"

I said, "I would like to see a doctor."

"Certainly," she said. "There goes one down the hall now. If you look quickly, you can catch a glimpse of him. See! there he goes!"

I looked and she was right—there *was* a doctor going down the hall. I could see him myself. I knew he was a doctor because he was wearing golf shoes and a sweater;

then he disappeared around a bend in the corridor. I turned back to the girl. "That wasn't exactly what I meant, I said.

"Well, what was it you meant?"

I said, "I would like for a doctor to look at me." "Oh," she said. "Why didn't you say so in the first place?"

"I thought I did," I said, but very softly.

"No, you didn't," she said. "And speak up. I can hardly hear you." She picked up her microphone and spoke into it. "Dr. Gibbon, puh-lease come to reception...." Then she put down her microphone and looked at me expectantly.

I did not say anything. I waited. After a moment, another man in golf shoes and sweater came out of one of the nearby doors and walked over to us. He looked at the girl behind the desk, and she said to him, "This gentleman would like a doctor to look at him."

The doctor took a step back and looked at me. He looked me up and down, then asked me to turn around and he looked at me some more. Then he said, "Okay," and walked back into his office.

1 asked, "Is that all?"

She said, "Of course, that's all. That's all you asked for. That will be ten dollars please."

"Wait a minute," I said. "I wanted him to look at my eye."

"Well," she said, "you should have said so in the first place. You know we're very busy here. We haven't got time to keep calling doctors down here to look at just anyone who wanders in. If you had wanted him to look at your eye in particular, you should have said so."

"But I don't want someone to just look at my eye." I said. "I want someone to cure it."

"Why?" She said. "Is there something wrong with it?"

I said, "Can't you see? The pupil has disappeared."

"Oh," she said. "So it has. Did you look for it?"

"Yes, I did. I looked all over for it—that's probably why I can't find it."

"Maybe you left it somewhere," she cooed softly. "Where was the last place you were?"

"I wasn't anywhere," I said.

"Well, maybe that's your trouble."

"I meant that I stayed home last night. I didn't go anywhere! And I don't feel very well."

"You don't look very well," she, said. "You should see a doctor."

"I already have," I said. "He went down that hall."

"Oh, that's right I remember now."

"Look," I said. I was starting to get a little angry. "Will you please get me an appointment with a doctor?"

"Is that what you want an *appointment?*"

"Yes, that is what I want."

"You're sure that's *all* you want now? You're not going to come back later and complain that we didn't give you what you want?"

"I'm, sure," I said. "I'm not going to come back."

"Good. That's what we want to be sure of."

By now, everything seemed to be all wrong. The whole world seemed to be slipping off sideways—all squished together and stretched out and tilted so that everything was sliding down towards the edge. So far, nothing had gone over, but I thought I could see tiny cracks appearing in the surface.

I shook my head to clear it, but all that did was produce a very distinct rattling noise—like a very small walnut in a very large shell.

I sat down on the couch to wait—I was still unable to think clearly. The fog swirled in thicker than ever, obscuring everything. Visibility had been reduced to zero, and the controllers were threatening to close down all operations until the ceiling lifted. I protested, no—wasn't the ceiling all right where it was?—but they just ignored me.

I stood up then and tried to push the ceiling back by hand, but I couldn't reach it and had to stand on a chair. Even then, the surface of it was hard and unyielding. (Although I was close enough to see that there were numerous cracks and flaws in it.)

I started to push on it again, but a strong hand on my shoulder and a deep voice stopped me. "Lay down on the couch," she said. "Just close your eyes. Relax. Lie back and relax."

"All right," I said, but I did not lie on my back. I lay on my stomach and pressed my face into the hard unyielding surface.

"Relax," she said again..

"I'll try," I said, forcing myself.

"Look out the window," the doctor said. "What do you see?'

"I see clouds," I said.

"What kind?"

"What kind???"

"Yes. What kind?"

I looked again. "Cottage cheese clouds. Little scuds of cottage cheese clouds." _

"Cottage cheese clouds—?" asked the doctor.

"Yes," I said. "Cottage cheese clouds. Hard and unyielding."

"Large curd or small curd?"

"Huh?" I asked. I rolled over and looked at her. She did not have on golf shoes, but she was wearing a sweater. Instead of the golf shoes, she had on high heels. But she was a doctor—I could tell that. Her shoes still had cleats.

"I asked you a question," she rumbled in that deep voice of hers.

"Yes, you did." I agreed. "Would you mind repeating .it?"

"No, I wouldn't mind," she said and waited quietly. I waited also. For a moment there was silence between us. I pushed the silence to one side and asked, "Well, what was it?"

"I asked whether the clouds were large curd or small curd."

"I give up," I said. "What were they?"

"That's very good of you to give up—otherwise we'd have had to come in after you and take you by force. By surrendering your misconceptions now you've made it so much easier for both of us."

The whole thing was coming disjointed and teetered precariously on the edge. Bigger cracks were beginning to appear in the image, and tiny pieces were starting to slip out and fall slowly to the ground where they shattered like so many soap bubbles.

"Uh—" I said. "Uh, Doctor—there's something wrong with my eye."

"Your I?

"Uh, yes. The pupil is gone."

"The pupil is gone from your I?" The doctor was astounded. "How astounding!"

I could only nod—so I did. (A bit too hard perhaps. A few more pieces came flaking off and fluttered gently to the floor. We watched for a moment.)

"Hm," she said. "I have a theory about that. Would you like to hear it?"

I didn't answer. She was going to tell me her theory whether I wanted to hear it or not.

"The world is coming to an end," she whispered conspiratorially.

"Right now?" I asked, somewhat worriedly. I still hadn't fed the cat.

"No, but soon," she reassured me.

"Oh," I said.

We sat there in silence. After a bit, she cleared her throat. "I think…" she began slowly, then she trailed off.

"That's nice," I said, but she didn't hear me.

"… I think that the world exists only as a reflection of our minds. It exists the way it does only because that's the way we think it does."

"*I* think—therefore *I* exist," I said. But she ignored me. She told me to be quiet.

"Yes, you exist," she confirmed. (I'm glad she did—I was beginning to be a bit worried—and this was the wrong day for it. The last time I looked this was Tuesday.) "You exist," she said, "because you think you do. And the world also exists because you think it does. "

"Then, when I die—the world ends with me …?" I asked hopefully, making a mental note not to die.

"No—that's nonsense. No sane and rational man believes in solipsism." She scratched at her eyeball with a fork and went on.

"When you die—*you* cease to exist," she said. "But the world goes on—it goes on because everybody else who's still alive still believes that it exists. (The only thing they've stopped believing in is you.) You see, the world is a collective figment of all of our individual imaginations."

"I'm sorry," I said stiffly. "I do not believe in collectivism." I unbent a little so as to sit up. "I am a staunch Republican."

"Don't you see?" she said, ignoring my interruption. "This mass hallucination that the world is real just keeps on going because of its own momentum. You believe in it because that's the way it was when you first began to exist—that is, when everybody else first began to believe you existed. When you were born, you saw that the world followed a certain set of rules that other people believed in, so you believed in them too—the fact that you believe in them just gives them that much more strength."

"Oh," I said. I lay there listening to her, trying to figure out some way to leave gracefully. My eye was starting to hurt, and I couldn't see the ceiling any more. The fog was rolling in again.

"Look at the church!" she said suddenly. "Huh?" I said.

"Look at the church!" she said it again, insistent.

I tried to. I lifted my head and tried to look at the church, but the fog was too thick. I couldn't even see my toes.

"Look at it, she said. "*Faith* is the basic precept of religion—faith that what they're telling you is true! Don't they tell you to have faith in the church, that faith can work miracles?!! Well, I'll tell you something—it can! If enough people believe in something, it becomes reality!"

By now, my eye was throbbing most painfully. I tried to sit up, but her strong hands held me back. She leaned closer and whispered intensely, "Yes! It's true. It is."

"If you say so," I nodded.

She went on. "Fortunately, the church long ago abandoned miracles in favor of conservatism—now, it's fighting to preserve the status quo! 'The church is one of the last bastions of reality—it's one of the few things holding back chaos!"

"Chaos?"

"Yes, chaos."

"Oh."

"The world is changing," she explained. "Man is changing it."

I nodded. "Yes, I know. I read the newspapers too."

"No, no! That's not what I meant! Man is changing his world unconsciously! More and more people are starting to believe that they really can change, their environment—and the more they believe it, the more drastically it changes. I'll give you an example—fossils!"

"Fossils?"

"Yes, fossils. Nobody ever discovered any fossils until people started believing in evolution—then when they did start to believe in it, you couldn't turn around without tripping over fossils."

"You really believe this?" I asked.

"Yes, I do!" she said intensely.

"Then it must be so," I said.

"Oh, it is," she agreed, and I knew that she really did believe it. She made a very convincing case. In fact, the more she talked, the more I began to believe it too.

"Why did you tell me all this?" I asked.

"Because we're in great danger. That's why." She whispered fiercely, "The world isn't changing uniformly. Everybody is starting to believe in different things, and they're forming pockets of non-causality."

"Like a pimple?" I offered.

"Yes," she said, and I could see a small one forming on the tip of her nose. "It works this way: A fanatic meets another fanatic, then the two of them meet with some other people who share the same hallucinations, and pretty soon there are a whole bunch of fanatics all believing the same thing—pretty soon, their delusions become real for them—they've started to contradict the known reality and replaced it with a node of non-reality."

I nodded and concentrated on wrapping a swirl of the fog securely around me.

"The more it changes, the more people believe in the changes, and the stronger they become. If this keeps up, we may be the only sane people left in the world—and we're in danger—"

"They're outnumbering our reality?" I suggested.

"Worse than that—all of their different outlooks area starting to flaw the structure of space! Even the shape of the Earth is changing! Why, at one time, it was really flat—the world didn't turn round until people started, to believe it was round."

I turned round then and. looked at her, but she had disappeared into the fog. All that was left was her grin.

"But the world is really pear-shaped," I said. "I read it in *Scientific American.*"

"And why do you think it's changing shape?" the grin asked. "It's because a certain nation is starting to believe that it's really bigger than it is. The Earth is bulging out to accommodate them."

"Oh," I said.

"It's the fault of the news media—television is influencing our image of the world! They keep telling us that the world is changing—and more and more people keep believing it."

"Well," I said. "With the shape of the world the way it is today, any change has got to be for the—"

"Oh, God not you too! All you people keep talking about the world going to pieces—falling apart at the seams"

And then even the grin was gone.

I was left there. I was also right. Other people had begun to notice it too. Great chunks of the surface *had* gone blotchy, and holes had appeared in it. More and more pieces were falling out all the time, but the waters had not yet broken through from the other side.

I poked my finger through one of the holes, and I could feel the soft gelatinous surface behind. Perhaps it hadn't thawed completely out yet.

So far, nothing had been accomplished about my eye—not only was it beginning to ache something fierce, but my I was beginning to twinge a bit also, and I had a feeling that that too might be going opaque.

"Have you found yourself yet?!" one of the speakers in the park demanded. (I hadn't even looked—and remembering my previous experiences with looking for things, I certainly was not going to initiate any kind of a search.) I walked on.

Farther on, there was, another speaker—this one on a soup box. "We should be thankful for this great nation of ours," the speaker woofed and tweetered, "where so many people are allowed to believe in so many different things."

I rubbed at my eye. I had an uneasy queasy feeling that great cracks were opening in the ceiling.

"Anyone can get up and speak for his cause—any group can believe in anything they choose—indeed we can remake the world if we want too! And in our own images!"

Things were teetering right and left—also write and wrong.

"But the truly great thing about it," he continued, "is that no matter how much we contradict each other, we are all working together for the common good! Our great democratic system lets us maximize our differences so that we can all compromise ourselves. Only by suggesting all the alternatives to a problem can we select the best possible solution. In the long run, this ultimate freedom and individuality will help all of us to achieve the most good for the most people!"

It sounded good to me.

When I got home, the workmen were just finishing with the wallpaper. It was amazing how solid the surface looked once all the cracks and flaws in it had been covered with a gaudy flowered facade.

I could no longer tell where the plaster had given way—and the bare surface of the understructure had disappeared into the fog. Indeed, the only thing was that the ceiling seemed to be much lower than before.

I paused long enough to stroke the cat. He waved as I came in. "Hey, man," said the cat. "Give me a J."

"I can't. I'm having trouble with my I."

"Well, then give me a dollar."

"What for?"

"For a trip," he said.

"Oh." I gave him a dollar, waited for the trip.

He dropped the bill into his mouth, lit it, picked up his suitcase and quickly rose to a cruising level of thirty thousand feet. Then he headed west. I did not quite understand this. The fog had gotten much worse, and the—controllers were not letting any traffic through. There had been something I had wanted to ask, but I had forgotten it. Oh, well—it couldn't have been very important. But I wish I could figure out—

The man on the TV was a Doctor. He sat on top of it with his feet dangling in front of the screen (his cleats were scratching the image) and said that the drugs were destroying the realities. Drugs could destroy a person's sanity by altering his perceptions of the world until he could no longer perceive reality at all.

"Just so long as it doesn't change what he believes in," I muttered and turned him off. Then I turned him out. It was getting late and I wanted to get some sleep. However, I did make a mental note not to have my prescription refilled. Already the wallpaper was peeling.

In fact, by now, only the framework of the structure is left, and it looks like it's made out of chocolate pudding. Maybe it is. Perhaps it *is* the drugs. Maybe they *are* altering our collective fogments—but I haven't noticed anything.

If real life was as heroic as the movies, we wouldn't need the movies.

THE FIREBRINGERS

The gunners, Taylor and Johnson, stood apart by themselves, whispering about something. I wondered if they were going to take their traditional good-luck piss under the tail of the plane before take-off. Would they even dare with all the guards looking on and all the brass who were supposed to be here? The rest of us stood around under the plane like we always did, smoking, worrying, and pretending not to care.

There were twenty armed marines spaced in a circle around the plane, so most of us in the crew stayed close to the boarding hatch and kept our eyes averted from their weapons. We weren't sure we appreciated the honor. Were the guards there to keep everyone else out—or us in?

We looked from one to the other and traded lights off each other's cigarettes. We talked about whisky, poker, women we had known, chocolate, beer, cigarettes, everything but what really counted. Our terror.

Meanwhile, the fog kept rolling in. It was so thick that even the specially outfit-ted B-32 above us was only a darker shape in the gloom. The ground crew would be putting out flares all the length of the runway. If we went. I was beginning to wonder. The case under my arm, with all my weather charts and maps was getting heavy. I didn't know if I wanted to go or not. I didn't want my work to be wasted. On the other hand....

The sound of an engine was followed by the ruddy glare of headlights, and then three trucks came rolling up to the belly of the ship. The middle one had a flat bed, with a tarp-covered shape clamped securely into place. The other two trucks were hooded and carried more armed marines. They spilled out of their vehicles in silence and quickly formed a secure circle around the loading operation.

Ollie, one of the two ordinance officers, climbed out of the shotgun side of the second truck and began gently cooing instructions to the bomb crew; he was so polite it was eerie. The scuttlebutt was that you could roll a Jeep over his foot and he wouldn't even say ouch. He was a corpulent man, but he moved like a dancer—and he was scrupulous about the loading, watching over every move like a mother hen with a single egg. He demanded precision and delicacy. Before the war, he and his partner, Stan, had been piano movers. Stanley was the quiet one. Once we were in the air, they'd actually arm the device.

Bogey, the bombardier, chewed an unlit stogie and looked skeptical. He'd had that stogie since the war started and he wasn't going to light it until he was sure he could get another one to replace it. He held a couple of steel ball-bearings in his right

15

hand, which he rotated nervously while he waited. Despite our incessant drilling and practicing and studying, Bogey remained outspokenly skeptical. He was only going along for the ride, he said. After the war, he was going to reopen his gambling salon in Morocco. Uh-huh. Most of us didn't believe he'd ever been further east than the Brooklyn Bridge. But it was his finger on the button. He'd look through the Norden bombsight, he'd press the release when the moment came. Maybe his tough-guy attitude was his way of not letting himself think about it too much.

While we watched, the bomb crew lowered specially designed clamps from the plane and attached them to matching hooks on the bomb, then they locked each one carefully into place, with two men checking each clamp. The clamps wouldn't be unlocked until just before release. They handed one set of keys to Lt. Bogart. The other set of keys would be given to Colonel Peck.

As soon as the last clamp was secured, they began the arduous and delicate process of hoisting the bomb up into the belly of the ship. The chains began to clank. The slack was taken up, there was a hesitation, and then the vehicle eased itself and sighed as the weight was lifted away. Simultaneously, the plane *groaned*. We could hear its back straining. That baby was *heavy*.

Slowly, slowly the bomb rose up, hanging precariously in the space between us. We watched its studied ascent with a mixture of curiosity and fear. We had all seen the test in Nevada. We were still dazed by the memory of that white-flashing roar of heat and wind. We were terrified what it would do to a city. White-faced, Jaeckel had screamed to Bogey, "Holy smokes! What is that?" Bogey had answered grimly, "It's the stuff that screams are made of."

Even now, it was still difficult to believe that so much destructive power could be contained in this solid black cylinder. Someone had written in bold white chalk on the side, "Heil *this*!" But as it rose, I saw that someone else had carefully inscribed in bright yellow paint: "*Sh'ma Yisrael, Adonai Elohainu Adonai Ehod.*" Beside it was a list of names—the men who had actually designed and built the bomb. I'd heard there had been quite a fight about the prayer and the names; but apparently Dr. Karloff and Dr. Lorre had told General Tracy, "No prayer, no names—no bomb." I couldn't imagine "Spence the Fence" saying no to either one of those two grand old gentlemen, and I was glad he hadn't.

But there were a lot of rumors floating around. We weren't supposed to repeat them, but we did anyway. We'd heard that Dr. Lugosi was already designing a more powerful bomb. We'd heard that Dr. Karloff was having second thoughts, that he'd written to the President and asked him to demonstrate the bomb on an uninhabited island so the Axis nations could see its power before we actually used it on a city. Rumor had it that Secretary of War Capra had advised against that as "too humanitarian." We needed to hurt the enemy *hard*—so hard that the war would come to a screeching halt.

President Cooper never said what he was thinking throughout the entire debate, but when the question was finally asked, he simply issued his characteristic "Yup" and that was the end of that. The prayer on the side of the bomb probably represented a compromise.

It bothered me. I understood—at least I thought I did—the urge behind it; but at the same time, I didn't think a bomb, and certainly not *this* bomb, was the right place to paint a prayer of any kind. But then again, I wasn't Jewish. I wondered how I'd feel about it if I were.

All of us were volunteers. At the beginning, we hadn't known what we were volunteering for, only that it was dangerous and important. Then they'd taken us out to Nevada and shown us. We were going to end the war. We were going to obliterate a city. We were going to kill a hundred thousand people in a brilliant bright flash of light.

We had dark goggles to protect our eyes. And radiation meters. Jaeckel, the new kid, would have the best view of all. He was the belly-gunner. He'd been issued a 16mm Bolex loaded with special Eastman-color film. He was supposed to photograph everything we saw. He was excited about the opportunity, even though it meant he had to wear lead-foil underwear.

And then, the bomb was secured and the trucks were rolling away. We still hadn't seen Colonel Peck. Or Colonel Reagan, our co-pilot, either. And the fog wasn't clearing up. Worse, it was getting thicker. My shirt collar was sticking damply to my neck. I checked my watch. So far, we were still on schedule, but time was tight. If we were going to get in the air at all this morning, it would have to be soon.

I was pretty sure that Colonel Peck was uneasy about the mission. I knew him too well, all his mannerisms. He'd been brooding about this ever since Nevada. And the closer we got to take-off, the more irritable he'd become. He kept ordering me to check the maps, over and over, plotting alternate courses, fuel consumption figures, alternate targets, everything. His tension was infectious. None of us were happy.

And now this. A morning so gloomy it felt like twilight. Could we even get off the ground?

We stood around underneath the plane, an uncomfortable clump of men in baggy flight-suits, and listened to the awful stillness of the fog. Far away sounds were simply swallowed up. Nearby sounds were amplified. Lieutenant Hope—I was suddenly struck by the irony of his name—wouldn't shut up. Even when I moved away to the other side of the bird, I could still hear his inane little jokes. "This is Bob 'fogged-in' Hope calling anybody. Is anybody out there? Say, did you guys hear the one about the leprechaun and the penguin?" There were groans and a *thump* as somebody hit him with a parachute. "Don't worry about me, fellas," he said, climbing back to his feet. "I'm goin' home after this. I'm not spending *my* Christmas with the army."

A chorus of hoots and catcalls greeted this response. I turned away in annoyance and saw the headlights coming out of the fog. I stubbed out my cigarette and called out, "Ten-*hut!*" The crew snapped to attention where they stood.

Generals Gable and Donleavy climbed out of the Jeep. Colonel Peck and Colonel Reagan climbed out after them, followed by the new sky-pilot. "At ease," said General Donleavy; he looked unhappy. General Gable stepped forward and spoke gruffly. "I just wanted to come out here myself and...wish you godspeed. I know some of you have been having second thoughts about this. I don't blame you. I would too. I've been having second thoughts about this since the day I was first briefed.

"But I want you to know that despite all my fears and concerns, that I fully support this operation. In fact, *I envy you.* You men are going to save a lot of lives today. If this device works as well as we hope, then millions of young men—on both sides of this terrible war—will not have to meet on the battlefield. You have it in your power today to save millions of lives, both civilian and military, and spare the world years of suffering and destruction. Just keep that thought in mind and you'll do fine." He glanced over at Captain Fonda. "If any of you want to see the chaplain before you take off...."

At first, most of us were too embarrassed, but then Stan and Ollie stepped over to Captain Fonda and bowed their heads. And then Bogey. And Colonel Peck. I followed. And the others came behind me. All except Taylor and Johnson, the skeptics. They strode down to the tail end of the plane and...upheld their military traditions. General Gable glanced over, decided not to say anything, and deliberately turned his back.

Captain Fonda was slim and gentle, almost too gentle for a war. He had a long, lanky way of speaking; the words came softly out of him like honey poured from a jar. He was a different kind of sky-pilot. He didn't talk about God so much as he talked about the spirit of God inside each and every one of us. "You know what's right in the world," he said. "Stand for it. And others will stand with you." It made me feel good to listen to him.

Afterward, I noticed, Jaeckel, the new kid, hung behind and knelt to confess. Captain Fonda made the sign of the cross over him, then helped him back to his feet with a friendly clap on the shoulder. That was what I liked about him; he knew how to be just an ordinary guy.

Colonel Peck collected his keys from Ollie, then the two of them, the pilot and the copilot, walked slowly around the plane, shining flashlights up into the wheel housings and looking for oil leaks under the engines. When they finished, they came back, saluted the Generals and shook their hands; then they ordered the rest of us up into the bomber. From here on out, the responsibility for delivering the device was all ours, nobody else's.

The solemnity of the moment left us all subdued. That plus the unusual circumstances of two generals and a chaplain coming all the way out to the end of the field for our departure. There was none of the usual wiseass chatter as we climbed into our seats, hooked up our oxygen, and buckled our harnesses. We went through our checklists without the usual banter. Even Hope kept his mouth shut for a change. Finally, Colonel Peck started the engines and they clattered explosively to life. They sputtered and smoked and then abruptly caught with a bang. The bird began to vibrate like a 1932 Ford on a rutted road. Colonel Reagan fussed with the fuel mixture to compensate for all the water vapor in the air.

We rolled out onto the end of the runway and turned into the wind. Colonel Peck closed his eyes for a moment—a silent prayer?—then picked up his microphone and asked the tower for permission to take off. The tower's reply was crisp. "Go with God." It would be our last communication. From here on out, strict radio silence would be observed.

Colonel Peck ran the engines up, louder and louder until the plane was howling like a banshee. He turned in his seat to look at the left wing; Reagan turned to look at the right. Satisfied, they both turned back. Colonel Peck put his hands firmly on the wheel, bit his lip, and let the plane leap forward. I glanced out the front windshield, but all I saw was a gray wall of haze. He had to be steering by the line of flares along the sides of the runway. I glanced out the side window and tried to gauge our speed by the passing red pinpoints. Faster and faster—they leapt out of the gloom ahead of us and vanished into the gloom behind. Colonel Reagan began calling out airspeed numbers.

At first I didn't think we were going to make it into the air. The bird was heavy and the air was thick and wet. The engines weren't happy. The bird was bouncing and buffeting. Colonel Peck must have been having a hell of a time keeping us on the concrete. And the end of the runway had to be getting awfully close...but at the last moment, the Colonel gunned it, grabbed hold of the sky, and pulled us up over the trees—so close, I could feel the branches scraping our belly.

We bounced up through the damn fog, shaking and buffeting and cursing all the way. But the bird held together and at last we climbed up into the clear blue sky above the gray blanket. Suddenly, the warm June sun poured down on us like a welcome smile, filling the plane with lemon-yellow light. The air smoothed out and the bird stopped complaining. Colonel Peck glanced back to me with a smile, I gave him a big thumbs-up.

We were on our way to Germany. And Berlin. And history.

Crossing the channel, we saw some fishing boats. Even in the midst of war, men still cast their nets into the sea to feed their families. I wondered if they looked up and wondered about us in turn. Did they ever think about the planes that crossed back and forth across the channel, and if so, did they wish us well—or did they just resent the burden of the war.

I scribbled notes in the log. Time, position, heading. At the opposite end of the plane, Van Johnson was probably writing another love letter to his fiancee,

June. He wrote one every mission and mailed it as soon as we landed. She wrote back every time she got a letter from him. We teased him about it, but we envied hm the letters and the connection to someone back home.

"Okay, Jimmy," Colonel Peck turned around to me. "What's it going to be? Paris or Amsterdam?"

I pulled out my lucky silver dollar, flipped it, and caught it on the back of my wrist. I lifted my hand away to show him. "Uh—ah—it looks like Paris," I said. I glanced at the compass. "Uh, you wanna come right about—ah, forty degrees, skipper."

This was part of the security around this operation. Once we were in the air, not even the ground stations were supposed to know where we were. We had been instructed to plot three separate courses to the target; we were forbidden to choose our final heading until we were out over the channel, away from all possible ground observers. Of course, all the flight crews knew that there were U-boats in the channel, tracking the comings and goings of all flights, but we didn't worry about it. Much. Colonel Peck and I favored two different courses, Amsterdam and Paris, each named for the city we'd head toward before turning toward Berlin.

Our group had been sending single flights out over the continent for months, spotting troop movements, checking weather conditions, dropping leaflets, taking photos, surveying bomb damage, all that stuff—a lot more flights than we needed to. They were decoys to get the jerries used to the sight of a single Allied plane crossing their skies. Some of the fellows resented the duty. They'd rather have been dropping bombs. Nobody could tell them why their flights were so important, but they were.

We'd flown a lot of the flights too, mostly the missions over Berlin and our secondary targets. In the past week, we'd even made two leaflet drops, dropping the package and then pulling up and away sharply to the right exactly as we would do later today. The leaflets had warned the Berliners to leave the city, because we were going to destroy it. We implied that we'd be sending a thousand planes across the channel, darkening their skies with the roar of engines and the thunder of bombs. We'd heard they were installing ack-ack guns from here to the Rhine and we wondered if they'd test them on us today.

Once, we'd also dropped an agent into Germany. A fellow named Flynn. His job was to contact members of the underground and warn them out of Berlin before the 6th. I wondered where he was now. I hoped he had gotten out. A nice fellow, I guess, but I wouldn't have his job. He'd seemed foolhardy to me.

Colonel Peck glanced at the altimeter, tapped it to make sure it wasn't stuck, and then spoke into his microphone. "All right, Stan, Ollie. We're at cruising altitude. You can start arming the device." He waited for their confirmations, then switched off again.

We'd heard that the Nazis had forbidden the civilian population to flee Berlin, but our intelligence sources were telling us that at least a third of the civilians had evacuated anyway and more were streaming out every day. Even if the bomb failed, we would still have seriously disrupted the economy of the Reich's capital. Most of the overlords of the Reich had already moved themselves away from the city—except for that pompous turnip, Goering. He had publicly boasted that not a single allied bomb would fall on Berlin. I wondered if he would be in Berlin today. I wondered about all the others too. Goebbels, Heydrich, Eichmann, Hess, Himmler, and the loudmouthed little paperhanger. Would they be close enough to see the blast? What would they think? What would they do?

Some of the psych boys said that they believed that Corporal Shickelgruber would sooner die in the holy flames of martyrdom than ever let himself be captured and put on trial for war crimes. Worse, he would take the nation down with him.

If the bomb worked—

Of course it worked. We'd seen it work in Nevada. I couldn't get it out of my head—that terrible mushroom cloud climbing into the morning sky, churning and rising and burning within. It was a preview of Hell. Afterward, we were given the chance to withdraw from the mission. None of us did. Perhaps, if we hadn't already been a crew, some of us would have, I'd have considered it, but I couldn't let the other fellows down. Later, we spent long hours talking among ourselves. If we ended the war, we'd be heroes. But...just as likely, we might be war criminals. Nobody had ever used a bomb like this before.

But never mind that—if the bomb worked the way we wanted it to, we'd paralyze the Third Reich. The armies would stop fighting. The Generals would surrender rather than let their troops be incinerated. Perhaps even they'd overthrow the murderous bastards at the top and save the rest of the world the trouble of hanging them. Perhaps.

And perhaps they'd do something else. Perhaps they'd launch a ferocious counter-attack beyond our abilities to comprehend. Perhaps they'd unleash all the poison gases and deadly germs they were rumored to have stockpiled. Who knew what they'd do if they were scared enough?

But that wasn't our worry. All we had to do was deliver the device. Behind us, taking off at fifteen-minute intervals, thirty other planes would be following; each one equipped with cameras and radiation-detectors. The visible aftermath of this weapon would be on movie screens all over the world within the week.

I tried to imagine what else might be happening today. Probably the French resistance was being signaled to do whatever they could to scramble communications and transportation among the Nazis. Our ambassadors were probably preparing to deliver informative messages to other governments. We'd entered the war in 1939. Everybody expected us to invade Europe before the end of the summer. I wondered if our troops were massing even now to follow us into Germany.

Lieutenant Bogart came forward then with a thermos of coffee. It was his habit to come up to the cockpit for a while before we reached enemy territory. Today, he had more reason than ever. Despite his frequent protestations otherwise, the thought of the bomb in our belly clearly disturbed him as much as the rest of us. Perhaps him more than anybody. He looked burnt and bitter. "Which way are we headed, skipper? We going over Paris?"

Colonel Peck nodded. "It's the long way around, but I want to give Stan and Ollie plenty of time to arm the device."

I looked at Bogey suddenly. There was something odd in his eyes, but I couldn't identify the look. Anger perhaps? Some long-remembered hurt?

"Uh, ahh-h—you've been to Paris?" I asked.

He nodded. "I was there. For a while. Just before the jerries moved in."

"I never made it myself. I always wanted to go, but something always came up. I had to stay home and help Pop with the business."

"After the war is over," Colonel Peck said, "We'll all meet for champagne on the Champs Elysees." He got a wistful look on his face then. "It's one of the most beautiful streets in the world. Lined with cafes and shops and beautiful women. You could spend your days just sitting and sipping coffee. Or you could stuff yourself with mushrooms and fish poached in butter. You could follow it with little thin pancakes filled with thick rich cream. And the wine—we had champagne and caviar on toast so crisp it snapped. I never had a bad meal anywhere in France. They could make even a potato a work of art."

He looked to Bogey for agreement, but the bombardier just shrugged. "I spent most of my time on the left bank, drinking the cheap wine. I didn't get to the same joints you did, Colonel."

"You saw a lot of Europe before the war, skipper?" Reagan asked.

Peck shook his head. "Not as much as I wanted to. But I have good memories." He stared off into the distance as if he were seeing them all again. "I remember the tulip gardens in Copenhagen—so bright they dazzle the eyes. And the dark canals of Amsterdam, circling around the center of the city, all the buildings are so narrow that the staircases are almost like ladders." He shook his head sadly. "I can still taste the thick layered pastries of Vienna. And I remember wandering through the sprawling parks of Rome—do you know there are wild cats living all over the ruins of the Colosseum? They've been there since Caesar's time. And the rumpled hills of Athens, the Parthenon looking down over the city, and ouzo in your belly like licorice fire. Berlin, the beerhalls and the nightclubs. The screech of the trains. The smell of coal. The old opera house. On Sundays, you could go to the afternoon concerts; if you were a student, you paid half price. That's where I first heard Beethoven and

Wagner. What a marvelous dichotomy the Germans represent, that they could produce such sublime music—and such incredible horrors too."

"Uh, ah—you've seen Berlin?" I asked. This was the first time he'd ever admitted it.

Colonel Peck nodded. "A long time ago." His eyes were shaded grimly. "It's a funny old town. When I was there it was full of students and workmen, shopkeepers and grandmothers in babushkas. No one was angry then. The streets were clean and the people were stolid and happy. It was spring and the world was green and fresh and full of butterflies and hope. It was a long time ago, and I was very...young."

Bogey and Reagan exchanged a look then. Worried. Was the Colonel having second thoughts?

Almost as if in answer to their question, Colonel Peck added, "It was the music. I was sure that Berlin had to be the most marvelous city in the world that such incredible music lived there." And then, as if realizing again where he was and what he'd just said, he shook his head grimly. "I've never liked this idea. Bombing a city. Civilians. It's—" He didn't finish the sentence. Instead he reached over and flipped the fuel tank switches. It was time to lighten the left side of the plane for a while.

After a moment, he turned around again and looked at the three of us. First Reagan, then me, then finally Bogey. "All right," he said. "What is it?"

"Ah, uh—are you feeling all right, skipper?"

Colonel Peck nodded with his chin, in that grim way of his. "If you're worrying if I can do the job, stop worrying. This is what we've trained for."

"Right," said Bogey, clapping one hand on the Colonel's shoulder. "We don't need Berlin. We'll always have Paris." I couldn't tell if he was joking or not.

Bogey was the weirdest one in the crew, always saying things that were either bitter jokes or just plain bitter. Colonel Peck wasn't sure what Bogey meant either. He just looked at him sideways for a long moment. The two of them studied each other the way two men do when they first meet, sizing each other up, getting a sense of whether they're going to be friends or enemies.

These two jokers had known each other for a long time, but right now, at this moment, it was as if they'd never really seen each other before. Bogey shifted the cigar from one side of his mouth to the other and grinned fiercely at Peck. Peck's expression relaxed, widened into a matching grin. And then suddenly, we were all grinning and laughing nervously.

"We're starting to take ourselves a little too seriously," said Peck. "Take over, Ronnie, I'm going back to check on the boys." He levered himself out of his seat and climbed past Bogey into the rear of the plane.

We waited until we were sure he was gone. None of us dared speak. Finally, I had to ask it. "Ah, ah—do you fellas think he's gonna be all right?"

Bogey shifted his cigar from one side of his mouth to the other, then back again. "I dunno. I've seen a lot of men do a lot of strange things. When the crunch comes, that's when you find out what a man's made of." He added. "He's got a look in his eye all right."

Reagan didn't say anything for a moment. He looked like he was rehearsing his next words. At last, he said, "I had a private briefing with General Donleavy last night." We waited for him to continue. "He said...he said that if for any reason Colonel Peck was unable to carry out the mission...I was to take over and make sure the device was delivered. I asked him if he thought that was likely. He said no, but...well, the top brass just wanted to cover every possibility, that's all."

"Ah, uh, you can't be serious," I stammered.

"Well, General Donleavy suggested that if I thought I had to do such a thing, I should talk it over with the bombardier and the navigator and maybe the flight engineer. I wouldn't have said anything, but—" He glanced backward.

"Uh—you *can't* do it," I said. "You just can't. The Colonel didn't mean anything by what he said. You saw him. He's just—I mean, anybody'd feel bad having to do this. You would, wouldn't you?" I looked to Bogey, alarmed at the way the conversation was going.

Bogey's expression was dark. "I'm not going to have any trouble dropping this bomb. I've seen the Nazis face-to-face." He looked to Reagan.

"Well," said Reagan. "I guess...a man's gotta do what a man's gotta do."

"Ah, uh, you can't do this, Colonel. You gotta give him a chance. You do this, you'll wreck his career—"

Bogey poked me hard in the shoulder then and I shut up just as Colonel Peck climbed back into the cockpit. If he'd heard anything, he didn't show any sign. He glanced around at us with gentle eyes, and I *knew* he knew.

"All right, men," he said. "Let's talk about it."

"Eh?" said Bogey, blandly. "We don't know what you're talking about."

Peck let out his breath in a sigh, glancing downward while he collected his thoughts. When he met our eyes again, his face was grim. "I wanted to have this talk with you before," he said. "But I realized that there was no safe way to have this talk until we were safely in the air. From here on in, this *thing* is our responsibility. It's up to us. We've been entrusted by our government with the single most important mission of the war. But I want you to think about something for a moment. There is a law that transcends the laws that mere men can make."

I glanced to Bogey, then to Reagan. Bogey's grim smile revealed nothing of what he was thinking. But everything Reagan was feeling was written on his face so clearly, he could have been a neon sign.

Peck saw it. He put his hand across the intervening space and laid it on Reagan's shoulder. "Ronnie, I want you to think about the precedent we're about to set. We'll be validating that it's all right to bomb civilians, to wipe out whole cities. This is the first atomic war. If we do this, it won't be the last. Yes, I've been thinking; maybe the most courageous thing we can do today is *not* drop this bomb. Maybe we should jettison it into the ocean. It'll be three months before the next one is ready. But we could take a stand today, that soldiers of the United States will not kill innocent civilians. And if we did that, our government leaders would have three months to change their minds about using the next one. Perhaps they'd think differently if we gave them a reason to reconsider—"

"And perhaps they'll just put us in Leavenworth and throw away the key," said Bogey. "Count me out. I've seen enough prisons, thank you."

"You're talking treason, sir," said Reagan.

"Yes, in one sense, I guess I am. But is it treasonous to place one's loyalty to God and all humanity above everything else? If our government is about to do something terribly terribly wrong, shouldn't we oppose it—just like all those brave men and women who have been trying to oppose the evils of the Third Reich for so many years? Do two wrongs make a right?"

"Ahh-h-h," I stammered. They all looked at me. "Ah, I hear the sense of your words, Colonel, but this is the wrong time to have second thoughts. The time to bail out of this mission was before we took off."

Peck looked to Bogey. He raised an eyebrow questioningly; what do you think?

Bogey chewed on the soggy end of his cigar for a moment before answering. "Colonel, you're one of the most decent men in the world. Perhaps too decent. You're certainly too decent for this job. And I wish I had your courage, because you're speaking what a lot of us have been thinking. But...I'm also a realist. And there comes a time when even decent men have to do indecent things. That's the obscenity of war. Especially this one. Lives are cheap. We drop this thing, they're going to get cheaper still. But if we don't—well, I don't see there's much decency in the alternative."

Colonel Peck nodded thoughtfully while he considered Bogey's words. He nodded and kept nodding. I could see that he was thinking through the logic step by step. That was Colonel Peck. Careful.

But he never got the chance to finish his thinking. Colonel Reagan unbuttoned his jacket pocket and pulled out a set of orders. He unfolded them and handed them to Colonel Peck. "Colonel, you are hereby relieved of command of this mission. I'm sorry, Greg. I was given those orders last night by General Donleavy. If you showed any signs of not being able to carry out this mission, he told me to place you under arrest and take over." And then he added, "I hope you won't make this difficult. Sir."

Colonel Peck read the orders without comment. "These appear to be in order," he said. He passed them to Bogey, who glanced at them, and handed them to me. I pulled my logbook around and wrote in the change of command. My hand shook as I did so.

"Colonel Reagan, your orders appear to be valid. The mission is yours." He folded his arms. "You've helped me make up my mind, and I thank you for that. The fact that General Donleavy felt that such an order might be necessary confirms the ugliness of this mission." He glanced at his watch. "We still have two hours before we're over Berlin. You might spend it thinking about what kind of a world we'll be living in after you drop that bomb. You too, Bogey, Jimmy." He looked to Reagan. "Do you want me to ride in the back?"

"If you promise not to interfere with the operation of this mission, I'd rather you stay up here, sir."

"Thank you. I'd like that."

Ronnie picked up his microphone then. "Attention, all hands. This is Colonel Reagan. Colonel Peck has been taken ill. I'm taking command. We will proceed with the mission as directed." He put the microphone down.

Colonel Peck nodded. "Thank you, Colonel Reagan."

"Thank you for your cooperation, Colonel Peck."

We flew in silence for a while. The plane droned across the bright green fields of France, heading toward the distant blue mountains and then the long run north toward Berlin.

"Colonel?" Lt. Laurel's softly accented tenor came through our headphones.

"Yes, Lieutenant?"

"Lieutenant Hardy and I would like to report that the device is armed."

"Thank you, Lieutenant." Reagan glanced at his watch. "You're ahead of schedule. Good job."

Reagan looked around at me, at Bogey. "Either of you fellows having second thoughts?"

I shook my head. "I'm fine." Bogey held up his thumb. *The* thumb. The one he'd use to press the button. I glanced at my watch, then wrote the time in the log. *Device armed.* The words looked strange on the page.

I wondered what the people of Berlin were doing now? Were they going about their daily lives without concern, or were they studying the skies and worrying? Did the husbands go to work this morning? Were they busy at their offices? Were the children reciting lessons in their classrooms? Were the wives and housekeepers out shopping for sausage and cheese? Were the students sitting in cafes, sipping coffee and arguing philosophy? Did the orchestras still rehearse their concerts of Beethoven and Wagner? Or was the music cancelled for the duration?

We flew on in silence. The engines roared and vibrated. The big machine talked to itself in a thousand different noises. We had our own symphony, here in the sky.

Colonel Peck looked curiously relaxed, as if he were finally at peace with himself. The bomb might fall, but it would not be his doing. Reagan, on the other hand, could not have looked unhappier. He must have felt betrayed by the Colonel. Worse, he must now be feeling the same burden that Colonel Peck had been carrying around for the last few months.

Reagan exhaled, loudly. I could tell he was trying to figure it out. "I don't get you, skipper. You're one of the smartest guys I know. How can you betray your country like this?" He had an angry edge to his voice.

"I'm not betraying my country. I'm holding her true to her principles. We're not killers."

"The Germans started this war," Reagan said. "The Nazis are an evil empire. This bomb will destroy them. We have to follow our orders."

Colonel Peck nodded. "Ron, it's an officer's duty to refuse to obey any order that he knows is wrong. We're about to drop the equivalent of fifteen kilotons of TNT on an unarmed civilian population. Do you think that's correct?"

Reagan didn't answer. Even from the back, I could see the expression on his face; he was so angry his hair was clenched.

"Maybe the whole idea of war has gone too far," Peck said. "Maybe it's time for someone to just say no."

"That's got to be the stupidest thing I've ever heard anyone say," Reagan replied, shaking his head. I could tell he wasn't thinking straight anymore. I'd seen him get like this before. He'd get so angry that he'd refuse to listen to anyone, even when he knew they were right.

"Maybe. Maybe it is—and maybe someday, someone else will have an atomic bomb—maybe the Russians or the Japanese or even some crazy little Arab hothead—and maybe they'll be thinking about dropping their bomb on an American city, maybe New York or Chicago or Los Angeles. I don't know. But whoever it is, they'll have the precedent of our actions today, Ron. They'll know *exactly* what the horror will look like. The whole world is watching. If we turn back today, we'll be saying that this bomb is too *terrible* for anyone to use.

"But—if we use it, then every nation will want to have one—will *need* to have one— if only to defend themselves against the United States, because we'll have demonstrated ourselves willing to inflict such horror on our enemies. Oh, if it were only the war, Ron, I'd drop the bomb. What's the difference between a bellyload of little blockbusters or one big city-killer? Only the size of the boom. But it's not just this war, Ron. It's everything. It's all the consequences. It's tomorrow and tomorrow and all the tomorrows that come after."

"We'll be over Germany soon," Reagan said to Bogey. He hadn't heard a thing that Colonel Peck had said.

Bogey grunted a noncommittal response.

Reagan looked to Peck. "It's time. Give him your keys."

Peck nodded. He unclipped the keys from his belt and handed them to Bogey. Bogey clapped the Colonel on the shoulder, a gesture of respect and affection, then ducked out of the cockpit.

We flew on. The engines droned and roared. I bent back to my table, my charts, my numbers, my logbook, my frustration. They were both right, each in their own way.

"How long to Berlin, Jimmy?"

"Uh, ah—ah-h, twenty minutes."

"Thank you." Reagan spoke into his mike. "Bombardier?"

Bogey's voice came through the headphones. "I've got a problem—I'm coming back up."

Reagan and Peck looked at each other in puzzlement. Peck glanced back to me. I shrugged.

Bogey pulled himself back into the cockpit, scratching the stubble on his chin. "I dunno how to tell you this, Colonel—" he said to Reagan. "—but I dropped the other set of keys. I can't unlock the bomb."

"Well, find 'em, dammit!" Reagan was getting red in the face.

"Uh, that'll be a little hard, Colonel. I dropped 'em out the window."

For a moment Reagan didn't get it. Peck realized it first, and a big grin started spreading across his face.

Reagan started to unfasten his seat-harness. "All right, I'll cut the damn chains if I have to—"

"That won't work either, sir. Stan and Ollie are already disarming the bomb." Bogey looked to Peck. "We're going to have to turn back."

"You'll be court martialed for this! Both of you!" Reagan snapped.

"Oh, hell," said Bogey. "Let 'em. If they want to put me in jail for standing for what's right, then our country's got a lot bigger problem than this little war. You and I, Colonel—our problems don't amount to a hill of beans in this crazy world. But if I let you take this plane to Berlin, I'll regret it for the rest of my life...."

Colonel Peck put his hands back on the controls of the aircraft. He looked over to Ron—

"Dammit! We have our orders—" Reagan protested.

"I know, Ron, I know." Colonel Peck said softly, regretfully. He picked up his microphone. "Lt. Hope. This is the Captain speaking. Break radio silence. Send the mission aborted signal. We're coming home." And then he began banking the plane around to the left.

Bogey took the cigar out of his mouth and grinned at me. "Hey, Jimmy, you got a light?"

THE MARTIAN CHILD

Toward the end of the meeting, the caseworker remarked, "Oh—and one more thing. Dennis thinks he's a Martian."

"I beg your pardon?" I wasn't certain I had heard her correctly. I had papers scattered all over the meeting room table—thick piles of stapled incident reports, manila-foldered psychiatric evaluations, Xeroxed clinical diagnoses, scribbled caseworker histories, typed abuse reports, bound trial transcripts, and my own crabbed notes as well: Hyperactivity. Fetal Alcohol Syndrome. Emotional Abuse. Physical Abuse. Conners Rating Scale. Apgars. I had no idea there was so much to know about children. For a moment, I was actually looking for the folder labeled Martian.

"He thinks he's a Martian," Ms. Bright repeated. She was a small woman, very proper and polite. "He told his group home parents that he's not like the other children—he's from Mars—so he shouldn't be expected to act like an Earthling all the time."

"Well, that's okay," I said, a little too quickly. "Some of my best friends are Martians. He'll fit right in. As long as he doesn't eat the tribbles or tease the feral Chtorran."

By the narrow expressions on their faces, I could tell that the caseworkers weren't amused. For a moment, my heart sank. Maybe I'd said the wrong thing. Maybe I was being too facile with my answers.

—The hardest thing about adoption is that *you have to ask someone to trust you with a child*.

That means that you have to be willing to let them scrutinize your entire life, everything: your financial standing, your medical history, your home and belongings, your upbringing, your personality, your motivations, your arrest record, your IQ, and even your sex life. It means that *every* self-esteem issue you have ever had will come bubbling right to the surface like last night's beans in this morning's bath tub.

Whatever you're most insecure about, that's what the whole adoption process will feel like it's focused on. For me, it was that terrible familiar feeling of being *second* best—of not being good enough to play with the big kids, or get the job, or win the award, or whatever was at stake. Even though the point of this interview was simply to see if Dennis and I would be a good match, I felt as if I was being judged again. What if I wasn't good enough this time?

I tried again. I began slowly. "Y'know, you all keep telling me all the bad news—you don't even know if this kid is capable of forming a deep attachment—it feels as if you're trying to talk me out of this match." I stopped myself before I said too much. I was suddenly angry and I didn't know why. These people were only doing their job.

And then it hit me. That was it—these people were *only* doing their job.

At that moment, I realized that there wasn't anyone in the room who had the kind of commitment to Dennis that I did, and I hadn't even met him yet. To them, he was only another case to handle. To me, he was... the possibility of a family. It wasn't fair to unload my frustration on these tired, overworked, underpaid women. They cared. It just wasn't the same kind of caring. I swallowed my anger.

"Listen," I said, sitting forward, placing my hands calmly and deliberately on the table. "After everything this poor little guy has been through, if he wants to think he's a Martian—I'm not going to argue with him. Actually, I think it's charming. It's evidence of his resilience. It's probably the most rational explanation he can come up with for his irrational situation. He probably feels alienated, abandoned, different, *alone*. At least, this gives him a reason for it. It lets him put a story around his situation so he can cope with it. Maybe it's the wrong explanation, but it's the only one he's got. We'd be stupid to try to take it away from him."

And after I'd said that, I couldn't help but add another thought as well. "I know a lot of people who hide out in fantasy because reality is too hard to cope with. Fantasy is my business. The only difference is that I write it down and make the rest of the world pay for the privilege of sharing the delusion. Fantasy isn't about escape; it's a survival mechanism. It's a way to deal with things that are so much bigger than you are. So I think fantasy is special, something to be cherished and protected because it's a very fragile thing and without it, we're so defenseless, we're paralyzed.

"I know what this boy is feeling because *I've been there.* Not the same circumstances, thank God—but I know this much, if he's surrounded by adults who can't understand what he really needs, he'll never have that chance to connect that everyone keeps talking about." For the first time I looked directly into their eyes as if they had to live up to *my* standards. "Excuse me for being presumptuous—but he's got to he with someone who'll tell him that it's all right for him to be a Martian. Let him be a Martian for as long as he needs."

"Yes. Thank you," the supervisor said abruptly. "I think that's everything we need to cover. We'll be getting back to you shortly."

My heart sank at her words. She hadn't acknowledged a word of what I'd said. I was certain she'd dismissed it totally. I gathered up all my papers. We exchanged pleasantries and handshakes, and I wore my company smile all the way to the elevator. I didn't say a word, neither did my sister. We both waited until we were in the car and headed back toward the Hollywood Freeway. She drove, guiding the big car through traffic as effortlessly as only a Los Angeles real estate agent can manage.

"I blew it," I said. "Didn't I? I got too...full of myself again."

"Honey, I think you were fine." She patted my hand.

"They're not going to make the match," I said. "It would be a single parent adoption. They're not going to do it. First they choose married couples, Ward and June. Then they choose single women, Murphy Brown. Then, only if there's no one else who'll take the kid, will they consider a single man. I'm at the bottom of the list. I'll never get this kid. I'll never get any kid. My own caseworker told me not to get my hopes up. There are two other families interested. This was just a formality, this interview. I know it. Just so they could prove they'd considered more than one match." I felt the frustration building up inside my chest like a balloon full of hurt. "But this is the kid for me, Alice, I know it. I don't know how I know it, but I do."

I'd first seen Dennis's picture three weeks earlier; a little square of colors that suggested a smile in flight.

I'd gone to the National Conference of the Adoptive Families of America at the Los Angeles Airport Hilton. There were six panels per hour, six hours a day, two days, Saturday and Sunday. I picked the panels that I thought would be most useful to me in finding and raising a child and ordered tapes—over two dozen—of the sessions I couldn't attend in person. I'd had no idea there were so many different issues to be dealt with in adoptions. I soaked it up like a sponge, listening eagerly to the advice of adoptive parents, their grown children, clinical psychologists, advocates, social workers, and adoption resource professionals.

But my *real* reason for attending was to find *the child*.

I'd already been approved. I'd spent more than a year filling out forms and submitting to interviews. But approval doesn't mean you get a child. It only means that your name is in the hat. Matching is done to meet the child's needs first. Fair enough—but terribly frustrating.

Eventually, I ended up in the conference's equivalent of a dealer's room. Rows of tables and heart-tugging displays. Books of all kinds for sale. Organizations. Agencies. Children in Eastern Europe. Children in Latin America. Asian children. Children with special needs. Photo-listings, like real-estate albums. Turn the pages, look at the eyes, the smiles, the needs. "Johnny was abandoned by his mother at age three. He is hyperactive, starts fires, and has been cruel to small animals. He will need extensive therapy...." "Janie, age 9, is severely retarded. She was sexually abused by her stepfather, she will need round-the-clock care...." "Michael suffers from severe epilepsy...." "Linda *needs*..." "Danny *needs*..." "Michael *needs*..." So many *needs*. So much hurt. It was overwhelming.

Why were so many of the children in the books "special needs" children? Retarded. Hyperactive. Abused. Had they been abandoned because they weren't perfect. or were these the leftovers after all the good children were selected? The part that disturbed me the most was that I could understand the emotions involved. I wanted a child, not a case. And some of the descriptions in the book did seem pretty intimidating. Were these the only kind of children available?

Maybe it was selfish, but I found myself turning the pages looking for a child who represented an easy answer. Did I really want another set of *needs* in my life—a single man who's old enough to be considered middle-aged and ought to be thinking seriously about retirement plans?

This was the most important question of all. "Why do you want to adopt a child?" And it was a question I couldn't answer. I couldn't find the words. It seemed that there was something I couldn't write down.

The motivational questionnaire had been a brick wall that sat on my desk for a week. It took me thirty pages of single-spaced printout just to get my thoughts organized. I could tell great stories about what I thought a family should be, but I couldn't really answer the question why *I* wanted a son. Not right away.

The three o'clock in the morning truth of it was a very nasty and selfish piece of business.

I didn't want to die alone. I didn't want to be left unremembered.

All those books and TV scripts... they were nothing. They used up trees. They were exercises in excess. They made other people rich. They were useless to me. They filled up shelves. They impressed the impressionable. But they didn't prove me a real person. They didn't validate my life as one worth living. In fact, they were about as valuable as the vice-presidency of the United States.

What I *really* wanted was to make a difference. I wanted someone to know that there was a real person behind all those words. A dad.

I would lie awake, staring into the darkness, trying to imagine it, what it would be like, how I would handle the various situations that might come up, how I would deal with the day-to-day business of daddying. I gamed out scenarios and tried to figure out how to handle difficult situations.

In my mind, I was always kind and generous, compassionate and wise. My fantasy child was innocent and joyous, full of love and wide-eyed wonder, and grateful to be in my home. He was an invisible presence, living inside my soul, defying reality to catch up. I wondered where he was now, and how and when I would finally meet him—and if the reality of parenting would be as wonderful as the dream.

—But it was all fantasyland. The books were proof of that. These children had histories, brutal, tragic, and heart-rending.

I wandered on to the next table. One of the social workers from the Los Angeles County Department of Children's Services had a photo book with her. I introduced myself, told her I'd been approved—but not matched. Could I look through the book? Yes, of course, she said. I turned the pages slowly, studying the innocent faces, looking for one who could be my son. All the pictures were of black children, and the county wasn't doing trans-racial adoptions anymore. Too controversial. The black social workers had taken a stand against it—I could see their point—but how many of these children would not find homes now?

Tucked away like an afterthought on the very last page was a photo of the only white child in the book. My glance slid across the picture quickly, I was already starting to close the album—and then as the impact of what I'd seen hit me, I froze in mid-action, almost slamming the book flat again.

The boy was riding a bicycle on a sunny tree-lined sidewalk; he was caught in the act of shouting or laughing at whoever was holding the camera. His blond hair was wild in the wind of his passage, his eyes shone like stars behind his glasses, his expression was raucous and exuberant.

I couldn't take my eyes off the picture. A cold wave of certainty came rolling up my spine like a blast of fire and ice. It was a feeling of *recognition*. This was *him*—the child who'd taken up permanent residence in my imagination! I could almost hear him yelling, "Hi, Daddy!"

"Tell me about this child," I said, a little too quickly. The social worker was already looking at me oddly. I could understand it. My voice sounded odd to me too. I tried to explain. "Tell me. Do you ever get people looking at a picture and telling you that this is the one?"

"All the time," she replied. Her face softened into an understanding smile.

His name was Dennis. He'd just turned eight. She'd just put his picture in the book this morning. And yes, she'd have the boy's caseworker get in touch with my caseworker. But... she cautioned... remember that there might be other families interested too. And remember, the department matches from the child's side.

I didn't hear any of that. I heard the words, but not the cautions.

I pushed hard and they set up a meeting to see if the match would work. But they cautioned me ahead of time—" Tthis might not be the child you're looking for. He's classified as 'hard-to-place.' He's hyperactive and he's been emotionally abused and he may have fetal alcohol effects and he's been in eight foster homes, he's never had a family of his own...."

I didn't hear a word of it. I simply refused to listen. The boy in the picture had grabbed my heart so completely that I'd suddenly expanded all my definitions of what I was willing to accept.

I posted messages on CompuServe asking for information and advice on adoption, on attention deficit hyperactivity disorder, on emotional abuse recovery, on everything I could think of—what were this child's chances of becoming an independent adult? I called the Adoption Warm Line and was referred to parents who'd been through it. I hit the bookstores and the libraries. I called my cousin, the doctor, and he faxed me twenty pages of reports. And I came into the meeting so well-papered and full of theories and good intentions that I must have looked the perfect jerk.

And now... it was over.

I leaned my head against the passenger side window of my sister's car and moaned. "Dammit. I'm so *tired* of being pregnant. Thirteen months is long enough for any man! I've got the baby blues so bad, I can't even go to the supermarket anymore. I find myself watching other people with their children and the tears start welling up in my eyes. I keep thinking 'Where's *mine*?'"

My sister understood. She had four children of her own, none of whom had ended up in jail; so she had to have done something right. "Listen to me, David. Maybe this little boy isn't right for you—"

"Of course he's right for me. He's a Martian."

She ignored the interruption. "And if he isn't right, there'll be another child who is. I promise you. And you said it yourself that you didn't know if you could handle all the problems he'd be bringing with him."

"I know—it's just that... I feel like—I don't know what I feel like. This is worse than anything I've ever been through. All this wanting and not having. Sometimes I'm afraid it's not going to happen at all."

Alice pulled the car over to the curb and turned off the engine. "Okay, it's my turn," she said. "Stop beating yourself up. You are the smartest one in the whole family—but sometimes you can be awfully stupid. You are going to be a terrific father to some very lucky little boy. Your caseworker knows that. All of those social workers in that meeting saw your commitment and dedication. All that research you did—when you asked about the Apgar numbers and the Conners scale, when you handed them that report on hyperactivity, which even they didn't know about—you *impressed* them."

I shook my head. "Research is easy. You post a note on CompuServe, wait two days, and then download your e-mail."

"It's not the research," Alice said. "It's the fact that you did it. That demonstrates your willingness to find out what the child needs so you can provide it."

"I wish I could believe you," I said.

She looked deeply at me. "What's the matter?"

"What if I'm really not good enough?" I said. "*That's* what I'm worried about—I can't shake that feeling."

"Oh, that—" she said, lightly. "That's normal. That's the proof that you're going to do okay. It's only those parents who don't worry who need to."

"Oh," I said. And then we both started laughing.

She hugged me then. "You'll do fine. Now let's go home and call Mom before she busts a kidney from the suspense."

Two centuries later, although the calendar insisted otherwise, Ms. Bright called me. "We've made a decision. If you're still interested in Dennis, we'd like to arrange a meeting—" I don't remember a lot of what she said after that; most of it was details about how we would proceed; but I remember what she said at the end. "I want to tell you the two things that helped us make the decision. First, all that research you did shows that you're committed to Dennis's needs. That's very important in any adoption, but especially in this one. The other thing was what you said at the end of the meeting—about understanding his need to be a Martian. We were really touched by your empathy for his situation. We think that's a quality that Dennis is going to need very much in any family he's placed in. That's why we decided to try you first."

I thanked her profusely; at least, I think I did; I was suddenly having trouble seeing. and the box of tissues had gone empty.

I met Dennis three days later, at the Johnson Group Home in Culver City. He was one of six children living at the facility; four boys, two girls. Because the caseworkers didn't want him to know that he was being *auditioned*, I would be introduced as a friend of the group home parents.

The child who came home from school was a sullen little zombie, going through the motions of life. He walked in the door, walked past me with no sign of recognition, and headed straight to his room. I said, "Hi." He grunted something that could have been "H'lo" and kept on going. For a moment, I felt somehow cheated. I recognized him, why hadn't he recognized me? And then I had to remind myself that I was the grownup, not him. I waited. After a bit, he came out from his retreat, looked me up and down, and said, "Do you want to play with me?"

We played air hockey. For the first few minutes, he was totally intent on the game. I didn't exist to him. Then I remembered an exercise from one of my communications courses—about simply *being with* another person. I stopped trying so hard to do it right, and instead just focused my attention on Dennis, letting it be all *right* with me for him to be exactly the way he was.

And yet, I couldn't turn off the analytical part of my mind. After reading all those reports, and hearing all the opinions of the caseworkers, I couldn't help but watch for evidence. I couldn't see it. None of it. All I could see was a child. And then that thing happened that always happens to an adult who is willing to play with a child. I rediscovered my own childhood again. I got involved in the game, and very shortly I was smiling and laughing when he did, returning the same delight and approval at every audacious play. And that's when it happened. He began to realize that there was a real human being on the opposite side of the game board. Something sparked. He started reacting to me instead of to the puck. I could feel the sense of connection almost as a physical presence.

Then, abruptly, it was time for him to do his chores. We loaded up the wagon with the cans from the recycling bin and walked them over to the nearby park. We talked about stuff. He talked, I listened. Sometimes I asked questions, sometimes he did. On the way back, he insisted that I pull the wagon so he could ride in it. By now, he was glowing. He was the boy in the photograph.

When we got back to the group home, however, the other children had arrived home from school and were already playing together in the back yard. As soon as he saw them, Dennis broke away from me and ran to the back of the yard. He flung himself into the corner of a large old couch and curled up in a ball. He was as apart from the other children—indeed the whole world—as it was possible to get.

What had suddenly triggered his unhappiness? Was it the thought that now that there were other children to play with, I would reject him? Did he have to reject me first? Or was there something else going on? From inside the house, I watched him as he sat alone. He was a very unhappy little boy. And he had stopped glowing. At that moment, I knew I couldn't leave him here. Whatever other problems he might have, my commitment was bigger. Or so I believed.

The group home parents invited me to stay to dinner with the children. I hadn't planned on it, but all the children insisted that I stay, so I did, specifically making a point of sitting next to Dennis. He didn't talk at all, he was subdued, as if he was afraid of losing something that he wanted very much—or maybe that was only my perception. He ate quietly and timidly. But then Tony, one of the more excitable children, suddenly piped up, "Do you know what Dennis said?"

Tony was sitting directly across from me. He had that look of malicious mischief common to children who are about to betray a confidence. "What?" I asked, with a queasy foreboding.

"Dennis said he wishes you were his dad." Even without looking, I could see that beside me, Dennis was cringing, readying himself for the inevitable politely worded rejection.

Instead, I turned to Dennis, focusing all my attention on him, and said, "Wow, what a great wish. Thank you!" There was more I wanted to add, but I couldn't. Not yet. The "game plan" required me to be Dennis's "special friend" for at least six weeks before I made any kind of commitment to him. He couldn't know that I had the same wish he did. I felt cheated at not being able to add, "So do I." But I understood the rationale, and I would follow it.

"Better watch out," Tony said. "He might make it a Martian wish, and then you'll *have* to."

At the time, I didn't understand what Tony had meant. So I forgot about it.

〰〰〰〰〰〰〰

The next time I heard about Martians happened thirteen months later.

I was in Arizona, at a party at Jeff Duntemann's sprawling house. Jeff is a two-time Hugo nominee who gave up science fiction to write books about computer programming. Apparently, it was far more profitable than science fiction; now he was publishing his own magazine, *PC-Techniques*. I write a regular column for the magazine, an off-the-wall mix of code and mutated zen. It was the standing joke that my contribution to the magazine was the "Martian perspective."

I was sitting on the patio, watching Dennis splash enthusiastically across the pool. He was doing cannonballs into the deep end. A year ago, I couldn't pry him loose from the steps in the shallow end; he wouldn't even let me teach him how to dog-paddle—now he was an apprentice fish. He spent more time swimming across the bottom of the water than the top.

A year ago, he'd been a waif—capable of joy, the picture proved that—but more often sad, uncertain, alienated, and angry. A year ago, he'd told his caseworker, "I don't think God listens to my prayers. I prayed for a dad and nothing happened." On the day he moved in, I asked his caseworker to remind him of that conversation and then tell him that sometimes it takes God a little while to make a miracle happen.

A miracle—according to my friend Randy MacNamara—is something that wouldn't have happened anyway. Now, after the fact, after the first giddy days of panic and joy, after the days of bottomless fears, after the tantrums and the testing, after a thousand and one peanut butter and jellyfish sandwiches, I understood what he meant. And more. A miracle takes real commitment. It never happens by accident. I'd had other miracles happen in my life—one which I'd written about, one which I may never write about—but this one was the best. I had the proof of it framed on my wall.

One afternoon I'd opened Dennis's lunch kit to see how much he'd eaten and found the note I'd packed that morning. It said, "Please eat your whole lunch today! I love you! Daddy." On the other side, written in a childish scrawl was Dennis's reply: *"I love you to. you are very specil to me. I realy think your the best. I love you very much dady I never loved eneyone more than you. I never new anyone nicer than you."* At the bottom, he'd drawn three hearts and put the word "dady" in the biggest of them.

So the miracle was complete. Dennis *could* form a deep attachment. And he could express it. And all I had to do was sit and glow and realize that despite all my doubts and all my mistakes, I was getting the important part of the job done right. I had passed from wannabe to gonnabe to finding-how-to-be to simply be-ing. I was glowing as brightly as the warm Arizona evening. Pink clouds were striped across the darkening twilight sky.

I didn't know anyone else at the party besides Jeff and Carol—and the world-famous Mr. Byte who was in the kitchen begging scraps he wasn't supposed to have. But that was all right. I was content just to sit and watch my son enjoying himself. And then I heard the word "Martian" in back of me, and without moving, my attention swiveled 180 degrees.

Four of the wives were sitting together—it was that kind of party; the programmers were talking code, the wives were talking children. I didn't know enough about either subject, I still felt like a dabbler in both fields, so I made the best kind of listener. One of the women was saying. "No, it's true. Since she was old enough to talk she's insisted that she's a Martian. Her mother has never been able to convince her otherwise. She asked her, 'How do you explain that I remember going to the hospital and giving birth to you?' and she said, 'I was implanted in your tummy.' She's twelve now and she still believes it. She has a whole story, an explanation for everything. She says UFOs are implanting Martian babies all the time."

The other women laughed gently. I found myself smiling to myself and watching Dennis. Remembering for the first time in a long while what he'd once told his caseworker—that he was a Martian too. Interesting coincidence.

Then, one of the others said, "We had a boy in my daughter's school who wore a T-shirt to school almost every day that said, 'I am a Martian.' He took a lot of teasing about it. The principal tried to make him stop wearing it, but he refused. All the kids thought he was crazy."

"That was probably the only way he could get the attention he needed."

"Well," said the fourth voice, "it's a common childhood fantasy—that the child is really a changeling or an orphan and that you're not her real mother. Adding Mars to it is just a way to take advantage of the information in the real world to make it more believable."

I didn't hear any more of that conversation; we were interrupted by Carol announcing that dessert was served; but a seed of inquiry had been planted. If nothing else, I thought it might make an interesting story. If only I could figure out an ending for it. Let's see, a man adopts a little boy and then discovers that the child is a Martian.

Hm. But what's the hook?

Horror story? Too easy. Too obvious—the Martian children are going to murder us in our beds. Besides, Richard Matheson could do it better, if he hadn't already. John Wyndham already had. A hidden invasion ? The Martians will take us over without our ever knowing? Fred Brown had beaten me to it by four decades. His story had even ended up as an episode on Hitchcock. Maybe something tender and gentle instead? Parenting a starlost orphan? That would be the hardest to write—and Zenna Henderson had already written it several times over. Sturgeon was another one who could handle that angle. I wished I could pick up the phone and call him. He would have had the most interesting insight for the ending, but the connect charges would have been horrendous. I could call Harlan, of course, but he'd probably bitch at me for interrupting him during *Jeopardy*. Besides, I didn't think he would take this question seriously. "Harlan, listen—I think my son's a Martian, and I'm trying to write it up as a story...." Yeah, right, David. Have you had your medication checked recently?

I made a mental note to think about it later. Maybe my subconscious would think about it during the drive home. Maybe I'd stumble across an ending by accident. I really couldn't do anything at all without an ending in mind. It's easy to start a story, but if you don't know the ending, you don't know what you're writing toward and after a while the story goes adrift, the energy fails, and you've got one more thing to be frustrated about. I had a file cabinet full of unfinished stories to prove that this was not the best way to generate pay copy.

◇◇◇◇◇◇◇◇◇◇◇◇◇◇◇◇

The next day... we were slicing across the desolate red desert, seemingly suspended between the blazing sky and the shimmering road, not talking about anything, just listening to a tape of Van Dyke Parks and sipping sodas from the cooler. The tape came to an end and the white noise of the wind rushed in to envelop us. Convertibles are fun, but they aren't quiet.

Abruptly, I remembered last night's conversation.

"Hey," I asked. "Are you a Martian?"

"What?"

"Are you a Martian?" I repeated.

"Why do you ask that?"

"Ah, obviously you're a Jewish Martian. You answer a question with a question."

"Who told you I was a Martian?"

"Kathy did. Before I met you, we had a meeting. She told me all about you. She said that you told her you were a Martian. Do you remember telling her that?"

"Yes."

"Are you still a Martian?"

"Yes," he said.

"Oh," I said. "Do you want to tell me about it?"

"Okay," he said. "I was made on Mars. I was a tadpole. Then I was brought to Earth in a UFO and implanted in my Mommy's tummy. She didn't know. Then I was borned."

"Ahh," I said. "That's how I thought it happened. Is that all?"

"Uh-huh."

"Why did the Martians send you here?"

"So I could be a Earth-boy."

"Oh."

"Can we go to Round Table Pizza for dinner?" he asked, abruptly changing the subject as if it was the most natural thing to do.

"Do Martians like pizza?"

"Yes!" he said excitedly. Then he pointed his fingers at me like a funny kind of ray gun. Most children would have pointed the top two fingers to make a pretend gun, but Dennis pointed his index and little fingers, his thumb stood straight up for the trigger. "If you don't take me out for pizza tonight, I'll have to disneygrade you."

"Ouch, that sounds painful. I definitely do not want to be disneygraded. Then I'd have to stand in the dark and sing that awful song forever while boatloads of Japanese tourists take pictures of me. But we're not going tonight. Maybe tomorrow, if you have a good day at school."

"No, tonight! " He pointed his fingers menacingly—both hands now—and for a moment I wondered what would happen if he pressed his thumbs forward. Would I be turned into a giant three-fingered mouse?

"If you disneygrade me," I said, "for sure you won't get any pizza."

"Okay," he said. Then he closed up both weapons, first one hand, then the other. First the little finger of his left hand, then the index finger; then the little finger of his right hand, then the index finger. Each time he made a soft clicking sound with his mouth. Finally he folded his thumbs down—and abruptly he had hands again.

Later, I tried to do the same thing myself. A human can do it, but it's like the Vulcan salute. It takes practice.

<hr>

I have a pinched nerve in my back. If I do my twisting exercises a couple of times a week, and if I take frequent breaks from the keyboard, and if I remember to put myself into the spa every couple days and let the bubbles boil up around me, then I can keep myself functioning pretty much like a normal person. It's a fair trade. Usually I wait until after dinner to sit in the spa. After the sun sets is a perfect time for a little skinny-dipping.

Several days after the Phoenix trip, Dennis and I were alone in the pool. The pool has a blue filter over the light, the spa has a red one; when the bubbles are on, it looks a little like a hot lava bath. Sometimes we talk about nothing important, sometimes we just sit silently letting the bubbles massage our skins, sometimes we stare up into the sky and watch for meteors; once we'd seen a bright red starpoint streak across the sky like a bullet.

But tonight, as he splashed in the bubbles, I found myself studying the way the light shaped his features. I'm not an expert on the development of children's skulls, but abruptly I was struck by the odd proportions of his forehead and eyes.

Before I'd adopted him, I'd been given copies of various doctor's reports. One doctor, who was supposed to be looking for fetal alcohol effects, had described the five-year-old Dennis as "an unusual-looking" child. I couldn't see what he was talking about. To me, Dennis had always been an unusually good-looking boy.

There are only two shapes of faces—pie and horse. Dennis was a pie-face, I'm a horse. In that, he was lucky because his smile was so wide he *needed* a round face to hold it all. He was blessed with dark blond hair which was growing steadily toward shoulder-length. His eyes were puppy-brown and hidden behind lashes long enough to trouble the sleep of mascara manufacturers. His complexion was as luminous and gold as an Arizona sunset.

His body was well-proportioned too; he had long legs and a swimmer's torso. He was thin, but not skinny. He looked like a Disney child. I expected him to be a heartbreaker when he grew up. The girls were going to chase him with lassos. Already I wondered what kind of a teenager he would become—and if I would be able to handle it.

Now... seeing him in the reflected red light of the spa—is this the same color light they have on Mars?—he did look a little *alien* to me. His forehead had a round-ish bulge toward the crown. His cheekbones seemed strangely angled. His eyes seemed narrow and reptilian. Probably it was the effect of the light coming from underneath instead of above, combined with the red filter, but it was momentarily unnerving. For a moment, I wondered what kind of a *thing* I'd brought into my life.

"What?" he asked, staring back.

"Nothing," I said.

"You were looking at me."

"I was admiring you. You're a beautiful kid, do you know that? "

"Uh-huh." And suddenly he was Dennis again.

"How do you know that?"

"Everybody says so. They all like my eyelashes."

I laughed. Of course. Here was a child who'd learned to work the system. He was a skilled manipulator. He'd learned real fast how to turn on his special smile and get what he wanted out of people. Of course he knew how much attention his eyelashes attracted.

But—for a moment there, he hadn't been Dennis the little boy. He'd been something else. Something cold and watchful. He'd noticed me studying him. He'd sensed the suspicion. Or was it just the power of suggestion at work? Most of the books on parenting advised not to feel guilty for wondering if your child is going to suddenly catch a fly with his tongue. It's a very common parental fear.

And then... whenever I had doubts about Dennis and my ability to keep up with him, all I had to do was ask myself one simple question. How would I feel if Kathy Bright said she had to remove him from my home? Ripped apart was the simplest answer. The truth was, I didn't care if he was a Martian or not, I was as *bonded* to him as he was to me.

But out of curiosity, and possibly just to reassure myself that I was imagining things, I logged onto CompuServe. The ISSUES forum has a parenting section. I left a message under the heading, "Is your child a Martian?"

> *My little boy says he's a Martian. I've heard of two other children who claim to be Martians as well. Has anyone else heard of children who believe that they're from Mars?*

Over the course of the next few days—before the message scrolled off the board and into the bit-bucket—I received thirty-three replies.

Several of the messages were thoughtful analyses of why a child might say such a thing; it was pretty much what that mother in Phoenix had surmised; it's common for children to fantasize that they have glamorous origins. In the past, children might have believed they were secretly princes and princesses and one day their real parents would arrive to take them to their golden castles. But because that mythology has now been superseded by starships and mutants, it's more appropriate for children to fantasize about traveling away on the *Millennium Falcon* or the *Enterprise*. But if a child was experienced enough to know that those stories were just fiction, he would also know that Mars was a real planet; therefore... Mars gave credibility to the fantasy. Etcetera. Etcetera. Local mileage may vary, but if the delusion persists, see a good therapist. It may be evidence of some deeper problem. Etcetera some more.

I knew what Dennis's deeper problems were. He'd been bounced around the foster care system for eight years before landing in my arms. He didn't know *where* he came from or *where* he belonged.

Several of the replies I received were from other parents sharing pieces of weirdness their own children had demonstrated. Interesting, but not particularly useful to my inquiry.

But... there were over a dozen private messages.

> *My sister's little girl used to insist that she'd been brought to Earth in a UFO and implanted in her mommy's tummy while her mommy was asleep. She kept this up until she was about fourteen, then abruptly stopped. After that, she wouldn't answer questions about it at all.*

> *My next door neighbors had a boy who said he wasn't from Earth. He disappeared when he was twelve. Without a trace. The police assumed he was kidnapped.*

> *My ex-wife was a child psychologist. She used to joke about her Martian*

children. She said she could tell how crazy New York was by the number of Martians she saw in any given year. At first she used to tell the parents that same old same old about children needing to fantasize about a glamorous background, but later on she began to wonder. The stories the kids told were all very similar. They began life as Martian tadpoles brought to Earth and implanted in the uteruses of Earth women. She always wanted to do a study on Martian children, but she could never get a grant.

I dated a girl once who said she was from Mars . She was very insistent on it. When I tried to get serious with her, she turned me down flat. She said she really liked me, but it wouldn't work out between us. When I asked her why, she said it was because she was from Mars. That's all. I guess Martians have a rule against marrying outside their species.

I heard about a Martian when I was in high school. He killed himself. I didn't know him. I only heard about it afterward.

I thought I was from Mars once. I even had memories of being on Mars. It had a pink sky. That's how I knew it was Mars. When the photos came in from JPL showing that Mars really did have a pink sky, just like in my memories, I thought that proved something. When I told my parents, they took me to see a doctor. I was in therapy for a long time, but I'm fine now. Maybe you should get your son into therapy

It was the last one that really got to me. I knew the person who sent it meant to be reassuring, but instead, his message had the opposite effect.

Okay, maybe it's me. Maybe it's because I'm a writer. I read subtext where none is intended. And maybe the cumulative effect of all these messages, especially the wistful, almost plaintive tone of the last one left me with a very uncomfortable feeling.

I replied to all of these messages.

I know this sounds silly, but please indulge me. What did your Martian friend/relative look like? Did he/she have any special physical characteristics or medical problems? What was his/her personality like? Do you know what happened to him other? Does he/she still believe that he/she is from Mars?

It took a week or two to compile the responses. Of the ten Martians specifically mentioned, two had committed suicide. One was successful in business. Three refused to talk about Mars. Two were "cured." The whereabouts of the others were unknown. Three were missing. Two of the missing had been repeated runaways during their teen years. I wondered where they thought they were running to.

Of the ten Martians, six were known to have had golden-brown skin, round faces, brown eyes and very long eyelashes. The hair color was generally dark blond or brown. That was an interesting statistical anomaly.

Of the ten Martians, five were hyperactive, two were epileptic. The other three weren't known.

I asked the fellow whose ex-wife had been a child psychologist if she'd ever noticed any statistical patterns among her Martians. He said he didn't know and he didn't even know her whereabouts anymore. She had disappeared two years earlier.

∞∞∞∞∞∞∞∞∞∞∞∞

I called my friend, Steve Barnes. He'd written one of the character references I'd needed to adopt Dennis, and because of that I regarded him as an unofficial godfather to the boy. We chatted about this and that and the other thing for awhile. And then, finally, I said, "Steve—do you know about the Martian phenomenon?" He didn't. I told him about it. He asked me if I was smoking dope again.

"I'm serious, Steve."

"So am I."

"I haven't touched that crap since I kicked out she-who-must-not-be-named," I said it angrily.

"Just checking. You gotta admit that's a pretty bizarre story, though."

"I know that. That's why I'm telling you. You're one of the few people I know who will actually consider it fairly. Geez—why is it that science fiction writers are the most skeptical animals of all?"

"Because we get to deal with more crazies than anyone else," Steve replied without missing a beat.

"I don't know what to do with this," I said, admitting my frustration. "I know it sounds like one more crazy UFO mystery. Only this one is something that can actually be validated. This is the kind of statistical anomaly that can't be explained away by coincidence. And I bet there's a lot more to it too. Like, what was the blood type of all those children? What was the position of the Earth and Mars when they were conceived? What was the phase of the moon? What are their favorite foods? How well did they do in school? What if there's something really going on here?—maybe not Martians, maybe some kind of social phenomenon or syndrome—I don't know what it is, I don't know what else to ask, and I don't know who to tell. Most of all, I don't want to end up on the front page of the *Inquirer*. Can't you just see it? 'SCI-FI WRITER HAS MARTIAN CHILD!'"

"It might be good for your career," Steve said thoughtfully. "I wonder how many new readers you could pick up."

"Oh, yeah, sure. And I wonder how many old readers I'll lose. I'd like to be taken seriously in my old age, Steve. Remember what happened to what's-his-name."

"I'll never forget old what's-his-name," Steve said. "Yeah, that was a real sad story."

"Anyway..." I said. "You see my point? Where do I go from here?"

"You want my *real* advice?" Steve asked. He didn't wait for my reply. "Don't go anywhere with it. Drop it. Let someone else figure it out. Or no one. You said it yourself, David. 'It's almost always dangerous to be right too soon.' Don't go borrowing trouble. Turn it into a story if you must and let people think it's a harmless fantasy. But don't let it screw up your life. You wanted this kid, didn't you? Now you have him. Just parent him. That's the only thing that's really wanted and needed."

He was right. I knew it. But I couldn't accept it. "Sure. That's easy for you to say. You don't have a Martian in the house."

"Yes I do." He laughed. "Only mine's a girl."

"Huh—?"

"Don't you get it? *All* children are Martians. We get thirteen years to civilize the little monsters. After that, it's too late. Then they start eating our hearts out for the rest of our lives."

"You sound like my mother now."

"I'll take that as a compliment."

"It's a good thing you don't know her, or you wouldn't say that."

"Listen to me, David," and his tone of voice was so serious that six different jokes died before they could pass my lips . "You're right on schedule. Have you ever really looked at the faces of new parents? Most of them are walking around in a state of shock, wondering what happened—what is this loathsome reptilian thing that has suddenly invaded their lives? It's part of the process of assimilation. The only difference is that you have a more active imagination than most people. You know how to name your fears. Trust me on this, Toni and I went through it too with Nicki. We thought she was a—never mind. Just know that this normal. There are days when you are absolutely certain that you've got a cute and stinky little alien in your house."

"But *every* day?"

"Trust me. It passes. In a year or two, you won't even remember what your life was like before."

"Hmm. Maybe that's how long it takes a Martian to brainwash his human hosts...."

Steve sighed. "You've got it bad."

"Yes, I do," I admitted.

∞∞∞∞∞∞∞∞∞∞∞∞

The Martian thing gnawed at me like an ulcer. I couldn't get it out of my head. No matter what we did, the thought was there.

If we went out front to swat koosh-balls back and forth, I wondered if the reason he was having trouble with his coordination was the unfamiliar gravity of Earth. If we went in the back yard and jumped in the pool together, I wondered if his attraction to water was because it was so scarce on Mars. I wondered about his ability to hear a piece of music a single time and still remember the melody so clearly that he could sing it again, note for note, a month later. He would walk through the house singing songs that he could not have heard except on the tapes I occasionally played. How many nine-year-olds know how to sing *My Clone Sleeps Alone* like Pat Benatar? I wondered why he had so little interest in comic books, but loved to watch television dramas about the relationships of human beings. He hated *Star Trek*, he thought it was "too silly." He loved the Discovery channel—especially all the shows about animals and insects.

There was no apparent pattern to his behavior, nothing that could be pointed to as evidence of otherworldliness. Indeed, the fact that he was making his father paranoid was a very strong argument that he was a normal Earth kid.

And then, just when I'd forgotten... something would happen. Maybe he'd react to something on television with an off-the-wall comment that would make me look over at him curiously. There was that Bugs Bunny cartoon, for instance, where the rabbit is making life difficult for Marvin the Martian, stealing the eludium-235 detonator so he can't blow up the Earth. In the middle of it, Dennis quietly declared, "No, that's wrong. Martians aren't like that." Then he got up and turned the television set *off*.

"Why did you do that?" I asked.

"Because it was wrong," he said blandly.

"But it's only a cartoon." One of my *favorite* cartoons, I might add.

"It's still wrong." And then he turned and went outside as if the whole concept of television would never be interesting to him again.

<hr/>

And now, almost two years to the day since I'd filled out the first application, the nickel finally dropped and I sat up in bed in the middle of the night. Why were so many adopted children *hyperactive*?

The evidence was all around me. I just hadn't noticed it before. It was there in the photo-listing books. It seemed as if every third child was hyperactive. It was acknowledged in the books, the articles, the seminars, the tapes... that a higher proportion of foster children have Attention Deficit Disorder, also called Hyperactivity. Why was that?

Some theorists suggested that it was the result of substance abuse by the parents, which is why we saw it more in abandoned and unwanted children. Some doctors believed that hyperactivity was the result of the body's failure to produce certain key enzymes in response to physical stimulation; therefore the child needed to over-stimulate himself in order to produce an equivalent amount of calming. Still others postulated that there was an emotional component to the disorder; that it was a response to a lack of nurturing. Most interesting of all to me was the offhand note in one article that some theorists believed that many cases of ADD were actually mis-diagnoses. If you were unattached and didn't know who you were or where you had come from or where you were going, you'd have a lot to worry about; your attention might be distracted too.

Or... what if the behavior that was judged abnormal for Earth children was perfectly normal for Martian children? What if there was no such thing as ADD... in Martians?

At this point, I'd reached the limits of my ability to research the question. Who could I tell? Who would have the resources to pursue this further? And who would take me seriously?

Suppose I picked up the *Los Angeles Times* tomorrow and saw that Ben Bova had called a press conference to announce that he'd been kidnapped by aliens and taken into space where they'd performed bizarre sexual experiments on him... would I believe him? Ben is one of the most believable men in the world. Once, he almost talked me into voting for Ronald Reagan. But if I saw a report like that in the newspaper, the first thing I'd do would be to call Barbara and ask if Ben were all right.

In other words... there was simply no way for me to research this question without destroying all of my credibility as a writer.

Even worse, *there was no way to research it without also destroying my credibility as a parent.*

Up until this time, I'd always been candid with the caseworkers and therapists; I'd talked to them about our discipline problems, about my feelings of frustration, about ever little step in the right direction and every major victory. But... suddenly, I realized this was something I couldn't talk to them about. Suppose I called Kathy Bright. What could I say? "Uh, Kathy, it's David. I want to talk to you about Dennis. You know how he says he's a Martian? Well, I think he might really be a Martian and..."

Uh-huh.

If the adoptive father was starting to have hallucinations about the child, how long would the Department of Children's Services leave the child in that placement? About twenty minutes, I figured. About as long as it took to get out there and pick him up. She'd pull him out of my house so fast they'd be hearing sonic booms in Malibu. And I wouldn't even be able to argue. She'd be right to do so. A child needs a stable and nurturing environment. How stable and nurturing would it be for him to be living with an adult who suspects he's from another planet and is wondering about his ultimate motives.

If I pursued this, I'd lose my son.

The thought was intolerable. I might never recover. I was sure that he wouldn't. For the first time in his life, he'd finally formed an attachment. What would it do to him to have it broken so abruptly? It would truly destroy his ability to trust any other human being.

I couldn't do that to him. I couldn't do *anything* that might hurt him.

And what about me? I had my own "attachment issues." I couldn't stand the thought of another failure. Another brick in the wall, as they say.

That was where I stayed stuck for the longest time. I walked around the house in physical pain for three weeks. My chest hurt. My head hurt. My legs hurt. My back hurt. My eyes hurt. My throat hurt. The only part of me that didn't hurt was my brain. That was so numb, I couldn't think.

I didn't know if he was a Martian or not. But something weird was going on. Wasn't it? And if it was just me—if I was going insane—then what right do I have to try to parent this child anyway? Either way I lose. If he's a Martian, I can't tell anyone. And if he isn't a Martian, then I'm going crazy.

∞∞∞∞∞∞∞∞∞∞∞∞

I started looking for local evidence. I began browsing through my journal. I'd been making daily notes of interesting incidents, in case I ever wanted to write a book about our experiences. At first, I couldn't find anything. Most of the incidents I'd written about were fairly mundane. Not even good *Reader's Digest* material.

For instance, the week after he moved in, I'd taken him to the baseball game at Dodger Stadium. For the first part of the game, he'd been more interested in having a pennant and getting some cotton candy than in what was going on down on the stadium floor. But along about the fifth inning, he'd climbed up onto my lap and I began explaining the game to him. "See that man at home plate, holding the bat. Wish for him to hit the ball right out of the park."

"Okay," said Dennis.

Cra-a-ack! The ball went sailing straight out into the right field stands. Someone in the lower deck caught it and the runner sauntered easily around the bases while the organist played, "Glory, glory, Hallelujah."

"You're a good wisher, Dennis. That was terrific. Want to try it again?"

"No."

"Okay."

Two innings later, the Dodgers were one run behind. I asked Dennis to wish for hits again. Four pitches later, there were runners at first and third.

It didn't matter to me who came up to bat now; I hadn't remembered the names of any ballplayers since Roy Campanella was catching for Don Drysdale and Sandy Koufax. As far as I was concerned, Who was on first, What was on second, and I Don't Know still played third. I liked baseball only so long as I didn't have to be an expert; but I'd never seen the Dodgers win a game. Every time I came to the stadium they lost; so I'd made it a point to stay away from Dodger Stadium to give them a fair chance at winning. I didn't expect them to win tonight; but Dennis's wishes had brought them from three runs behind.

"Okay, Dennis," I said, giving him a little squeeze. "It's time for one last wish. See that guy at the home plate, holding the bat. You gotta wish for him to hit a home run. All the way out of the park. Just like before. Okay?"

"Okay."

And just like before—*cra-a-ack*—the ball went sailing deep into right field, triggering a sudden cluster of excited fans scrambling down across the seats.

The Dodgers won that night. All the way home, I kept praising Dennis for his excellent wishing.

⸎⸎⸎⸎⸎⸎⸎⸎⸎⸎⸎⸎⸎⸎⸎

A couple of weeks after that, we were stopped at a light, waiting for it to change. It was one of those intersections that existed slightly sideways to reality. Whenever you stopped there, time slowed down to a crawl. Without even thinking, I said, "Dennis, wish for the light to turn green please."

"Okay," he said.

—and abruptly the light turned green. I frowned. It seemed to me the cycle hadn't quite completed.

Nah. I must have been daydreaming. I eased the car through the intersection. A moment later, we got caught at the next red light . I said a word.

"Why'd you say that?"

"These lights are supposed to be synchronized," I said. "So you only get green ones. We must be out of synch. Why don't you wish for this light to change too please."

"Okay."

—green.

"Boy! You are really a good wisher."

"Thank you."

A minute later, I said, "Can you wish this light to turn green too?"

"No," he said, abruptly angry. "You're going to use up all my wishes."

"Huh?" I looked over at him.

"I only have so many wishes and you're going to use them all up on stoplights." There was a hurt quality in his voice.

I pulled the car over to the side of the road and stopped. I turned to him and put my hand gently on his shoulder. "Oh, sweetheart. I don't know who told you that, but that's not so. The wish bag is bottomless. You can have as many wishes as you want."

"No, you can't," he insisted. "I have to save my wishes for things that are important."

"What's the most important thing you ever wished for? " I asked, already knowing the answer.

He didn't answer.

"What's the most important wish?" I repeated.

Very softly, he admitted, "I wished for a dad. Someone who would be nice to me."

"Uh-huh. And did you get your wish?"

He nodded.

"So, you see, sweetheart. There's no shortage of miracles."

I didn't know if he believed me. It was still too early in the process. We were still learning who each other was. I noted the conversation in my journal and let the matter slide. But it left me with an uncomfortable feeling. What has to happen to a child to make him believe there's a limit to wishes?

A year later, I looked at the words I'd written glowing on the computer screen, and *wondered* about Dennis's ability to wish. It was probably a coincidence. But maybe it wasn't. That time we'd matched four out of six numbers in the lottery and won eighty-eight dollars—was that the week I'd asked him to wish real hard for us to win?

Maybe Martians have precognitive or telekinetic powers... ?

<hr/>

Dennis likes cleaning things. Without asking, he'll go out and wash the car, or the patio. He'll give the dogs baths. He'll vacuum the rugs and take the Dustbuster to the couch. He'll mop the floors. His favorite toys are a sponge and a squirt-bottle of Simple Green. I've seen him take a rusty old wrench he found in a vacant field and scrub the rust off of it until it shone like new. One night after dinner, after he finished methodically loading the dishwasher, I sat him down at the kitchen table and told him I had a surprise for him.

"What?"

"It's a book of puzzles."

"Oh." He sounded disappointed.

"No, listen. Here's the game. You have twenty minutes to do these puzzles, and then when you finish. I add them up and we'll find out how smart you are. Do you want to do this?"

"It'll really tell you how smart I am?"

"Uh-huh. "

He grabbed for the book and a pencil.

"Wait a minute—let me set the timer. Okay? Now once you start, you can't stop. You have to go all the way through to the end. Okay?"

"Okay."

"Ready?"

"Ready."

"One, two, three... go."

He attacked the first three puzzles with a vengeance. They were simple. Pick the next shape in a series: triangle, square, pentagon... ? Which object doesn't belong: horse, cow, sheep, scissors? Feather is to Bird as Fur is to: dog, automobile, ice cream... ?

Then the puzzles started getting harder and he started to frown. He brushed his hair out of his eyes and once he stopped to clean his glasses; but he stayed interested and involved and when the timer went off, he didn't want to stop. He insisted that he be allowed to finish the puzzle he was working on. What the hell. I let him.

"What does it say?" Dennis asked as I computed the percentile. He wanted to grab the test book out of my hand.

"Well... let me finish here. " I held it out of his reach as I checked the table of percentiles.

The test showed that he had above-average intelligence—not unexpected; hyperactive kids tend to be brighter than average—but well within the normal range for a nine-year-old. "It says that you are fifty-two inches high, that you weigh sixty-six pounds, and that your daddy loves you very much. It also says that you are very smart."

"How smart?"

"Well, if this test were given to one hundred children, you would be smarter than ninety-two of them."

"How good is that?"

"That's *very* good. You can't get much better. And it means we should go out for ice cream after dinner. What do you think?"

"Yeah!"

Oh, that was another thing. He didn't like chocolate. He preferred rainbow sherbet. I'd never seen that in a kid before.

∞∞∞∞∞∞∞∞∞∞

A couple of weeks later, we played another game. I made sure to pick a quiet evening, one with no distractions. "This game is even harder," I explained. "It's a kind of card game," I explained. "See these cards? There are six different shapes here. A circle, a square, a star, three squiggly lines, a cross, and a figure-eight. All you have to do is guess which one I'm looking at. See if you can read my mind, okay?"

He frowned at me, and I had to explain it two or three more times. This was not a game he wanted to play. I said okay and started to put the deck away. If he didn't want to cooperate, the results would be inconclusive. "Can we go for ice cream after we do this?" he asked abruptly.

"Sure," I said.

"Okay, let's do it then."

"All night. We have to do it five times. Do you think you can do it that many times?"

He shrugged. I laid out a paper in front of him, showing him the shapes so he would be able remember them all. I told him he could close his eyes if it would help him concentrate. The test conditions were less than perfect, but if there were any precognitive or telepathic powers present, five trials should be enough to demonstrate them.

Half an hour later, I knew.

Martians aren't telepathic.

But they do like rainbow sherbet. A lot.

∞∞∞∞∞∞∞∞∞∞

There were other tests. Not many. Not anything too weird. Just little ones that might indicate if there was something worth further investigation. There wasn't. As near as I could determine, there was nothing so unusual about Dennis that it would register as a statistical anomaly in a repeatable testable circumstance. He couldn't levitate. He couldn't move objects. He couldn't make things disappear. He didn't know how to *grok*. He could only hold his breath for thirty-three seconds. He couldn't *think* muscles. He couldn't see around corners.

But—

He *could* predict elevators. Take him into any building, anywhere. Take him to the elevator bank. Let him push the up button. Don't say a word. Without fail, the door he stands in front of will be the one where the first elevator arrives. Was he wishing them or predicting them? I don't know. It's useful only at science fiction conventions, which are legendary for recalcitrant elevators. It has little value anywhere else in the world.

He could make stop lights turn green—sometimes. Mostly, he waited until he saw the lights for the cross street turn yellow before he announced his wish. Maybe he could still make the Dodgers score four runs in two innings—but it wasn't consistent. We went back to Dodger Stadium in May, and either Dennis wasn't wishing or he really had used up all his wishes.

He *could* sing with perfect pitch, especially if the lyrics were about Popeye's gastrointestinal distress. He could play a video game for four hours straight without food or water. He could invent an amazing number of excuses for not staying in bed. He could also hug my neck so hard that once I felt a warning crack in my trachea. My throat hurt for a week afterward.

I began to think that *maybe* I had imagined the whole thing.

On school nights, I tucked him in at 9:30. We had a whole ritual. If there was time, we read a storybook together; whatever was appropriate. Afterward, prayers—

"I'm sorry God for... I didn't do anything to be sorry for."

"How about sassing your dad? Remember you had to take a timeout?"

"Oh, yeah. I'm sorry God for sassing my dad. Thank you God for... um, I can't think of anything."

"Going swimming?"

"No. Thank you God for Calvin, my cat."

"Good. Anything else you want to say to God?"

"Does God hear the prayers of Martians?"

"Uh... of course he does. God hears everybody's prayers."

"Not Martians."

"Yes, even Martians."

"Uh-uh."

"Why do you say no?"

"Because God didn't make any Martians."

"If God didn't make the Martians, then who did?"

"The devil."

"Did the devil make you?"

"Uh-huh."

"How do you know?"

"Because... I'm a Martian."

"Mm," I said, remembering a little speech I'd made just about a year ago. *Let it be all right for him to be a Martian for as long as he needs to be.* "All right," I said. "But let me tell you a secret," I whispered. "The devil didn't make any Martians. That's just a lie the devil wants you to believe. God made the Martians."

"Really?"

"Cross my heart and hope to die. Stick a noodle in my eye."

"How do you know?" He was very insistent.

"Because I talk to God every night," I said. "Just like you, I say my prayers. And God made everything in the world."

"But Martians aren't from this world—"

"That's right. But God made Mars too. And everything on it. Just like she made this world, she made a whole bunch of others, and Mars was one of them. Honest."

"How come you say 'she' when you talk about God?"

"Because sometimes God is female and sometimes God is male. God is everything. And now it's time for you to stop asking questions and go to sleep. Hugs and kisses—?"

"Hugs and kisses."

"G'night. No more talking."

"I love you."

"I love you too. Now no more talking."

"Dad?'

"What?"

"I have to tell you something."

"What?"

"I love you."

"I love you too. Now, shhh. No more talking, Dennis."

"G'night."

"Sleep tight—"

Finally, I got smart. I stopped answering. Control freaks. We each wanted to have the last word.

◇◇◇◇◇◇◇◇◇◇◇◇◇◇◇

I padded barefoot down the hall. I stopped in the living room long enough to turn off the television set, the VCR, and the surround-sound system. I continued on through the dining room and finally to my office. Two computers sat on my desk, both showing me that it was 9:47. The monster-child had manipulated an extra seventeen minutes tonight.

I sat down in my chair, leaned back, put my feet up on my desk, and stared out at the dark waters of the swimming pool in the back yard. The pool glowed with soft blue light. The night was... silent. Somewhere, a dog, barked.

Somewhere—that was his name, yes. He was a writer's dog—lived under my desk. Whenever I said," Let's go to work," wherever he was in the house, Somewhere would pick himself up and laboriously pad-pad-pad into my office where he'd squelch himself flat and scrooch his way under the desk, with a great impassioned Jewish sigh of, "I hope you appreciate what I do for you."

He'd stay there all day—as long as the computer was on. Somewhere would only come out for two things: cookies and the doorbell... and the doorbell was broken. It had been broken for as long as I'd lived in this house. I'd never had the need to get it fixed. If someone came to the door, the dog barked.

Somewhere, the dog, barked.

That was why I loved him so much. He was a living cliché. He was the only possible justification for one of the most infamous sentences in bad writing. It was just a matter of placing the commas correctly.

Somewhere had just enough intelligence to keep out of the way and more than enough intelligence to find his dinner dish—as long as no one moved it. He spent his mornings resting under my desk, his afternoons snoozing behind the couch, his evenings snoring next to Dennis; he spent the hours before dawn in the dark space underneath the headboard of my bed, dreaming about the refrigerator.

Almost every night, just as Dennis began saying his prayers, Somewhere would come sighing down the hall, a shaggy, absent-minded canine-American. He'd step over everything that was in his way, uncaring if he knocked over a day's worth of Lego construction. He'd climb onto the bed, over my lap, over Dennis, grumbling softly as he found his position next to Dennis. With his prehensile tongue, he could slurp the inside of Dennis's right ear from the left side of his head, taking either the internal or external route.

Tonight, though, he knew I wasn't finished working. I had some serious thinking to do. He remained under the desk, sighing about the overtime. "You're in super-golden hours," I said to him; he shut up.

Whenever I'm in doubt about something, I sit down and start writing. I write down everything I'm feeling or thinking or worrying about. I say everything there is to say until there's nothing left to say. The first time I did this was the day after my dad died. I sat and wrote for two days. When I was finished, I had a Nebula nominated story, *In the Deadlands*. To this day I still don't fully understand what the story was about, but the emotional impact of it is undeniable. It still gives me the shudders.

But the lesson I learned from that experience was the most important thing I've ever learned about storytelling. Effective writing isn't in the mechanics. Anyone can master the mechanical act of stringing together words and sentences and paragraphs to make a character move from A to B. The bookstores are full of evidence. But that's not writing. Writing isn't about the words, it's about the experience. It's about the *feeling* that the story creates inside of you. If there's no feeling, there's no story.

But sometimes, there's only the feeling without any meaning or understanding. And that's not a story either. What I was feeling about Dennis was so confusing and troubling and uncertain that I couldn't even begin to sort it out. I needed to write down all the separate pieces—as if in the act of telling, it would sort itself out. Sometimes the process worked.

When I looked up again, three hours had passed. My back and shoulders ached. The dog had gone to bed, and I felt I had accomplished nothing at all except to delineate the scale of my frustration.

Why would an alien species come to this planet? The last time I spent that much time on this question, I came up with giant pink man-eating slugs in search of new flavors. Why would Martians send their children to Earth?

The most logical idea that I came up with was that they were here as observers. Spies.

Haven't you ever been pulling on your underwear and realized that your dog or your cat is watching you? Haven't you ever considered the possibility that the creature is sharing your secrets with some secret network of dogs and cats? *"Oh, you think that's weird? My human wears underwear with pictures of Rocky and Bullwinkle on them."*

But dogs and cats are limited in what they can observe. If you *really* want to know a culture, you have to be a member of it. But an alien couldn't step in and pretend to be a member of this culture, could he? He'd have to learn. He'd have to be taught....

Where could a Martian go to get lessons in being a human? Who gives lessons in human beingness?

Mommies and Daddies. That's right.

◇◇◇◇◇◇◇◇◇◇◇◇◇◇◇◇

"You're too paranoid," my sane friend said. He asked me to leave his name out of this narrative, so I'll just call him my sane friend.

"What do you mean?"

"You think that aliens are all motivated by evil intentions. You've written four novels about evil aliens eating our children, and you're working on a fifth. Isn't it possible that you're wrong?"

"M*oi?* Wrong?"

"Do you ever think about the cuckoo?" my sane friend asked.

"No," I said.

"Well, think about the cuckoo for a moment."

"Okay."

"How do you feel about the cuckoo?" he asked.

"It's an evil bird," I said. "It lays its egg in the sparrow's nest. The cuckoo chick pushes the other babies out of the nest. The sparrow ends up raising it—even at the expense of her own young. It's a parasite."

"See, that's your judgment talking—"

"That's the truth—" I started to object.

"Is it? Is that what you tell Dennis about his birth-mother?"

"Uh—I tell him that his birth-mom couldn't take care of him. And that she loves him and misses him. And that's the truth. Sort of...whitewashed."

My sane friend grinned at me.

"Okay," I admitted. "I'm protective of my son. So what?"

My sane friend shrugged. "How do you think the cuckoo feels?"

"Birds don't feel."

"If it could feel, how do you think it would feel?"

I thought about it. The first image that came to mind was the silly little bird from the Dr. Seuss story; the one who flew off, leaving Horton the elephant to hatch her egg. I shook my head. "I'm not getting anything useful—"

"How do you think Dennis's mother feels?"

I shook my head again. "Everything I've heard about her... I can't empathize."

"All right, try it this way. Under what circumstances would *you* give Dennis up?"

"I'd die before I'd give him up," I said. "He makes me happier than anybody I've ever known before. Just looking at him, I get an endorphin rush. If anybody started proceedings to take him out of my home, I'd have him on a plane to New Zealand so fast—" I stopped. "Oh, I see what you mean." I thought about it. "If I wasn't able to take care of him, or if I thought I was hurting him, or if I thought I wasn't doing a good enough job—" There was that old *familiar* twinge again. "If I thought he'd *really* be better off with someone else, I'd want him to have the best chance possible. But I just can't see that happening."

"Uh-huh...." My sane friend grinned. *"Now*, how do you think the Martians feel?"

"Huh?"

He repeated the question.

I thought about it for a while. "I'd have to assume that if they have the capability to implant their children in human wombs that they would have a highly developed science and technology and that implies—to me anyway—a highly developed emotional structure and probably a correspondingly well-developed moral structure as well. At least, that's what I'd like to believe."

"And if what you believe is true..." he started to say.

I finished the thought for him. " ... then the Martians are trusting us with their children."

"Aren't they?" he asked.

I didn't answer. I didn't like where that train of thought might lead. But I followed it anyway.

"Would you trust your child to apes or wolves? " my sane friend asked. "No," I said. "You know what happens to feral children."

He nodded. "I've read the same books you have."

"So, if the Martians are trusting us with their children... then that implies that either they don't care about their children very much—or they do."

"You want my best guess?"

"This is where you resolve everything for me, isn't it?"

"No. This is where I tell you what I think. I think they're engaged in a long-term breeding experiment... to upgrade the level of intelligence and compassion in the human race."

"Yeah?" I gave him my best raised-eyebrow look. "Remember what happened to Spock? He was a half-breed too. His parents wanted to breed a logical human. Instead, they got an emotional Vulcan."

"Have you got a better guess?"

"No," I admitted. "But what kind of Martians *are* we raising?"

"What kind of Martian are *you* raising?" he corrected.

And that really did it for me. That was the question. "I don't know," I finally admitted. "But—he is mine to raise, isn't he?"

"Yep," my sane friend agreed.

That thought echoed for a long long moment. Finally, I acknowledged the truth of it with a grin. "Yeah," I said. "I can live with that...."

∞∞∞∞∞∞∞∞∞∞∞∞∞

As a literary puzzle, this is incomplete. As a story, it doesn't work. There's no ending.

There isn't enough evidence for me to even *suggest* a conclusion. What do we know about the Martians? For that matter, what do we really know about ourselves? There's nothing to extrapolate. And if the Martians are really engaged in some kind of large-scale genetic engineering we won't really know what their intentions are until the Martian children start reaching adulthood. Dennis will be old enough to vote in 2005. And that raises *another* question. *How long* have the Martians been planting their babies in human homes? Maybe we *already* live in a Martian-influenced world?

Maybe the Martian children will be super geniuses, inventing cold fusion and silicon sentience and nanotechnological miracles—Stephen Hawking and Buckminster Fuller. Maybe they'll be spiritual saviors, bringing such superior technology of consciousness that those of us brave enough to follow will achieve the enlightenment of saints. Maybe they'll be demagogues and dictators. Or maybe they'll be madmen and all end up in institutions. And maybe they'll be monsters, giving us a new generation of serial killers and cult-leaders—Jack the Ripper and Charles Manson.

All we can do is wait and see how it works out.

∞∞∞∞∞∞∞∞∞∞∞

There's one more thing.

In reviewing the material for this story, I came across a curious coincidence. Kathy Bright had given me several huge stacks of reports on Dennis, written by various therapists and counselors. I hadn't had time to read them all, and after the first few, I stopped—I didn't want *their* experience of Dennis; I wanted to make up my own mind. But as I paged through the files, looking for Martian stuff, one of them caught my eye. On Saturday, June 27th, 1992, Carolyn Green (the counselor on his case at the time) had noted, "Dennis thinks God doesn't hear his prayers, because he wished for a dad and nothing happened."

I first saw Dennis's picture on Saturday, June 27th, 1992, at about two in the afternoon. According to Carolyn Green's report, that was the exact time of his weekly session. I cannot help but believe that he was wishing for a dad at the exact moment I first saw his picture. *A Martian wish*. Was that what I felt so strongly?

Does it mean anything? Maybe. Maybe not. In any case, I know better than to argue with Martian wishes. Tonight, at bed time, he wished for me to be happy.

I had to smile. "Was that a Martian wish?" I asked.

"Yes," he said, in a voice that left no room for disagreement.

"Then, I'm happy," I said. And in fact, I was.

I hadn't realized it before, because I hadn't acknowledged it, not even to myself; but as I walked back down the hall to my office, I had to admit that I was glowing. I'd gotten everything I'd wanted, a wonderful son, a profound sense of family, a whole new reason for waking up in the morning. So what if he's a Martian, it really doesn't matter, does it? He's my *son*, and I love him. I'm not giving him up. He's *special*.

When Dennis puts his mind to it, he can predict elevators and make stoplights turn green and help the Dodgers win baseball games. He can make lottery tickets pay off (a little bit, four numbers at a time) and he can wish a father into his life. That's pretty powerful stuff.

I think we might experiment with that a little bit more. We haven't bought any lottery tickets in a while. Maybe we should buy a couple tonight. And if that works, who knows what else he could wish for. I was thinking of asking him to wish for a Hugo award for his dad—just a test, you understand—but this morning, he announced he was going to wish for a mom instead. I'll be *very* interested to see how that one works out.

AFTERWORD

This story is, to the best of my knowledge, a work of fiction.

Yes, I have an adopted son. Yes, his name is Dennis. No, he is not a Martian.

I asked him if he was. He said he wasn't. Then he came over and whispered in my ear, "I said no because we're not supposed to tell."

This is a true story. It isn't science fiction. It isn't fantasy. It isn't magical realism or anything else. This is word-for-word what happened.

PICKLED MONGOOSE

Once upon a time, I'd had this fantasy, I wouldn't tell my mother anything at all about the impending adoption—then one day, I'd show up at her house with a little boy. She would look at him ask, "Who's this?" And I would reply, "Your new grandson." Just for the look on her face and the resulting shriek of surprise.

Of course, it couldn't work that way. The caseworkers needed to know that the extended family would be supportive of the adoption, so everybody had to be on board, even before they met the child.

On the other hand, telling a Jewish mother she has a new grandson, but can't meet him yet is almost as exquisite. On the scale of unbearable anticipation, it outranks the first trip to Disneyland. It's right up there with chocolate, redheads, and honeymoons.

Mom and Harvey lived fifteen minutes away. Three miles east, three miles south on the 405, 2 miles east on the 101—

Summer evenings in California are surly, with the hot breath of the wind breathing down the back of your neck like a giant Labrador Retriever. In an open convertible, the air roars past, all dry and leathery. It always makes me think of Raymond Chandler's literary housewives fingering the edges of kitchen knives and studying their husband's necks.

As we slid through the glimmering night, Dennis asked, "What's she making for dinner?"

Without missing a beat, I deadpanned, "Pickled mongoose."

I might just as well have switched on an air-raid siren: *"I don't want pickled mongoose. I don't like pickled mongoose. I'm not eating pickled mongoose—"*

"Have you ever had pickled mongoose? How do you know you don't like it if you've never had it?"

"I don't want pickled mongoose. I don't like pickled mongoose. I'm not eating pickled mongoose—"

"You'll take one taste. You'll try it. Maybe you'll like. Grandma Jo makes the best pickled mongoose in the whole world. She does this thing with cobra sauce—"

"I don't want pickled mongoose. I don't like pickled mongoose. I'm not eating pickled mongoose—"

Uh-oh. He was taking me serious.

This was a double whammy. I wasn't used to people taking me serious. And worse, it meant that Dennis didn't understand jokes. Not good.

The ability to joke is the difference between sane people and crazy people. Crazy people don't do jokes. I wondered just how big a problem this was going to be—

"I don't want pickled mongoose. I don't like pickled mongoose. I'm not eating pickled mongoose—"

By now, we were in serious risk of Dennis shattering large chunks of air out of the sky. I had no idea what the limits of his lung power might be. This could go on for days—

I remembered an old piece of engineering wisdom: "If you don't know where the *off*-switch is, don't press the *on*-button." It applied to children too.

We got off the freeway at Van Nuys Blvd. Turn right, turn left, turn left and we're there. Dennis was still going strong. Sooner or later, he would have to take a breath—

I let him out of the car and pointed him toward the rear of the complex. "See those stairs? Grandma Jo and Grandpa Harvey live at the top." He rushed up the stairs ahead of me, then stopped and waited.

I knocked on the screen door and hollered, "Hello! Burglar—where do you hide the gold and jewelry?"

"Come on in. The gold is in the safe, the jewelry is under the bed."

Dennis followed me in. Grandma Jo was in the kitchen; she turned to us, wiping her hands on a towel. Dennis went straight to her, skipping all introductions. "What are you making for dinner?" he demanded.

"Chicken. And salad. And smashed potatoes."

"You're not making *pickled mongoose*—?"

She didn't even blink. To her credit, she had always been fast on the uptake; it had only taken thirty years for her to figure out that her first-born son was *meshuge*. (This may have been why there was no second-born son.)

"Pickled mongoose? Oh, no." Dennis shot me a look of angry accusation. And then she added, "The store was all out of mongoose. I'll make it next time."

Dennis's expression turned back into a suspicious frown. He looked back and forth between us with narrowed eyes. Maybe he was starting to figure it out. I hoped so.

Harvey handed me a tumbler of scotch. I took a sip. The Chivas 100 Blend. Not available in the States. I'd picked up two bottles at the duty free store on my way back from England a year ago and given one to Harve for Father's Day. "Mm, the good stuff. What's the special occasion?"

"You are."

"Well, we do have some news. Dennis, do you want to tell them?"

"David's gonna 'dopt me. He's gonna be my dad—and you're gonna be my Grandma and Grandpa!" He practically shouted the news.

"Oh, good," Mom said, "That means I get to hug you—" She swept him into her arms and he grabbed her around the waist and held on tight. It was a perfect fit.

Grandpa too. I couldn't tell who was happier. I promised myself this kid was going to spend a lot of time with his grandparents; it was all part of my secret plan to give him as many happy memories as possible.

And for a moment, I thought of my own Grandma. I hadn't realized until now how much a part of my life she'd been and how much I missed her...and how much she would have loved Dennis.

And then, of course, the inevitable Grandma moment. "Well, you must be very hungry. Sit down and I'll serve—"

Dennis eyed his dinner suspiciously.

"Relax, it's chicken," I said. "Nobody can torture a chicken like your Grandma Jo. That was chicken, wasn't it, Mom?"

"That's what it said on the wrapper."

"I dunno...it tastes like rattlesnake to me. Doesn't it taste like rattlesnake to you, Dennis?"

"No!" he insisted. "It tastes like chicken!"

"Or maybe iguana?"

"Chicken!"

"I can make iguana for you sometime, then we'll see—"

"No!"

I decided not to pursue it. Probably a wise decision.

As soon as he finished eating, Dennis asked quietly, "Can I wash the dishes?"

My mother looked at me, eyebrows raised. *This is the monster child you were so worried about?* To Dennis, she said, "Of course, you can, sweetheart."

We watched as he very carefully cleared the table, taking all the dishes to the sink. He made three deliberate trips. Then he turned on the water and began sudsing and scrubbing.

"Do you rent him out?"

Very softly, I said, "He's trying to show us how much he wants to fit in. He's terrified it won't work."

"Of course, it's going to work," she said, not bothering to whisper. "He's a good kid."

Harvey added, "All you have to do is love him."

"Well, that's the game plan—"

"You're going to have to find a school for him," said Harvey.

"And he's going to need new clothes," said Mom. "Shoes, shirts, pants. What size is he? I'll take him to the mall—"

"Just a minute here," I interrupted. "If you want to spoil a kid, spoil your own. This one is mine to spoil—"

Dennis walked out of the kitchen, a dish and a towel in his hand. His expression was serious. Very soft and very polite, he said, "She could spoil me if she wants to." His timing and delivery were perfect. He returned to the kitchen without further comment.

Mom and Harvey looked at him, then to me. Mom said, "I think you've met your match."

Harvey added, "He's going to fit into this family, just fine."

"I think so."

"Does he ever smile?" Harvey asked softly.

"Give him time. He hasn't had a lot to smile about yet. That's first on my list of things to do."

On the day he moved in—*officially* moved in—Kathy told me she'd never seen him so happy. I asked her to remind him of that conversation he'd had with the counselor. "Remember when he said, 'I don't think God listens to my prayers.' Tell him that sometimes it takes God a little while to make a miracle happen."

Dennis moved in with a small battered suitcase, half full of worn-out hand-me-downs; and a large cardboard box, less than half full of pieces of broken toys. His entire life could be carried in one trip.

Unpacking his few belongings was painful. Everything was tattered. Everything was precious. A too-small T-shirt autographed by Luc Robitaille and Wayne Gretsky. A sad and faded, dirty-with-age, stuffed gingerbread man named Eric. A few photographs of a long-ago trip to the Los Angeles County Fair. The only evidence of a past. Not much evidence of a life though.

He had only a few pairs of underpants. Three of them had pockets sewn onto the front. "What's this?" I asked.

"That's for the buzzer. If I wet the bed, it buzzes and wakes me up."

"We're not going to do that here," I said, tossing the underwear aside. "You won't be wearing those again." We put the T-shirts in one drawer, the shorts in another, and we were through unpacking.

"We can throw this out," I said, holding up his small battered suitcase. It was pretty much falling apart.

"No," he said firmly. "I'll need it when I move out."

"No, you won't. You're not moving out. This is *it*."

"When I have to go back to Mars," he said. He took the suitcase from me and put it into the closet.

Dennis needed *everything*.

We spent the week shopping.

Shoes. Underpants. T-shirts. Shorts. Socks. A jacket. A new teddy bear. Some storybooks for bedtime. Not too much, but enough. Christmas was coming soon, Santa was going to be very very good to this little boy.

It wasn't just his miracle, it was mine as well. I was terrified that it wasn't real, that somebody somewhere was going to realize that they'd made a horrible mistake placing him with me, and that suddenly one day, they'd come and pack him up and take him away, and the adventure would be over.

I spent the first three or four weeks with him in a state of absolute wonder that I had this wonderful little person in my life. I read him a story every night, tucked him into bed, hugged him, kissed him, told him how special he was to me, turned off the light and tiptoed out. I'd wait fifteen minutes, get a box of Kleenex, then tiptoe back in and sit and watch him sleep for an hour or two. It was better than television—and it was one of my few chances to see what he actually looked like; the rest of the time, he was mostly a blur with a smile.

I developed a routine for the mornings. First I'd turn to the little voice in my head that was muttering in amazement, "There's a seven O'clock in the morning too?!" and say, "Thank you for sharing that, now shut up."

Then I'd wake Dennis up and before his blood sugar could remind him that he was hyperactive, I'd hand him a glass of orange juice and pop him into the tub and start a hot breakfast. Hot cereal. Or pancakes, Dennis loved pancakes. Or scrambled eggs and bacon. Toast and jelly. But no waffles. For Christmas, I'd bought a waffle iron that made waffles shaped like Mickey Mouse—but Dennis wouldn't eat anything that looked like a giant grinning mongoose.

I gained five pounds. The last time I'd actually eaten breakfast, it had been an unwitting mistake—brought on by crossing the International Date Line on a sixteen hour red-eye.

And then, one morning, right on schedule, it was time to test the rules. He decided he didn't want to eat breakfast. I told him he had to. He said no, and then abruptly he announced, "The adoption is off, I'm moving out." He went to the front door, walked out, and closed it behind him. I waited thirty seconds, then followed. He was standing on the front porch, waiting for me.

Very calmly, I said, "You can't move out until you finish breakfast."

So he came back in and ate.

As he was finishing, I said, "Why don't you go to school now, and you can move out after you get home from school, all right?"

He went to school.

When he got home from school, I handed him a peanut butter sandwich, and said, "Listen, why don't you wait and run away from home on the weekend. You can go farther."

I kept that up for three days, until he finally said, "I'm not going to run away from home." That night, I made a note in my journal: "Sighted manipulation, sank same."

I had a plan. Affirmations—lots of little reminders, like pebbles in the stream, to let him how much he was loved—that he was finally *connected*. And choices—opportunities to feel in control, to give him back a sense of power over his own life; the system had stolen that from him, yanking him around from place to place like a case-file shuffled from desk to desk. And most of all, *a safe place* just to be—so he could have an emotional ground of being, and a sense that he wasn't alone anymore.

That last one would be the hardest to achieve.

The supermarket was always a challenge. He had to push the cart. No one else was allowed to touch it—*Gran Prix de Vons*. Up one aisle and down the next at mach 8 and a half. And always, strange things kept finding their way into the cart.

It amused me, how my shopping list had suddenly transformed. White bread instead of sourdough. Peanut butter. Jelly. Spaghetti. Tomato sauce. Hamburger. Cookies. Cheerios. Oatmeal. Cream Of Wheat—that was my favorite when I was little. Malt-O-Meal. Ice cream. Hot dogs. Buns. Mustard, ketchup, relish. Chocolate for Daddy. Apples, bananas, grapes. Dog biscuits. "You and Somewhere will have to share these."

"I don't like dog biscuits."

"Then Somewhere will eat your share."

And in the middle of all this shopping, I had a flash of recognition—I was *being* Daddy. This was what it looked like. This was what it *felt* like.

Kewl.

I could get used to this. This was good.

On the drive home, I asked. "What should I make for dinner tonight? How about pickled mongoose?"

I should have known better—

"You're making fun of me—!"

"Huh? No, I'm not!"

"I don't like it when people make fun of me! The kids at school used to make fun of me all the time. 'You live in a group home. You live in a group home.'"

I pulled the car over to the side. "I'm not making fun of you, sweetheart."

He was adamant. *"Yes, you are—"*

sigh

This part wasn't in the manual.

For some odd reason, I had a picture in my head of John F. Kennedy discovering that there were nuclear missiles in Cuba, in October of 1962. His reaction? "This is the day we earn our salary."

"Dennis, let me explain something to you about jokes. People don't tell jokes to make fun of each other. People tell jokes because they like each other. Jokes are a way of playing together."

"I don't like it! It feels like you're making fun of me! Everybody always makes fun of me!"

"Sweetheart, I'm not making fun of you. I will *never* make fun of you. You're my favorite kid in the whole wide world. And you need to learn something very important here. You're in a family of people who love to tell jokes. It's our way of saying, 'I love you, play with me.' So you're going to have to learn how to tell jokes too."

"I don't know any jokes—"

That stopped me for a moment. A kid who didn't know any jokes? "Okay, I'll teach you one."

He fell silent. I went rummaging frantically through the attics of memory for the easiest and silliest joke I had.

"Okay, ready? Why do elephants have such big trunks?"

"I dunno."

"Because they don't have glove compartments."

"What's a glove department?"

Right.

We had a lot of work to do.

"See this thing here in front of you? It opens up. That's a glove compartment. It's called a glove compartment because you put gloves in it."

"I don't have any gloves."

"Nobody in California does. It's against the law. But the cars are all made in Detroit or Tokyo, where everybody wears gloves. So that's why they put glove compartments into cars. So now you know why elephants have such big trunks—"

"Because they don't have glove departments."

"Close enough. Very good. Now you tell that joke to everybody you meet."

"Will they laugh?"

"I'm sure they will. If they don't, we'll return the joke to the manufacturer and get a full refund."

For the next few weeks, he told that joke to everyone he saw—Grandma and Grandpa. Our neighbor, Roz. The waitress at the corner coffee shop. Julieanne, his therapist. Aunt Alice. Susie, my assistant. And it didn't even matter if he got it right. "Why don't elephants have glove departments—because they have trunks?" "Why don't elephants have trunks—because they have glove departments?" Where do elephants put their gloves? In their trunks." And everybody he told it to laughed. Every time.

It was basic Communication Theory: Jokes are a way of producing a happy response in people. If you want to be liked, tell jokes; it shows you want to play. And that's all that any of us really want—the chance to play together.

Dennis had been given one of the keys to the universe, and he was unlocking everything he could.

"Knock knock."

"Who's there?"

"Orange?"

His eyes narrowed. "Orange who?"

"Orange you glad I didn't say 'banana?'"

He made me sorry I taught him that one—I had to hear it a dozen times a day for the next two months. Some jokes are funny once. Some jokes are funny every time. It depends on who's telling them. But if you're only eight years old, it doesn't matter. The fun is in the telling, not the punch line. The fun is in the laughing.

And then one morning, while I was getting him ready for school—we were still only a few weeks into this adventure—I put him into the bathtub, a naked little toothpick of a child with puppy-dog eyes and Liz Taylor eyelashes. A little bubble bath and he was happy. He could wash himself, but he liked being taken care of. I wondered if anybody had ever really taken care of him before.

Okay, time to go start some water boiling for hot cereal. I stopped and asked, "What do you want for breakfast? Cream of Wheat? Or Malt-O-Meal?"

He looked up at me, with an expression so innocent, you could have used it as icing on a birthday cake. Very softly, very shyly, he said, "Pickled mongoose...." And waited for my reaction.

I blinked.

"Um—" For half an instant, I was annoyed, because he hadn't answered the question I'd asked, and then the enormity of what had just happened sank in. I grinned. "Okay. Pickled mongoose, it is." And then, as an afterthought, "Do you want the Cream of Wheat flavored pickled mongoose or Malt-O-Meal flavor?"

"Cream of Wheat flavor."

"Okay, Cream of Wheat flavor pickled mongoose, coming right up." And we both smiled.

Halfway to the kitchen, in the middle of the hall, where not even the dog could see me, I stopped for a quick, silent victory dance, punching the air with both fists in one-two triumph. *"Yes!"*

That's what miracles look like.

AUTHOR'S AFTERWORD:

Miracles have to be shared. If you don't share them, nobody knows they happened.

I always wanted to write old-fashioned science fiction, the kind that filled the pages of the great SF magazines of the 50s, especially Galaxy and F&SF. This story comes closest. It's intended as a thematic sequel to one of Theodore Sturgeons' best, "Mr. Costello, Hero."

THE FURTHER ADVENTURES OF MR. COSTELLO

Haven? Yeah, it used to be a nice place, great place even.

You could raise a podful of kids and not have to worry about traffic and cities and taxes—we didn't have any. In the evening, we'd sit out on the front porch and watch the suns go down, double sunsets worth staying up late for—one red, one blue, and sometimes the two of them together would edge the howling green sky with orange and yellow streamers so brilliant you had to put on goggles. The best was when they lit up the spiral rings that arced across the southern sky, shimmering the night for hours.

There was a fella one time, he said, "There ain't no Earth-like planets, there's only wishful thinkin.'" Well, maybe so, but he never saw Haven. It's as close to the homeworld as I ever found, and I bounced across fifty planets before finally coming to rest on this one. It's an unlikely planet in an unlikely place—an ephemeral zone of livability around a binary dance, but somehow all the unlikelies cancelled each other out and Haven was the result. A 37-hour day, 93% Earth-gee, a dollop more oxygen, a thirty-seven degree tilt on the axis which made for some spectacular seasons, and a temperate zone that stretched around the planet's equator like a slippery cummerbund. Yeah, I know what a cummerbund is. Second time I had to wear one, it was time to move on.

I bounced lucky and ended up in a contract family with four beautiful wives and two strong husbands—well, most of the time, except when we switched around, which wasn't too often, unless one of us wanted to get pregnant, which hadn't happened yet because we weren't ready to start a tank-farm and didn't want to rent a gestation bottle somewhere else, either. As a family, we only had one rule: nobody ever goes to bed hungry or angry; the rest was details. That rule lasted as long as the contract did. Which was quite a long time, and probably would have been a lot longer if it hadn't been for him.

Some people can't handle contracts, no big deal to me, I like 'em when I find one that suits me. A few years in a can wrestling vacuum, you learn how to live close with others. Some people don't learn, and that buys them a one-way ticket out the airlock. I knew several captains more than happy to sign the warrant. That's how they got well-behaved crews.

On Haven, though, if you and a neighbor started bumping heads, either he got up and moved or you did. One or t'other. Wasn't that hard; most of the houses were already on wheels. Our closest neighbor was a fella named Jasper, ten klicks to the west, but as long as he kept to himself we all got along fine. He was a good man, when he was a man, and a good woman the rest of the time. Called herself Jasmine then, Jas for short. Never borrowed anything she didn't return the next week, never spoke bad of anyone, never slept in where she wasn't invited, and didn't deserve the shit that came down when it did. None of us did.

But that's a story for another time and it happened long enough before Costello arrived that it doesn't matter here. This is about Costello—him and his fancy orange suit. First we heard of him, we thought he was just another star-grazer. Folks pass through Haven all the time, get caught up in her, and start planning resorts or industries or grand utopian communities—their utopias, of course. We listen politely, then go home and get back to the real work. Star-grazers are good entertainment, not much more; though every once in a while, we have to explain to one of them how an airlock works dirtside and why it would be a good idea to build his resort or his industry or his utopia *somewhere else.*

We didn't meet Mr. Costello until Midsummer Jubilee. We unhitched and drove in to Temp, short for Temporary, which was all the name that place was ever going to have. Midsummer was the best time for restocking medicines and spices and any other stuff we couldn't lab ourselves. The weather was calm, traveling was easy, and the bots could manage the crops while we were away.

Temp wasn't the best-stocked place, but it was a lot more convenient than driving three days to the other side of the mountain, to Settlement, and then driving three days back. We always ordered ahead anyway, and anything Temporary didn't have, they'd get Settlement to toss it on the next truck over, so we made out okay. I'd only been to Settlement once and had no wish to go there ever again. I don't do crowds. Not even small ones. And any place big enough to need a jail was no place I wanted to stay. I learned that lesson a long time ago.

Temp is half a day across the Rumpled Hills, up Narrow Canyon and down Abysmal, and then follow Occasional River for another half day. We leave the day before and camp overnight at Empty Meadow. We talked once about carving a road from here to there, but it was a very short discussion. Construction would use up the better part of a year and even if it might shorten our trip to only a few hours, it'd also open up the slopes for traffic. When you build a road, people drive it. And traffic would annoy the glitter-bushes enough to disrupt their breeding—plus careless tourists would encourage the horgs to aggressiveness. The conversation ended when Grampa (his title, not his description) said that roads are too much like civilization and we didn't come to Haven to be city-folk, did we? But there wasn't anyone in the family arguing for it anyway.

We crossed the river at the shallows and drove up onto the common track that thirty years of trucks had worn into the turf. We could tell from the ruts, wider and deeper, that traffic from the landing ports was up again. Not a good sign. Tourists are trouble; immigrants are worse, even rich ones.

Thirty klicks along, we came over the crest of the hill and there was Temporary. A busy day. Too many rigs linked in. Even worse, the Jacklins had added an extension to the public dock. Bad news, that. This was the new normal. Regular traffic. It wasn't unexpected—there was a new station up on the southern ridge, far enough away it wouldn't bother us and mostly good folks, tho it did make for bigger gatherings.

But Temporary was still the right size for a visit. The Jacklins had started with a six-pod spider and connected it by weather-tubes to a scattering of inflatable domes, all sizes. Each dome wrapped a different cargo drop, the leftovers from when Temporary was a landing site for a resource-development company. The Jacklins bought it after the company was persuaded to pull out by a series of unexplainable delays.

After the first winter, the Jacklins sprayed the domes with a meter of shelter-foam, so now, despite the name, the domes were permanent until further notice and sturdy enough to stand up by themselves, even with three or four meters of snow, ice, and occasionally a few centimeters of frozen carbon dioxide piled on top of that.

One of the larger domes served as a public swap and meeting place. Two of the others had long since been emptied and served now as occasional habitats for migrant workers and transients. Plus the inevitable call-boys and -girls working the western circuit. During the summer, with the Jacklins' grudging permission, various pass-throughs and unsettleds used a few of the old mineshafts as a retreat. During the winter, too. I say grudging because it's bad business to kill off customers, but some customers need to be killed. They used the tunnels that weren't habitated as storehouses and winter-bunkers. The bots had dug a whole network of tubes and tunnels inside the mountain, but the topmost part of Temporary still looked haphazard, unplanned, and accidental.

Most folks land at Settlement or at the bigger port farther north where the beanstalk touches down. They put wheels on their pods and head east and then south. The dumber ones head south first, and then east. Those are the ones who come through Temporary, and sometimes we all make a bit of money off them, especially from towing them out of ditches and ravines, repairing broken axles, or just hiring ourselves out as guides to the caravans and wagon trains. A train can be as many as twenty or thirty family-rigs—standard cargo pods laid horizontal and mounted on six or more fluffy polymer spheres two or three meters in diameter, depending on the terrain. It's standard practice to use bright colors; it helps identify your rig from a distance, especially if it's surrounded by snow. Our family colors were Florentine, equal stripes of red and yellow on the trucks and tires.

A cargo pod makes a good house—or a truck. Or both at the same time. Whatever you need. They're designed to be reused after landing. A standard unit can house six in comfort, eight if they're friendly, ten if they're small. If you're homesteading, you can drop one or two or three on a site, depending on how many of you there are and how much room you need. You can connect as many as eight to a central nexus and call it a spider. And you can link one spider to another to make an estate; I've seen linked clusters and chains of twenty or more spiders, but that's too many people for me. That's practically a city.

Once a pod is down, after twelve hours of unpacking you're ready to settle in; sooner if the first thing you unpack are the bots. If you're smart, you'll mount the rigs on wheels and give yourself mobility. As the saint says, "A man should be prepared to move fast at least three times in his life." It's a lot easier if you can just put the house in gear and drive to the dustoff—something I didn't expect to do on Haven, at least not until my third or fourth rejuvenation. And that was just the way I wanted it. This planet is far enough out that people don't drop round because they're in the neighborhood; Haven is a destination, not a rest stop.

But as much as I dislike crowds, I will admit that other people have their uses. For one thing, making love is better with a partner. And it's easier to find a partner in a crowd than a wilderness. If you're looking. I'm not. Not anymore. Not since my husbands and wives picked me out of a lineup, married me, and dragged me into the living pod. It was storm season, which is also honeymoon season for most folks, so we didn't come out for three weeks and that was only to check the anchor blocks on truck two. It wasn't the storm making it move, so we went back in and resumed what we'd only just begun. By first thaw we'd slowed down a bit, and by spring had pretty well finished 'mooning for awhile. By Midsummer, the new bots were trained well enough that we could take a week off for Jubilee. Lot of work to do before autumn, so we unchocked the bubbles on truck two, unlinked, and rolled. The break would do us all good.

As we bumped downslope, we saw a big black rig that none of us recognized—three industrial pods in a train, like a traveling factory, maybe a bio-refiner, and a couple more drones parked off-site. They had to be passing through, on their way to the richer territories southeast. The huge bulk of the rolling stock loomed over all the other vehicles like a cluster of broodysaurs.

For the most part we can tell who else is in attendance by the other rigs in the field, but sometimes we see a few strangers—not always newbies, this isn't that kind of neighborhood, just folks just passing through on their way to places they believe are going to be better than the places they left. Over the years, we've seen geologists, zoologists, biologists, mappers, trappers, huskers, buskers, peddlers, meddlers, tinkers, dinkers, migrants, handicrafters, and the occasional salesman. Once in a while, even a tourist, though there isn't really a lot to see, just trees and savannah and occasionally a horg in the distance. But you can see horgs at Settlement; they have a zoo, not a big one, but big enough to maintain a family of horgs, and if you're a tourist, that's what you come to see. Horgs. Once, a circus passed through, but I don't think they made much money. They only stayed for a day. Temp is not a place where anyone stays, not for long; it's just a place to rest overnight before heading deeper into the continent.

Grampa drove us in and found our dock. Most of the time, you just take whatever slot is open, but for Jubilee, the Jacklins always reserve key slots for local families. It's not just a question of good will—it's good management. When trouble breaks out, as it sometimes does, the locals are right there to handle it quickly.

The outside air was warm, by Haven standards, and clean enough that we could have parked and walked. Jackets and air filters would have been enough protection, but anyone who's lived on Haven longer than a week knows how hard it is to keep the inside air filtered and clean with folks coming in and out all the time. And one thing you learn real fast, running an airlock costs, especially bio- and particle-filtering, and the more you run it, the more it adds up. So as a courtesy to our hosts—Mik and Jik and Tilda Jacklin, the only real permanents at Temporary—we linked to the public access and ran our own airlock.

There's a ritual to follow. First you all go to the big common dome and say hello and share a beer and catch up on any gossip that's happened since you last logged on to the community. Then, if you're living in that kind of a family—I'm not, I'm in a closed contract, but some people are—you start filling out your dance card, who you're going to sleep with tonight. Then, and only after you've taken care of all the social business, then you can start talking about what you're looking to buy and what you brought to trade or sell. Otherwise, you look rude. Or worse, desperate. And people take advantage of you when you're desperate. So it's not a good idea to be impatient. The merchandise will still be on the shelves an hour from now, but the seller's good feelings might not.

Finn and I always shop together. The rest of the family goes looking for practicals, but Finn and I like to start with the clothing aisles. Of course, there's not a lot on the hangers that we can wear outside. As good as either one of us might look in a kilt or a pinafore, those are party clothes, not work detail. And Finn is a lot bigger than me, almost burly. But we still like to fantasize, and sometimes it's fun for whoever's being a husband this season. This trip, we contented ourselves with some fancy underwear. We'd take turns wearing it for each other.

During melting-season, that's when the hard work begins. Especially if you're ranching/farming. We had the long downslope of Restless Mountain, the western side, hence the spectacular sunsets. But the other side was Bareback Ridge. With that behind us, sunrise isn't until 9 or 10am, depending on the time of year, just a few hours of bright sky first, bright enough that we can get out early with the bots and start herding the glitter-bushes up and down the fields, making sure they get more sunlight per season than they would if they just sat in one place and brooded.

We spend most of summer harvesting, then start moving the bushes up toward higher ground. It's like herding cats in slow motion, but it's necessary to the survival of the herd. We have to do it before first autumn, because that's when the bushes start slowing their metabolism, saving their summer fat and closing up before long winter settles in. That's when they're most vulnerable to the horgs. A horg-pack can shred most of a herd in a matter of days, even digging down through the frozen ground to rip out the fatty stores at the heart of each bush.

Left to itself, a glitter-bush will take root inside a grove of tall wailing trees. It's not that the bushes don't like sunlight, they do, but swarms of spider-bats nest in the wailing trees, and at night, just before taking to the air, they all drop their guano. The bushes raise their roots to collect the rich fertilizer, so whenever a glitter-bush gets hungry it heads for the shade of a wailing willow, hoping to secure the best feeding spot for itself. Generally, the bushes only venture any distance into the meadows during midsummer because that's when the intense sunlight excites them to breed.

By having the bots herd them back into the fields where we can bright them, we're forcing two or three extra breeding cycles in a season, but that exhausts the bushes, so they strive for the trees even harder—despite us bringing them our own rich fertilizer, a lot more potent than the bat-shit they're accustomed to. One good garbage-refiner can generate both burnable oil and a lot of nitrogen-rich granules.

A determined glitter-bush can cover almost a klick a day. But a more determined bot can herd it by using mirrors to focus even more sunlight on the bush. The bush will reverse course and head back to the center of the meadow and the rest of its community.

An individual bush will breed continually, but when they're raised in herds, they breed in synchronized cycles, releasing clouds of spores. That's why we wear masks outside. The air on Haven is breathable, but glitter-spores can take root in your lungs. Not hard to kill, but who wants to inhale that much ammonia?

Because we brighten them, our bushes grow taller and thicker than the wild ones and their seedpods get two or three times as big. And with the bots patrolling the perimeters, we don't lose many to marauding horgs. Mostly, horgs don't come up this high, but dry season always sends them uphill, so midsummer usually brings excitement as well as magic.

This year, it brought Mr. Costello.

We were still looking at clothes when Trina came to get us. Finn was holding up a blue longshirt he thought would look good on me—more of a dress than a longshirt, but it could be worn either way. I smiled in embarrassment and said I wasn't planning to shift back for a while. He said he didn't care, he'd buy it for me and I could wear it now, it would show off my calves. I admitted it was pretty, but when I looked at the price tag, I told him no, we weren't that rich yet. Trina came up behind me and said it was cute and she and I could share it and yes we could too afford it and I said, "Only if Grampa approves," and that was the end of it for now. I was still the newest member of the family and they were still spoiling me a little, but I wasn't going to be a spoiled brat.

After Finn hung the dress back on the rack, Trina grabbed both our arms. "You don't wanna miss this. There's a guy bragging he's got a better way to commit suicide."

She dragged us into the big dome which doubled as bar, restaurant, dance floor, auction hall, and flea market, depending on the time of day. A small group had gathered around a stocky man in an orange suit. He had a thick fringe of black beard framing a round, unweathered face. He looked too innocent to be here, but here he was anyway. He had two blank-faced companions sitting at the table beside him. One was dressed in a tight black suit that looked vaguely military; the other looked like some kind of tech.

"—and when each person does their part, everybody makes money. Everybody wins."

That's when Tilda Jacklin came up behind him and tape-measured the width of his shoulders.

He turned around, puzzled. "What are you doing?"

"Measurin'. Makin' sure I got a body bag your size. Ye wanna pay fer it now? Discount it ten percent if ye do."

Give him credit, the stranger didn't get angry. He reached up and patted Tilda on the shoulder and said, "You have a fine sense of humor, young man. Very fine. Are you looking for a job?"

Tilda smiled, shook his head, and did a quick vertical measure of the man. "Not even two meters. Got plenty in stock. I'll put one aside fer ye." Then he went back behind the counter and poured three beers for Finn, Trina, and me.

"What's all that about?" Finn asked.

"Horgs," said Tilda.

"What about 'em?"

"That's Mr. Costello. Says he can sell 'em."

"Really . . . ?"

"Ayep."

"Gotta catch 'em first."

Tilda grinned and scratched the top of his head, the way he did when he was amused. "Ayep."

"How's he gonna do it?"

Tilda shrugged, making that wide-eyed, stretched expression he makes when he's reacting to stupidity. "Dunno. Says he needs two-three helpers. Says he's got buyers upside. Says he can fill a pod every ten weeks, send 'em right up the beanstalk. That's what he says. And he's already scheduled two empties and a truck."

Finn frowned, shook his head. "Ain't possible." Trina agreed with a snort.

I was already figuring in my head. "That's a lot of tonnage. Even to fill one pod. He's gotta be talking at least forty, maybe fifty head."

"He says sixty."

"Not possible," said Trina.

"Ayep. But he says his buyer is payin' three hundred a ton. So he's lookin' to gross fifty-thou per pod, at least six times a year, he says. Mebbe more. Temptation like that, a man'll go beyond crazy to pure unadulterated stupid."

"Ain't never gonna happen," said Finn. "No way to round up even a dozen of those bastards."

"Ayep. Horgs is horgs."

What Tilda said—you hear that everywhere on Haven. It's a way of saying this is what it is and there ain't no way of changing it. Rocks is hard, water is wet, and horgs is horgs.

Horgs are . . . well, they're big, they're ugly, they smell bad, and they're meaner than anything else on the planet, even humans, especially when they're in rut. Horgs have only one sex—they don't mate, they fight until exhausted. Or dead. The winner stabs the loser with a spiked penis. The sperm make their way through the bloodstream to the egg sac, where a litter of little horgs gets started. Sometimes the broodhorg survives, sometimes it doesn't.

Horgs aren't choosy, sometimes they poke other things—even humans. When they do that, when there's no eggs available, the sperm self-fertilizes, turns into minihorgs, and the litter eat their way out. Not pretty. You get a couple hundred rat-sized critters. The big horgs eat 'em. And if it's a horg with ripe eggs, they get fertilized that way. Crazy biology, but it works.

Some people think Horg meat is a delicacy. I'm not one of them. Some people say that if horg meat is fixed right, it's delicious. They can have my share. I've seen what an angry horg can do. And a horny one.

But offworld, horgs are a commodity. People pay a lot for them—dunno why, there are better things to eat, but there's a steady market. And that's why the Jacklins do a fair business in body bags, funerals, and estate planning. There's always some fool with a plan.

If there's a safe way to farm horgs, nobody's found it yet. If there was a safe way to herd them, if there was a safe way to round them up, I'd export every last horg from the planet. And most everyone else feels the same way. But we can't, and even if we could, we wouldn't, because you don't take the apex predator out of an ecology unless you want it to collapse. Without the horgs, we lose the glitter-bushes and everything else that makes Haven so interesting.

It's complicated, but horgs are essential. Spider-bat swarms feed on the insects that live on horg-droppings. No horgs, no droppings, no insects, no spider-bats, no guano. If the spider-bats starve, the glitter-bushes don't bloom, and one of Haven's main crops disappears. And that's only the first domino.

But Mr. Costello wasn't the first idjit to think he knew how to make a profit on Haven. He certainly wouldn't be the last. We'd probably have to dig a few more holes and lay a few more wreaths at Settlement's own Idjits' Field before he was done. I just hoped it wouldn't be anybody I cared about.

So, of course, it was Grampa.

He told us after second supper. We had arrayed ourselves at one of the long tables, the space next to the wall, so we had some privacy for conversation. Grampa was smiling happily about something but he wouldn't say what. "Not here, not here," and he resumed slurping his soup.

I started to press, but Trina shook her head. She touched her lips with a forefinger, then touched the same finger to her ear, and pointed at both the table and the wall. Someone might be listening.

I didn't think the Jacklins would eavesdrop unless it was necessary, like someone with a history of trouble, but you never knew who else passing through might have stuck a button under the table or into the rough paneling of the big common room. So Trina was telling me this was family business and it had to stay private.

Back in the truck, Grampa tamped his pipe carefully and puffed it to life. "Well," he said, "we found us a rich idjit. That fellow Costello. He offered to buy our entire year's crop of glitter-bush seedpods. Twelve percent over market, plus travel and delivery expenses—"

"He's the one says he's going to catch and sell horgs?" asked Finn.

"Ayep. That's the one."

Finn shook his head. "He'll be dead the first day he steps out the hatch—"

"That's fine, too. I told him there's a rich tradition of horg-wranglin' out here, so he'd have to pay in advance. The fool didn't even flinch. Paid the first half right then." Grampa patted his vest pocket, as if the actual money was resting next to his tobacco. "We get the other half on delivery."

Finn pursed his lips, looked around at the rest of us—me, Trina, Marlie, Charlie, and Lazz who'd just gone male again—then back to Grampa. "I wish you'd talked to us—"

"Wasn't any time. Couldn't find all of you. Had to make the deal then. Too rich to say no. And he did pay up front." As if that settled the matter.

Grampa had seniority because he'd staked the family to get it started. He was the majority shareholder. Even better, he was smart enough with the numbers to keep us buoyant and the way he explained it, it did sound better than trucking the loads all the way to Settlement for transshipment up the beanstalk. I wasn't going to say anything because I was the junior-est partner, but I could see by everybody's faces I wasn't the only one in my head about it.

"All right," said Grampa, "why's everybody lookin' so twisted?"

Finn glanced at Trina, then at me—we'd seen Mr. Costello in the common dome too. He was waiting for either of us to say something, but as the second-ranking male, it was his responsibility first. "It's like this," he began. He took a deep breath. "It sounds like a good deal, I mean, it really does. But we saw Mr. Costello in the common room and . . . well, I don't think he knows what he's doing. I think he's gonna get people killed."

"Ayep," said Grampa. "That's my thinkin', too."

"Takin' advantage of a dead idjit like that—it don't sit right."

Grampa puffed a cloud of sweet smoke. "He ain't dead yet. And until some horg pokes him with a litter, his money's just as good as the next idjit's."

Finn shook his head in resignation. He knew he wasn't going to talk Grampa out of anything. Grampa had already made the deal. We were stuck with it.

Trina spoke up then. "It really isn't that bad. I mean, not really. That's a lot of money. And if he gets killed early, we'll still have half a crop to sell. We could buy another pod or start a dome or . . . maybe even get a gestation tank and start a baby."

"Ayep," said Grampa.

"And . . . " she added slowly, " . . . if we don't take the deal, someone else will. Then we lose twice. It's money we don't make and it's money someone else makes." She didn't have to say who. We were all thinking the same thing.

"Yeah, okay," said Finn. "Okay, okay." He gave up with a shrug. "When and where do we deliver?"

"Ten days after harvest. The high savannah, the north end, Little Summerland. Then twenty klicks west into the bush. Reckless Meadow."

Finn swiveled around and brought up a navigation display. He studied the map for a moment, scratching his head. "Terrible close to the mating fields. It's a heavy-grazing area."

"Ayep. If you wanna catch horgs, you gotta go where the horgs are."

Finn turned back to Grampa, folding his arms. "He doesn't expect us to help, does he? Because otherwise—"

"Not to worry. Told him that up front. We're not wranglers. We'll sell him the crop, nothing else. No bots. No riders. No shooters."

"And he agreed?"

Grampa puffed his pipe some more before answering. "Says he doesn't need bots, riders, or shooters. Just a couple of cargo-loaders."

"Then how's he plan to—?"

"He didn't say." Grampa grinned. "Gonna be a fun time, huh?"

With the up-front money from Mr. Costello, Grampa and Finn and Lazz bought three new bots, replacement parts, a new toolkit, two heavyweight weapons, two suits of body armor, several cases of repellents, four banks of high-powered dazzlers, a hundred meters of shock-fence, and several cases of extra fuel cells. We restocked the larders and the med-kits as well.

And we updated our libraries, too. Winter was long and brutal. We had to create much of our own entertainment. Last year, we'd staged *A Midsummer Night's Dream*; this year we were plannin' a suite of Third symphonies—we'd agreed on Beethoven, Copland, Saint-Saëns, but were still arguing about Tchaikovsky, Brahms, Shostakovich, Williams, Sibelius, and Mahler. We'd probably end up doing them all. Winter was long and brutal.

Meanwhile, Mr. Costello was busy on his own, circling around, taking advantage of the Jubilee gathering, meeting as many families as he could. We figured he was making other deals, but nobody was talking. We had a nondisclosure clause, so we assumed everyone else did, too. Eventually, Mr. Costello had some mysterious crates choppered in from Settlement and loaded immediately into his big black trucks.

Jubilee lasted two extra days; we weren't the only ones buying and loading, and a lot of us had to wait for the trucks from Settlement to arrive with everything the Jacklins didn't have to hand. Mr. Costello had pumped a lot of cash into the local economy and most folks were happy to tilt an extra pint or two in his name. By the time the last kegs had been drained, Jacklin's shelves were just about spare. Everybody bought gifts for everybody. We passed out our family gifts on Goodbye Morning, right after first breakfast, just before dawn, with all the usual teasing and laughter.

Finn surprised me with that blue dress he said showed off my calves. I bought him hair and body brushes for the shower, along with the promise that I'd personally demonstrate their proper use. He grinned and said, "You didn't buy those for me, you bought 'em for you." I ducked my head so he wouldn't see me smiling and blushing, but he was right.

It was tradition that we all chip in to buy Grampa a fresh supply of his favorite sweet-smelling tobacco and a new pipe to smoke it in. We couldn't pull out until he puffed it to life and pronounced it good. "This is good," he'd say. "Life is good. Okay, let's roll. Let's see what happens next."

The trip back to Homestead was uneventful. Charlie and Marlie had been monitoring and managing the bots the whole trip. Except for one busted voltivator, swarm-confidence was high and the bushes were sparkling. It looked like an early harvest—a big harvest, too.

Glitter-bush leaves are long. Morning dew collects on the leaves, the leaves curl lengthwise to hold the wetness in. As the day heats up, the leaves dry into needles. Bite the end of a needle and you can suck out the water—not much, but you won't die of thirst, either. Chew a lot of needles and you can rehydrate almost as fast as you sweat. That's why horgs and all the other critters come hunting. It's easier than searching for a water hole.

But if the needle is left alone, if no one eats it, it starts to secrete its oils into the water, and what you get is kinda like honey, only better because bees didn't walk around in it. And if you wait long enough, each needle develops a seed within the oil-honey, and the seeds are even more valuable. That's why glitter-bushes are such a profitable crop. The leaves are edible, the honey is perfect, and the seeds are delicious.

Not all the seeds germinate, though. Only the ones that pass through a horg's gut. So there's the other reason we need horgs. Just not too many. But the numbers cycle up and down, up and down, because that's the way the whole thing works, so when they're up, we have to cull the herds the best we can. If we get to the carcass quick enough, we'll butcher it—but usually the rest of the herd is right there. They're omnivores. They're not just carrion-eaters, they're cannibals. Another reason to be disgusted.

But if we can get in there fast enough to slice off the drumsticks, the tails, the shoulders, the flanks, the ribs, and the belly muscles, sometimes the heart and tongue, we'll hang the meat, cure it, smoke it, age it, whatever, and maybe make a bit of cash off it. But we won't eat it ourselves.

Some people—mostly offworlders—say horg steak is a delicacy. That's because they don't know horgs. They say the meat has a sweet aftertaste, probably from the glitter-bush needles. Like I said, they can have my share. The one time I tried it, I puked it all up—and I had diarrhea for three days, too. Horg is tough and greasy and gamey. You have to tenderize it and marinate it and cover it with sauce to make it edible. But there's some people who like that, I guess. Or maybe it's just that it's expensive and exotic. Or maybe it's because of the side effects. Dunno. Supposedly something in the meat is mildly hallucinogenic and just as supposedly it makes people horny, too, so even if they're not crazy about the taste, that's not the reason they're eating it.

Anyway—summer storms chased us all the way back to Homestead. Not the worst we'd ever seen, but ferocious enough to slow us down. Flash floods scoured Narrow Canyon and the Rumpled River was raging impassable. We had to take the long way around, crossing at The Hump, and we spent the better part of the night parked lee side of Ugly Ridge. Frustrating to be so close to Homestead, but it couldn't be helped.

We'd spent two extra days at Jubilee and lost another half-day coming back, but after the storm passed, the forecast promised a few weeks of milder weather, so we wouldn't have to dock and lock the trucks. We could start rigging them immediately for the trek to Reckless Meadow.

When we finally did get back, dawn was just turning the eastern sky pink and the underside of the cloud-ceiling loomed purple. It wasn't the best start for the day but it could have been worse. Three of the bots were mired in mud and the rest were worrying around, trying to keep the bushes from leaving the meadow.

We unpacked the new bots first, activated them, then rushed to extract the ones that were stuck. It took the entire morning, all of us scrambling to contain the herd, barely getting them settled in and re-rooted and watered before the heat of midday. We didn't even try to plan harvest until after siesta and second lunch.

Charlie and Marlie woke up early to switch out the herding reflectors on six of the bots, installing the new harvest tools and collection baskets. I ran some numbers, and if the ground dried out enough we could complete most of the harvesting in two nights.

After harvest, the bushes would start getting hungry. We could take a few days to herd them back to the willows, or make up the time by dredging a couple loads of guano and delivering it to the meadow. That'd given us good results before, plus a head start on the next harvest, but it would also upset the local balance. We might have to let these fields go fallow for a season or two, maybe plant some darkberries up here and let the bushes gather on the lower slopes instead—that would mean extra work patrolling for horgs, but if Mr. Costello was right, he'd be thinning out the herds enough to give us a break in the up-down cycle. But using the lower slopes for a whole summer would open up a lot more range, meaning we could raise more bushes and expand the homestead.

If Mr. Costello didn't get himself killed first.

Right now, we figured him for just another fellow with more money than sense, but if he wanted to throw some of that cash in our direction, we'd bring out the big baskets to hold it all.

As soon as the bots were charged and refitted, we set them trimming. You don't want to take too many needle-leaves—the bushes need the water—but you want to take the fattest and sweetest pods because the horgs are picky and those are the ones they like most. Those are the ones most likely to germinate after a quick trip through the gut.

The best harvest time is siesta and afternoon, while the pods are heat-sealing. Charlie and Marlie and Lazz napped midmorning so they could work through siesta. Finn and Trina and I took the afternoon shift. We ate first supper when the shadows started stretching east and then began prepping the trucks for Restless Meadow, packing everything we knew we'd need and a bunch more stuff we hoped we wouldn't. Always makes for an easier trip that way. We finally pulled out with five vans full of ripe pods, chilled but not frozen.

The journey down to Restless Meadow took two and a half days, stopping along the way to install several new monitoring stations and a couple of drone-nests. Sky-balls are useful but the weather on Haven limits when they can fly. There's maybe a hundred-klick range on good days, that's a three-hour window. So we put the drone-nests in a hexagonal grid with overlapping edges and try to get coverage whenever the winds permit. We can track the local herds and are getting better at predicting the migratory packs. Some horgs migrate, some don't—still working that out, but we think it's the brooding horgs that get territorial.

By the time we arrived, Mr. Costello had already set up his camp, with his big black trucks parked on the slope overlooking the meadow. One of them opened onto a large deck with a roof of silk-looking fabric. There were chairs around a table, and even a pitcher of lemonade and glasses laid out.

Mr. Costello signaled us to pull up beside. We anchored our trucks, dismount-ed, and met him on his deck. He invited us to sit with a wave and poured lemonade for all of us as if this were just another autumn day in back-home dusty Illinois—a place we'd all heard of but none of us had ever been. What the hell, it was lemonade.

"Things are going very well, very well indeed," he said. "You should be very pleased, very proud, indeed, yes." One of his two associates—the one who looked vaguely military—came out then with a fresh pitcher of lemonade, and Mr. Costello introduced her. "This is Mikla. Mikla, please welcome our new partners. Please tell me if I have all your names right—"

Mr. Costello went on to explain, "Mikla will be handling the accounting, mak-ing sure that everyone is taken care of. And Jerrid, he's our tech—he's working on the communications gear. We have such good news to share. Jerrid has created a new communications web."

Finn grunted. "We already have one—"

"Yes, of course. But Jerrid believes we should have a private web just for our part-ners. He says we need secure channels for our business operations. If other people can see what we're doing, we'll have competition. Don't you think we should delay that as long as possible?"

Grampa nodded, but Finn looked skeptical. "Most folks don't go pryin' into other folks' business. Ain't polite. There's not a lot of secrets on Haven, anyway.

Maybe secrets are an offworld thing. But if it concerns y'that much, y'could just use the regular channels with a smidge of encryption. Nobody'll bother then."

"A very good suggestion, yes. Thank you, Finn." Mr. Costello pretended to think about it, then frowned and said, "But don't you think a flurry of encrypted messages might make people suspicious? Suspicious enough to want to find out what we're up to?"

"Aye, there is that." Finn shrugged.

"This way they won't even know that we're talking to each other. Wouldn't you agree that'll be safer for everyone?"

Finn nodded—reluctantly, but he nodded. "I see your point."

Mr. Costello reached over and poured Finn more lemonade. "Thank you, Finn. Jerrid worked very hard to set up a private communication network for us. He'll be pleased that you see the value of his work."

We sat there for a while longer, exchanging pleasantries, until finally Charlie asked, "But the horgs, Mr. Costello—how do you intend to catch them? You know, it's not safe to go out hunting them. The whole herd will turn on you."

Mr. Costello nodded agreement. "Yes, thank you. You're not the first to point that out. I was thinking—well, Jerrid and Mikla and I were thinking that it would be easier if the horgs came to us."

"So you're gonna lure 'em here with glitter-pods . . . ?"

Mr. Costello pointed down the slope. Three of his bots were already at work, installing two thick masts about fifteen meters apart, anchoring them in the ground as deep as they were tall. The pylons looked heavy enough, even our worst winter storms wouldn't budge them. They glinted like carbonized-polycrete, the bots were wrapping them in tree-bark to hide the metallic finish. But Mr. Costello pointed past them. "You see that level area, down there? Just beyond the posts? Where the bots have laid a polycrete floor? That would be a good place to put out some glitter-pods, yes?"

Charlie shrugged. "One place is as good as another. The horgs'll find 'em wherever."

"How much do you think would be a good appetizer?"

"I dunno. I never thought about feeding horgs before. Mostly, I don't want 'em feeding. Not as much as they want to, that is. They'd eat the whole crop to the ground if they could."

"See? That's my point. You know horgs much better than I do. So what's your advice? If you wanted to get the horgs to come to you, how much would you put out?"

Charlie said slowly, "Well, it all depends. I guess if you want to see most of the herd, you'd put out fifty, maybe a hundred kilos. They'd finish it off right quick, but they'd make a real mess of it and the smell would keep 'em snuffling around for a while searching for leavings. Sometimes they ain't too smart."

"That's what I'm counting on—that we are smarter than horgs." Mr. Costello continued, "Why don't we try your idea? We'll put out a hundred kilos tonight." He suddenly remembered something. "There are lights on top of those masts. Do you think we can leave them on? Or will the light drive the horgs away?"

Marlie leaned forward then. "I never knew a horg to resist a free meal. Once they figure out there's food, they'll come. And once they figure the lights are where the food is, they'll come whether there's food or not. Just in case." She pushed her glass forward and Mr. Costello happily refilled it.

So that was that.

Grampa asked Mr. Costello and his partners to join us for dinner. Lazz and I cooked up a Storm—actually, the full name of the stew was Shit Storm, but not everybody got the joke so we just called it a Storm for short. It's a familiar recipe. I've heard it called Leftover Stew, Ingredient Soup, Glop, Bottomless Pot, Slumgullion, Scouse, Irish Cesspool, Gutter Slime, Desperation, and Oh God, Not Again.

But Lazz is pretty good with spices and I don't do so bad myself with the basics— rice, beans, and noodles. And we had five truckloads of fresh pods—we could serve up a mess of those as well.

Pods have another virtue in the kitchen, too—it's one of the better tricks of Haven cuisine. You can add curry powder, red pepper, blue pepper, jalapenos, haba- neros, Pot Douglahs, Trinidad Moruga Scorpions, Carolina Reapers, and a few other spices with Scoville ratings so high they melt the equipment—it doesn't matter. You can neutralize most of the heat with glitter-bush pods, leaving only the flavor and just the slightest hint of sweetness. Mostly, though, we stop at habaneros. The other peppers are better used in horg-repellent sprays. It slows 'em down. Sometimes. But one of the attractions of Jubilee is the spice-cookout. You bring in your hottest dish and see who can eat a whole bowl of it. The survivors win free medical care until they can walk again.

We opened up our own deck, set out tables and chairs, dropped the side-silks to slow down bugs and dust, laid the table for everyone, and rang the triangle. Everyone was already gathered, but it's part of the ritual. The weather on Haven doesn't always encourage eating outside, but when it does, you do. We still had another hour of sunset.

Mr. Costello praised the Storm as if it was a culinary discovery of the first order. Jerrid and Mikla even asked for seconds and extra bread to mop their bowls, so we knew tonight's Oh God, Not Again had been a success.

After they headed back to their own trucks, after both the suns had finally dipped below the western horizon, we all retreated inside for the Circle. It's how we keep ourselves centered. We sit around the table with coffee or tea, and we go round and round until we're done.

One by one, first we acknowledge whatever might be gnawing at us, hurts and upsets, simmering frustrations, whatever. You have to say what you want and need to make things right. Nobody interrupts. Nobody gets to offer advice. Nobody gets to play peacemaker. All of those things are arrogant and disrespectful. You have three minutes to say whatever you have to say. Then to the next person, and the next.

On the second round, whatever upsets might have come up—you get to take responsibility for your part of it, you get to offer support to those who need it, you get to be a partner to whoever needs partnership. The second round keeps going round and round until the air has been cleared and everything that needs to be said has been said.

Usually, the first round is about the frustrations of the day's work, not about our frustrations with each other. While it's not a firm rule, if any two people in the family have an upset with each other, they're supposed to resolve it before we get to Circle. So first round is usually about outside annoyances and second round is about creating strength to deal with them. But if a personal upset doesn't get resolved before Circle, if it's that important, we deal with it there.

Finally, third round is about completion. We go around and each person acknowledges the strengths they see in the family, the gifts they see in others, the gifts they wish to be to the whole. By then we're usually on the second or third cup of coffee or tea. We finish by all holding hands and reminding ourselves that being in the family is a gift and a privilege. Then we have whatever special dessert or treat we've saved for ourselves.

That's when the real fun begins. We share all the best gossip we've heard, all the most interesting stories and jokes, all the news that's come down the channels. And . . . we also take some time to make sure we're all on the same page about the business at hand. Those discussions sometimes go on for an hour or longer.

This night, we talked about Mr. Costello and his partners. We tried to figure out who they were and what they were planning and whether or not we could trust them—and most of all, what they weren't telling us. We speculated, we guessed, we imagined, we goggled the web and came up empty. Finally, we paired off for the night, our usual couplings, and headed to our bunks.

I lay down next to Finn and sighed, mostly happy to be with Finn, but also concerned for no reason I could identify. "What I said in Circle. I still feel that way. Mr. Costello makes me uneasy. I don't know why. There's just something about him."

Finn didn't answer immediately. He was rubbing my back, my shoulders, my neck, working out the tensions of the day. When he finished, I would do the same for him. Finally, he said, "I think it's because he's too nice. It's like he's trying too hard."

I had to think about that for a while. "If he's trying too hard, isn't that a kind of lying? Maybe he doesn't trust his own plan?"

"No, I think he trusts his plan. But I wonder if maybe the plan he's showing us is only the top part of the plan he isn't showing us." He patted my shoulders affection-ately, "You're done. My turn."

He sprawled face down on the bed and I straddled him, digging into his spine. He was all muscle and I had to use all my weight and all my leverage. After a while, I said, "You and Grampa have been here longer than anyone. You've seen a lot of schemers and scammers come through here—"

"Yep. Most of 'em are buried on Idjit Hill."

"—so why do you trust Mr. Costello?"

"I don't. But his money spends just as good as anyone else's. What Grampa said—if we don't take it, someone else will. So far, I haven't seen any reason to distrust him. Maybe his manner is just the way he is." He grunted as I worked his shoulders. "He's a starsider. Maybe that's how they behave on other worlds."

I thought about my next words, decided to say them anyway. "I've been on a lot of planets, Finn. More than I've told you about. You haven't asked and I haven't volunteered. Because I've done some things—"

"We don't care about who you were before you got here," said Finn. "We care about who you are now. If we didn't, you wouldn't be in this family. You wouldn't be here in this bed tonight. And you wouldn't be screaming my name to the ceiling."

"I'm not doing that."

"Not yet, but you will—"

"First let me finish what I was going to say. I've bounced around a few systems and I've never met any starsider who behaved like Mr. Costello. No, let me say it another way. Maybe I've seen a few—he reminds me of some of them. Some of them ended up the guest of honor at an airlock dance."

"You *have* been around—"

"If you really want to know—"

"Do I need to?" Even in the dark, I could see the expression on his face. "Or will it hurt you to tell more than it would hurt me to hear?"

I didn't answer. That was answer enough.

He grabbed me, rolled me over on my back, and pushed my knees up toward my nipples. He leaned his weight on my bent legs so he could look down on me. "This is where I want you, right here, right now. Is that enough?"

I barely had time to gasp my answer.

Sometime after first sleep, when we were all awake for midnight meal, Lazz powered up two bots and had them dump a hundred kilos of pods in the center of Mr. Costello's polycrete floor. The lights on the pylons blazed down from the two nearest corners. There were cameras there as well, so we had an excellent view of the entire field.

"How long do you think we'll have to wait?"

"Dunno," said Marlie, and swiveled to face a wall of screens. One display showed our location. Another tracked the herd. "They're not directly downwind but they should catch the scent soon enough. See? There—" Marlie pointed. "Some of the outliers are turning."

"They're at least ten klicks away," said Charlie. "That's an hour, minimum, more likely two."

"We gonna wait up for 'em?"

"Might could," said Grampa. "Then again, just as easily I might could go back to sleep. If they got pods to eat, they ain't comin' up the hill to see what we're doin'." A thought occurred to him. "You sprayed those trucks good, Finn?"

"Five coats, all the worst peppers. I spent two hours in that damn suit. I sprayed until the paint blistered. If any horgs can sniff the pods in our trucks, they're welcome to 'em. At this point, I ain't gonna argue. My eyes are still burning. And that was two days ago."

"Told y'to wear the goggles."

"I did. Even with the goggles, even with the mask, even with the hood, even with the O-tanks, that spray gets through. Y'know, people have died just breathing downwind from that crap."

"Ayep," said Grampa, lighting his pipe and grinning.

In the morning, while Lazz and Trina fixed first breakfast, the rest of us reviewed the night's videos. Only a few horgs showed up, mostly outliers, mostly curious. Maybe a dozen. Maybe a few more. I didn't count. They sniffed around the piles of pods cautiously—probably the unfamiliar scent traces of machines and humans made them suspicious—but after a bit, they bent their massive heads and inhaled the pods like so much dandelion fluff.

Horgs are sloppy eaters. They snuffled around, spreading pods every which way, smashing them under their feet, smearing the honeyed juices everywhere. The monitors showed their excitement rising as the scent grew stronger. Even after the last few pods had been slobbered away, they still licked eagerly at the now-oily surface of the polycrete. If they weren't horgs, it could have been adorable.

But they were horgs and it was disgusting.

Horgs look like the mutant offspring of a rhinoceros and a warthog, only a lot bigger and ruddier and fatter and flatter and hairier. They have sharp razorback armor all along their spines, extending from the ends of their thick flat tails forward to their thick plated skulls. That's where the armor splits and curves downward around their jaws, finally turning into two savage curving tusks. They have big paddle-like feet, so they can swim as well as they gallop—not fast, but pretty much unstoppable. On the deep savannahs, they travel in herds that can sprawl as wide as a hundred kilometers. They have to—they'd overpower the local ecology if they massed any closer together. Few predators are big enough to bring down a horg, but there are swarms of little things that can worry one to death.

Away from the plains, in the foothills and the forests, horgs become loners. And that makes them even more vicious, because they attack everything. It has something to do with not being able to sync their biological cycles with their fellows. They turn into psychopaths.

Horgs are omnivorous. They eat everything. Mostly, they eat grass, flowers, trees, bark, glitter-bushes, wailing willows, insects, grubs, roots, fungi, mushrooms, snakes, worms, lizards, birds, carrion, and any small horgs that get in their way. Loners tend to overeat, not just because they're hungry, but because they need to build up bulk in case of a mating fight. Away from the herd, the majority of matings are injurious or fatal.

And those are their good points.

In the morning, after first breakfast, we all walked down to the feeding deck with Mr. Costello's group and examined the aftermath. One of the smaller horgs had lost an argument with one of the larger horgs. There were still traces of blood everywhere and carrion birds were picking at the few remaining scraps of skin and bone.

Mr. Costello found that very interesting. He didn't approach the scavengers. They looked feisty, so he studied them from a distance. Mikla and Jerrid frowned and whispered between themselves. Finally, Mr. Costello turned back to us and waved his cigar at the bloodstains on the polycrete. "How many did we lose?"

Finn was studying the blood smears, too. He shook his head. "Hard to say. I'd have to process the video to be sure. And even then, I dunno. Once the fighting started, it was a scramble—impossible to tell what was happening. All I can say for sure is that there were a lot fewer horgs leaving than arriving. Mebbe five or six fewer."

For the first time, Mr. Costello looked unhappy. "This was unexpected. Very unexpected." He turned to Grampa. "This—this cannibalism. Is that normal behavior?"

Grampa shrugged. He took a moment to light his pipe while he considered his answer. "Well, there's a lot of theories about that. Horgs get hungry, they eat what's in front of 'em. But—" he paused to puff thoughtfully "—sometimes these critters work themselves into a feeding frenzy. Sometimes it's hunger and sometimes it's rage and sometimes the mating fights get out of control—" another puff, another thoughtful pause "—but in this case, mebbe you overstimulated them. In the wild, they don't get big piles of pods. They have to work a bit for every mouthful. But you gave 'em a big fat feast. Drove 'em crazy, mebbe. Leastways, that'd be my guess."

Grampa didn't guess. Grampa never guessed. But Grampa rarely spoke in declarative sentences, either. He let you do the work—kind of like Mr. Costello. The difference? Grampa was Grampa and Mr. Costello was Mr. Costello. That's the only way I can explain it.

Mr. Costello considered, then nodded his agreement. "Hm. That sounds likely. Is there a way to slow them down?"

Grampa frowned in thought. "Now, that depends on what you want to do. I don't mind horgs eatin' each other if it thins the herd a bit. But it sounds to me like you want to feed 'em without getting 'em all worked up and agitated, right? You don't want 'em killin' each other."

"We can't sell horgs we don't have, can we?"

"Nope," agreed Grampa.

And that's how it went for a while. Back and forth, back and forth, with neither one ever quite saying anything in the clear.

Finally, Finn spoke up again—I could tell he was getting frustrated. It's bad enough having to deal with Grampa's roundabout talk, but having to listen to the pair of them dancing around the subject like they didn't know what they wanted, or more like whoever said it first would have to pay extra for the privilege of saying it first—Finn was exasperated.

"Listen," he said. "We'll send a few bots up into the trees, have 'em bring down some branches. We'll put 'em through the shredders and mix 'em into the pods. It'll mean they have to do a lot more chewing. And instead of putting it all in one big pile, we'll spread it out in a lot of little piles all over the feeding floor. We could try that."

Mr. Costello looked to Grampa. Grampa looked to Mr. Costello. They both were nodding thoughtfully, each waiting for the other to say, "Let's do it."

Finn didn't wait. He turned to Lazz. "Unpack the lumberjack gear. Use bots four and six, they'll have enough capacity. Number seven can do the shredding." Some people named their bots, Finn didn't. He insisted that people are people, machines are machines—mixing them up gets dangerous. I had to agree with that. I'd seen what happens when people forgot. Or worse, when machines forgot.

Finn and Lazz talked for a bit about what kind of branches to cut down and how many and where. The rule was not to take from more than one tree per acre and never more than one of a kind, unless it was a monoculture. There was still too much we didn't know about Haven's ecology—all the different ways that all the different plants and animals interacted. Based on the evidence of history, both here and elsewhere, even stepping on a butterfly could have unintended consequences.

By the time that conversation finished, Mr. Costello's people had adjusted their plan as well. Jerrid was directing his construction bots to put up two more towers, these at the two remaining corners of the feeding floor.

"Yes, that's a very good idea," said Mr. Costello. He turned to us. "You'll have more cameras now with different angles on the creatures as they feed, so you'll get better information on their behavior. That should be very useful." Back to his own people. "Thank you, Jerrid. Thank you, Mikla. How long do you think all this will take?"

I spent the next part of the day with Charlie, bringing the family's finances up to date. Mostly, I handled the day-to-day stuff, paying bills, allocating shares, ordering necessities, coordinating deliveries—if something was urgent, we'd send out a drone to pick stuff up from Settlement or Temporary, if the weather permitted flight—otherwise we'd let the goods arrive on the Monthly. Eventually, Charlie would entrust me with access to the investment portfolios. I hadn't been married in long enough to qualify for a permanent share, but another year or two, the others would vote. If they didn't grant permanence, it would be a gentle way of saying, "You are free to leave whenever you want."

I wasn't worrying about it now. I'd learned that it's more important to focus on what you can give than what you're going to get. That works in finance almost as well as it does in bed. And that was another conversation I wanted to have with Finn—

By the end of the day, the two new pylons had been set and hardened, and the bots were more than half-done pre-chewing the night's meal for the horgs. This time, we'd be putting out only fifty kilos of pods and a hundred and fifty kilos of shredded bark and leaves. Lazz had selected six small trees across the edges of the forest—one anchorwood, two redbarks, a whitemarch, a wailing willow, and a bower-tree.

After taking a few branches from each, he'd scattered fresh seeds in fertilizer pods to apologize for the assault. Forest horgs were known to chew into all of these species during the barest periods of winter, but most of the rest of the year they ignored them, so we knew the chaff would be edible without being overstimulating.

Because of the day's efforts, dinner was flashed from the freezer. Charlie baked fresh bread and Lazz whomped up some of his best tomato-gravy and we washed the whole thing down with Grampa's special beer, which was only special because he said so. It had the same familiar honeyed overtaste as everyone else's special brew.

That night's video revealed a scattering of horgs feeding placidly. Not a whole herd, but enough to justify the effort. Maybe two dozen. The important thing, no fights broke out, although the monitors reported that the animals were experiencing more irritability than we would have liked. Lazz and Charlie decided to reduce the proportion of glitter-bush pods even more for the next day's feed.

After second breakfast, we met again with Mr. Costello. While he didn't express any disappointment—on the contrary, he remained delighted with the progress we were making—he did wonder aloud that the horgs were finishing the feed too quickly, leaving nothing to attract the rest of the herd. Eventually, Finn realized he was asking us to put out more food to attract more horgs. But it was our idea, of course. We had enough chaff to handle tonight's feed, but we'd need a lot more for the days to come.

Lazz and Charlie took one of the trucks north to select more trees. They planned to hit several different groves and would be gone all day, perhaps even two days. Mr. Costello asked why they couldn't just take whole trees from the nearby slopes and they had to explain to him that the tree roots held the soil in place. If they deforested a slope, the winter storms would wash the entire hill down into the valley below. Aside from the inconvenience that might represent to those of us who lived in the area, it could also change the migratory patterns of various small herds—and nobody would appreciate having horgs wandering through their fields. Most settlers had chosen their sites specifically to stay away from the migration routes.

Marlie and Trina put out the evening feed for the horgs, spreading it thin and wide. That took a few hours, more time than anyone expected, so the rest of us made do with sandwiches and coffee. It was a long night. Because Charlie was gone, I handled the day's journal-keeping. Not just the personal stats and billables, but the log as well. We logged everything. The family journal was a way of not having to depend on anyone's memory. The notes we were making about horg behavior would be very valuable—not just for us, but for anyone else who wanted to download the public half of our records. We didn't make a lot of local money from our logs, but we had a sizable offworld audience and the royalties did add up over time. Grampa wouldn't let us spend any royalties unless it was an emergency—that money always got folded back into the portfolio. The job was to be self-sufficient on what we could make from the land. I had a thought we might be worth a lot more than Grampa ever let on, but I had no right to ask. Not yet.

We were reviewing the videos even before first breakfast now, gathering around the displays with coffee and fresh donuts to watch an accelerated record, only slowing down to real time if something interesting or unusual popped up on any of the screens. Today we were seeing a much bigger gathering of horgs. At any given time, there were thirty-some animals on the stage, but the total was greater than that—at least a dozen moewsnuffled cautiously around the edges. Not the hundreds Mr. Costello had promised, but certainly enough to demonstrate that he could attract a crowd.

Too much of a crowd, actually. Horgs are always hungry. After cleaning the floor of the feeding deck, they started snuffling up the slope toward the trucks. While it was unlikely that any of the animals would attack the vehicles, they could still do considerable damage. They could knock a vehicle on its side and rip out the under-carriage, just out of pure horgish malevolence. There was a lot of history—with pictures suitable for Goblin Night. Also known as Gobblin' Night, when all the mini-horgs swarmed. We usually had two or three days' warning, enough time to get home, lock all the doors and windows, and hide under the blankets.

But right now we had curious horgs wandering up the slopes. Not far enough—not yet, not last night—but tonight? Maybe. And the next night—certainly. Hungry horgs search and scavenge. Wake up a horg's appetite and you're asking for trouble. Something else Mr. Costello didn't know.

We had an emergency meeting on his deck. He served iced tea and English biscuits. "Oh my, yes, the video was very disturbing. It's a good thing the video cameras have a three-hundred-sixty-degree view or we'd have never known the creatures were wandering up the slope. Thank you, Jerrid, for your wonderful cameras." He looked to Grampa. "Will we have to stop feeding them now?"

Grampa didn't bother with his pipe today. He said, "It won't do any good. Three nights now you've been laying out glitter-pods. Even if the place didn't already reek with the scent of the crushed leaves, they'll still be coming back. Looking for more. They ain't stupid. You train 'em to come for food, they'll come."

"Well . . ." said Mr. Costello. "Well, well, well. This will be a challenge. Perhaps there's some way to keep the horgs from wandering off the feeding floor, some way to keep them from wandering up the hill, some way to keep them where they are and away from the trucks."

"We could put a fence up," said Finn.

"Do you think that would work?" Mr. Costello's face lit up.

Finn was thinking it over. "We could carve out a berm. I suppose we could have a 'dozer lifted out. It'd be expensive, though. And I'm not sure it would stop 'em. If a horg is determined to go over something, he goes over it. If he wants to go through it, he goes through it. Those paddle-feet, they have claws as long as your forearm—they're good for slashing open each other's bellies, but they're also for digging into the ground, especially frozen ground—that's how the horgs survive the outer-winters. They dig into huge communal burrows. You know those holes you saw from space, the ones that looked like craters? Horg-nests."

Mr. Costello listened patiently to Finn's monolog, then turned to Jerrid. "I think you packed something that might work—"

Jerrid nodded. "We have twenty bolts of carbon monofilament, triple-knit—" He looked to Finn. "It's very lightweight and essentially unbreakable. We can spray it with shelterfoam and it'll harden nicely." He pointed at the silk-looking hangings that sheltered Mr. Costello's deck. "I brought plenty, in case we needed to build a tented enclosure—"

"Ahh," said Finn. He looked down the slope. "I see . . . we stretch a length of it between the first two towers, from one to the other and back again, then spray it to harden it, and we create a visual barrier between the feeding deck and the slope."

"That's a marvelous idea!" Mr. Costello clapped his hands in glee.

Jerrid looked to Finn. "You know horgs. Will it work?"

"Only one way to find out."

Before the sun hit zenith, Jerrid's bots were stringing the first lengths of triple-knit. By the time siesta was over, they were already prepping the shelterfoam tanks. We watched them from the deck while we ate second lunch. "That's gonna be a tall wall," said Grampa.

Finn said, "It's a visual cliff. It should keep them focused on the food instead of the hill."

Grampa puffed his pipe. "If nothin' else, Mr. Costello has proven that you can train a horg to eat. Whether or not he can train 'em to butcher themselves, that'll be a whole other thing, won't it?"

Charlie and Lazz arrived late in the day with three huge trailers of wood for the shredders. They'd circled through six forests, taking branches from the outliers and the rogues. They'd left the mother-trees alone. No sense pissing off the woodlands. The trees on Haven could be friendly—or they could make life hell for you. As soon as a forest felt alarm, the surrounding trees would start releasing threat-pheromones. That would attract huge swarms of things that bite. It would also encourage local bugs and birds, lizards, and slugs to transform into their more hostile forms. An angry forest was no place for any creature not part of the rage. And if the forest got angry enough, all those different swarms would go into a feeding frenzy. Even the horgs wouldn't be safe—that's how the forests protected themselves from aggressive herds. Checks and balances everywhere. Don't push the on-button if you don't know where the off-button is.

All of us worked late into the evening, shredding wood, mixing in glitter-pods, and spreading small piles of feed across the polycrete. Well, the bots actually did the work, but we stayed up to supervise. It was a big job and we couldn't risk a bug in our programming.

The horgs were already gathering downslope even before the last bot trotted out of the way. They snuffled and grunted, annoyed but curious. They approached cautiously. Horgs are suspicious by nature. The lights, the wall, the piles of feed—that was alien to their experience. But on the other hand, a free meal is a free meal.

Finn wasn't certain that a single fence would deter the horgs, so he stayed up late to keep watch. He armed two bots with pepper spray and positioned them at the top of the slope. But most of the horgs were too interested in dinner to be concerned. A couple sniffed around the edges of the fence, looking to see if there was food beyond, but Finn had sprayed the perimeter upslope of the fence, and that appeared to be enough to deter further exploration.

By the time the rest of us woke up for mid-meal, Finn was ready to crash. Trina volunteered to take over the rest of the watch, and after updating the logs, I went back to our compartment in the second truck, expecting to find Finn snoring like a jelly-badger. Instead, he was awake and waiting for me.

"I haven't showered," I protested.

"No problem. I'll shower with you. We'll save water."

There's only one way to win an argument with Finn. You wrap yourself up in his arms and say, "Yes, honey, you're right." So I did. And we did. And then we did it again, just to make sure.

And finally, afterward, with me lying on top of his big broad chest, feeling very satisfied and very comfortable, I said, "Aren't you sleepy yet?"

"I took a wide-awake."

"Why?"

"Why not?"

"Not good enough. Why'd you stay up?" I repeated.

"For you," he said, stroking my back. "For us. For this. I don't want us to get so busy we forget to be us. What about you? Are you tired?"

"I'll stay up with you. For as long as I can."

He stroked my brush cut. "I miss your hair."

"You liked it long?"

"Very much."

"You never said. All right. I'll let it grow out." I kissed his left nipple. Then the right one, so it wouldn't feel neglected.

He knew me too well. "You don't like having your hair long?"

"It's extra work, especially if I color-glow."

"You don't have to do it for me."

"If it makes you happy—"

"Will it make *you* happy?" Even in the dark, I could see the intensity of his expression.

"Making you happy makes me happy."

"I can see I'm not going to win this argument—"

"Oh? Are we having an argument? Wait. I'll get my flak jacket and helmet. No kissing below the belt—"

He pulled me back down on top of him. "You do whatever you want." He held me there for a long time, making that purring noise in his chest that attracted me to him in the first place. He never told me how he did it and I suspected an augment he wasn't telling me about.

Finally, I lifted up, I straddled him, and looked down. "I do have to ask you something?"

"Uh-oh, I know that tone."

"No." I slapped his chest playfully. "This is serious."

"What?"

"Would you like me to change back? Do you like me better as a boy or a girl?"

"I like you in my bed. Isn't that enough?"

"No. It isn't. I want to be the best you ever had. I want us to be perfect. I'm—" I looked at the ceiling but the answer wasn't there, either, so I looked back to him and admitted, "It's what you said. I don't want us to stop being us."

He sighed. Not quite exasperated. Not yet. But I knew that sigh. "Aren't you happy?" he said.

"I'm the happiest I've ever been in my life—"

"Then why are you worrying about the plumbing?"

"Because I want to make you as happy as I am—"

"You've already done that." He said, "If you want to change, then change. If you don't, then don't. Whichever, I'll still find a way to make you scream loud enough to wake up Grampa." Abruptly, he stopped and stared up at me. "Wait—are you asking me if I want to change?"

"Huh? No. I just—" My turn to stop and stare. "Do you want to change?"

"I wasn't thinking about it. At least, not until now. Would that make you happy?"

I collapsed onto his chest, playfully frustrated. "Oh, great—I had to ask. Now we're going to have gender confusion every time we get in bed. Finn, my sweetheart, my playmate, my lover, I am fine if you're fine. I only asked because if it was something you wanted, it would be all right with me. Whatever—"

He kissed me lightly on the top of my head. "You can stop now. I'm fine. You're fine. We're fine. If you want to change, do it for you, I'll still be fine. If you would like me to change, that might be fun too. But for now, right now, with all this other business going on, let's just take things one day at a time—okay?"

And that's how that part of the conversation ended. The kissing part went on for a lot longer. And somewhere after that, I fell asleep in Finn's arms, which was always my favorite place to fall asleep. My ears turned off as I cycled down and Finn could snore like a horg all night long if he wanted.

After first breakfast, Mr. Costello and his folks wandered over for a meeting. Nothing important, just an affirmation that everything looked like it was working out well. He agreed that we should continue feeding the horgs. The rest of the herd seemed to be gravitating this way. Perhaps within another few days we might see as many as a hundred or two hundred animals feeding each night. Perhaps we should increase the amount of feed we were putting out.

Somehow, the way he talked about things, the way he drew us into the discussion, it always felt like we were creating the plan, not him. But that was good—it gave us ownership. It put the responsibility on us to make things work. You couldn't fault him for that.

Afterward, once that was settled, he sat down with me and Charlie and Finn and Grampa. "Jerrid has been working on something else. Mikla, too. They're both so very smart about these things."

We listened while he meandered his way toward the punch line.

"Y'see, this whole enterprise has to be a partnership, a team effort, don't you agree?"

We nodded politely, already wondering where this was leading.

"And from time to time, we have to acknowledge that there are skills we need to add to the team. Jerrid pointed this out. Mikla, too. We've succeeded so well already. We've proven that we can direct the attention of a herd of horgs."

"We can feed 'em, yes," said Finn. He did not say what his tone suggested he was thinking: *Any idjit can do that.*

"If I might interrupt," Mikla said politely. "We need to prepare for the next phase of the operation, which is to set up a processing plant for the horg meat."

"Ah," said Finn.

"We'll need to bring in processing equipment, extra bots, and a team of operators."

"Of course."

"And that means expanding our partnership."

"I see . . . " Finn said. He didn't. Neither did the rest of us.

"It doesn't affect our contracts with you, of course. You're already locked in as a supplier."

Jerrid spoke up then. "Mr. Costello has negotiated contracts with several other families, all of whom are ready to provide services for processing, packing, shipping, and so on."

"That's a good idea," said Grampa, nodding. "It's convenient. And it's good for the local economy."

Mikla said, "However . . . the larger the team gets, the more complicated all of the interrelated accounting becomes. So—" Mikla looked to Jerrid.

Jerrid said, "We'd like to streamline the financial channels. We already have a private web, to which our new partners will be added as they come aboard, of course. We'd like to use it as our primary financial network as well."

Finn looked to Grampa. I looked to Charlie. We all looked to each other. The question didn't have to be asked, but I did anyway. "Why is that necessary?"

"Well, for one thing," Mikla said, "secrecy. Just as we're keeping our business chatter isolated, we think we should take the same precautions with our financial transactions as well. If money is moving around, other people can use that information, possibly to our disadvantage."

"That kinda makes sense," said Charlie.

"I always thought our existing networks were secure," said Finn.

"For most things, they are," said Jerrid. "But it only takes one leak to sink a ship."

Mr. Costello spoke up then. He had been looking from one to the other of us, especially Mikla and Jerrid, with a happy expression on his face. Now he said, "Don't you think with this much money at stake, we should take every precaution possible to protect all of our interests?"

Grampa nodded. Despite the half-scowl on his face, he nodded.

"Wonderful, wonderful. I'm glad you agree. Mikla will set up accounts for all of you today. We'll run our own private bank—with secured deposits for all pending contracts held in an independent escrow."

"A local escrow, please," said Finn.

"Of course, of course. We have to make sure that everybody is well taken care of or this won't work. Not at all. Not at all."

After they left, we all looked at each other. "Well," said Charlie, "it does make sense."

Finn snorted. Grampa puffed furiously on his pipe. I said nothing. Finally, Grampa took his pipe out of his mouth and said, "Used to be, a man's handshake was enough. All these secrets—it makes a man wonder." He put his pipe back in his mouth and resumed wondering.

I said, "The way I heard it, a contract is a list of all the ways two people don't trust each other."

Finn smiled. "That sounds about right. If Mr. Costello doesn't think other people can be trusted, maybe it's because he knows he can't."

Charlie said, "I've been studying all these protocols, all the riders, all the guarantees. A lot of it is boilerplate, but I don't see anything dangerous here. I'm not getting any red flags."

Lazz hardly ever spoke. He was the quiet one, but now he said what we were all thinking. "It's just not the way we're used to doin' business."

"He's an offworlder," said Charlie. "Maybe he doesn't know any better. Maybe he's been burned before—maybe he's learned he needs strong fences to keep horgs out of his fields."

"That's probably it," said Finn. "Still, it makes the back of my neck itch."

"I think we're all a little uneasy here," Marlie said. "Perhaps it's just having so many horgs sniffing around—one wrong smell and we could have a stampede or a frenzy."

"Yep," said Finn. "I think I'll spray around the trucks again tonight. All of 'em. Might want to make sure the windows and vents are sealed, too."

The next few days, we fell into an easy routine—easy only because we were still waiting. Mr. Costello hadn't said anything about how we were going to get the horgs into the processing plant. But each night, the crowd of horgs gathering to gorge themselves continued to grow. Trina and Marlie went off to gather more wood. This time they went southeast so as not to assault the same forests as Charlie and Lazz had visited.

By the time they got back, we were seeing 70 or 80 horgs coming out of the trees each night. They jostled past each other with the usual snuffling and grumping, occasionally giving deep warning rumbles as they milled about, but by now there was a real order to the process. The largest of the animals approached first. They sniffed around, inspecting the various piles of wood chips and seedpods on the feeding deck. When they were finally satisfied—a process that usually involved selecting the largest piles for themselves—they grunted their approval. The others then followed and feeding began.

The next day, the first trucks from Settlement arrived. We knew the Hellisons, we recognized the Herkles—they were an all-male family, except when they needed to make a baby—but we didn't know the Maetlins except by reputation. They were big and brawny, the family you called in when you meant business. We had a little meet-and-greet when they arrived, but they were impatient to set up their camp and went straight to work.

I suppose I should mention that a lot of families go unigender except when it's baby-making time. I can see the logic of it, it makes for a different kind of emotional stability when you don't have all those unaligned hormonal and emotional cycles in conflict, never really achieving stability, all the different relationships having to be constantly refreshed. But I can argue the other side of it, too—high-maintenance has its virtues. It demands continual reinvention.

But even as I chugged along on that train of thought, I realized what was happening to me—I was assimilating my rejuve. My past was starting to assert itself again and my old ways of thinking and being were coming back. I'd have to watch myself now. I'd have to spend some time apart, so I found a place on the slope that was off the main paths, where I could sit and watch. That was probably a bad idea, too—but I could lose myself in the watching.

The Maetlins started by leveling an area at least as big as the feeding platform, just on the other side of the first wall. They staked it out and raised two conjoined inflatables, giving themselves a good-sized warehouse right next to the feeding floor. Shelterfoam followed, then airlocks and vents. No windows. Even before it hardened, they started off-loading various ominous-looking pieces of machinery. Too many blades and hooks for my liking. They said it would take at least a week to assemble the line.

While they did that, we prepared the biggest pot of Shit Storm we'd ever cooked. The whole family worked on it, cutting vegetables, tasting, adding spices, scrounging ingredients. Everybody contributed. The Hellisons had a half-finished kettle of turkey. The Herkles carved a big chunk of beef from the shoulder they were growing in one of their meat tanks, the Maetlins gave us a fresh spice rack, and we turned the gathering Storm into Last Chance Chili.

After we ate, the newcomers finally asked to see what we had accomplished. They didn't look impressed, there wasn't much to see—at least not until the horgs arrived.

By now, the assembling crowds of horgs were large enough that as the feeding subsided, many of the animals were still hungry, so they started searching beyond the feeding deck. Occasionally, several ventured around the edges of the fence and stared uphill, growling. A couple of sniffs of the ground, however, and the blistering stink of Finn's pepper spray was usually enough to dissuade them, but it always made for an uneasy few moments.

On the third day of that behavior, we met again with Mr. Costello. The short version—it was agreed to put up another fence, this time between posts two and three. The horgs hadn't minded the first fence, they probably wouldn't mind the second. We'd find out soon enough.

That night, most of us stayed up late to watch the monitors. The horgs arrived as usual but didn't immediately rush to the feeding platform. The three largest snuffled forward and sniffed the new fence, then after they satisfied themselves that it was not a threat they turned their attention to the piles of glitter-pods and wood chips. At the first satisfied grunt, the other animals trundled forward. We all breathed a sigh of relief.

But the pack was larger than ever, and Finn said, "We might have to put up a third fence soon. Look at the size of that pack—they'll wander off the edges of the platform unless we can contain them."

And as he said that, I realized exactly how Mr. Costello planned to conquer the herd. But I didn't say anything. Not then. Not so anyone else could hear.

Besides—

There was something else I didn't want to tell him. And that was more important. I knew the red-haired Herkle twins. I'd met them the week I arrived on Haven. The Herkles were one of the families I'd applied to. The Herkle boys had bedded me—but no invitation had followed. I felt used. I never shared that with anyone, not even Finn.

But in all the hustle and bustle of everyone settling in, meeting and greeting, sorting things out, sharing news and gossip, trading tools and whatever, the Herkle boys had somehow tracked me to the south end of the slope.

One of the parts of our contract with Mr. Costello—we got first dibs on the dung. Glitter-bush seeds need to pass through a horg's gut to germinate. All that dung—there should be enough fertile seeds to start three, maybe four new meadowlands. This was a side benefit that Grampa had smartly added to our arrangement with Mr. Costello and Mr. Costello had agreed without argument. Either he didn't understand or he didn't care. Whatever, this was the real reason Grampa had so readily accepted Mr. Costello's initial proposal.

See, you could follow the herds and hope to gather dung from areas rich in glitter-bushes. Or you could put out piles of feed near the herds and hope you collected the right dung. Or you could hope that a few passing animals would drop by and eat just enough pods from your crop to give you enough fertile seeds for the next season. More than that, if you had extra seeds that had been fertilized, you could sell or trade them anywhere.

Yeah, there are artificial ways to force a seed to germinate, I guess, but most folks around here don't think much of lab-germinated. General opinion holds that lab crops are missing something, they're stunted and flavorless. Mebbe good for industrial use, mebbe good for animal feed, but not exactly a quality product. If anybody has done a real study, I haven't seen the report, and I haven't seen any lab crops myself, so I have to take Grampa's word for it.

Anyway, I went down to the south end, where three of the agri-bots were picking up the dung balls, weighing them, scanning them, and measuring the various compositions—this was all useful information about the health of the herd—and if there were any fertile seeds inside, they'd toss the dung ball into a hopper. The useless dung balls were shredded and spread, which would make it easier for the various soil bugs to go to work faster. The bots could have done the job without me—or I could have monitored their progress from the truck, but I was tired of the truck, I was tired of Mr. Costello, I wanted to get away—and I wanted to see how this worked first hand. I didn't want to watch screens all the time.

It was a mistake—one I quickly realized. The stink on this field was bad, terrible, even under the hood I wore. But I was too proud to turn around and march back up the hill, so I followed the bots and tried to figure out how they could tell which dung balls were good and which were not. I was beginning to sense that size had something to do with it when the Herkle twins showed up.

Kind of surprising that they found me. I hadn't gone looking for them. If anything, I'd been avoiding them, deliberately moving to the opposite side of whatever assembly they joined. So I figured they had to be tracking me specifically, and this meeting wasn't an accident.

I was right.

I never could tell the difference between Dane and Dyne, even when they wore dissimilar earrings, even when they wore different hairstyles and hair colors. I always just called them Herkle. It didn't matter, either would answer.

I didn't want to talk through the hood and I certainly wasn't going to have this conversation on any channel, wireless or otherwise. I'd learned the hard way about people listening in. Actually, I was in no mood to talk to them at all, so I marched up the hill away from them.

They didn't take the hint. They followed me across the polycrete—which was starting to show some serious cracking from the pounding weight of the horgs—and up into the corner of the fences, out of anyone's line of sight, before I pulled off my hood and turned around, annoyed. "What do you want?"

Both of them flashed dazzling grins. The one on the left said, "We kinda feel bad you didn't join our family."

"I never got an invitation."

They looked confused. "But we sent you one."

"No. You didn't."

"Yes, we did."

"I never got it."

They looked at each other, even more confused. "Well, uh, okay. There must have been some mix-up. But the invitation is still there, still open. Any time you want to be a Herkle—"

I didn't have a bad opinion of the Herkles. They were mostly a good family. They kept their word, they paid their bills on time, and they were always there for anyone in need. I just didn't have a good feeling about the twins. They acted like you weren't allowed to say no to them, and if you did, they couldn't understand why you'd said it. They weren't bad in bed, though, I couldn't say it wouldn't be fun. And one thing was well known: the Herkles ate good.

I stood there, looking back and forth between them, trying to figure out what they really wanted—and at the same time listing in my mind all the reasons I should slap their faces and walk away.

I'd already earned some credential in Grampa's family. And whatever happened with Mr. Costello, I could see that we were still going to do very well off this exercise. And I was happy in Finn's bed. So the only advantage in going to the Herkle twins' bed would be . . . what? I'd be just another toy they shared. I'd be back to zero seniority and there were over a dozen invested members in the Herkle brood, so my cut would be proportionally smaller. They were a rich family, but not so rich as to make the offer dazzling.

So . . . why the invitation? Why now?

Apparently I was taking too long. The one on the right said, "We like having you between us. Even if you don't want to take up our invitation now . . . well, we have an empty cabin in truck three. If you want to visit tonight, we could have some fun."

Well, that was blatant. I said, "Sorry. I'm married."

"So are we."

"Not to me." And I strode away, feeling confused, frustrated, angry—and a little horny. Because, dammit, those two were gorgeous, exciting, and energetic. Also spoiled rotten.

The only thing I could figure—they wanted to pump me. For information, too. Only there probably wasn't anything I could tell them that Mr. Costello hadn't already.

I didn't know if I should tell Finn about it. I didn't want to upset him. I certainly didn't want him to get angry. We didn't need a fight with another family, especially not here, not now. I took a long hot shower, put on the blue dress that Finn had bought—the one he'd said we'd take turns wearing, this was the first time either of us had put it on—and went in to help with dinner. Trina noticed the dress but said nothing. Neither did anyone else. I guess they figured this was between Finn and me.

But during Circle, Grampa looked across to me and said, "You wanna dump it? Or you wanna let it fester?"

I started crying. I didn't know why. It was everything and nothing. It was silly and I felt stupid. I thought—after all the stuff I'd been through before getting to Haven—that I'd hardened myself. Now I realized the only person I'd been fooling was me.

Next thing I knew, Finn picked me up and carried me back to our cabin. The door slid shut behind us and he put me gently down on the bed. He didn't say anything, just popped open a water bottle and handed it to me. He sat down opposite and waited, a concerned look on his face—not judging, just ready to listen.

"I'm not a good person, Finn. I don't know why you took me into your family, but you're the best people I've ever known and I'm grateful for the little bit of time I've had here. You should probably invite me out now, before I hurt you."

"You can't hurt us," he said. "No, that's not true. The only way you could hurt any of us would be by leaving. We love you. We care about you. Whatever it is, we have your back."

"Yes, that's the right thing to say. You always know the right thing to say, but you don't know who I really am—"

"Yes, I do—"

"I've been lying to you. Lying to the whole family."

"Sweetheart, stop it. Just stop." He tilted my head up and looked me in the eyes. "You haven't been lying. You've just been afraid. With good reason. We know your real age, we know about the rejuve, we know how old you really are. We don't care. We know what you did on Flatland, we know what you did on Myrva, we know who you were on Borran. We've known all along. We don't care. We know who you are on Haven. That's the only thing we care about."

"You've known—?"

"We figured you'd tell us when you were ready. And if you never told us, well—that would be fine, too. We've all done things—"

"I killed people, Finn. I was—"

"Stop." He put a finger across my lips. "Are you planning to kill anyone today?"

"No. No, of course not."

"Then it doesn't matter."

"But it does—"

"Another time, another place. You put it behind you. You put everything behind you when you rejuved. You've got the body and the spirit—and the confusion—of a brand-new adolescent. You'll be another ten years growing up again. But here's the thing, sweetheart. It was necessary, it was the right thing to do—it was the only way you could abandon your past. And it's one of the things that convinced us to take you in. Even after the way the Herkles treated you—"

"You know about that?"

"Yes, I do. The Family does. That's one of the reasons we watch out for you so closely—we know how fragile you are. Everybody your age is fragile, even when you're doing it for the second or third time. Because you're so full of life and hope and energy and enthusiasm—it overwhelms all the stuff you thought you knew, all the stuff you thought was worth knowing. You know how you say, 'I wish I'd known this when I was young'? Well, guess what—knowing it doesn't slow down the impulsiveness of the adolescent spirit."

He pulled me into a hug and held me close. "Now have a good cry, as much as you need to—but those had better be tears of happiness." After a bit, after we finished kissing too, he said, "By the way, I was right. The blue dress really does look good on you."

"I wore it for you."

"I know." He nuzzled my ear. "I knew what it meant. I was glad to see it." He helped me take it off, pulling it up over my head, hanging it carefully on a hook.

"Next time, you wear it," I said.

"Promise," he said.

And then we stopped talking for a while.

Two days later, we put up the third fence. It didn't slow the horgs down. By now, they were so eager to eat they barely noticed it. They had a nice comfortable U-shaped enclosure with the biggest piles of feed located at the back wall of the U.

And it was finally obvious to everyone what the next step would be. Jerrid and Mikla were already prepping it. But right now, we were just waiting to see how many horgs would show up to feed in a night. We were counting as many as ninety.

Our camp was growing. Another dozen trucks arrived and set up shop, three more families to help with the processing, packing, and pickling. While it didn't affect our accounting, I could see that Mr. Costello's bank channels were picking up a lot more traffic.

So at the afternoon meeting, it didn't surprise me that the Herkle twins—probably at Mr. Costello's coaching—stood up and suggested we needed some rules and regulations for our settlement as well as for our business. "Just so we'll all know where we stand. So there won't be any misunderstandings later on."

Mr. Costello smiled and said, "Having rules is a good thing, yes. These boys are very smart, they are."

And because no one wanted to argue with Mr. Costello, the vote was unanimous. A committee was set up to determine appropriate guidelines for establishing property limits—and for personal boundaries, too. That was a week's worth of wrangling, sometimes heated, because there were a lot of people here now, not everybody knew everybody, and different folks kept imagining various ways to get their toes stepped on.

We kept out of most of it. Mostly because Grampa didn't like crowds. Neither did any of the rest of us, but Grampa was worst. He kept to his cabin a lot—enough that we were starting to worry about him. But he showed up for dinner and he was okay during Circle, so as much as we worried, we knew he was staying close and connected.

I was feeling a lot better, too. At midnight meal, I went to each member of the family and just hugged them close. There was nothing that needed to be said, the hug said it all. And they hugged me back and kissed me and told me they were proud of me, and that was the end of it. Grampa was funniest, though. He whispered in my ear, "Next time I rejuve, I'm gonna want you to wear that blue dress for me." And I whispered back, "I promise I will." He didn't flirt with me often, but when he did, it was his way of saying, "You're good with me."

Meanwhile, after laying out the feed, five hundred kilos a night now—and more wood than we felt comfortable shredding—we focused ourselves on gathering as much horg-dung as we could. We had six bots working the downslope and we kept them out there all day and all night, only pulling them back when the horgs were around. We chilled the dung balls as fast as the bots collected them and were close to filling the first trailer. Lazz was already talking about driving it back home to empty it into the main cellar.

The Maetlins had their warehouse lit up all the time now, and one afternoon they invited everyone to walk through the installations to see how the carcasses would be hung and fed into the disassembly line, where all the separate machines would skin, cut, separate, slice, grade, and process the horg meat. They were ready to go, anytime. They just needed a horg-sized tunnel from the feeding pen into the first machine, the killing machine.

And finally, on the last day, a few more trucks arrived—looky-loos and wan-nabes, curiosity-seekers and even a few tourists—all of whom had heard the gossip about Mr. Costello's marvelous horg-catching operation. They'd all come out to see this idjit get himself good and killed. Tilda Jacklin was running a pool.

Afternoon meeting got a little heated, tho. Finn and Charlie and me always attended. Trina usually stayed home with Grampa. Lazz and Marlie kept busy, mon-itoring the dung-bots.

This day tho, the Maetlins started talking about offal rights. You cut up a carcass, the intestines—or whatever the horgs use as intestines—spill out. The upper part of the tract is mostly full of undigested food, but the lower part is packed with dung that hasn't been dropped. And a lot of that dung is fertilized seedpods.

By rights, that dung belonged to us, and Charlie stood up to voice our claim. The Maetlins argued otherwise. Their contract gave them rights to all parts of the creature that were not immediately saleable, and that included the undropped dung. We knew they were being paid on a per-carcass basis, plus a percentage of Mr. Costello's sale price, a very fair deal. They were also getting the ingredients for bone meal and various fertilizers, which was their bonus. So Charlie argued that if they took the dung, they were taking part of our bonus. The Maetlins argued back that if the dung wasn't dropped, it was still part of the animal and covered by their contract. Obviously, they knew the value of fertilized seedpods.

We already had enough to corner the market—enough to crash the market if we wanted to—but that wasn't information anyone else knew and we intended to keep it that way. But if the Maetlins got fertilized seedpods from the undropped dung, they'd have enough to be a serious competitor. They could drive the prize down if they wanted to. And they might want to, just because they could. It wouldn't be the first time they'd savaged another family. If they saw an advantage for themselves, they took it. That was their reputation and it was well earned. There were some aban-doned farms to testify to that.

So we argued, first Charlie, then Finn. I kept my mouth shut and made notes. It got pretty ferocious there for a bit and I was afraid a fight might break out. We had a hospital truck. The Hellisons managed that. And surveillance, too. But the kind of injuries the Maetlins were capable of inflicting—I put my hand on Finn's forearm and he sat back down.

Harm Maetlin noticed it, and I knew he was about to ask who wore the balls in our family—but Arle Maetlin stepped in front of him. The Maetlins might be feisty but they're not stupid. A fight was the last thing they needed right now.

In fact—just the possibility of a fight sidetracked that meeting, Mr. Costello stood up and said it worried him terribly that we had gotten to such a sad position. Perhaps we needed to consider what kinds of mechanisms should be put in place?

Well, that's how we got a police force. And a judge. And a mechanism to enforce the application of our new settlement's rules and guidelines. It all happened so fast, it would have been head-spinning. Except Mr. Costello just happened to have the boilerplate. Because a good businessman is always prepared. And Mr. Costello was a very good businessman. He didn't say so, he didn't have to, but he'd been planning this from the beginning.

And that's how the settlement got named, too. Costello. Of course. In honor of the man who made it happen.

Mr. Costello accepted the position of mayor. And judge. Of course. And as his first ruling, he cut Solomon's baby in half. We got the offal. The Maetlins got the responsibility of running the police force. They would be paid appropriately for their efforts. The rest of us would be charged a pro-rata user fee for the provision of police salaries, as well as the billables of the judge and mayor, who—because Mr. Costello was so thoughtful and generous—would only be compensated for hours actually served.

That night, while the horgs were feeding, Jerrid and Mikla rolled the last huge section of fence around and slammed it shut with a satisfying clank, penning in a hundred and twenty-three grunting, grumbling mountains of ugly meat. The horgs were so busy scraping the glitter-pods off the deck, they never even noticed.

Almost immediately, the Maetlins started spraying liquid nitrogen into the air above the pen, forming huge clouds of cold steam. A cross-spray of water created flurries of snow, which fell onto the backs of the uneasy creatures like a quiet blizzard. And just as quickly, the horgs started huddling together, their instinctive response to winter.

The monitors showed us that their metabolic processes were slowing, slowing, turning the animals into huge docile lumps. Using nothing more than a bucket of warm glitter-pods, a single man could lead a near-slumbering horg to the receiving gate, through a short tunnel, through the airlocks, and finally into the killing room of the processing plant. Harm Maetlin had the honor of leading the first. The other beasts would follow, one at a time. When the line was fully up to speed, they'd be able to process—kill and butcher—thirty-six horgs a day.

From the hill above, cheers and applause. Mr. Costello had captured a herd. Mr. Costello was going to pack and ship several hundred tons of horg meat. Mr. Costello was going to make us all rich. Mr. Costello, hooray.

Mr. Costello!

I could still hear the clank of that last piece of fence slamming shut. That's when the uncomfortable little itch at the back of my neck became a lot more than an uncomfortable little itch.

We watched for a bit, then walked silently back to our trucks. Nobody said much. We ate in silence. Cold sandwiches. We'd just seen the future of Haven. It wasn't pretty.

The videos of what we'd accomplished at Costello Township were already circulating across the public webs. Within hours, new partnerships, new alliances, new collectives of all kinds would be announced—all with the intention of cashing in. The giant herds would be slaughtered, sacrificed to the greed of little men. They'd be annihilated within a generation and the ecology of Haven would collapse.

It's okay to take one or two. It's not okay to take a thousand or ten thousand. It's not okay to wipe out an apex predator. I stayed up late, running simulations. Without enough mates, the horgs would self-fertilize. Without any parents to feed on them, the mini-horg swarms would run out of control. They'd decimate the countryside, eating everything they could, leaving deserts behind, and wiping out every species that depended on the devastated land. The only good news? They'd wipe out most of the human population, too.

The next morning, we had an emergency meeting with Mr. Costello. Just me and Finn, Charlie and Grampa. We told him about our fears.

Mr. Costello looked sad. Very sad. "Yes, of course. Of course," he said. "You're very smart to share your concerns with me. This is why I'm so glad we're business partners. You're all so intelligent and insightful. So please let me put your minds at ease." He motioned to Mikla, who arrived with two fresh pitchers of lemonade, his signal that this was going to be a long but pleasant meeting.

"From the beginning, I realized that if our techniques worked, they could be copied. So I incorporated a holding company, patented the mechanics of the entire operation, and transferred the patent to the corporation. That corporation will sell licenses, materiel, and equipment to any other prospective horg-trapping collective. They will only be allowed to take a limited number of horgs in any given year. Their license requires them to sell their catch only to licensed shippers, and the corporation takes a percentage from both packagers and shippers. So there will be a limit on the number of beasts killed and the amount of meat shipped. That will also keep the prices high. The enforcement protocols are all in place. For the protection of the species . . . as well as for the protection of the market, nobody will be able to ship a ton of horg-meat off this planet without buying a license from me. Well, from my corporation."

Finn leaned back in his chair. He looked to Grampa. Grampa looked to Charlie. Charlie shook his head.

Mr. Costello sensed our unease. Hell, even a rock would have noticed. "You still look unhappy. Did I do something wrong? How can I make it up to you? You've been paid, haven't you? You even got bonuses. Was it not enough?"

"No, you've been fair," Grampa said. "You kept your word."

Mr. Costello relaxed in his chair.

"But—" Grampa continued. "To be honest, we kinda expected you to get killed. We was even bettin' on how it would happen. You weren't the first idjit to come down here with a brilliant idea. You probably won't be the last. So we never expected you to get this far. But your money was good and what the hell—we went along for the ride."

"So what's the problem?"

"Nothing. Everything."

I raised my hand politely to interrupt. Grampa nodded to me.

I said, "You've hanged the world. And I'm not sure—*we're* not sure it's going to be for the better."

Mr. Costello looked honestly confused. "Oh my. Oh dear. Yes. You must think I'm planning to leave and take all my profits with me. Oh, no. No, no, no. We're going to lay tracks and build a railroad from Costello Town to Settlement so we can ship horg-meat all year long. Restless Meadow is perfectly situated to draw horgs off the main migratory track. This will be a permanent base for expansion. We'll have a hospital, a school, a year-round marketplace. Eventually, we'll extend the railroad across the continent and establish Costello Towns on every major migratory track. That's where the other collectives will be allowed to build. Liftcore has already agreed to drop a second beanstalk, and we've got sites picked out for three and four as well. And you'll be senior partners. You'll be among the richest people on Haven. No, please don't thank me—I'm happy to do it. Haven will no longer be a backwater world. Soon it will live up to its name. Millions of people will want to settle here."

Well, you can't argue with good news. And I suppose all that good news should have made us happy, but it didn't. Finn and Grampa headed back to the truck, their footsteps quiet on the new sidewalks the Hellisons had installed.

Charlie shook his head and walked on down to Jacklins' Outpost to see what new goods Tilda had driven in from Temp.

Me? I stood alone, shaking. Trying to figure out what to do next.

Was I the only one who could see it?

Bait and walls. First you put out bait. Something juicy. Then you put up a wall. You put out more bait, you put up another wall. Do it enough, you have a cage. Costello did it to the horgs, he did it to us. Glitter pods. Money. Something juicy. No difference at all. Bait and walls. Money and banks, then courts and police. We all get captured.

Mr. Costello saw me on the sidewalk and invited me to join him for a stroll. Some of the horgs were warming up, getting a little agitated. He wanted my opinion on whether or not they needed to be cooled again.

I didn't know, but what the hell. I followed him.

Yes, the remaining horgs were waking up. Yes, they were getting agitated. I didn't need the monitors to tell me that. They were hungry and annoyed. They'd definitely need to be fed and cooled. Already a few were pushing themselves against the fences, testing their imprisonment.

We climbed up onto the catwalk that overlooked this side of the pen. "Aren't they beautiful?" Mr. Costello said. His smile was broad and beneficent. In the afternoon light, he glowed like a saint.

I had to admit—if you looked at them the right way, horgs could be beautiful.

"Someday . . . " he mused. "Someday, there will be a city here." He turned to me with a serious expression. "Tell me something. Do you think they might put up a statue of me?"

That's when I kicked him into the pen with the horgs.

No one saw. And apparently someone had conveniently turned off the cameras without leaving any prints.

It was time for me to move on, anyway.

Finn caught up with me at Settlement and pulled me out of line for the bus to Beanstalk. "Like hell you will," he said, and wrapped me in his arms.

I didn't argue. He was wearing the blue dress.

AUTHOR'S AFTERWORD

First, let me acknowledge and thank the Theodore Sturgeon Literary Trust for permission to continue the adventures of one of Theodore Sturgeon's most memorable characters. I hope I have done him justice. If you haven't read the story that inspired this, "Mr. Costello, Hero," you should seek it out now. It is a classic. It will stick to the roof of your mind like mental peanut butter.

Now, let me acknowledge the gifts that Theodore Sturgeon represented to the community of science fiction authors—and to me as both a writer and a friend.

One night, when a group of us were gathered at a local restaurant, I asked him about style. He generously showed me one of the most marvelous mechanisms for creating voice and style in a story. He called it metric prose, and it's a tool I continue to use today.

There's not enough room to share the details here, but the short version— Ted showed me how it's possible to write with a poetic meter that carries from one sentence to the next to create a specific mood. When you change the meter, it changes the emotional tone of the prose, as if you're moving from silk onto sandpaper (his metaphor). Google Sturgeon's interviews or read James Gunn's writings on Sturgeon for more information.

But the most important lesson I learned from Ted wasn't about writing as much as it was about how to be a human being. I can't sum that up easily, either—the best I can say is that in its expression, you find yourself living at the center of your soul, unafraid and joyous, discovering over and over that the very best stories one can write are about what happens in the space between two human beings.

THE WHITE PIANO

Last night I had the dream again.

I dreamt I was a child. I dreamt I was in bed, waiting to fall asleep. The walls of my room were gray and featureless, except for a black door. On the other side of the door was a long dark hall. I don't know how I knew this. The door was closed. Something was coming down the hall. When it reached the door, it started scratching to get in.

◇◇◇◇◇◇◇◇◇◇◇◇◇◇◇◇◇

When mother went into the hospital, our grandmother came to take care of me and my sister. We were both very young. Neither of us understood why our mother had to be away for so long, but we trusted our grandmother. She fed us, bathed us, and tucked us in every night. She kissed us and stroked our heads and told us that Mama was getting better and would be home soon, we just had to be patient a little longer.

Then she'd tell us a bedtime story, a different tale every night. She never read from a book. She only told us true stories.

One day, Grandma got a phone call that made her very sad. When we asked her what was the matter, she didn't want to say. But finally, she gathered us in her arms and told us that Mama would not be coming home after all. She had not gotten better in the hospital and this morning she had passed away.

"Did she go to Heaven?" we asked.

Grandma hugged us close and said, "Nobody knows where you go after you die, because nobody has ever come back to tell us. No matter what anyone says, nobody knows. That's why it's so scary. We don't like not knowing." Grandma was not very religious. She said that a loving God would not have allowed so much evil and cruelty to happen in the world, so she was going to take her business elsewhere, to a better class of deity. But she never told us who that was.

That day, however, we didn't care about God. We all hurt too much and we cried and cried for a very long time. I didn't even know why I cried so much. I hadn't seen my mother in so many months that she had turned into a memory of a different time. I had learned to live without her. But I cried just the same. Finally, we all climbed into bed together and just held onto each other until we fell asleep.

In the middle of the night, I thought I heard a scratching in the wall. I mentioned it to Grandma the next morning. She said it must have been a mouse. The house was

107

very old and every winter, there were always a few mice looking for warmth. This was the first winter without a cat, we had not yet replaced Winston, maybe we should do that soon, so it must have been a mouse.

We slept with Grandma for another two nights before she made us go back to our own beds. She laughed and said, "You two snore too loudly." But it was really Grandma who snored. She sounded like a great grumbly bear hibernating in a deep dark cave. When I said that to Emma we both laughed.

And then when Emma told Grandma what I'd said, Grandma made a squinched-up scary face and growled horribly at us. Then she chased us around the bedroom insisting she was going to eat us all up, while we shrieked and laughed and ran back and forth around the bed, until finally we scrambled underneath it, thinking we'd be safe. But no—she crawled under the bed with us and gathered us into her arms and we all had another long cry.

I didn't want to go back to my own bed, but Grandma put me into one of her big flannel nightgowns and said that would be just the same as her holding me close all night long. It wasn't the first time she'd popped me into a nightgown, sometimes my pajamas were still in the laundry or hadn't come out of the wash on time, but tonight was different. She said this was Grandma-magic, she'd put a blessing on the nightgown and it would keep me safe all night long.

It was a strange feeling not wearing pajamas, not having that band around my waist, my legs feeling free and naked. I wasn't uncomfortable, but I wasn't ready to fall asleep either. I was confused and my head was full of churning thoughts.

That's when I heard the scratching again.

I listened as carefully as I could, but it didn't sound like a mouse, not to me. It sounded familiar, but I couldn't place the memory. It was like one of those bits of melody that pops up in your head—you know you know it, but you don't know where it came from. It sounded close, like just outside my room, but then after a while it went away.

In the morning, Grandma asked me how I slept. I told her okay. She frowned and squinted at me. "Didn't my nightgown keep you safe and warm?"

I said the nightgown was okay. It was nice and soft. But I heard scratching again.

Grandma made a face. "I didn't hear anything." She thought about it. "Maybe it was the branches from the big tree rattling against that side of the house. It must have gotten windy. I'll bet that's what you heard. I'll have Mr. Lopez come out and trim them back."

"It didn't sound like branches to me."

"What did it sound like?"

"I don't know. It just didn't sound like branches. It sounded like something scraping. Like scrubbing a pot. Or maybe sharpening a knife."

"Well," she said. "Yes. I suppose it could sound like that. I'll call Mr. Lopez after breakfast."

Mr. Lopez came out that afternoon. Emma and I stood a safe distance away and watched him as he climbed his ladder and cut off branches with a chainsaw.

The limbs of the tree fell crashing to the ground, raising little clouds of dust and dry autumn leaves. After a bit, he climbed down from the ladder and cut the branches into smaller pieces. He loaded everything into the back of his truck, and put an envelope into Grandma's mailbox, his bill.

It was getting dark when he finally drove away. Clouds were piling up in the distance. The air smelled cold and damp, but not like rain. Grandma said it wasn't ready to be a real storm yet.

That night, when it was time to get ready for bed, I started to reach for my pajamas, then changed my mind. I looked at Grandma's nightgown and frowned. No. It wasn't Grandma's nightgown that would make me feel safe.

I walked down the hall to Mama's room. Nobody else was around, but I closed the door behind me anyway. Mama's nightgowns were all in the top drawer of her dresser. Feeling like a thief, I sorted through them until I found the one I wanted. It was very light, very pale and silky-smooth. It was almost blue, but not quite, and if you looked carefully, there were tiny flowers printed into the material.

I took it out of the drawer reverently, like something sacred. I put it on top of the dresser and gently closed the drawer. Biting my lip, I looked at Mama's nightgown for the longest time. Finally, I reached out and stroked it with my fingertips. I'd never felt anything so soft. A minute longer and I gave in to temptation. I picked it up and held it to my nose. It smelled like Mama. I hadn't realized how much I'd missed her until just this moment. I buried myself in the faint smell of her perfume.

I wasn't planning to put it on, or maybe I was. I told myself I just wanted to keep it next to me because it still smelled like Mama. But once in my room, I wondered what it would feel like to wear it, to feel this incredible smoothness against my naked skin. Mama wouldn't mind, I knew. It would be like having her hug me all night. And that would be better than Grandma.

I told myself I shouldn't, but then I told myself that if I didn't I'd always be left wondering what it felt like, what I'd missed, so finally I took off all my clothes and pulled on Mama's nightgown. It was almost too big for me, hanging down to my feet, the sleeves falling past my hands, I didn't care.

Feeling daring, I turned and looked at myself in the full-length mirror—it made me feel confused, wicked, embarrassed, ashamed, and delicious, all at once. I stood there for I don't know how long, until all the different feelings became too much.

Then quickly, before anyone could see, I jumped into bed and snuggled under the covers feeling very special, maybe even a little rebellious. For a moment, I didn't move at all, then finally I let myself feel the softness of the material, stroking it against my chest and belly and legs and everywhere and feeling oh so very luxurious—but also feeling sad and strange and close to tears, wrapped in the sweet smell of my lost mother.

About the time I started to drift off, I heard the noise again. Something scratching. I rolled up on one elbow and listened. I wondered if I should get out of bed and go look. It sounded like someone scraping something hard off of old linoleum. Or maybe someone sharpening a knife on a grinding wheel. Or maybe—

There was a story I'd read once. Downstairs, we had a room filled with wonderful old books and I was allowed to read any book I wanted, but only if I showed it first to Mama or Grandma and asked for permission. Mostly, I did, but sometimes I didn't. One of the books was a collection of stories by Edgar Allan Poe. It was called *Tales of Mystery and Imagination*. Grandma said I wasn't old enough to read it yet, so I only read it when she was out of the house and wouldn't catch me.

One of the stories was about a man whose hearing was so intense, he could hear the sounds coming from the chambers beneath the house, where his sister was scratching at the lid of her coffin, frantically trying to get out.

I wondered if that was the noise I was hearing.

Maybe Mama hadn't really died. Maybe Grandma was lying to us. Maybe she was in a box underneath the house, screaming and scratching in desperate frenzy.

The more I thought about it, the more certain I became that the noise was coming from the basement. Forgetting what I was wearing, I crept out of bed. I almost tripped on the hem of my nightgown, Mama's nightgown, then grabbed the front to hold it up. I crossed to the door and peeked out of my room. The whole house was so dark, it must have been past midnight. Only the vaguest hint of illumination outlined the hall.

I listened for the scratching again.

I stepped into the hall, started cautiously toward the stairs—then caught a glimpse of something pale moving at the far end of the corridor, something ghostly. I yeeped and ran back to my room, slamming the door in fright—until I remembered there was a full-length mirror at the end of the hall and I'd seen my own reflection. I'd seen Mama's nightgown. I would have laughed out loud if my heart hadn't been pounding so hard.

When I caught my breath again, I counted to ten, then I counted to ten again just to be sure, then I opened the door of my room, very very slowly, so slowly it creaked, and finally finally, even more slowly than I had opened the door, I peeked around the heavy wooden frame to look down the hall.

There was nothing there.

Of course there wasn't.

Maybe just the slightest hint of a face, a distant pink blur.

I waved my arm and something in the distance waved back.

Bravely, I stepped out into the hall and so did my reflection. I waved my arms first away from my sides like an animated Jesus, then over my head like a victory cheer. So did my reflection. Again. And again. I giggled.

I held out the sides of my nightgown and waved them like wings. A distant angel waved back. A minute more and I was twirling and dancing, capering with my faraway twin, feeling deliciously free and dangerous.

I pretended I had a twin brother dancing and giggling with me, someone who knew and shared everything without my ever having to say a word, someone who was my other half so complete that I would never have to feel alone again, someone who liked me completely because we were both the same. He was another me.

So I danced with my ghostly brother down the hall until—abruptly, I heard a sound that wasn't me and I dashed back into my room and carefully closed the door. After a minute, I peeked out again.

There was no one in the hall.

Except—

Down at the far end of the hall, even beyond that—in the faraway dark distant reflection in the mirror, something pale and soft still fluttered and twirled and danced. It looked like a woman.

She waved to me.

I ran back into my room, nearly tripping in the nightgown, pulling it off as fast as I could and flinging it aside—*it was haunted!*—I scrambled naked into bed, pulled the covers up over my head, wrapped myself tight in the blankets, and then shrieked and sobbed into my pillow, shaking and trembling in terror so intense I thought I was going to die.

I must have fallen asleep sometime. The next thing I knew, the morning sun was screaming in through my bedroom window. Not streaming, screaming. That's how I experienced it—a howl of angry dawn. I was so snarled in my sheets I couldn't move. I had to roll out of bed and onto the floor with an ugly thump, pushing and kicking at the shroudlike embrace. I felt like a mummy.

Somehow I twisted free and leapt backward away from the tangled mess as if I had escaped from the jaws of some hideous beast. Standing there naked, I remembered what had happened the night before. I saw Mama's nightgown on the floor, and Grandma's too. I picked them both up and shoved them quickly into a bottom drawer, embarrassed.

I grabbed some clothes from the closet and pulled them on hastily. I was confused and exhausted and feverish, I knew I had to get out of the house immediately. I had to get away as far as I could.

Cautiously, I opened the door, I peeked down the hall. Bars of light slanted across the corridor from the open window at the end. The soft yellow daylight revealed everything. The noise I'd heard, the one that startled me—that was the wind blowing an unlocked window open, the tall one that led out onto what Grandma called "the widow's walk," a second story porch that wrapped around the old house. Grandma called it an architectural horror, I thought it was a great place for watching the world. The window had swung inward, lifting the light summer curtain—it was still blowing across the mirror, fluttering and dancing. And waving.

That was what I'd seen. Nothing more.

I rushed the last few steps to the window and pulled the curtain away from it and shut the window as quickly as I could and locked it firmly. The curtain fell back into place, once again shading the light and muting the bars of drifting dust-motes. The hall was safe again.

But I didn't feel relieved. No. Something had caused the window to open when it did. That's how these things worked. I'd read enough ghost stories by then to know. Whatever supernatural thing happens, it has to look like a natural event. That way, only the believers will see what's really happening. The ones who don't believe—they're the ones who always get caught unawares and unprepared.

I wondered if I had caused it—if by putting on Mama's nightgown I had somehow angered her. I didn't want Mama to be mad at me.

After breakfast, after Emma went outside to look for autumn leaves to press into her scrapbook. I stayed with Grandma at the breakfast table while she finished her tea. I asked her if there were such things as ghosts.

She put her teacup down and looked at me, "Did something happen last night?"

"I thought I saw a ghost." I didn't tell her about putting on Mama's nightgown, but I did tell her about the scratching I heard and what I saw when I opened my door. "I looked down the hall and saw something waving at me. I thought it was Mama—Mama's ghost."

Grandma didn't say anything. She poured herself another cup of tea. "Lots of things happen in the world we can't explain. That's why there are scientists. It's their job to look for explanations. Did you find one?"

I told her how the window had blown open in the night, letting the curtain flap in front of the window.

"There, you see."

She waited for me to agree.

I didn't answer. I just bit my lip and stared at my hands in my lap.

"What?" She didn't say it loudly, she didn't have to, it was still a command. "Tell me, sweetheart."

When I still didn't answer, she reached over and patted my arm. "All right. You don't have to if you don't want to. If you change your mind—"

"Grandma," I blurted, "I think Mama's mad at me. I think she blew the window open on purpose."

"Now, why on Earth would your mother be angry with you? She loved you very much. More than you know. All she wanted was to come home and be with you and Emma." I noticed that she didn't tell me there were no such things as ghosts, that Mama couldn't have been there in the hall, couldn't have opened the window.

I balled up my hands into fists and held them against my belly. Tears ran down my cheeks as I admitted, "I took her nightgown out of the drawer. It smelled so much like her, I wanted to wear it and sleep in it, so she could have her arms around me like you did. But I think Mama's mad at me for taking it, for putting it on, for everything. I'm so sorry, Grandma—"

All these years later, I can see that my grandmother was a very pragmatic woman and a very loving one too. She didn't care about the nightgown. All she saw was a little boy blubbering in distress. She pulled me to her and held me close and let me sob into the huge pillows of her bosom. I can still remember how safe I felt in her arms.

"Sweetheart," she said, "you go ahead and keep your mother's nightgown. You go ahead and wear it whenever you want to feel close to her. I'm sure that's what she would have wanted. I know it's what I'd want if you needed to feel close to me."

I sniffed hard and looked up at her. "Really?"

"Really," she said.

"But what about the ghost?"

"Ahh, yes. What about the ghost? Well, you let me think about that for a bit, okay?"

"Okay."

We sat there in the kitchen for a while, talking about nothing in particular. Grandma stroked my hair, she said I had such beautiful hair it made her jealous. She asked me which nightgown I'd taken. I told her the really soft one, the blue one. She said that was a good choice, that's the one she would have chosen too, and that's when I realized it really was all right with her.

After a while, Emma came back in, carrying two huge red leaves she'd found in the back yard. When she saw me in Grandma's lap, she put them carefully down on the kitchen table and announced, "My turn now." I slipped out of Grandma's hug and Emma climbed up onto her lap with a happy expression.

"Was he crying?" she asked.

"No, course not," Grandma said. "But it would have been all right if he did. Boys can cry too."

"Oh, okay." And then she buried her face against Grandma's neck. After a minute, she pulled back and looked into Grandma's face. "When I grow up, I want to have big shaky bosoms like you. They're nice and warm."

Grandma laughed at that, we all did, and we kept laughing about it all the rest of the day. Every time Emma wanted to make us giggle, all she had to say was, "I'm going to have big shaky bosoms too."

Even funnier was when I said it and Emma frowned at me and said, "You won't have any place to put them," and I snapped right back, "I'll put them on my girlfriend." That made Grandma howl with laughter. I wasn't sure why that was funny—whether it was the big shaky bosoms or the idea that I might someday have a girlfriend. I didn't know.

∞∞∞∞∞∞∞∞∞∞∞∞∞

After dinner, after our lessons, after our practice at the piano (and after Grandma showed us how that part of the concerto should really sound), after our cocoa and biscuits, it was time for story and bed.

Grandma said we should each put on our favorite nightgown, she looked directly at me when she said it, so I knew what she meant. She was saying it was all right, and we'd all snuggle up together for a very special story.

I went to my room and dug out Mama's nightgown. I put it on slowly, then made my way back down the hall to Grandma's room, knowing it was all right but embarrassed anyway. When I came in, Emma looked at me and screwed up her face in confusion. Finally she said, "Isn't that Mama's—?" But Grandma said, "Shh, honey. It's his now. Mama wanted him to have it, so she could hug him all night long, even when she's not here. Now, come snuggle up with me."

We both got into bed with her, one on each side, and Grandma wrapped her arms around us, pulling us close. "I am going to tell you a story that I have never told anybody before. It's a true story and it happened to me when I was your age." I wasn't sure if she meant me or Emma, I didn't ask. Maybe she meant it that way for each of us.

"It's a very long story and it's very complicated, so you'll have to pay close attention. But if there's anything you don't understand, you just ask, and I'll explain as I go."

◇◇◇◇◇◇◇◇◇◇◇◇◇◇◇◇

There's a hotel in New York, Grandma said, called The Algonquin. It's very famous.

Grandma said she stayed there once when she visited the city. It was her honeymoon. She said it was a very nice hotel, but all she remembered was that it felt old and dark and dusty.

But in the twenties, the Algonquin was a place where a cluster of self-indulgent writers and actors would gather for lunch and repartee every day. Some of them were columnists, and whenever they had nothing important to say, they wrote about each other. They called their gatherings The Algonquin Round Table.

This made them famous for being famous.

The most famous was a lady named Dorothy Parker, but the circle included Robert Benchley, George S. Kaufman, Heywood Broun, Harold Ross, and Alexander Woollcott. Sometimes people like Tallulah Bankhead, Edna Ferber, Estelle Winwood, and Harpo Marx would join them. I don't know if Harpo said much though.

Grandma said that there were even more important gatherings of writers and artists in Europe. She mentioned several cities, but I remember only Berlin and Paris.

The Paris salon, she said, was started by Gertrude Stein. It included F. Scott Fitzgerald, Sinclair Lewis, Thornton Wilder, Ezra Pound, Georges Braque, Henri Rousseau, Henri Matisse, Pablo Picasso, James Joyce, and of course, Alice B. Toklas. Although they didn't meet as regularly, they also had a favorite gathering place, a bistro on the left bank of the river Seine.

While Ernest Hemingway was still a struggling author, he would show up to cadge drinks and meals from the others, but very quickly he established himself as an efficient reporter, and even demonstrated some skill with short stories. Occasionally, publishers dropped by. Sometimes they paid for meals. Sometimes they even bought the writers' stories.

"Did you know Hemingway?" I asked.

"No, I did not," Grandma said, "but I almost knew his German publisher. I lived in his house for a while. He'd made a lot of money printing German translations of Hemingway and other authors."

It was the twenties and even if they didn't know it then, it was a marvelous time to be alive. It was the first generation with radios and telephones and automobiles and record players. There was music everywhere. People were discovering a different way of life.

But it was also the first decade after the Great War, and it was a terrible time for Europe. A whole generation of young men had died in the trenches and even though no one really knew how to explain what they were all feeling, there was a terrible emptiness everywhere. So they tried to cover it up with wild parties, drinking and dancing and lots of casual sex instead of learning how to fall in love.

Germany had lost the war, so the German government was forced to sign a peace treaty at Versailles. Germany couldn't build any more warships or guns and they had to pay the Allies for the cost of the war, billions of dollars. This impoverished the country, leaving almost no money for anything else.

The Nazi Party blamed the economic turmoil on the Jews. They blamed the Jews for starting the war. Although the Nazi Party had begun as an extremist movement, by the end of the decade it had won nearly a third of the seats in the Reichstag.

Fearing darker times ahead, some of Germany's Jews began emigrating, quietly making their way westward. Some ended up in Paris, others passed through on their way to America or other places.

After Hitler became Führer, the trickle of refugees grew rapidly. Some sold off as much of their goods and property as they could. Others, those who could afford it, brought their art and furniture with them. One of these was a publisher who had been very successful all over Europe, so he was a very wealthy man. He had translated and published many of the writers in the Paris group so he was welcomed into their ranks. His wife owned a beautiful white piano and they brought it with them to Paris at great expense. The piano had been his gift to her when they married.

The publisher's wife had been a famous concert pianist, almost a prodigy. Before the Great War, she had played concerts all over Europe—Vienna, Paris, Berlin, all the major capitals. Audiences marveled not only at her sublime technical skills, but were also deeply moved by the emotional depth of her performances.

As the story goes, on their wedding night, instead of taking her to bed, her new husband took her to the room in his house that had previously been his private study, but unknown to her, he had ordered it remodeled into a special room just for her, a music room, and in it he'd installed the most beautiful grand piano she had ever seen, all gleaming white with exquisite gold trim. It had been designed and built for an extravagant movie musical, but the movie was never filmed because the writer and director had left Germany for America.

The publisher's new wife sat down at the keyboard and began to play for him. She played her favorite piano pieces—Beethoven and Mozart and Liszt. He sat and listened, enraptured. She played for hours and they did not go to bed until dawn finally lit up the curtains with the pink light of morning. It was, they both said, the most romantic wedding night in the world.

By the middle of the thirties, it was apparent that a reinvigorated Germany was preparing for war again. There was a civil war in Spain and German weapons were being used to crush the anti-Franco factions. Among the members of the Paris Salon, there was a gloomy awareness that this was a preview of Germany's renewed military strength. Pablo Picasso painted a terrifying mural called *Guernica*, to portray the horror of a Spanish town subjected to aerial bombing by Germany's Nazi Luftwaffe.

With all this talk of a new war, Paris didn't feel safe anymore, so the publisher and his wife retreated again, this time to England. Of course, they brought the piano with them, again at great expense. They bought a small estate near Durham and installed the white piano in a spacious parlor. But the wife died of pneumonia that first winter and the husband covered the piano with a heavy sheet, locked up the parlor, and never went in there again.

Later, when the Nazis began bombing London, thousands of children were evacuated and sent to live in the country. Even so, one in ten people killed in the Blitz were children, not all of them were as lucky as Grandma.

Grandma and her younger brother and sister were sent to live in the publisher's house, a small manor not too far from the Scottish border. The publisher was off in some place called Bletchley, working for the British government as a translator, so the house stood empty except for a small caretaker staff.

For whatever reasons, Grandma was never sure why, she and her two siblings were the only children boarded in that house. The two younger ones were safely established in an upstairs nursery, but Grandma was put in an unused room downstairs. It was a large L-shaped room at the southwest corner of the house. Other than her bed and a chair, all the other furniture in the room was draped with sheets.

Charlotte-the-housemaid showed her where to unpack. She was a big red-haired Irish lady who had no children of her own, never having found a man big enough to sweep her off her feet, or so she said. Consequently, she was delighted to finally have some children to take care of, especially ones old enough to be out of diapers.

"I'll have to get you some sheets and towels," she said, and hurried off to find them. Grandma hadn't even put down her suitcase yet, everything was happening so fast. She dropped it on the rug and turned around, staring. She couldn't help herself. The walls were almost all bookshelves, except for several old portraits of men and women. The men were all standing sternly, the women all sitting politely. That made Grandma laugh.

Around the corner was a huge piano-shape covered with a large white sheet. Curious, Grandma lifted up the edge of the sheet to peek. As soon as she saw it was a grand piano, she cried out with delight and clapped her hands. Quickly, she pulled the sheet off and let it fall to the floor forgotten, amazed at what she saw.

No longer gleaming, the fabulous piano had turned a faded gray. The damp air of northern England had not been kind to it. The beautiful instrument's once-glamorous paint was now streaked with deep cracks, even peeling away at the edges, but in the gloomy afternoon light, it looked magically silver to Grandma. It was an enchanted fairy piano, wonderful and mysterious.

Carefully, she walked around it, touching it gently with her fingertips, tracing the gold trim. When she got to the front, she opened the fallboard and let her fingers stray across the yellowing ivory keys. They felt as smooth and seductive as if they were made out of silk. Grandma couldn't help herself. She started playing "Für

Elise," which Ludwig Van Beethoven had written for a little girl named Elise. All these years later, nobody is sure who Elise really was. It's still something to argue about.

"Für Elise" is easy to play and almost every beginning piano student learns it sometime—that and "Twinkle, Twinkle, Little Star," which started as a nursery rhyme but ended up being part of Haydn's "Surprise" symphony. Mozart wrote some variations on it too.

But Grandma didn't get very far into the piece before Charlotte-the-housemaid came running in, red-faced and shouting, "Oh, no, no, no!" She closed the fallboard, almost slamming it down on Grandma's fingers. "You must never play this piano," she said. "Never." She started gathering up the sheet from the floor.

"Why not?" Grandma asked.

"Because you mustn't. It's forbidden," Charlotte-the-housemaid said, clutching the sheet to her chest. "This piano belonged to the Missus. It was her favorite thing in the whole world. She used to sit in here and play for hours, the most beautiful music you ever heard. But then she took sick suddenly and died and the Mister ordered that no one should ever play this piano again, because it was hers."

"But it's such a beautiful piano. And I know how to play the piano. I used to practice every day. It isn't fair that it's here and I can't play it. I like playing the piano. I need to practice my lessons."

That's when Charlotte-the-housemaid said, "If it were up to me, I wouldn't mind. But..." She lowered her voice, "...You don't want to make the ghost angry, do you?"

"Is there really a ghost?" Grandma asked.

Charlotte-the-housemaid had come from a large family in Dublin. She had helped raise two little sisters, so she was very good with children. Now she lowered her voice even more, down to the quietest whisper—she looked around in all directions, very conspiratorially, and said, "Now, I'll tell you, sweetie, I don't believe in ghosts, but I think maybe the Mister does, because every few months a man comes up from town just to tune the piano, even though no one's allowed to play it, so maybe the Mister wants to keep the ghost happy—what do you think?"

"I think it's not fair," Grandma announced. "I want to play the piano." Grandma was always very stubborn, even as a little girl. She said she once out-stubborned a cat, but that might have been another of her stories. But this time, however, she sat on the bench and folded her arms—and stuck out her lower lip. And that was always a sign of trouble. Emma does it too.

It must have worked because Charlotte-the-housemaid said, "Now, sweetheart, you know I'm not supposed to go against Mister's instructions." Then she took a big deep breath and added, "But he's not here and you're right, it is a perfectly good piano, and maybe what he don't know won't hurt him, will it?" She sat down next to Grandma on the bench and opened the lid for her. "Maybe a little bit, just for right now?"

So Grandma started to play her favorite piece. She didn't need the music. She knew it by heart. She played it every time she sat down at a piano. It was called "The Aquarium" and it was written by a Frenchman named Camille Saint-Saëns. It's part of a larger suite called *The Carnival of the Animals*. There are thirteen other parts, each one dedicated to a different animal—elephants, asses, swans, kangaroos, hens and roosters, tortoises, and even pianists who I guess are some special kind of animal too. But Grandma's favorite part was "The Aquarium."

If you close your eyes, you can almost see the fish moving through the rippling water, drifting above the rocks, nibbling and bubbling, lurking beneath lily pads, and looking back at you with black lidless eyes. Fish don't blink. That always makes me wonder what they're thinking. Do fish even think?

When Grandma is in an angry mood, she plays Beethoven, usually the *Pathetique* sonata, which is much harder and has lots of ferocious pounding. She says that's how she works out her upset, but Emma and I think it's how she warns everyone to leave her alone for a while.

But this time, this night—back when she was little—sitting at the keyboard of that strange and wonderful piano, she played "The Aquarium," and sitting there next to her, just listening, Charlotte-the-housemaid started weeping.

Grandma stopped, frightened and concerned, but Charlotte-the-housemaid touched her arm and said, "No, no, honey. Keep playing. Keep playing." She took out her handkerchief and wiped at her eyes while Grandma played through the piece. When she finished, Charlotte whispered, "Again, please." And then once more after that as well. Grandma played "The Aquarium" three times before Charlotte-the-housemaid gasped, as if in pain, and said, "No more. No more for now." She reached over and closed the fallboard.

"That's my favorite piece," said Grandma.

"It was her favorite too," Charlotte-the-housemaid said. "She used to play it all the time." She nodded to the portraits of the lady. There were two.

The portrait on the left showed her as a beautiful young woman, her hair piled high on top of her head in the style of the time. All dressed in white with just a bit of neck and bosom revealed, she sat quietly in front of the piano, hands resting primly in her lap. Her smile had an impish quality and according to Grandma, you could almost see the twinkle in her eyes.

The portrait on the right showed her as she was the year before she died, thicker around the waist, hair all white now to match the dress, a different dress, much more prim, a higher lace collar around her throat, but the same pose of course, sitting in front of the piano with her hands held quietly in her lap. The smile was older, kinder, less mischievous, but the twinkle in her eyes was still there—if you looked for it.

"She was so beautiful," Grandma said.

"Yes, she was. The Mister loved her very much. We all did. She was kind to everyone. And always laughing. Always so happy." Charlotte-the-housemaid stroked the top of the fallboard. "Never a day went by that she didn't come in here and play, sometimes for hours and hours. The house was filled with music always. You could hear it everywhere, even to the farthest corners of the second floor, and even down in the pantry, everywhere."

"She must have been very good."

"Oh, she was. Very very good. She said it was because she practiced every day. She had to if she was going to play for kings and queens. The Mister once invited her to take a walk in the garden—it was such a beautiful day—but she said she needed to practice. He said that nobody would hear the difference if she skipped a day, but she just smiled at him and said, 'I would hear it.' That's how good she was."

"I'd like to be that good," Grandma said.

"You'd have to practice every day," said Charlotte-the-housemaid.

"Could I?" Grandma asked.

Charlotte-the-housemaid stared at the two portraits on the wall, first one, then the other. Finally, she patted Grandma's hand. "I miss the music. We all do. I guess it would be nice to have a little music here again."

"But won't the ghost get angry?"

"Only if you miss a note or play it wrong," Charlotte-the-housemaid said sadly. "That was the only time I ever heard her say a cross word—that was toward the end, when her hands weren't working right anymore. Hush, no more questions now. It's time for you to go to bed."

The music room bent around the southwest corner of the house. Grandma's bed was in one leg of the L, the piano was in the other, so Grandma couldn't see it around the corner, but she said it was nice to know it was there. She was so excited to have a piano again, she couldn't sleep. She could hardly wait for morning. There were huge stacks of music piled up on the shelves behind the piano. She wanted to sort through all of them. Maybe staying here in Durham wouldn't be so bad after all.

Grandma said she fell asleep imagining a great big concert hall, and a silver piano in front of a thousand people, all the women so beautiful in evening gowns, all the men so handsome in shiny black suits, and she was on stage, all in white like the lady in the paintings, and of course she was playing her favorite piece, "The Aquarium" by Monsieur Camille Saint-Saëns. She could hear it as clearly as if she were actually there in the hall.

In the morning, the whole household gathered for breakfast. Grandma said the kitchen was enormous. There was a huge wooden table in the middle of it where Cook pounded out the dough for the day's bread or carved slices off a big ham. The table was surrounded by tall wooden chairs for the kitchen staff and hanging over everything and everywhere, to hear Grandma tell it, were all kinds of pots and pans, cutlery and sieves and spoons and stirrers, anything that Cook might need to grab in a hurry.

The far wall of the kitchen was a giant fireplace, deep enough to walk into, and wide enough that if you wanted to serve roast herd, you could lay the fire for it here and still have room left over for wild boar on a spit.

But today, there were only fried eggs and sausages, toast and jam, but no butter. The only reason they had eggs, there was a coop with six chickens in back of the house. Grandma said Cook was very unhappy about having three children in the house, not because she didn't like cooking for children, but because if the children all had eggs for breakfast, there wouldn't be any for staff, including her. But Charlotte-the-housemaid told Cook to hush up with her complaints. She poked Cook's overstuffed waist and said, "Besides, you've already had enough eggs in your life." Cook waved a huge wooden spoon at her, as if it was a club, but then grumbled away to stir the porridge.

As soon as Cook's back was turned Charlotte-the-housemaid turned to Grandma with a stern look on her face. She lowered her voice and said, "You mustn't play the piano in the middle of the night anymore. You'll wake everybody up."

That confused Grandma. She said, "I didn't. I was in bed all night long."

Charlotte-the-housemaid frowned and said, "Don't you tell me no lies, Missy, or we'll not be getting along very well."

That made Grandma cry and she ran from the kitchen in tears. "I'm not lying, I'm not!" She went to her big L-shaped room and threw herself on her new bed, sobbing. That was where Charlotte-the-housemaid found her.

"Now stop that crying this minute. I won't have it, you hear me?"

Grandma sat up stubbornly and glowered at Charlotte-the-housemaid the way only a little girl can glower. "I didn't lie," she shouted angrily. "I didn't. I didn't get out of bed last night, it would have been too cold, and I wouldn't have been able to find my slippers in the dark anyway. And I wasn't playing that stupid old piano. It must have been the ghost."

And that's when they both stopped talking at the same time and just looked at each other, stunned by what they were both thinking.

Grandma spoke first. "I'm sorry. It's not a stupid old piano. It's a beautiful piano. It's the most beautiful piano I've ever seen. And if I were a ghost, I'd want to come back and play it too."

Charlotte-the-housemaid looked stricken. She walked around the corner, Grandma following, just to look at the piano. It stood alone at the other end of the room. The morning sun gave it a silvery-gray sheen.

"I dunno. Doesn't look all that ghostly to me," said Charlotte-the-housemaid, but not very convincingly.

"Maybe it's only ghostly at night," said Grandma. Then she added, "In the daylight, it just looks magical. Maybe it's not haunted, maybe it's enchanted. Maybe that's why the ghost comes back? Because it reminds her of what made her happy in life...?"

"Well," said Charlotte-the-housemaid, "The Missus did like to laugh a lot. You can see it in her eyes. In both paintings."

"So there," said Grandma, as if that proved something. "I'm not going to be afraid of any ghost who plays the piano and neither should you."

"It's still a ghost," said Charlotte-the-housemaid.

"We're all ghosts," Grandma decided. "We just ride around in meat-wrapped skeletons until we're tired of them. Then we leave them behind and go on without."

"Is that what you say?" asked Charlotte-the-housemaid.

"Yes, that's what I say, because that's what I think." Grandma folded her arms and put on her stubborn face.

"Well, all right then." Charlotte-the-housemaid was smart enough not to argue with Grandma. Instead, she said, "But in the meantime, let's ask the ghost to please not play too loud in the night, so she won't wake up Cook and have her blame you. All right?"

"All right," said Grandma. "I will. In fact, I'll even write her a note. Will that do?"

"If it works for The Missus, it works for me. Good on ya, then."

Grandma wrote a very nice letter, thanking The Missus for letting her play the piano, but very politely asking her not to play loud enough to wake anyone up. She signed it and put it on the music rack so the ghost wouldn't miss it. Then, satisfied that she had behaved properly, she began looking through all the scores on the shelves.

For most of the afternoon, Grandma sat on the floor sorting through stacks of sheet music. There were popular songs and ballads, concertos and suites, even Franz Liszt's transcriptions of Beethoven's nine symphonies. There were piano concertos by Mozart, Grieg, Tchaikovsky, and of course Beethoven again. And surprise, there were even some Scott Joplin ragtime numbers. Most of the classical pieces had too many pages and looked very complicated and difficult, but Grandma was excited to see such complex melodies and harmonies captured on paper. She wanted to hear how they sounded, but she couldn't pick which one to try first. Whatever she chose, she knew it would be a lot of work—and take a lot of practice.

Finally, she settled on Beethoven's "Pathetique" sonata, not the whole piece, but the second movement, because it was slow and wistful. Grandma said she liked wistful music, and that's why "The Aquarium" was her favorite, but I think she just liked slow music because it was easier to play than fast music.

Grandma explained to us that when she was just beginning, she invented her own way of practicing. She'd take two or three bars of music and play them over and over and over, like she was teaching her fingers to find out where all the notes were on the keyboard. Then she'd go on to the next two or three bars and play them over and over the same way. When she reached the end of the page, she'd go back to the beginning and play the whole page over and over until she felt she could get through it comfortably. Grandma said she had to learn a piece of music one note at a time, one bar at a time, one page at a time. It must have worked because I never heard her miss a note.

Once I asked her how she played the piano so well. She just smiled and said, "All you have to do is hit the keys in the right order. The piano does the rest." But I don't think Grandma ever noticed how hard she worked at the keyboard because she was always too busy concentrating. When she played the piano, she puckered up her face in a terrible frown, focusing as hard as she could to touch every key just right.

That day, she practiced the "Pathetique" all day long, just the second movement. Played at the right tempo, it should only be five minutes long, but Grandma was still finding her way through it and playing it very slowly. She didn't notice how much time had passed until the room had turned rosy with sunset and Charlotte-the-housemaid came in to call her to dinner. Beans and potatoes and bits of ham and cheese on toast.

That was when Grandma realized they had skipped tea. That only happened when something bad occurred and everybody was so upset they just stopped in shock.

There was terrible news of the war. There was news every night, and sometimes music too, sad or triumphant—or music that was supposed to be inspiring. But this evening the news was very bad. The radio in the kitchen spoke in many serious voices. Grandma forgot all about Ludwig van Beethoven and his marvelous concerto.

The night before, German planes had bombed the town of Coventry. The voices on the radio said that thousands of buildings had been destroyed. Hundreds of people had been killed, including many women and children. It could have been much worse, but most of the town's residents had escaped death and injury in Coventry's air-raid shelters.

Cook was grim-faced and red-eyed as if she had been crying all day. Charlotte-the-housemaid stomped around like an angry bull. The groundskeeper came slamming in, stared around the room for a moment, saw three children sitting wide-eyed and afraid at the kitchen table, then slammed out again without saying a word, probably because the words he wanted to say weren't fit for children's ears.

Coventry was only 160 miles south of Durham. Grandma said she didn't have a good sense of distance at that age, but she got the feeling that Coventry was close enough that the people in Durham were worried they might be targeted tonight. Cook and Charlotte-the-housemaid talked back and forth that maybe everyone should move down to the basement for shelter and sleep there a few nights, but Charlotte-the-housemaid said that were several good air raid sirens in the town, loud enough to wake everyone up. If there was an air raid, they'd all hear them in plenty of time to go down to the root cellar or the basement, so everybody should sleep in their own beds tonight and not be afraid of some silly Nazi bogeyman.

It turned into a terrible argument between Cook and Charlotte-the-housemaid, without either of them ever saying the words specifically—"the safety of the children"— but finally Charlotte-the-housemaid won out. She said she had already made up enough beds today, she wasn't going to make up any more in the basement. Cook said she'd go down and sleep in the basement anyway. Charlotte-the-housemaid said Cook could go sleep in Carfax Abbey for all she cared. That made Cook very angry and she stormed out of the kitchen. Grandma and her younger siblings laughed at that, even though they didn't know why Carfax Abbey was so funny, but for many days afterward, "go to Carfax Abbey" was their way of saying "go to the bad place."

Grandma didn't go back to the piano after dinner. Charlotte-the-housemaid read them a story from Beatrix Potter—about a rabbit named Peter who got himself into some terrible trouble in Mr. McGregor's garden, but still got out all right and came home to a nice cup of chamomile tea. Not Grandma's favorite story, she would have preferred *The Wind in the Willows*, but her younger brother and sister liked it, so she sat with them and listened quietly.

After the story, Charlotte-the-housemaid decided to take the two younger children down to the basement for the night after all. Despite her earlier objections, she had made up three beds, but Grandma said she wanted to stay upstairs with the piano. Charlotte-the-housemaid said she might allow this only if Grandma promised to come down to the basement immediately if the air raid sirens sounded. Grandma agreed.

There was no air raid that night, but Grandma woke up anyway. She thought she heard something—music. Someone was playing the piano, very softly.

It was the "Pathetique" sonata. Second movement. Not too fast, not too slow. Not the way Grandma had practiced it, but the way it should be played—the way a master pianist would play it, turning the dispassionate notes on the page into breathtaking moments of emotion. Grandma sat up in bed and listened, enchanted—and too appreciative to get out of bed to see who was at the keyboard. And yes, maybe she was a little bit scared as well. After all, no one else in the house could play the piano—certainly not like this. It had to be the ghost.

Grandma listened while the ghost—or whoever it was—played the whole sonata, not just the second movement. Some people, Grandma said, play the sonata ferociously, like they're angry. Grandma admitted she plays it that way when she's angry, but the "Pathetique" sonata isn't about anger. It's about grief. It's about loss. It's about the terrible feeling of emptiness that scourges your soul when you've lost that very special someone you love so much it hurts all the way down to the bottom. It's about the rage you feel inside because there's nothing you can do to recover yourself—and it's about accepting that the past is gone forever. It's about coming to terms with whatever is still left to you, however meager it is.

And—Grandma said, this was her interpretation—it's also about saying goodbye, because life is one long process of saying goodbye, over and over and over, until it's your turn to go. When she said that, I realized for the first time just how much she must still miss Grandpa. Even after all these years.

Grandma said she didn't know if there were ghosts or not, but maybe sometimes some part of a person's spirit is so strong that it can't die. It stays in the world for a long while, only fading away slowly as time and memory evaporate. Maybe that's why she heard music in the night—it was the part of the lady that couldn't die, couldn't go away yet.

In the morning, there was more news about Coventry, about rescue workers going in, about recovering the bodies, many of them so badly burned that identification was impossible. Four hundred dead, maybe more, they wouldn't know for sure for days, not until they finished digging through the wreckage. Hundreds more injured. The whole town reduced to rubble. A terrible disaster. Another reason to hate the monsters on the other side of the Channel. The monsters were already bragging about how effective their war machines had been against Coventry and how even more destructive they would be when they turned their attention back to London.

Cook burned the eggs and toast. Charlotte-the-housemaid was unusually quiet. She hushed the children sternly when they started to giggle about something. Everyone was upset about everything. The groundskeeper was nowhere to be found—he'd probably gone into town and gotten raging drunk like a lot of the other old men, especially those who'd survived the Great War, he was probably still sleeping it off somewhere. Fortunately, the November weather was still unseasonably mild—mild enough that if he'd fallen asleep in an alley or passed out behind the pub, at least he wouldn't have frozen to death.

Later, when Charlotte-the-housemaid was making up the beds, Grandma asked her if she had heard any of the music in the night. Charlotte-the-housemaid shook her head. "Too much hurt and too much sorrow, sweetheart. I took a pill to help me sleep. You could have played the *1812 Overture* with real cannons and it wouldn't have roused me."

That afternoon, Charlotte-the-housemaid, Cook, and the groundskeeper all went into town, carrying bundles of clothes, sheets for bandages, blankets, and anything else they could find to help the survivors of Coventry. They took the two younger children with them, but Grandma said she wasn't feeling well and Charlotte-the-housemaid thought she did look poorly, so after another argument between Cook and Charlotte-the-housemaid, Grandma was allowed to stay behind.

As soon as they left, she went straight to her room and the shelves behind the piano. She sat down on the floor and began sorting through the sheet music. She did want to go back to the "Pathetique" and begin learning the other two movements, especially now that she had heard the sonata the way it should be played. But at the same time, she wanted to try something different, something that wasn't so sad. She didn't have the right word for it, she said—not then—but she wanted to play something that wouldn't hurt to hear, something that would make the tears all right. Something peaceful, something that would be an island of calm in her small, troubled world.

She finally settled on another Beethoven sonata, Piano Sonata No. 14 in C-sharp minor, the "Moonlight" sonata. The first movement. It's slow and it has its own wistful quality, but the way Grandma plays the piece, it's about the shimmering reflection of the moon on the surface of a quiet lake, somewhere high in the mountains. Maybe there are snowcapped peaks visible, both in the distance and seen upside down in the silent water. The music is about a woman, or maybe a man, sitting on the shore, staring out over the barely rippling waters, reflecting on her own life, her past, her future, her possibilities. She's at peace with her choices. It's a moment of contemplation, maybe even contentment, before she goes back to the brighter world that waits when dawn comes again.

Cook had left a cold plate for Grandma in the kitchen, in case everyone had to stay in town to help with the rescue efforts for Coventry. They wouldn't know how much needed to be done until the emergency teams reported back—so if there were sheets to be torn for bandages or boxes of food to be packed, they might need to spend the night helping. Grandma had decided the ghost wasn't going to hurt anyone, so she wasn't afraid to spend the night by herself, but she had to spend a lot of time reassuring Charlotte-the-housemaid that she would be all right and that she could take care of herself.

After she ate, she returned to the piano. She had set aside a whole stack of music that interested her. "Au Claire de Lune," of course, and Erik Satie's *Gymnopedie No. 1*, and "Solace" by Scott Joplin. She'd heard of Mr. Joplin, she'd even heard some of his music in films, but she'd been told by her piano teacher that Mr. Joplin's music was not for polite society, and certainly not for little girls. Her teacher had not explained why. So when Grandma found the music for "Solace," she definitely had to put it in the growing stack of pieces she wanted to learn.

She also found Bach's Prelude and Fugue in C major, which was also the accompaniment to Gounaud's Ave Maria, and maybe that would be a good thing to practice too, considering what had happened in Coventry. She added Mozart's Piano Sonata No. 16 in C major, the first movement, Bach's Minuet in G major from the *Notebook for Anna Magdalena Bach*, and was looking at Chopin's Polonaise in A Major, trying to decide if it might be too difficult, when she noticed the piece immediately below it—George Gershwin's *Rhapsody in Blue*.

She knew it would be much too difficult for her, but she couldn't resist. Maybe there was a piece of it, even a little bit, that she could learn. She took it to the piano, sat down with it, and turned the pages back and forth, frowning. She'd never seen music like this before. She tried a few phrases. Her hands weren't big enough for some of the chords, but she really wanted to know what the music would sound like. She'd heard it on the radio once, before the war, when they'd still lived in London, and she'd sat before the speaker, mesmerized by the dramatic syncopation. *Rhapsody in Blue* was one of the reasons she'd wanted to learn how to play the piano. And now, here in her hands, she finally had the music. How could she not want to play it?

Grandma said it wasn't the hardest piece of music she ever had to learn, but it was the hardest piece of music she ever tried to play—because she wanted so much to get it right. There were parts of it that she just couldn't manage, not yet, but there were a few places where she did evoke a small sense of Gershwin's magic.

At last, though, she had to put it aside. She turned her attention instead to "Solace" by Mr. Scott Joplin. Although it was ragtime, it was a more thoughtful exploration of the form than anything she had heard before. Grandma worked her way through it carefully, paying special attention to the recurring phrase that suggested a quiet stroll in a garden, or perhaps a pleasant carriage ride through a shady green.

When the great clock in the hall struck eleven, Grandma realized she had stayed up much later than she was supposed to. Reluctantly, she closed the fallboard and went to bed, wondering if the ghost would show up and play this very modern music.

The way Grandma tells it, she was so tired, she slept through the entire night. But she had a dream, and in her dream there was music—marvelous music. She was standing alone in a great room, a golden hall, and in the distance, there was the piano all gleaming and white, just as it had been when it was new, and sitting at the keyboard, a beautiful woman in a beautiful white gown, so elegant and gracious, her hands dancing across the keys almost too fast to see. And the music she was playing—it was the most exquisite music Grandma had ever heard.

And then the woman finished the piece. She stopped, she rested her hands lightly on her lap for a moment, then she closed the fallboard to indicate she was done. She looked up from the piano, she looked directly down the length of the room to Grandma...and smiled and nodded. Then she stood up, she wasn't tall, but she wasn't short. She wasn't thin and she wasn't fat—she had the stoutness of age and the grace of confidence. Her white hair was piled high in a bun and that made her look taller than five feet. Then she turned and left the room, disappearing into the shuttered French doors as if they weren't there, passing through them to a place that wasn't on the other side.

In the morning, Grandma fixed herself tea and toast with jam for breakfast. Cook and Charlotte-the-housemaid and the groundskeeper showed up shortly before noon, tired but satisfied they had made a difference. Grandma's younger brother and sister were excited to tell her about everything they had seen in Durham proper. All the inns and hotels were full to overcrowded, so they had stayed overnight with Cook's daughter, everyone sleeping on the floor in front of a huge open fireplace.

Many people in Durham had opened their homes to the refugees from Coventry, there were lorries and buses going back and forth all day and night. People arrived on every train, still black from the smoke of the fires, many of them carrying what little they could salvage from their burned-out homes. Some people had to be carried from the train on stretchers. The hospitals were already full but more and more injured were arriving with every train. There were so many people arriving in Durham, they were sleeping on the floor of the college gymnasium.

Later, when Charlotte-the-housemaid got around to asking Grandma if she had managed all right, Grandma said she had. When Charlotte-the-housemaid came into her room to make up her bed, Grandma asked her about the sheet music on the shelves. Did she know where it had all come from?

"Oh my, yes," said Charlotte-the-housemaid. "Before the war, Mister and Missus went to London regularly, sometimes twice a month. Every time there was an important concert or show, they took the train down. Sometimes the Mister was already in London and Missus had to travel alone, so I went along with her when she needed a travel maid. I went with Missus to her favorite music stores. Oh, such a lady she was. She picked through the music as if she could hear it with her eyes. Sometimes she would sit at the piano in the store and play a piece to see how it sounded. Everyone in the store would stop and listen. Oh my, you should have seen how the clerks loved her. Everyone did. Wherever she went, it was a concert. And then we'd come back home with her luggage full of music—every trip, and sometimes mine too if there wasn't enough room in hers—oh, we had such fun. Missus was a very famous pianist, she played all over Europe, even for some of the crowned heads, she did. Missus had trained with some of the very best teachers in Vienna and Berlin, but she had a—oh, what would you call it? She had a wonderful curiosity, a fascination with all the new music coming from America. She said it was very exciting what the American composers were creating, that they were inventing new kinds of music. I'm sure she could hear things I couldn't, it all sounded like music to me, but when she sat down to play, you just wanted to stop and listen. Oh, listen to me now, I'm starting to sound like I know what I'm talking about. I'm getting above myself, but... well, I did love traveling with her. Whenever I went with, we would sit together and she would very patiently explain the music to me, what it was about, and why it was important. It wasn't just that it made the train rides feel like no time at all was passing—it was like we were just two old friends chatting away. She was a dear woman, she treated everyone the same, it didn't matter if you were a lady or a servant. Oh, and she had the most delicious way of speaking—such a thick accent, all German and Jewish, what they call Yiddish, it was great fun to listen to her talk—and she always looked so elegant, until she opened her mouth and sounded like a—like a Russian babushka. The Mister worshipped her so much. He had the same accent, only thicker than hers, so to listen to them chatter back and forth—especially if they were disagreeing about the details of some silly little thing that had happened in Düsseldorf or was it Straussburg or maybe it was Brussels, no I'm sure it was Marseilles, because there was that little café that served those funny little cakes you liked so much, until finally he would look across at her and say with such a twinkle, yes whatever, my dear, I'm sure you are right, his way of saying he loved her too much to argue. They were so cute, they were. Oh my, we all miss them every day. This big old house is too empty without them." Then Charlotte-the-housemaid patted Grandma on the head. "It's been so much better since you arrived. All of us like having someone to take care of."

Then Grandma remembered something from her dream. She pointed to the shuttered French doors at the west side of the room, behind the piano. "What's out there?" she asked.

"Oh, that was Missus' own private garden...." Charlotte-the-housemaid said. "She would go out there with the Mister whenever he came back from London. The two of them would just sit with each other, holding hands like a couple of newlyweds, and catch up on all the things they wanted to share. They were such a perfect pair, him with his cane and all, and she—oh my, she always dressed herself up for him like it was the most special day of their lives, she always dressed in white—you can see that in her pictures—she always said a lady should be a lady, if you know what I mean, except at the piano, she said, where a pianist should be everything from a delightful sparkle to a ferocious monsoon. I think that's why she liked playing the piano so much—because it let her be everything she couldn't be inside a corset and a white dress. She liked to bust loose, she did."

"Can we open those big French doors?" Grandma asked.

Charlotte-the-housemaid hesitated. "Those doors haven't been opened since—" She took another breath. "Missus is buried out there. In her garden. The Mister won't go out there anymore. I think maybe he wants to believe she's still here in the house."

"I think we should open the doors and let the sunlight in. It's too dark and gloomy in here."

"Yes, it is, but—"

"But the Mister isn't here, is he? And maybe the ghost doesn't want to feel locked out? Maybe ghosts are ghosts because they're lonely? Maybe she misses him as much as he misses her?"

Grandma pushed past Charlotte-the-housemaid and began unlatching the big French doors. Charlotte-the-housemaid fussed a little more, but made no move to stop Grandma from throwing open the doors to let in the sunset. Wide steps led down to a circle of precisely trimmed rose bushes, where a few red and pink and white flowers still bloomed, even this late in the year.

Charlotte-the-housemaid followed Grandma down the steps, past the bushes, past a circle of benches around a pond and a fountain, to a quiet hedged-in sanctuary and a simple marble monolith. Carved into the face of it was the outline of a grand piano, and below that, a name and two dates.

"This is where she rests," Charlotte-the-housemaid whispered.

"Only in the daytime," Grandma said with the certainty only a young lady could have. "At night she likes to play the piano."

Charlotte-the-housemaid looked at Grandma with a raised eyebrow. Was Grandma making something up or did she believe what she just said?

Grandma turned to the marker and said, "Please come back and play some more. I want to learn to play as well as you." Then she turned back to Charlotte-the-housemaid. "This is a very pretty garden, I think I would like to come out here just to sit and enjoy the day, wouldn't you? I don't think the Missus would mind if we came back. Everything you tell me about her, she must have been very nice." Then Grandma remembered her manners and said, "Maybe sometime, we could have tea out here? For the Missus?"

That night, after dinner, after the radio concert, after she was washed and brushed and ready for bed, Grandma went to the piano part of the room and picked up all the music she had set aside for herself. She put the pages on top of the piano, spreading them out in a fan so all the titles were visible.

Then she sat down on the bench and waited. She must have dozed for a while. But then suddenly, she was awake. And there, sitting next to her, was a kindly-looking, white-haired old lady—a little bit transparent, but very real.

Grandma didn't know what to say, but the ghost did.

"So, dah-link. Vat vould you like to play tonight?"

Grandma said it so perfectly, we laughed and laughed and snuggled in next to her, still giggling. After that, all Grandma had to say was, "So, dah-link. Vat vould you like to play?" and we would all start laughing again.

But finally, I asked, "Was that a made-up story? Just to make us feel better?"

Grandma gave me the Grandma look, offended. "I never make up anything. Every word of it was true."

The next morning, we dressed up in our best clothes and went to Mama's funeral. It was very somber. And very sad. But neither I nor Emma cried. Everybody said we were very brave, but we knew better. There was nothing to be sad about. Mama was still with us. Laughing quietly in a way that only we could hear.

I still have my mother's old blue nightgown in my drawer, just a keepsake now. Sometimes, when I'm feeling lonely, sometimes when I'm feeling down, I take it out and hold it against my cheek. It reminds me of a time when I felt safe. It reminds me of people long gone, even a lady I never met.

Tonight, I didn't close the bedroom door. Tonight, I left it open.

And tonight, I did not hear something scratching. Instead, I heard music.

I don't have a piano, I gave up playing years ago.

But Grandma never stopped.

ENDLESS CITY

She was beautiful.

Of course.

They almost always are. Nobody picks ugly. At least, not the people I deal with.

My office is on the second floor of a run-down building in a shabby mid-century neighborhood. Last century. It's part of the mystique. Either you get it or you don't. She got it. She was dressed to the forties. Muted red dress, fox stole, auburn hair piled forward in perfectly sculpted waves.

I waved a chair at her. She sat, crossing her perfect legs perfectly. I caught a whiff of her perfume. *The Rose of Time*. Nice. And very expensive.

"There's going to be a murder," she said.

"On average, there's one every seventeen minutes," I replied. "The most recent one was two minutes ago." I had a display on the wall behind her. She couldn't see it, of course, but it was already reading out her statistics for me, at least the ones she was willing to share.

"No, this is serious. The expansion is going to be approved."

"And the sun will rise tomorrow."

"Have you seen the map?"

I nodded.

The city was going to expand, a dozen klicks south and east. The disruption would be one of the biggest in history, but going to 128-bit granularity would create a vast new range of terrain. Bad news for some, great news for others. If the disruption index went high enough, there would be a lot of murders. It wouldn't solve anything, but a lot of people would feel vindicated—not satisfied, but vindicated. The difference is profound. It's what keeps me in business.

I took my time studying her. The view was magnificent. Finally, "What is it you want from me? Prevention? Detection? Revenge? I have to tell you up front, I'm out of the murder-for-hire business—it makes me a target. And besides, I make more money this side of the law."

She didn't answer. Instead, she lit a cigarette. She fixed it in a long black holder, then waved it curtly to light. She took a puff and stared at me. Cigarettes are great props. Especially if you look like Marlene Dietrich. Or a young Tallulah Bankhead. Her appearance was somewhere between the two, a nice morph-job.

She took another puff. "Well...I don't need a murderer. Not now anyway. But I do need someone who knows how to find a murderer."

"Any particular murderer?"

"Yes," she said. "Because it's a very particular murder."

I leaned back in my chair. It gave me a better view up her skirt. "That might be worth my time. Is it a clever murder?"

"The murder...? Not clever, just nasty. But the murderer—? That'll be the hard part."

"And after I find this person...?"

"You'll know what to do." She leaned forward, giving me a spectacular view down the grand canyon of her cleavage. "You're my last hope."

She was impossible to refuse. "Who's the victim."

Another puff. She exhaled golden smoke. "I am." She pinned me with steel-blue eyes.

I took a moment to consider that. "Why?"

"I've done bad things. I've made enemies."

"Who hasn't? See that filing cabinet over there—?"

"I'm not interested in your problems. Are you interested in mine?"

"It'll be expensive—"

She had a tiny purse on her lap. She opened it now, dipped delicate fingers into it, pulled out an envelope larger than the purse itself, passed it across to me.

"You'll find a retainer in there. There's more in the escrow account. You'll have the right to draw on it for billable hours and expenses. My banker will audit."

I opened the envelope. I would have raised my eyebrows, but I had facial expressions turned off. It's more in character.

"There will be a bonus, of course, if you solve the case quickly. If not...well, the amount in the escrow account should be sufficient for an extended investigation. The numbers are based on a performance analysis of your last six years of investigations."

I closed the envelope. "You've done your homework." I put the envelope down on my desk. "But let me ask you something. Why don't we work on preventing the murder—?"

"That's no longer possible—"

"Why?"

"Because the murder is happening now—"

She finished the last word and winked out.

Shit.

◇◇◇◇◇◇◇◇◇◇◇◇◇◇◇

The problem goes back to the founding. Nobody expected the city to get this big. But it did.

Endless City is semi-spherical. It's a three-dimensional rectangular grid that curves around on itself in all directions—pick one, if you travel far enough, long enough, you'll end up back where you started. Convenient, but self-limiting when it comes to expansion.

That's why the sysops can't just drop in a block of new addresses wherever they want. They have to add X, Y, and Z — the row, the column, the depth. That splits any settlement that spans any affected part of the grid.

Nobody cares if a lake gets stretched or an ocean gets wider—but if your view suddenly retreats, if your access to a desirable neighborhood is compromised, if your sky-haven is suddenly on the ground or in the stratosphere, or if your private community is abruptly sliced in half, it matters.

Already the petitions were piling up, requests to have the addresses reassigned— so that sections on one side or the other of the split would remain adjacent to their most desirable neighbors. Most of those would be granted, except where it might conflict with a travel corridor.

The new space would start as a vast empty plain, several orders of magnitude larger than the current size of the city. The city would become a gigantic oasis in the middle of near-infinite blankness. But just in case it filled up anyway, there would now be delineated vertical and horizontal equators where additional addresses could be installed in the future with minimal further disruption.

Meanwhile, a lot of people were about to be very unhappy. And some of them already were.

∞∞∞∞∞∞∞∞∞∞∞∞∞

She was right. The murder was serious—more serious than I had expected. This was not a death she was going to recover from. It had occurred in meatspace.

Her name was Edward Ferguson, Cobie to his friends. He was found collapsed in his holosphere, one of the newer models. Death had been slow, moderately painful. The murder weapon—oh, she'd been right. It was nasty. And a bit sloppy too.

Cobie's holosphere had included a multi-function sextable, again one of the newer models. It was a horizontal array of vibration pads, with a matching frame above. You lay down on it, you put your face in the audio-video display, and the pads would massage and manipulate, rub and stroke and titillate to match any fantasy you could create.

A variety of programs were available, from gentle snuggling to rough trade. Male or female simulations were programmable, top or bottom, or both at the same time. The experience was generally better than the real thing because the programs monitored and responded to the physical reactions of the consumer.

Illicit programs, rape simulators, were also available. That's how Cobie had been murdered—raped to death, top and bottom simultaneously. There was blood and shit everywhere.

I did not visit the crime scene, no need. The forensics team had been very thorough. And Cobie's death-insurance covered the cost of unlimited access to all pertinent investigations. Cobie had seen to that, so that suggested he knew he was in danger for quite some time. But if he knew he was in danger, then why didn't he identify the source of the threat?

That was a good question. There wasn't a lot of other evidence. The only tangible corroboration was the sextable. Someone had replaced Cobie's copy of "Frat Boy

Shenanigans" with "Death by Oompah!" Cobie wouldn't have done it himself—not deliberately. Only by mistake.

Backtracking the channels wasn't a dead-end, but it was an infinite labyrinth. The malware had been routed through several hundred thousand ephemeral nodes created on the fly to pass on the code, then erased immediately after. Most of those nodes had played Ping-Pong with the Trojan a few million times, bouncing it around various private networks, encrypting and decrypting it millions of more times, before sending it on. If Cyber-Pol's monitors had kept up, they might be able to trace the message traffic all the way back to the source—but even if they could, it would take months, just to sort through the sheer number of transactions, and at the end, they'd find little more than a burner ID. The best they might come up with would be the cell-tower where the Oompah had begun—most likely the wi-fi in a public library.

No, this was not an ordinary cyber-murder. This was carefully planned—and it was deliberately vicious. An online persona could be rebooted, but wetware termination was permanent.

Okay, go back to the victim. Start from there.

Damn, but Cobie had been one beautiful woman. He knew how to work it. He was good. So good, I'd have hooked up with her.

I wasn't the first to discover this, it was common knowledge—a woman designed by a man knows exactly how to please another man, usually better than a woman. Sorry, ladies, but there are all those peer-reviewed studies. Of course, the reverse is true too—and the male ego is unlikely to ever recover.

So...Cobie had been playing female for years. He knew what he was doing. Start with that.

So...who would want to murder a crossplayer? No. Wrong question. Who would be enraged by a crossplayer? Or why? Crossplaying was so common it wasn't an issue for most people—only a few religious fanatics might be offended and they weren't likely to visit Endless City. That left a cliché so obvious even fan-fic wouldn't go there—a man, had fallen for Cobie's female avatar and then become enraged when he discovered Cobie had a meatspace penis. Nope. Only a studio producer would buy a storyline that shallow.

The not quite so obvious answer—could it have been a TERF, a Trans-Exclusionary Radical Freak? Some of them were online violent, they made excellent assassins if they approved of the target, but there weren't many meatspace incidents. This didn't fit their pattern.

Everybody in Endless City was an avatar—a performance. Even if you were a puristan and your avatar was an accurate rendition of your physical body, you were still running an avatar. Any rational player would have known that. An irrational player—someone so damaged they believed the reality of the avatars—yeah, there were those too. Furries, aliens, morphs, posers, replicants, repetitions, celebrocities, historicals, fictives, presenters, fluids, there weren't enough words for all the variants.

Not a problem, most of the outliers clustered, and someone too far off the mean would be easy to identify and track—

Okay, leave that, it's not low-hanging fruit. If necessary come back later. Work through the evidence first. What story does it tell?

Cobie had a high-end sextable. You don't spend kilobucks unless you're in deep. So, what was his kink? Had he used the bot for solo adventures? Or had he paired up with an online partner? Maybe several? It would have had to be someone with a compatible rig, another high-ender, Cobie's rig was new, not compatible with older models. Okay, check the connections, see if Cobie had partnered.

There's a thought.

Maybe "Death by Oompah" hadn't been planted by malware. Maybe Cobie had a hookup, a regular one, someone he trusted. Maybe the hookup had said "Let's share a fantasy," and sent him a kink. And then, our little Cobie, trusting the hookup, not noticing it had been flickering around the net, had plugged it in and—

But, no—that's stupid. If you're planning a murder, you want to make sure you leave no fingerprints, especially not digital ones.

Okay, wait—

Consider. The hookup knows he's going to kill Cobie—so he builds a burner identity. It has to be a sophisticated one, with an elaborate history, one that would fool even a high-level sniffer. And if Cobie had a high-end bot, then he'd likely have a high-level sniffer. And it would have gone off like a fire alarm if it didn't trust the source.

So no. That didn't make sense.

Okay, wait—

Let's say, the hookup created it, bounced it around, sent it to himself—herself?—and then sent it on to Cobie from the burner identity. Yeah, maybe. That might work. And as soon as Cobie died, the burner identity would vanish.

Um, no. There'd be a record of the identity—there just wouldn't be a trackable source for it. It would probably have gone through the same maze of connections as the kink.

Hmm. Hm. Hm.

I might have to leave the office for this one.

Crap.

Okay. Time to put on my legs. I rolled over to the sideboard and waved at the walker. It lit up, stood up, took three steps forward and held itself in place. I lifted myself up from the roller, angled my thighs into position and dropped into the exolegs. It took a moment for everything to settle into place, then I was ready to go—I could walk, run, stroll, stride, slide, saunter, stagger, shuffle, shamble, scramble, amble, toddle, totter, trot, truck, tango, boogie, march, waltz, polka, or pirouette. The pirouette would not be graceful, however—I'm not balanced for it.

<hr />

There are things I know how to do, but it's cheaper and easier and faster to hire someone else for certain tasks.

I went to see Miranda.

No, not in person. Nobody sees Miranda in person. You go to a public access, an emporium, a café, never the same one twice. You get a private booth, you punch in the number Miranda has given you, then you wait. Miranda gives a different number to each of her customers, that's how she knows who's calling—by what line you come in on.

If Miranda wants to talk to you, the screen flashes with another number—a burner, a proxy, a labyrinth. You take that to another booth, not close by either, tap that and you're connected. Or not. Sometimes Miranda will take you through two, three, a dozen separate burner-tracks.

If you don't follow Miranda's rules, if you try to trace Miranda, if you ask the wrong questions, you get permanently blocked. Miranda disappears from your world. Forever. Instead of a number, you get a "no results" screen. And no, you can't go through proxies either, human or otherwise—once you're blocked, you're blocked. Miranda's a tracker. If she blocks you, she assumes you're an enemy and she watches you very carefully.

Some people speculate that Miranda's not human, just a very good A.I. Or maybe she's a conglomerate. She could be, she charges enough—I don't speculate. I just pay for her services.

Miranda lit up quickly. Today, her avatar was a very skeptical Bette Davis. Very Margo Channing, cigarette holder and all. "Cobie Ferguson," she said.

"Yes."

"You want him deep-traced, all transactions. Meatspace tracking, Endless City, and any associated activities. How far back?" She took a puff for effect.

"A year should do it."

"Six months should be enough," she said. "But I'll look for anomalies at least three years back. That's the larger window of probability. Anything else?"

"Special focus on relationships, please. I'm looking for motives."

"Of course. I'll send you an invoice. Do you want a cap on expenses?"

I considered it. "The client is covering the cost."

She paused. She was searching. "The client can afford it. No problem." Another pause. "Interesting. The client prepared for his own murder. I'll include all of that too. It'll be waiting for you when you get home. You might want to fasten your seat belt. It's going to be a bumpy ride." She clicked off, leaving me wondering if she was being sarcastic, or if that had been a warning.

I found out soon enough.

◇◇◇◇◇◇◇◇◇◇◇◇◇◇◇

My physical office is in a building identical to the one in Endless City. The interior is a match as well, a dusty corner office with a couple of dirty file cabinets and various framed papers on the wall.

It's a deliberate match, another part of the performance. Everything is performance. I haven't been inside the building in seven months.

In truth, I'm in the building across the street and two floors down. In the afternoons, I park myself at the corner table of the outdoor café. I have a lettuce-and-tomato sandwich on whole wheat and coffee while I study the news. I don't see clients in meatspace, only in the City. Realtime is for research.

My professional persona is a burner identity, constructed on top of several proxies. Miranda could trace the path, I doubt anyone else could—probably she already has, otherwise she wouldn't have taken my business. I'm pretty sure a lot of what Miranda does is too deep in the wires to be legal, but I'm too smart to ask.

I pulled out a burner pad and downloaded Miranda's reports. As soon as I tapped to open the file, the second floor of the building across the street—my office—blew up. The corner windows shattered outward, south and east, gouts of fire and glass and smoke, knocking down pedestrians, sending cars skidding and screeching.

Nice. Very nice.

Another clue. Someone didn't want me to read Miranda's report. Someone smart enough to know I would link to Miranda, but not smart enough to know that my office was a Potemkin. Obviously, someone who spends too much time in Endless City. Someone smart enough to put a tracker on Miranda—she wasn't going to like that. Unless this was her doing. Whatever. I couldn't trust her again. Not until this was sorted out. One way to find out if she was responsible—call her and see if I'm blocked. But that would have to wait till later.

I got up quickly, and headed toward the back of the café, not so fast as to draw attention, but fast enough to disappear from the scene. Out through the kitchen, past the dishwashers, into the alley, two doors down, and in, up the back stairs. I had maybe two minutes, I needed only one—

Stepped in, hit the red button on the wall, opened the closet, pushed the side wall of the closet open, stepped through to the matching closet of the apartment on the other side. Behind me, an entire identity was evaporating. Everything. It would take less than thirty seconds to shred that existence.

This apartment was intentionally bare. Merely a transfer station. I stripped off my clothes, dropped everything—all my hardware too—into the shredder, then naked back into the closet—touched the wall the right way and the floor dropped me into the closet of the apartment below, then slapped back into place. An easy fall, I bounced on the trampoline

Overkill? Yes. Searchers would certainly find the first escape route, they'd assume I'd changed clothes and gone out the back door. By the time they realized that was a dead end, I should be on the other side of the city, on my way out of the state.

Padded to the shower, pulled myself out of my exo-legs, hung onto the grips, and punched for decontamination. Went through the cycle three times, prayed it would be enough, and waited for the blowers to finish drying me.

I hated to lose the legs, they were expensive and I hadn't finished breaking them in, but I couldn't trust them anymore. I couldn't even buy another set. If they—the mysterious "they"—were tracking buyers, the same set of legs would be a big red arrow pointing at me.

I whistled for—god, I hate them, but no choice—the fat lady. Two flubbery dark elephant props. Not graceful, but...you want to be invisible, be a fat black lady waddling off to some night job cleaning toilets for people who think their money deodorizes their turds. The disguise took a while, too many parts to it—the fat suit, the dress, the hidden compartments in the legs, under the tits, under the folds of flesh, even behind the big fat ass, and a few other places too—and then power up the new identity, hoping to hell it hasn't already been compromised, grab the purse and two huge shopping bags that pass for luggage when you're scraping poor—

If it got me out of the city, it was fine. I'd pass through at least two more identities before I came up for air and looked around. Four blocks away, a circuitous route, there was a recycling station—the fat lady would go in, a teenage screwhead would wander out, a skinny junkie-hustler with a peg below the knee. He'd shamble aimlessly for a while, then take the tube north toward the Jumble, and somewhere in there he'd vanish too. Max Blankman—not his real name—just a transfer identity would catch a train or a bus or maybe a ferry across the river—

And three days from now, a fluffy little old lady with a couple of robot cats would purchase a little pink gazebo in Lavender Meadows. Her wife had died a few months previously and she still hadn't figured out what to do with the rest of her life. Zoe Elaina Kilmartin had been a librarian once, a specialist in arcane research of all kinds. Occasionally she still accepted part-time work from authors and filmmakers, so she maintained a T-3 bandwidth.

Lavender Meadows was not specifically part of Endless City, but it used some of the same data-pipes. A skilled wirehead could proxy through. Of course, Ms. Kilmartin couldn't possibly know that the access in her gazebo had been proxied by a skilled wirehead several years before—and any deep search of her hardware would reveal that most of the research jobs she'd taken on were deliciously kinky, but nowhere near dangerous or illegal. But, oh those proxies—

If they held up even a week, they'd be gold.

I could afford it, but I was still pissed. Disappearing, transferring, reinventing—it was time-consuming, it was expensive. And I was no closer to solving the case. If anything, the case had gotten far more complicated.

Someone had found a perversely ingenious way to commit murder—he or she or whatever had killed Cobie Ferguson. But Cobie Ferguson had found out somehow. He'd discovered he was in danger—and he must have taken steps to protect himself, but just in case he'd also taken care to provide for the subsequent investigation. He'd put a lot of key pieces in place—he'd hired me. But he didn't know who the murderer would be, that was weird in itself, and now someone—probably the same murderer, but don't make assumptions—had tried to stop me from investigating.

Had to think about that. I'd assumed that the person who'd planted the bomb wasn't smart enough to find me in meatspace—but what if I was mistaken about that? What if he was—and the bomb wasn't an attempt to kill me, just scare me off?

But...no, I don't get scared off. Not that easily. If anything, the disruption of my business, the destruction of a carefully constructed identity, had pissed me off—enough that I was more committed than ever to crack this one.

I still had Miranda's report. I'd relayed it to a safe haven, scanned it and stripped it of all tracking macros. Now, I finally had time to study it in depth.

Miranda's research had been through, but it still didn't reveal much. Cobie's online identity was respectable, too respectable—obviously he'd run himself through a cleaning service, probably several. There weren't any connections that called attention to themselves either. Probably, the circles he moved in, they all had continuing cleaning services.

I sat in the little pink gazebo, studying the wraparound display, frowning to myself, tapping my teeth, and saying some very unladylike things.

Miranda's reports were always hyper-detailed. Sometimes she pointed out interesting anomalies. Sometimes she left them for me to discover myself. And sometimes they just leapt out of the display and shouted, "Here I am!"

Let's start with an assumption, a logical one—that whoever planned to kill Cobie Ferguson had been tracking his movements, stalking him in Endless City, stalking him in meatspace. So, if we track Cobie's movements for the past six months and expand that to include an area-search of everyone who passed within his local radius, eliminating all the randoms, minimizing the residents, we should be able to reveal any unusual patterns that are semi-congruent with Cobie's. Every traffic-cam, every security monitor, every smartphone, every ad-tracker, every functioning device plugged into the net, and every app on all of those devices—every photo or video or audio captured within Cobie's radius was rawdata if you had the resources to tap into all those separate data-feeds. Miranda did—and had.

Eezy-peezy, right?

Wrong.

Because the next part of the assumption was that if someone could upload "Death by Oompah" to a high-end sextable, they'd also be smart enough to know that simply stepping out onto a public street would create a permanent record of their every movement. Their every step and gesture—every fart, sneeze, and exhalation—would be logged somewhere. There would be only one protection—a blocking field.

Blockers are usually licensed to celebrities, politicians, corporate leaders, billionaires, and various government agencies. Ordinary citizens have to demonstrate a compelling need—witness protection, stalkers, restraining orders, that kind of stuff. Anyone else has to pay a hefty premium—because why would you want to hide your movements if you weren't doing something unlawful?

A blocking field interrupts the local flow of packets associated with your image, your voice, your location, everything. All the data going back and forth between your devices and the rest of the world is triple-encrypted. You show up on the displays as an empty space.

But even an empty space reveals a lot—especially if it's ambulatory.

If the blot tracks to the restroom, did it center on the men's, the ladies', the neuts', or the morphs'? That's useful information. If the blot goes into a store, what kind of a store? Clothing? Male? Female? Uni? If the blot moves from here to there—did it take a bus? A taxi? The tube? What does that tell you about its income? Does it suburb or supra? Or does it disappear into the Jumble—that's another slice of information. Just finding the home-locus of the blot is critical. If the blot abruptly disappears—who's in the suddenly revealed space, there's your list of suspects. Track them now.

If the blot doubles back, twists and turns, moves across the map in an erratic pattern to make sure it isn't being followed, it still gives itself away. It reveals it has a secret to hide.

Just one problem.

Yes, there was a blot—but it wasn't following Cobie Ferguson. It *was* Cobie Ferguson. Every time it shut down, there was Cobie. No other suspects.

Miranda was good. Cobie thought he'd been careful, he'd only shut down his blocker when he thought he was in the presence of other blockers. But Miranda tracked everyone leaving the blank areas and Cobie's presence was the only repeating factor.

Well, crap.

The case just got a whole lot weirder. I was now looking for an invisible murderer—one who wasn't blotted but still didn't show up in any data-feeds. One who could track his target even when the target was inside a blot.

Okay, let me think about this. If the answer isn't in the evidence you're looking at, it has to be in the evidence you're not looking at. Miranda had brute-forced the raw data, she'd minimized all the randoms and all the residents, and anyone else who might have had business in the area.

So...the man or woman or newt that I was looking for was probably a shifter, like me—someone who could burn through a dozen identities in a week. A lot harder to track, but not impossible. It requires some pretty deep scanning, but you can find identities that are too shallow, too perfect, too well constructed—or just too good to be true.

Miranda had flagged identities she trusted, individuals who'd existed in her own databases for three years or longer. That eliminated more than half of the randoms. Others were minimally suspect candidates—too old, too young, physically disabled, medically impossible, emotionally unfit, intellectually impaired, chronically ill, and so on—all the different outliers.

And then there were the ones with big ripples—deep family ties, long-term business connections, anyone with a hint of celebrity, those were the least likely to be burners.

Burner identities tended to be disconnected, enclosed, not a lot of interaction with the rest of the world. Yeah, that includes a lot of shut-downs, introverts, hiders, and agoraphobes. And a lot of petty crooks, farmers, dealers, and distributors. But those are traceable too. The problem gets harder when you're dealing with pros. A good burner is usually connected to at least a few dozen other good burners to create the illusion of a life.

Miranda had eliminated at least two thirds of the randoms, leaving only two dozen on the list of possibles. Not a bad winnowing, but still a time-consuming effort.

Put that aside for a moment, consider something else instead. Why had Cobie blocked himself in meatspace? What was he hiding from? And as good as his block-ware had been—and it was state-of-the-art—then how had he been tracked? The easy answer, the obvious one, was that he hadn't been tracked—he'd invited the killer in. And the killer had installed "Death by Oompah."

A thought occurred to me—

Yes, Miranda had uploaded Cobie's autopsy report.

Cobie had been hard-wired into the machine. He was getting direct stimulation to the brain's pleasure center. And just in case, his blood had high levels of pain blockers.

Cobie had died happy—very happy.

So...the murderer hadn't been vindictive. That suggested a whole other set of motives.

I leaned back in my chair—in meatspace. Mrs. Kilmartin did likewise in her pink gazebo.

There's this:

If you live in Endless City, everything is recorded. Everything. There is no privacy—anyone with a warrant can prowl.

If you retreat to meatspace, you can have the illusion of privacy. You can lock yourself in your apartment, live off the Basic, and have all your meals delivered.

But that's still not enough.

Every time you turn on the electricity, you leave a data-trail. Every appliance. Every light bulb. Every electrical socket. Everything. Everywhere.

If you go to the circuit box and flip all the breakers, that's still no defense. If you have anything in your pocket or your purse that runs off batteries, if it connects to anything else, if it taps into, if it reports, if it monitors—that's a data-trail too.

If you go lo-tech, disconnecting from the grid, generating your own life-support, you can still be observed—from the sky, from across the street, and even through the walls of the apartment next door. Lasers can read the vibrations on your window glass, thermal detectors can tell how many people are in the room, and microwaves can monitor your movements.

There is no privacy. There is no anonymity.

Put on a burka and walk down the street, you still leave a data-trail. Even if you wear a mask or a hood, cameras will still record your height, your gait, your body-movements, assembling a personality-pattern that will be matched with the paths you take, the purchases you make, the signs that catch your attention, everything.

Someone smart enough to be completely invisible would also have been smart enough to plan a perfect murder. He hadn't.

What's a perfect murder? One that doesn't get discovered, one that no one ever knows about—no one except the murderer.

So... Cobie's killer wanted the murder to be known. Why?

It didn't make sense.

Maybe the murderer wasn't invisible.

There was no evidence that Cobie had invited anyone into his penthouse apartment. There was no trace. No physical evidence. No data-trail. Nothing.

And there was no evidence of anyone leaving afterward, not even a blot.

Which brought me back to the first question...how did "Death by Oompah" get into Cobie's sextable?

Malware? Not with Cobie's level of hardware. He would have had multiple state-of-the-art firewalls. So he would have had to install it himself....

Did he think it was "Frat Boy Shenanigans"—or did he know it wasn't?

Because—the son of a bitch had been wired in like a screwhead and narked like a man strapped to an execution table. It was painless because he wanted it to be painless.

Son of a bitch.

But why then, follow that train of thought, it doesn't make sense...would he want me to investigate a murder that didn't happen? And why would he blow up my office?

Unless...

That was a little far-fetched, but—

All right, back to Miranda's reports. There was something I'd missed.

But now I knew what I was looking for. I had to backtrace the movements of Cobie's blot, only a few days were needed—he'd taken a trip, not too far, but far enough. He'd gone to a place where his blot overlapped with another blot. Then the other blot disappeared. They'd merged. Then his blot went home.

So...backtrace that other blot—and it goes all the way back to the Jumble.

Crap.

And crap again.

Mrs. Zoe Elaina Kilmartin said some very bad words and winked out of her beautiful pink gazebo.

I'd need to switch to a burner identity. Hell, I'd probably have to burn through half a dozen.

This was going to take some thought, and some careful preparation.

◇◇◇◇◇◇◇◇◇◇◇◇◇◇◇◇◇

The Jumble is all proxies and untraceables. The whole area is blotted—it's splattered with multiple overlapping blots. And they stack.

There are few visible cues. Endless City is woven in and out of its structure so deep, it's impossible to navigate without plugins.

Nothing is what it seems. Nobody is who they pretend to be. If Endless City is one relentless performance, the Jumble is its physical counterpart. It's Kowloon's Walled City reborn—with a vengeance. The Jumble exists where three, or maybe more, jurisdictions fail to overlap—each one retreating from the responsibility of governance. The result is a hole in the fabric of responsibility, a gigantic ungoverned enclave, sprawling like a cancerous amoeba across several square kilometers of broken terrain. Ancient buildings lean against each other for support, bridges to nowhere span the gaps and canyons, cables and tubes, balconies turned into shops, staircases transformed into vertical habitats, banners and canopies everywhere, tangles of wires leading every which way, vertical farms of all kinds, blankets for walls, ladders, rickety staircases, an ancient aqueduct, twisting alleys wind through various pretenders to street level, and beneath everything abandoned tubeways where trains no longer run, crumbling sewers, the whole a tottering slum, clinging to unfinished concrete towers, a gaping triangular spire, heli-decks, windmills, and open catch-barrels for the monsoon rains—a wild collection of humanity, clustered in its walls, morphs and newts, cross-players, gendernauts, inflatos, slendermen, barbies, twinkles, bearables, mandroids, femminoids, remods, rejuves, sportsters, shifters, grifters, xenoids, saleables, whatevers—there's no directory. If you have to ask, you don't want it badly enough.

The Jumble is a self-contained paradox, simultaneously the most connected and the most disconnected place in the urban sprawl. It exists, it continues to exist because no authority wants responsibility of the physical realm, no agency dares to attempt cyber-control—not any more. No one wants the economic burden, the legal burden—no one wants to inherit the morass of the Jumble's bizarre societies and ungovernable residents. In short, no one knows what to do with it, so the Jumble exists, a great machine of self-evolving survival.

Within its walls, the Jumble is anything and nothing, sanctuary, brothel, casino, hideaway, drug den, fantasyland, shops of all kinds—tattoo artists, mutation parlors, transformatories, fetish-holes, meal-vendors, cafes, tailors, bootmakers, indigo marketplaces, purple holes, exo-printers, fabbers, xeno-labs, crack-doors—everything. The Jumble has its own unwritten rules, you're safe as long as you follow them. Don't take what isn't yours. Don't ask what you don't need to know. Don't go where you have no business. Whatever you want or need, it's here—buy or trade, cash only, no credit. No wires, no traces, thank you. Next, please?

Old identities disappear into the Jumble. New ones come out. And Cobie Ferguson had done a lot of business here. The money wasn't traceable, but Miranda's data-diving had revealed large sums converted into cash over a three year period. Gambling losses, he said, but there weren't many trips to the Endless City casinos—none that could be tracked. No, he told his taxman that he gambled in the Jumble. There were certain games within its walls not available anywhere else. The taxman didn't ask for details—and if he had, Cobie wouldn't have answered. Because he wasn't gambling. You didn't stay as rich as Cobie Ferguson if you had that kind of gambling habit. No, he was investing in something else—not illegal if you intend to use it legally, but definitely illegal if you don't.

There were only three practitioners of this art in the Jumble—well, only three that I knew of—but only one of them had a reputation for clean hands. I'd start with

Her. Him. Whatever. Depending on the moment. Because there was no Him, Her, or Whatever—there was only the convenient avatar, created for the day and worn by whichever member of the crew was on desk duty.

Max Blankman got off the tube at 13:13 o'clock. Not deliberate, just ironic. The Max Blankman ID was a public domain, open-source identity. Anyone could wear it. It wasn't suspicious, unless it was. Usually it was as innocuous as a Charles Manson T-shirt on a recently liberated teener. (Hint: The revolution is not a fashion statement.) If you were serious about hiding out, you didn't go as Blankman, not Max, not Minnie, not any of their offspring.

He. She. Whatever did not have a name. Like Miranda, access was exclusive. I had it, because I had money to spend. Enough. Most people don't have that advantage. Most people never have enough. And it collapses their thinking from "I don't have enough" into "I am not enough." It's that kind of mindset that keeps me in business, provides me with customers. I should be grateful, but I'm not. I spend too much time with the wrong kind of people.

Goggled, half in meatspace, half in Endless City, I made my way quickly through the Jumble. Worst thing you can do is hesitate. All the signs, all the rules and warnings, all the directions, all the arrow-trails were available only in the Endless City overlay—you saw only the overlays you were allowed to see. I saw a much more intricate and complex map than most people. This iteration of Max Blankman was probably getting a lot of attention because of that. Somewhere—a lot of somewheres—a lot of someones were poking someone else and saying, "Hey, look at this, we've got a Max who can see us." There must have been a hundred sets of eyes on me, my only protection. Nobody was going to assault me with that many witnesses.

I followed a blinking red arrow up an escalator, one of the few that worked, the rest were just stairs, halfway up, then right along "the becauseway"—called that not because it was a causeway, but because it was a "becauseway." Because. You either got it, or you didn't. Maybe you had to be there.

Stopped at a noodle shop, put a copper coin on the counter and ducked behind the curtain, still following the blinking arrow, through six interleaved apartments, then out onto a balcony overlooking a steep atrium—I'd never seen this before, didn't even know it was here. But the red arrow never led me the same way twice.

Once, the balconies had been separate domains. Now the railings were gone, makeshift platforms linked them all, one to the next, and it was an elevated walkway. All the way around to the other side, then right turn through a meet-rack where naked avatars lounged along a railing. The double-vision of meatspace revealed the unappetizing truth—another reason why sexbots and sextables had become so popular. If you could afford them. If not, avatar-whores were cheap.

Up, down, around, in, out—the arrow finally led me to a simple dark room. Yellow silk drapes, artfully decorated with dancing and reclining and copulating naked people, all combinations, all positions. Red paper lanterns. I could have been in the foyer of an expensive Happy House, where unique designer fantasies were created for wealthy aesthetes with specific erotic tastes. Well, yes. I was.

There were two backless chairs in the room. Padded cylinders, one on each side of a low table. A Eurasian boy came in carrying a ceramic tea service on a wooden tray. He couldn't have been more than thirteen. He was beautiful, dressed in a soft red kilt and a flowing white shirt. His avatar flawlessly matched his physical presence. He sat down opposite me and placed the tray exactly between us with mathematical precision. Then he carefully, meticulously poured tea into two small red cups. Steam rose like a warning.

He folded his hands into his lap and waited patiently. I took the closest cup. I cradled it in my palms so as to minimize the heat coming off it. I inhaled the fragrance of the steeping leaves. I returned the cup to the table without drinking. I only look stupid.

"I have questions," I said.

The boy was impassive. He waited.

"I want to know if something is possible."

I knew I wasn't speaking to the boy. I was speaking to his puppeteer. He was a Cyranoid—taking his instructions from someone offsite. His features were perfect, his skin was pink and golden and shining—as clear as porcelain. His hair was pure blue-black and shining. His eyes were stunning blue. His physical presence was already an answer to my question.

When the boy spoke, his voice was lyrical. He said quietly, "You're here. Therefore you have permission. Ask."

"How much would it cost to grow a body? A life-size clone. How long would it take?"

A pause. "You did not ask if such a thing is possible."

"I already know it's possible. I want to know how much and how long."

The boy hesitated, listening to his master again. "We can grow fully functioning new legs onto your stumps in six months."

"That's not the question I asked. How much for a whole body? Head and brain included."

"You do not have a life-threatening disease. All of your organs are functioning well. You will have no need of an organ replacement for at least a decade or longer."

"How much? How long?"

"For what purpose do you need a clone of yourself?"

Now it was my turn to pause while I considered my reply. How much should I say?

"Even a small meat-tank is big enough for a full-size male body," I began. "Scanning and sampling is less than an hour. You can print the collagen matrix in three days. Two weeks to grow and seed the stem cells. I'm guessing two months for the bones, four to six months for organ maturity and function, the last three will be spent exercising and toning the various muscle groups. Six months, right?"

The boy didn't answer.

"As for costs? Okay, there's the cost of nutrients, that's minimal. Tank rental, again minimal. Security—that's not minimal. Skillage required to manage the various processes, I'm guessing six to ten specialists, maybe another twelve assistants for scut-work. Plus all the different bits and pieces of equipment, the bots, the maintenance, the electricity, plus overhead—" I quoted a number.

The boy did not reply. His failure to react was just as informative as if he had spoken.

Finally. "What you ask is possible." Another pause. "However..."

"Yes?"

"Your cost estimate is too low. We would have to establish a specific facility. You would have to assume that overhead." He quoted a number.

"I see. Your current operations are at capacity?"

The boy didn't answer.

It didn't matter. That he had actually quoted a price told me what I needed to know. He. She. Whatever. Didn't offer a service unless they could deliver it. That meant they'd already done it. At least once and probably more than once. And probably enough times that their tanks were full and they had a waiting list. And as soon as they found a customer desperate enough to pay for the cost of a new facility, they'd move him to the head of the line.

I nodded. "I will get back to you on this. I'm only the agent of inquiry."

I left the tea untouched on the table, a terrible insult, but one I had to risk. The other risk was greater. If they—the mysterious "they"—were capable of tracking Miranda's feed to me and blowing up my office, might they also be just as capable of tracking me here?

In any other case, the unfinished tea would have been a signal that our business was not yet complete, but here in the Jumble it implied a darker message. I do not trust you.

Max Blankman disappeared on the southward train. I shadowed with a traveling blot for several blocks, changing clothes and posture and the gait of my legs, as I went. Reversed my jacket, pulled up the hood, popped on disposable goggles, deflated the fat suit by ten kilos, and a few other tricks I don't like sharing.

So...now I knew. Ninety percent certain anyway. Cobie hadn't died. He'd faked his own death.

He'd grown a clone, perhaps even swapped most of his organs for fresh ones, then murdered the donor in his place. It would have been a perfect crime, but at the last moment, Cobie must have developed some kind of emotional bond. He couldn't bear to cause his donor-toddler any pain. So he'd killed it painlessly.

That was his mistake. A real murderer would have wanted the victim to suffer.

Okay, next question. Why had Cobie gone to so much trouble? Why did he need to go invisible?

Only one way to answer that question.

Ask Cobie.

Right. Find the invisible man. Eezy-peezy. He's only got a three-day lead.

If I go back to Miranda—she'll know I'm still alive. She probably already knows, but maybe not. If Miranda planted the bomb, then contacting her lets her know she failed—but how could she have planted the bomb so quickly? So, probably it wasn't Miranda. It would have had to have been Cobie.

Okay, ninety percent sure it was Cobie who blew up my office—the space I pretended was my office. But why? Why kill the guy you've just hired to investigate the fake murder you've staged?

Ah—that one's almost obvious. You kill him to keep him from discovering the murder was staged. And it clouds the investigation with another false track.

God, I'm good.

Or stupid.

But Cobie had distracted me. The way he'd crossed his perfect legs so perfectly—and I'd bought into it. I'd had so many clients who were painfully shallow, I'd begun to believe they all were. Cobie might have set me up, but he had my help.

Time to call Miranda.

It took me a while to get through, she bounced me through a dozen numbers and three calling locations, the most I'd ever experienced, but finally—

Morticia Gomez. The Anjelica Huston iteration. "You've been compromised," she said.

"Yeah, I noticed."

She said, "Your office line was tapped. About two weeks ago. A very sophisticated piece of work. The tap didn't go active until after Cobie died—"

I thought about telling her it wasn't Cobie, decided to wait until she finished. The bomb had been planted the same time as the tap. The tap itself was a physical device attached to the line outside the building. Once the bomb went off, the tap self-destructed. It would have looked like part of the bomb damage. Except it left software traces of itself in the system. "A very sophisticated piece of work," Miranda said. "But shallow. The cleanup wasn't deep enough. The author didn't realize that I was monitoring your feeds."

"For how long?"

"Long enough to notice there were hiccups in your reception."

"So you knew about the bomb?"

"I knew about the tap. The bomb was a surprise."

"The tap triggered it."

"I made a mistake. I assumed the trigger was simply an alert. I was wrong."

"I could have been killed."

"Yes. That would have ruined my whole day. I hate losing customers."

"Thank you for your concern."

"So—are we looking for the bomber now?"

"No. Yes. We're looking for Cobie Ferguson." I told her about the clone farms in the Jumble.

"I'm aware of the practice. Most of the clones have been organ donors, several have been sexual partners. Two have been used for vicarious revenge. This would have been the first murder—or staged murder. But you have no direct evidence."

"No. What I have is a hunch."

"Yes?"

"Cobie was—is—rich. Rich people don't abandon their wealth. They take it with them. They're stupid that way. Follow the money."

"That's not a hunch," Miranda said. "That's logic."

"Anyway, that's my question. Where is Cobie's money?"

"The report is on its way." She added, "To your current account."

"I have to ask. Are there any taps?"

"None that I am aware of. Nevertheless, you should stay alert."

"Thank you."

It turned out that Cobie didn't have wealth. He had *access* to wealth. Those are two very different things.

I have access to wealth. I know. I have multiple client accounts I draw on. As long as I can present an auditable invoice for billable hours, as long as my maintenance expenses remain reasonable, as long as I spread the expenses across multiple accounts, I have access to wealth.

In return for my services, which are considerable.

As Cobie Ferguson was about to find out.

I parked myself in realtime in the middle of a crowded plaza, and plugged into Miranda's findings. Cobie had been a beneficiary of three trusts and two foundations. He drew from two of those resources. Now all I had to do was find out who else was drawing and how much—and where they were now.

If Cobie was smart, he would have plugged in his alternate identity some time ago and created a financial backstory. But again—the giveaway was how far the ripples had spread.

The details are irrelevant. It was mostly a process of elimination.

I found Cobie in the next penthouse up. That was why we had no record of him—blotted or otherwise—leaving his building. He hadn't. He'd burned his past and walked up one flight of stairs.

I knocked on the door.

After a moment, he opened it. He was wearing a silk dress, a kimono. No makeup. Just a crossplayer at home. He looked nothing like his avatar, just an ageless young-old man. He looked down the hall past me, both ways, then stepped aside to let me in. "That was fast."

"You were stupid." I walked into the apartment. It wasn't bare, but it wasn't lived in yet either. I turned around to face him. "The surgery went okay?"

He shrugged. He looked tired. "I'm still adjusting." Then, "Where did I screw up?"

"At the beginning."

"Is it a long story?"

"No."

He looked disappointed. "You want something to drink?"

"I'm fine," I said.

He went to the bar anyway, picked up the soda gun, and filled a tall glass with super-carbonated water. He hesitated before putting the soda gun down.

I said, "Your blocker isn't as good as you think it is. Miranda is recording everything. So if you're still thinking about shooting me with whatever is concealed in that soda gun, I wouldn't recommend it."

He sighed, shrugged, picked up his glass, and walked over to one of two black leather chairs. He sat down in one, gestured at the other.

"No thanks, I'll stand." I took an envelope out of my pocket. "Here's an invoice for my services. And an additional contract. You're buying my silence. It's not exorbitant. You can afford it. It's certainly cheaper than any of your other options." I tossed it at him, he let it fall to the black coffee table between the chairs.

"Really?" He looked skeptical.

"Really," I assured him. "It's certainly cheaper than killing me."

He sipped at his water. He leaned forward and put the glass on the table. He picked up the envelope. He opened it and studied the two papers, first one, then the other. He nodded. "You're fair. I'll give you that. I'll set up an automatic payment."

"Thank you." But I didn't head for the door.

"Is there something else?"

"Maybe. It's up to you."

"How much?"

"That's the right question to ask." I crossed to the bar, hefted the soda gun, studied the buttons for a moment, then filled a glass of my own. I carried it to the chair opposite him, sat down and drank.

"Let's say that I have a pretty good idea who's after you. What's it worth to you to stop them?"

He studied me for a long moment. "You are good."

"I did the job you hired me to do. You said after I found the murderer, I'd know what to do. You were right. I do know what to do. Do you want me to do it?"

"Tell me more."

"The expansion is going to be approved. It's going to be a very large expansion. Good for some. Bad for others. The horizontal and vertical equators are going to cut through some valuable territory. The value of land bordering the new equators is going to go up. But the value of certain other parcels divided by the equators will collapse. Even if all the petitions for adjustments are approved, it's still going to be ugly. Some people are going to make a lot of money. Others are going to lose a lot."

"Every screwhead on the street knows that. They're all scrambling for advantage. Tell me something I don't know."

"You have pro-rata shares in more than a thousand cyber-properties, spread across a hundred different holding companies—your share is funneled through five financial instruments, of which you've only been tapping two. You've been keeping a very low profile for a long time—probably because if you die, some other people's shares will increase. In most cases, only a point or two. But in a couple of other cases, as much as 20% will be divided among the survivors. Enough to make your death a lucrative proposition. Your staged death does not alleviate the danger, because you've assigned your shares to a new holding identity, funneling the dividends through another set of instruments until they finally arrive here. All you've done is prolong the search and delay the inevitable. Those who want you dead are going to follow the money, just like I did. And...my guess is that they have access to even more sophisticated resources than I do."

"Then why haven't they found me yet?"

"Because—" I counted off the reasons for him, "First, they're trying to figure out which of them killed you. It'll take them two or maybe three days to convince themselves that none of them got their hands dirty. Two, they're not going to believe it was suicide either, because—three, as soon as they discover your shares are not being divided among themselves, but were presold to a holding identity, that will lead them directly to four—that you are still alive and hiding out, at which point, five, they will start searching in earnest. This is clever—plugging into your own security, you've been able to watch every stage of the investigation. But—as clever as you are, six—guys like me do this for a living. We know all the tricks, usually because we invented most of them ourselves."

"How long do I have?"

"I got in, didn't I? If they're not already landing on the roof, they will be some-time in the next three days. They're not stupid."

"But you're smarter?"

"No, I'm not. I'm just faster. I don't have to take as many meetings to explain what I'm doing. Whoever is searching for you probably has to report to a commit-tee. The committee has to argue for a while before approving the next step. That's why you're still alive. Shall we go?"

"Huh?"

"You're not safe here. If I could find you, a three year old could. It would just take a little longer. Now, seven—let's go. I assume you have your next hideout prepared? We'll start there, just long enough to muddy the trail, then I'll take you through the labyrinth. That'll buy us time for what comes next—the messy part."

There were two golems in the hall. I burned them from behind, I'm not proud, I'm a survivor. Cobie gave me a look—he didn't have to say it. Where the hell did that come from? Your scan came up clean. "Trade secret," I explained.

And we were off.

This was going to be a bigger job than I expected. I was already counting shekels in my head. I should be able to make enough to retire.

Except guys like me, we don't retire. We just keep going until the some other guy catches up—because that's how it works in Endless City.

THE ONES WHO WALK AWAY FROM THE ONES WHO WALK AWAY

When we reached the last oasis, we stopped to give the animals a well-deserved rest. We made a meager meal of hard-bread, dried meat, and beer, before retiring to our separate tents to escape the heat of the day.

Ogilvey and I had been late to join the caravan, Captain Bledsoe and the others had already made their own accommodations, so despite our mutual differences Ogilvey and I had no choice but to share a tent. Grudgingly, we made the best of it. I knew that Ogilvey was more resistant to the idea than I was, but as was his usual manner he kept his darker thoughts unspoken.

The senior guide was a leathery man named Ahmed or Ammad, I was never quite sure, because of his thick pronunciation, had repeatedly cautioned us that despite the fabled city's reputation of magnificence, its glory existed more in story than in fact. We should not expect much.

Ogilvey had listened politely and without comment, but later, after we had traveled a bit, he became more talkative, finally sharing his own thoughts with the members of the expedition. "This journey has been difficult, no question, but it is long overdue. My colleague and myself are grateful to you, Captain Bledsoe, for including us. Whatever the truth of the fabled city, magnificent or disappointing, I am certain that the effort will be worthwhile, the knowledge gained will be a significant addition to our understanding of this region.

"Whatever the case, we should be cautious in our investigations. We will be on strange ground, in unknown territory. It is likely that Ammad speaks the truth. Perhaps the fabled city is simply a much embellished story. We cannot know until we see it ourselves. If that is the case, then this expedition is not for our benefit as much as it is for the goods we bring to an impoverished village.

151

"But that does not explain the almost violent resistance of the local tribes to this caravan. We had to make our purchases through shadowy agents. We had to sneak away under cover of night. Why is that? There is a mystery here and perhaps we shall uncover it."

Captain Bledsoe and the other members of the party nodded in quiet agreement, albeit with some hesitation. The five of them had organized this journey together, it had taken them many months and whatever enthusiasm they had initially brought to the effort had long since faded into exhaustion.

Ogilvey and I had learned of their efforts only by accident. When one of the Captain's colleagues learned we were passing through the area, he met us at the train station to ask for our assistance. He hoped that Ogilvey's experience with the local languages and my own researches into the history of the region might be of some value.

Bledsoe had not been not pleased that his colleague had come to us. He did not greet us warmly. It was common knowledge that Ogilvey had tried to arrange a similar expedition several years before, and had experienced the same stubborn resistance that Bledsoe was now dealing with. The locals seemed to hold a low regard for foreigners, especially explorers.

Ogilvey was generous enough to acknowledge Captain Bledsoe's efforts, but he also suggested there would be no shame if he could not arrange a caravan. Perhaps the obstinance of the locals was nothing more than a refusal to engage in a futile and possibly fatal undertaking. They did not part on good terms.

But when Captain Bledsoe was finally ready to give up the quest, when he begin making plans to return home, he was discreetly approached by a group of quiet men. They wore robes of brown, orange, and white, a manner of dress unknown in this or any other region. Their leader was a dark man named Ammad. He said, "We will take you where you want to go, but you will not be happy with what you find. Here is what you must bring." They provided a list of goods, nothing extravagant; oddly, the majority were items of the most mundane use.

When Ogilvey heard of Bledsoe's renewed efforts, he went to the Captain and demanded an audience. He was extremely agitated, annoyed that Bledsoe had made contact where his own efforts had produced no result. I do not know what was said, I was not present for that meeting, but Ogilvey informed later that the discussion was prolonged and intense. Only after Ogilvey had stressed the necessity for academic verification of any find, did Bledsoe finally relent. Reluctantly, he allowed Ogilvey to join the expedition—and myself as well.

I was surprised at the invitation, especially when I found out it was Ogilvey who had arranged it, but I did not inquire too deeply into his reasons. Despite our overlapping areas of study and specific explorations that sometimes required that we cooperate, Ogilvey and I had never been on the best of terms, dealing with each other only when we had to, and only with deliberate courtesy. Perhaps Ogilvey believed that our common academic background had created some kind of partnership and that I would act as a necessary ally if any disagreement with Captain Bledsoe were to develop.

The discord between Ogilvey and myself was not a recent affair. It had begun at Oxford. Ogilvey had come from diminished circumstances and that had affected his perceptions of class differences. He resented that I had enjoyed the privileges of what he believed to be an excessive family fortune as well as the occasional patronage of the dons. As a result, he felt that my work had not required the same effort as his. Though we had both endured same the rigorous challenges of university life, it was his belief that I had benefited from unfair advantage. He had never made any secret of his feelings.

Considering all that, the invitation to me must have been a reluctant one, not just by Ogilvey, but Captain Bledsoe as well. The Captain would not be comfortable knowing that Ogilvey's reputation would significantly overshadow his own, and of course, because of my family name, my presence as well. Nevertheless, the partnership could prove mutually advantageous; so despite Captain Bledsoe's ill-concealed displeasure, the significance of the opportunity was undeniable. Once more, Ogilvey and I put aside our own differences and made arrangements to join the expedition.

There was also this. While Ogilvey's intention was academic in nature, possibly a defining achievement in his field, Captain Bledsoe made no secret that he was much more interested in the fabled city's legendary wealth. Perhaps that was why Ammad and the other guides had been so insistent that we would be disappointed. Forewarned that the fabled city would be much less than its promise, Captain Bledsoe and his team would not be able to claim that they had been deceived.

We would know the truth of the fabled city soon enough.

Days of rugged travel brought us to the last oasis. Ahead, lay mountainous waves of treacherous dunes, one after another, stretching without remorse or respite into terrain so desolate it had never been charted; but somewhere beyond, according to our guides, the desert finally gave way to a more hospitable realm. First, we would see the dark edges of distant peaks on the horizon. Eventually we would reach sparse grasslands and even occasional streams, mostly trickles, the furthest reach of the mountains' gift to the land, the glacier's summer tears.

But before that, the sands would be perilous and we would have to proceed with extreme caution. The heat of the day would be ferocious and unrelenting. We would wait in the shade of our tents until the sun drifted into the western haze. Then we would mount our beasts and travel across the moonlit slopes as far as we could, until Luna's silent orb finally disappeared behind us.

Before we could begin that most dangerous part of the journey, Ammad confronted Bledsoe and the others. "Here, this last oasis—this is the edge of the world. What lies beyond, there are no maps. From this place on, you will have to trust us. If you have any doubts at all, we will turn back."

Bledsoe's reply was immediate. "Whatever doubts any of us might have, we have come too far to turn back. Let us proceed."

Ammad nodded. "Then here we rest. At twilight, we go."

It took us three long nights to cross the dunes. The journey was not easy. The air was dry and cold. The sands whispered beneath the pads of the camels. And when the wind rose, we had to wrap our heads against the sand. But when the moon was high and bright, when its cool light illuminated the slopes in shades of enigmatic blue and indigo, it was eerily beautiful. Deadly the dunes were, but also magnificent.

In the first morning after, the distant mountains stood like a wall on the horizon. From here the fabled city would be a half day's journey. We rested by a tiny trickle of a stream, a welcome respite from the dry sands behind us. We refilled our water skins before heading on.

At last, we saw the first pink hints of habitation, a cluster of rose and gold towers. They glistened in the afternoon sunlight. Lush greenery hugged them all. Closer still, we saw alabaster domes beneath the minarets, shining pearls in a jeweled garden. A blue river sparkled with dancing light.

But as we grew closer, the undeniable signs of ruin and decay became evident, shattered walls and fallen roofs, debris scattered in the avenues, vacant windows and cracked surfaces. Everywhere, weeds broke through the stones of the streets, tenacious vines climbed forsaken walls.

The fabled city was long abandoned, deserted to the seasons, a fallen monument to its past, an empty shell of itself. Rasped by the relentless wind, baked by the unforgiving sun, chilled by uncaring nights and scoured by the blistering days—

Our guides would not let us approach. They said the bridges weren't safe. They said the city was evil. They said ghosts roamed the ruins. They said that those who disturbed the sleep of the city would be cursed forever.

To have come this far, to behold such magnificent desolation and not be allowed to examine these wonders closer—we felt frustrated and more, we experienced a profound despair, but our guides were firm in their insistence. They argued so aggressively that we must keep our distance that even Ogilvey fell silent, reluctant to argue.

It was clear that had we defied them, had we crossed the river, had we walked those avenues, they would have abandoned us immediately. We would have no safe passage back. We would end up as all the others who tried to cross the angry desert alone, missing, unmourned, and forgotten, our sufferings unknown.

They had told us at the beginning that we would be disappointed. They spoke true. Not being able to enter, we were bitterly disappointed.

We made our studies of the fabled city from the closest hillside allowable. We attempted a few sketches, but nothing that could do justice to the scene, and in the end, our guides implored us to destroy our efforts. They feared that these rough drawings, crude as they were, if they were circulated at all, would only lure others to this site—others who would ignore the warnings, who would disturb the silence of the city and awaken whatever evils might still sleep there.

Reluctantly, we put our drawings in the fire and settled in for the night. Across the river, the city rested. When the moon rose, the ruins took on an unholy glow, as if spectral beings had risen from their daytime rest and now wandered through the empty streets, searching for their brighter past. Ogilvey had little to say. From time to time he would scribble something frantically into his notebook, but whatever he was thinking he wasn't ready to share.

I did not sleep well. Strange visions disturbed my dreams. In the morning, the more candid members of the party admitted their nights had not been restful either. For two of them, sleep had been a churning stew of disquiet, but the others kept an uncomfortable silence, refusing to discuss what rough beasts had troubled their slumber.

It was no small matter to settle ourselves. Our distress was palpable. A return to rational action was not easy to come by, but as responsible representatives of our world we could not allow ourselves to give in to our emotions and certainly not in front of our guides, who had already begun to mock the weakness they presumed in us.

We turned our minds again to the fabled city before us, speculating on the reasons for its abandonment. It could not have been a lack of water. The river provided as clean a source as one could wish for. Nor would it have been drought or famine. The fields surrounding the city were lush and fertile. And it could not have been ravaged by war. No army would have crossed this desert for such a small and distant prize, and none of the buildings that we could see showed any injuries of a siege.

So why had the city's citizens abandoned it?

It was a mystery, a question that couldn't be answered without a closer examination of the ruins and that had been specifically denied us. Our guides were reticent to speak of the city. We suspected they knew more than they would admit, but when we tried to question them, they simply shook their heads in response, only acknowledging that the fabled city had been abandoned for as long as anyone knew.

When at last we had concluded all of our separate tasks, when there was nothing more to be seen or spoken, when we were finally and reluctantly ready to depart, we set out for a nearby village, apparently the village of our guides, where we would spend a quiet evening, resting and refreshing ourselves before continuing on our journey. We had to travel several leagues upstream, far enough up into the foothills that the empty city was no longer visible.

But here we came upon a small community, a scattering of simple houses, circular in shape, with conical roofs, steep and black. The walls were baked clay bricks painted with layers of hardened red clay and decorated with intricate designs of brown, orange, and white. The homes lacked windows and instead of wooden doors, there were dark-colored curtains. Every hut had a tall pole in front of its door where a long banner flapped in the breeze. The colors were simple, possibly limited by the availability of local plants from which to produce dye.

A much larger structure, similar in design, sat in the center of the village. In front of it, a wide open space attended a rugged fountain, obviously fed by the mountain streams. The village lacked the elegance of the fabled city, but it certainly seemed rugged enough to withstand the rigors of the harshest seasons.

The residents themselves looked healthy and comfortable, and not given to excessive ornamentation or decoration. Their garments were as plain as their homes, mostly red and brown robes, but several wore strings of colored beads, shells, and feathers. The Chieftain greeted our guides with familiar affection, but regarded the rest of us with cautious civility. It was an understandable reaction, we were strangers, unknown to them, and they had no way of knowing what discourtesies we might represent.

But they did not treat us badly. We had come prepared for just such an encounter, and we presented the villagers with tokens of our appreciation. Curiously, they were unimpressed with the hand mirrors that the other travelers presented and they seemed honestly repelled by the bright-colored beads that they offered, but the iron needles and silk threads that Ogilvey produced were accepted with great enthusiasm. The villagers were not much impressed by Ogilvey's compass, they were far more interested in the magnifying glass that covered it; apparently they'd seen such a lens before and knew that it could focus the sun's rays to start a fire. The villagers accepted our gifts with quiet polite nods. But the thing that they greeted with the most excitement was a bag containing several pounds of salt. This far inland, salt was a rare commodity. The Chieftain shouted and held it aloft.

They spoke a dialect that we could understand, not easily because it was not a common derivation, but one of several that Ogilvey had examined and written about in several of his papers. It was a derivation of a much older tongue, so even though communication was halting at first, within a short time, after we had determined the specific shifts in pronunciation, we were able to understand each other fairly well.

When they were finally satisfied that our intentions were friendly, the villagers led us to the large hall at the center of their town. As we had surmised, it served as a primary gathering place. It was cool and well appointed inside, though not luxurious. Simple oil lamps hung from the ceiling, others were mounted on tall wooden stands, all suffusing the chamber with a deep orange luminance.

The walls were not ornately decorated. It was as if these people had deliberately chosen to avoid extravagant adornments of all kinds, preferring instead a simpler existence. They were not without art, but Ogilvey noted that it was a more contained and muted expression than he would have ordinarily expected. It was another curious aspect.

The townspeople made us comfortable and several young men and women brought us mint tea to refresh our thirst and our souls. Of course, we had many questions, but our guides cautioned us to be patient. By the respect that we had shown, by the practicality of our gifts, and by the fact that several of us could actually speak their language, we had made an excellent impression. Therefore, we had earned a rare privilege. The village chieftain had called for a gathering. There would be a recitation for us tonight. Be patient, our guides assured us, it will be worth it. But they would not say more.

The evening meal was a simple but hearty stew of mutton, potatoes, and onions, served in wooden bowls. and accompanied by huge mugs of honey-sweet wine. For all of their apparent austerity, these villagers lived and ate well. At least twenty of them joined us for the evening feast, men and women ranging in age from youngster to ancient crone. There was no common factor.

Our guides explained that these were the elders of the village—the attendants of history. Each had taken the solemn duty of keeping the past alive. Each had performed the recitation of time lost, some in their youth, others when they were called. The performance was given at the celebration of the spring solstice, but sometimes for favored travelers like ourselves.

Ogilvey took out his notebook and started to write, but when several of the villagers frowned, I touched his arm and whispered, "I don't think that's a good idea. They think it's rude." He nodded and made a little show of closing the book, waving his hands over it three times as if blessing it before putting it away. He made it look like a personal ritual. The disapproving expressions faded and the service proceeded without further incident.

At last, when the broad planks of food were finally cleared away and the great skins of wine removed, seven musicians came into the hall, settled themselves along the front wall, lifted their instruments, and began to play, quietly at first, but as the chatter in the room drifted into silence, their music swelled. Two of the musicians had carved wooden cylinders that they hammered as drums, two blew wistful melodies on polished wooden flutes, two had lyres that they plucked so gently the notes sounded like sparkles, and the last brought a collection of bells and rattles to punctuate the whole. The music had an alien sound, dry and ancient and plaintive, but the melodies had a mysterious playful quality as well. All of us were drawn into the spell of it.

But soon the tune became slow and somber, it was such a natural progression we felt it first in the shift of our emotions. And even though the hall was lit only by the oil lamps, it seemed as if the front of the room had somehow become brighter. A boy stood there, barely a teen, half-naked, dressed only in rags and soot.

The music stopped and the room fell silent.

"I will tell you the tale of the child," he said.

"Long ago, but not so long that memory has yet faded into legend, the western desert was not a desert, but a violent sea. Here, a great city overlooked a beautiful blue bay. Nestled in the arc of eighteen snow-capped peaks, the city was blessed. It was not an easy journey, there were brutal storms, nevertheless ships baring the flags of many nations filled the harbor and trade was good.

"The city produced elegant fabrics and colorful dyes, flavorful spices and teas that could be found nowhere else in the known world. So the people lived well, wealth was easy here and all took pride in their fortune. They lived as kings, celebrating themselves in glorious festivals and joyous parades. They wore the finest silks and linens. They decked themselves with silver and gold and ornate jeweled headware, necklaces and pendants, sashes and bracelets and belts, everything crusted with sparkling gems, even their shoes.

"It was a place of splendid halls and spacious gardens. Graceful trees lined the avenues, music filled the parks. Beauty was celebrated everywhere. Their public buildings were decorated with bright mosaics portraying their greatest ideals. The streets were paved with yellow and red bricks. The city was fabled, its grandeur was legendary, many songs and stories celebrated its beauty and its wealth. But here, so distant, so remote, so difficult to reach by sea and even more difficult by land, the city stood alone."

The boy spread his arms wide, as if to hold the whole world. "So why would anyone leave such a paradise?" He hung his head in silence and after a moment, the musicians filled the air with long drawn-out notes that felt like a long sorrowful wail of despair.

Abruptly the music stopped and the young man raised his head again. When he finally spoke, his words burned. " "All of that magnificence—that city, that shining city on the hill—it was built on a dreadful lie." He lowered his voice now. "Yes, that part of the story has been told—that there was a child. Only one. But that too is a lie.

The boy held up the rags he wore. He held out his dirty hands for all of us to see. "I speak for the first child. And I speak for all the children who came after. I speak for all who dwelt in the squalor beneath the city."

He pointed toward the distant ruins, as if he could see them clearly through the walls of the building, as well as through the haze of time. "There were many of us. All the ones they didn't care about." He held out his arms to include everyone in the room, everyone in the village, and the ghosts of all those who were no longer here to listen. "But it was us. All of us."

For the listeners this had to be a familiar tale, but even though they would have heard these words countless times before, the reawakened misery still echoed in their hearts. They wailed and moaned in counterpoint to the young man's recitation.

"I am the children," he said. "Hear my pain. Feel me. I am naked and cold and hungry. I am afraid. Everything hurts. I have sores and scabs and bruises. We have scars where they whipped me. I am hidden far beneath their tall sparkling towers. I am locked away in deep dark chambers.

"As soon as I was old enough to work, they came in the night and took me away from my family. They put a hood over my head, so I wouldn't know where I was taken. They ignored my screams and my struggles. I was locked away in the dark, chained in filth."

He raised his arms in angry defiance. "Listen to me. Listen all of you. I was there. And I will never forget. I will share it with the children and the children of my children, unto the last generation—until the last day of the world. Let the shame of the great city be told forever.

"I burned in the summer and I froze in the winter. I knew illness and hunger and pain. Whatever they demanded, whatever work they didn't want to do themselves— if I didn't sweat for them, I didn't eat. If I didn't work hard enough, I was beaten. If I didn't work, I died. They didn't care.

"Where do you think their magnificent silks came from? The colorful dyes for their lavish robes? Their beautiful adornments, their glistening shoes? All the limitless fineries of wealth?" He held up his hands, and now what looked like blood dripped from his fingers. "I made them all. Myself and all the other selves that stand before you. We made them. We dyed their fabulous cloths. We stirred boiling vats in sweltering chambers until we fell exhausted from the heat. We washed their soiled undergarments, scrubbing and rinsing, scrubbing and rinsing, twelve and fourteen hours a day. We fell ill, coughing and choking from the foulness they carried. We died and they replaced us. Always the children.

"And there is more," he said. At this, the wails and moans of his listeners rose and became an anguished chorus. When the sounds subsided again, he said, "If the days were bad, the nights were worse—yes, this must be told as well—sometimes, I was taken up, taken and washed, taken to their beds where they used my body to satisfy their lascivious desires. Girls or boys, whatever they wanted they took—they left us nothing. Nothing. We had nothing.

"Not even names."

He finished his recitation amid the cries and sobs of his listeners—and stepped back into the shadows.

The musicians filled the silence with a mournful howl, a wail of sorrow, while the drummers pounded in rage.

"Is that it?" I whispered to our senior guide.

"Hush," he said. "It hasn't even begun."

Now, another stepped forward, a woman, tall and elegant, dressed in layers of fine cloth. She came forward proudly, unashamed.

"Yes, we knew," she said. "Everyone knew. It was never a secret. We brought our own children down the stairs, just so they could see that this was how the city flourished. This was where the wealth was made. It was a necessary thing, it was a good thing."

She opened her hands wide, a gesture of kindness and welcome. "Perhaps it seemed unfair that some children lived in luminous towers while others toiled below. But the children who worked, they would not have had worthwhile lives. We gave them purpose. It was a good thing we did. It was good, yes."

The musicians interrupted her with a discordant screech. She took a deep breath of annoyance. But before she could speak again, another person stepped forward, an old man, stooped and wearing only a simple brown robe. He took a deep breath. He lowered his eyes for a moment, perhaps remembering some specific moment, some point he needed to make. When he looked up again, his voice took on a dark tone.

"But sometimes—yes, sometimes; not often, but sometimes—some of us could see the pain. We saw the wrongness. We saw. The wretched conditions, the crying, the dying, the misery, it burned our souls to see it—"

Another screech from the musicians, and now the boy was back, bleeding now, and limping on a makeshift crutch. "Yes, you saw the wrongness, you felt the pain, and when we looked up, when we saw you, when we saw that you understood, for a moment, just that briefest moment, we had hope. But then what did you do—?"

And now, a chorus from the watchers filled the room. "What did you do? What did you do?"

The man whispered his answer. He said it slowly. "We couldn't stand to see it. We couldn't stand to know it. We did the only thing we could. We … walked … away …."

The musicians punctuated this admission with a yelp of despair, and as it died away into silence, the boy spoke directly to the man. "You … walked … away …. " And then he turned to the room, to the rest of us. He pointed at the man, a searing accusation. "They … walked … away…."

And the man … walked away, off the stage, and back into the darkness that surrounded all of us. It wasn't just shadows anymore.

The boy's voice rose in anger. "They walked away! They came, they saw, they knew—and then they left us anyway!"

From the darkness, the man's voice, almost plaintive. "We couldn't do anything, could we? But we couldn't stay, could we? We can't change what we can't change—"

"You didn't even try!" The boy shouted back. "We were dying. You knew we were dying. And you walked away!"

The whole room wailed with him, cries of rage and despair and anguish, a dreadful sound that filled me with fear. Even our guides seemed shrunken into their robes, and they must have seen and heard this recitation many times before.

The boy waited until they finished responding—to catch his breath or recapture his rage? Perhaps both. But when at last the anguish of the villagers subsided he continued, this time almost calmly. "Why did they just walk away? Why? Didn't the knowing go with them? Did they think they would be free of it, just by leaving?" He stepped forward and looked around the room, speaking to each and every one of us. "The pain in the heart does not vanish with either time or distance. A person carries it forever, wherever they go. But even if they knew that, they still walked away. To whatever lies beyond the mountains—they walked away."

The boy looked around again, this time with even more pain in his voice. "But the way that it is told—and there are people who repeat it as if it's true—they say that walking away was an honorable thing to do. They say that if a person cannot bear the knowing, they should leave and it's good that they leave."

The boy shifted his weight on his crutch and started to turn away, as if he had finished, but no—he hadn't. He turned back abruptly and spoke his next words with a bitter vengeance. "And we were left without even hope."

Now he pointed into the darkness where the man and the woman had retreated. "I stand here, alone, dirty, in rags, bleeding. I bear witness to the crime of my imprisonment. My jailers justified their crime and I can hate them for that. They were greedy and selfish and cruel." He took a deep breath. "But I bear the greatest rage and fury against those who walked away. There is no honor in that. It is no more honorable than staying. Staying continues everything, but walking away changes nothing!" He raised his fist and shouted, "It changes nothing!"

This angry boy now looked enflamed. He advanced to the center of the room, he turned around and around, looking at each of us, as if looking into our hearts and examining our souls. We could not escape the fury in his eyes. "Cowards!" he shouted. "Cowards! They walked away and left us alone and naked in our filth and our chains. They knew and did nothing. They ... walked ... away."

He took another deep breath and paused for a long moment. Long enough that we began to wonder if he was done, but he was not. He took a second breath and a third. "Alone, we died. Used and abused and despised, we died alone in the darkness."

He hung his head and stood that way for a long sorrowful moment.

The musicians remained silent.

But the boy had nothing more to say. Finally, he turned and limped back into the shadows.

After a long soundless moment, the village Chieftain stood up from his seat. He stepped quietly to the center of the room.

"So how did we get here? Listen. I will tell you how the story ends. Because it does end.

"One day, one amazing day, it came everything stopped. One day, as if by some untold magic, all of the children together, as if they spoke in a single voice, they said, 'No, I will work no more. I am done.' And they stopped. All of them together. They simply stopped. And when they stopped, the city stopped.

"The city had taken away their power. One day, they took it back.

"Oh, yes—the good people of the city tried to make the children work again. They whipped them. That didn't work. They stopped bringing food and water. And many died. That didn't work either. That was when the children knew their power. The city could not thrive without them. When they stopped, the city stopped.

"And it stayed stopped.

"And after a while, the city died. Not all at once, a little bit at a time, but it died. It died in pain. A different kind of pain. The pain of power and privilege denied. First, the fountains stopped. No water flowed. Soon the breezes turned into hot dry winds, stinging and scouring. The sea retreated, leaving a stinking swamp of decay. The boats with their bright sails could not reach the docks, they brought no fish, they brought no goods from faraway lands. And soon, the blazing sun baked the fields dry, the crops withered and died. The storehouses emptied. The city withered.

"Some people left. They walked away too. Not because they cared, no—they walked away because they had gotten so used to the ease and comfort of their cursed wealth, they couldn't live without it. They thought it was hardship, so they went off in search of some other place of cursed wealth.

"Others believed their troubles could be endured, that their good times would eventually return. So they stayed and waited, but the good times were over. They would never return. The city died and those who stayed died with it. They crept into their crumbling rooms and closed their doors behind them. They laid down in their beds, wrapped themselves in their soiled silks and blankets—and never rose again.

"And at last, there were the foolish men and women who believed themselves that reason should prevail. Everything would be made right again and the city could be restored to its fabled glory if only the children understood. They said it to each other so many times they began to believe it. If the children could see how badly the city had suffered, if they could see how necessary their labors were, they would go back to work, it would be their civic duty.

"These foolish men and women, with their strange convictions—they descended into darkness and unlocked the chains and opened the stairways. They led the children up into the light, saying, "You need to see the damage you have done to the city.

"But the children—those who survived—when they finally climbed out of the darkness, out of the filth and sewage and stink, when they finally found themselves in the bright morning, they raised their arms and covered their eyes. Sunlight was unknown to them. It blazed down on them like a brilliant scream. The glorious radiance dazzled them, paralyzed them. They cried in surprise. Tears came to their eyes.

"It was wondrous to them. They had never known such things were possible. But—" Here, he paused. "...It wasn't beautiful. They had ascended to an empty and abandoned world. There was just as much rot and despair in the streets as they had left below. They had climbed out of one prison into another and the only difference was the burning sky above."

The Chieftain smiled. "That was the day we walked away. All of us. We ... walked ... away.

"We walked away and never looked back. And when we left, we left the pain behind. We came here to live. We have no gold, no jewels, no silken robes. We have no gaudy avenues, no splendid parks. We have no towers and temples, no ornate decorations. And we never will.

"Here, the sun blesses us every day with light and warmth. The evening blesses us with cool breezes and bright stars. It is a good place because it is our place. And our work is good because it is our work. We belong only to ourselves. And that is enough."

The Chieftain stopped to let the music rise around him, gentle chords that suggested completeness and satisfaction and even a hint of triumph. But he wasn't done yet.

"Out there, beyond the lonely hills, the winds blow through empty streets. All the trees have died and the sands of the desert now cover the parks. Climbing vines are slowly and surely pulling down the stones of the towers. What remains is a warning. Wealth that stands on misery is no wealth at all—it is only the sickness of an empty soul."

And now, he approached us, Ogilvey and myself and the others. He looked directly at us where we sat.

"The tale of city has now been told. We have shared it many times to many people. You are not the first, nor will you be the last. Every listener has their own way of hearing it. Some hear it as a challenge, others as a warning. Some do not hear anything.

"But in the end, when the tale is told and done, when quiet returns to these halls, when the sun rises again, everyone walks away. Whatever story you might have heard or thought you heard, in the morning you will still walk away. And that is the real truth of the fabled city.

"Nothing is changed when you walk away."

He finished with a sigh. "I am done now." Straightening, he moved to join the other elders as they filed out silently. The musicians stood then and followed them out. And the villagers as well.

None of us slept well that night. In the morning, we packed up in silence. We headed out across the desert, none of us speaking of what we had seen and heard.

It was early evening when we arrived at the first waterhole. We made camp in silence. We had been well-provisioned by the villagers with baskets of fruit and dried meat, and while our meal wasn't sumptuous, it was more satisfying than the meager fare we had traveled with before.

After our supper, after we had each had our ration of wine, we began to discuss what we had seen and heard. Our travels had given us distance and a reprieve from the spell of the fabled city. The liquor released our reluctant thoughts.

Captain Bledsoe, of course, was in the darkest mood. His drunken mutterings soured the conversation, turning it from disappointment to smoldering anger. He had not been allowed to approach the city. He had nothing to show for his effort. He felt he had been cheated by the guides.

Ogilvey began to assuage him with calm rationality. "We were warned that we would be disappointed. We should not have begun this effort with expectations that could not be satisfied. Obviously, the history of these people is shrouded in strong emotion. I suspect that what we heard was not the whole story. Nor even an accurate one.

"The key part of the story is that there were significant changes in the environment. That's probably the real explanation for the abandonment of the city. The retreat of the ocean must have been caused by some distant shift in the land. Perhaps some great quake closed an isthmus to the sea. The waters would have slowly dried away, but we would need the opinion of a geologist for that."

"But I must point something out," he continued gravely. "Origin stories always exist as a cultural necessity. A community does not exist as a community until it invents an identity-story that affirms its existence. A creation story is almost always told as a moment of liberation, an escape from some intolerable oppression—and that's certainly the case here. Whatever the actual events of the original exodus from the prosperity of the city, probably famine, the ritual that we saw last night has to be seen as an affirmation of self-righteous poverty. A very evocative tale, indeed, but one that must be met with considerable skepticism, yes?"

He brushed nonexistent dirt off his hands, a dismissal, then turned to Captain Bledsoe. "Let me suggest something to you. I have studied this region for many years, and I am certain that there are more lucrative opportunities further south. And since Ammad has agreed to take us as far as—"

Ogilvey obviously intended to go on at some length. I could already sense what he was planning. He would convince Captain Bledsoe that there were other and better opportunities and their partnership would continue until both were either satisfied or exhausted.

I excused myself and walked away from the gathering.

I had previously become friendly with two of the guides. I found them tending to the animals. When I made clear to them my intentions, they nodded. They understood. They would take me back to the village of the children.

Perhaps the children would let me stay for a while. Perhaps not. I didn't know. But whatever they said, I knew I had to walk away from the ones who walked away.

THE BAG LADY

The street stank of garbage and sweat, but it was still early. Later, as the day warmed up, the smells of garlic and bacon would seep out of the corner diner. Traffic splashed through spring puddles. The last white patches of winter still resisted the glare of the sun, but if this was not their last day, it would be their last week.

The bag lady shuffled painfully along the sidewalk, pushing an overloaded shopping cart with one broken wheel. She didn't walk as much as she staggered. She was a shapeless lump, an ambulatory heap of clothing, new layers added on top of the old, sweaters, sweatshirts, torn coats, a blanket, another coat, the whole stuffed with old newspapers for insulation—she was an oblate spheroid of rubbish and rejection. Her swollen ankles made it difficult for her to move, even harder to push the cart. Her feet were wrapped in more layers of dirty cloth.

The woman's skin was leathery and lined, burned and scoured, eroded by the relentless weather. Her graying hair was a tangle of greasy ropes. If she'd ever had a name, she hadn't heard anyone speak it in years. Her eyes were rheumy and blood-shot—wherever she looked, she seemed to be staring at something on the other side of reality.

Several people passed her by, none of them saw her. She was invisible to them, not even scenery. Oblivious to her anguish and embarrassment, they hurried on about their business—exhaling puffs of breath like human locomotives, they chugged along the unbreakable rails of their lives.

The bag lady didn't care. She had more important matters to attend to. She did not often push her way onto this street, the business owners frowned at her, turned their hoses on her, chased her away with epithets and sometimes even threats of violence. But today—

She frowned, she sniffed, she looked up the street and back again. Something wasn't right. No, not here. Not there, but close. Something in the universe smelled wrong. And it wasn't her.

And then, she spotted it—

The dirty van, the dirty dark grey van. A panel van parked at the curb. No windows at the rear or sides. The front windows were tinted dark. No markings to identify the vehicle, no bumper stickers, no ads painted on the side. Just a featureless block.

It smelled wrong.

She looked down the street, all the way down to the end of the street, where a little girl in a pink winter coat had just come bouncing around the corner. A cherub, she glowed with innocence—the world was still bright and beautiful to her. She was singing and skipping, trailing one mittened hand across the frosty store-fronts, leaving sketchy streaks in the hoar-frost.

And as it always did, the moment clicked into clarity. The bag lady made a decision. She pushed her heavy cart forward. She put all her strength into the effort, squelching desperately forward.

Finally, unable to move any further, she stopped, her cart inconveniently blocking the passenger door of the van, her reeking body blocking the sliding panel door on the side. Someone on the inside made a noise, it sounded like a curse.

The bag lady grunted in sudden annoyance. She leaned against the panel door of the van for balance, her wrinkled hand sliding and leaving an ugly smear—and then a stream of urine ran down her left leg, puddling at her feet, steaming on the icy pavement.

The moment was perfectly timed. The little girl came dancing by, her song abruptly stopping as she glanced over. She made a face, an expression of disgust and disapproval, then she broke into a run and scampered on toward school.

The bag lady still leaned against the van, frowning, concentrating on something more than her own body now. The left tail light of the van abruptly shattered. No repair shop would ever be able to make it light again. Every police cruiser that noticed would pull this vehicle over to cite the driver for the broken light—but no, that wouldn't be enough. She needed to do more.

She muttered a few words—barely finishing the curse before the van pulled angrily away. The greasy handprint on its side would not wash off—not easily and not for a long time. But the handprint was only the smallest part of the spell. The van and its unseen occupant were now afflicted with a fetid malcharisma. They would never go unnoticed again—it might be enough. The bag lady couldn't be sure.

In the great grand scheme of things, this little shift of possibility was so small as to be infinitesimal in its reach—but to the little girl in the pink coat, the unknowing recipient of this reversal of entropy, it was an unknown coup, a victory of life-changing proportions—simply because she would live to see tomorrow.

But for the bag lady, it was going to be a very expensive triumph. The avalanche of entropy is unforgiving and the effort to shift it even a millimeter would cost her dearly.

Already, she was groaning with new pains. She grabbed onto the handle of her shopping cart to keep from falling. It was so heavily loaded it was an anchor to her sudden dizziness. For a moment, she did not know who she was or where she was. She knew only pain, the bottomless well of icy fire that gnawed at her gut, the first warnings of the waves of despair to come.

Somehow, she managed to make it across the slippery sidewalk to the nearest doorstep, where she sank down to her knees, collapsing in her rags, sagging against the frame of the door. She knew she couldn't stay here long. She knew the proprietor of this shop was an unforgiving tyrant, a small and petty excuse for a human being, interested only in the amount of commerce he could attract, never in the people he might serve. Soon, he would come bursting angrily out of his sacred warmth to chase her away.

But right now, she was overcome with the simple effort of breathing. In. Out. In. Out. She gasped for breath, strove to regain some sense of herself, but failing. This was going to be a bad one. Very bad. She couldn't help herself, she had to see. Still puffing, she began laboriously unwrapping the coils of cloth around her right leg, around and around, all the way down, until she finally revealed the mottled skin of her left foot. It was stippled with ugly blotches of green and yellow, blue and purple. There were new sores appearing, pus-filled boils, inflammations that grew even as she watched. Blood oozed from old scabs.

She searched desperately for the first telltale signs of gangrene, but was quickly disappointed. As eagerly as she hoped—no, not yet. This wasn't the one. Not even close. Not big enough. Not yet. She was going to survive. She was going to live another day. She wept.

She could remember another time—so long long ago—a time of naïve ignorance, but that was before the flashes began, before the smells and the flavors and the clamoring sense of wrongness overwhelmed her with a terrible compulsion to do something—*anything*—that might restore even a small balance to the world.

"It isn't fair! Why me?" she wept. "Why me? What did I do to deserve this—?"

But even as the words dribbled out of her torn mouth, she already knew the answer. Because. Because. Because she'd brought it on herself—with her own outraged scream of anguish at the universe. "Why doesn't somebody do something?"

And the universe had answered. "Why don't *you*?"

So tomorrow, just like today, just like yesterday, just like all the days and years before, freezing through the unrelenting winter, burning and baking beneath the heavy blanket of summer, nevertheless she'll lever herself up again, every day paying the ugly price of her compulsion one more time. She has no choice—

The bag lady will pull herself up from the unforgiving pavement, stumble to her feet, wheezing and groaning, her bones crackling resentfully, all stiff and resisting—racked with pain and hunger, driven by desperation, she'll go out and search the streets and the alleys, looking for the big one, hoping, always hoping—every day hoping that today will be the day she can finally earn her death.

ENTERPRISE FISH

"The only constant in the universe is change and even that isn't constant."

— *Solomon Short*

Finally, the pilot said, "There it is."

"Where?"

"Straight ahead. That gray mass on the horizon." He tapped a screen, zooming in. The picture was still indistinct.

Barksdale stood up and went downstairs to peer out the passenger windshield. I didn't bother. Neither did anyone else. But I'd known how close we were for the last half-hour. The others hadn't noticed the smell, wouldn't notice it until we began our descent. Without augments, bio or cyber or worm, most humans don't smell anything until they rub their own noses in it.

We were flying up the wind-signature of the event. Not intentionally; it was unavoidable. Ten square klicks of fetid biomass churning through the stages of death and recomposition, drew a dark red stain across the map. Ugly stuff. Sticky stuff. They'd have to decontaminate the aircraft, or every flying, crawling, leaping, scrabbling red thing that liked that particular set of pheromones—and that was pretty much every flying, crawling, leaping, scrabbling thing with Chtorran genes—would come flying, crawling, leaping, and scrabbling after it.

General Anderson was about to turn to me. There's an instant of anticipation in a body's posture that occurs long before any movement; most humans can't sense it, but it's like a neon explosion of information to me. I swiveled to face him, simultaneous with his own action. "I wish you wouldn't do that," he said. I could have apologized, but I didn't. I'd given up pretending to be human. It had never really worked all that well for me *before*. Now, I just didn't see the point in it. I wasn't human. Had stopped being human a long time ago. Would have stopped being human even if I hadn't fallen down to the bottom of a Chtorran nest.

"Can you smell anything yet?"

"I can smell everything," I said. "I've been tasting it for fifty klicks. Ever since we crossed the Arctic Circle."

Anderson looked annoyed. He didn't like me. I didn't blame him. I didn't like me all that much either. But he had at least five good reasons to dislike me. And three of those were my reasons too. It didn't matter, we still had to work together. So I said, "It's soup. I'm still sorting out the flavors. Tomato. Clam. Garlic. Parsley. Swordfish. Mercury...." I shrugged, a physical punctuation mark, performed more as a courtesy than as any actual representation of how I felt or thought. "It's Boullibase." And then I added, "Not very good Boullibase either."

"Eh?"

I held up a hand. Another courtesy. But humans communicate through nuance as much as through language. So if I wanted to be understood, I had to practice nuance. "Have you ever tasted something for the first time, but even though it's the first time, you've never tasted it before in your life, you still know there's something wrong with it?"

He considered the question. That was one of the good things about General Daniel Anderson. He didn't speak without thinking. Well, not as often as most people. "You're saying there's something wrong with the smell, so there's something wrong with the biophysical processes?"

"I'm saying that's how I'm experiencing it."

He nodded.

General Barksdale came back up from the downstairs cabin, wrapping his outer-coat tighter around himself and making a great show of shivering. "Brrr brrr brrr. It looks cold out there." Unnecessary. And grating. He leaned on the back of Anderson's chair and asked, "So, how are we doing here, boys? Figured out the Enterprise Fish yet?"

Anderson looked annoyed, partly at Barksdale's stupid interruption, and partly because Barksdale's impressive weight had pushed his seat uncomfortably backward. Barksdale was looming over Anderson to lean in toward me and Anderson didn't like being cramped by his size or his manner. Even a human could read that tableau.

"It's not a fish," Anderson said quietly.

"Yeah, yeah, I know," said Barksdale. "It's a gigantic colony of adaptive symbi-otes in multiplex synergistic relationships." He looked at me. "Did I get it right? I know the fancy language for it. But it still looks and acts like a fish. So we can think of it like a fish, right?"

Anderson was watching for my reaction. I didn't display because I didn't have a reaction. I'd figured out Barksdale a long time ago. He hadn't climbed any farther up the evolutionary ladder than he'd needed to. His grandfather's business acumen had bought the rest of the family an enviable comfort zone. Although David Hale Barks-dale had displayed little interest in a military career, the war had necessitated his assumption into the highest ranks of the Civilian-Military (an astonishing oxymo-ron, but humans had passed beyond astonishment the day that Chtorrans showed up in downtown Manhattan.)

What was left of the community of governments on the North American conti-nent had welcomed the creation of the Civilian-Military as a viable way of securing a self-sustaining response to the Chtorran infestation; overlapping the military onto the pre-existing corporate-clusters of the defense industry should ensure an uninterruptible chain of supply and command. At least, that was the projection. If, along the way, it meant shifting to a system of no-bid contracts, that was small price to pay. Actually, it was a large price to pay, but who was counting the cost anymore. Now that Plastic Dollars, Credit Dollars, Chocolate Dollars, and Oil Dollars had all collapsed, the economists were inventing a new economy based on Future Dollars. But given the nature of the war, the value of the dollar was irrelevant.

Some people speak because they have something to say. Others speak because they have to say something. Barksdale's mouth was still going. "I mean, as far as I'm concerned, if it looks like a fish, if it swims like a fish—it's a fish. It's simple."

I met his gaze. "It isn't simple. Only stupid people say things like that." I didn't have to be polite to Barksdale. I didn't have to be polite to anyone. I was a nation-state unto myself. The united state of McCarthy. I don't do diplomacy. Behind my back, they call me Mr. Tact.

Barksdale didn't take it personally. He didn't take anything personally. He just laughed genially. Everything was a joke to him, a big friendly joke. "For the record," I added, "It doesn't look like a fish and it doesn't act like a fish. It floats in the ocean. After that, any resemblance is coincidental. It's a mobile ecological domain." I looked across to Anderson. "Do you want to explain?"

Anderson showed the faintest hint of a smile. He had to be polite to Barksdale, it was part of his job. Not mine. But that didn't stop him from appreciating the moment. "No, you go ahead," he said.

I looked at Barksdale. "You haven't read your briefing books." A statement, not a question.

"Who has time? We've got a war to win. Do you know how busy I am?"

Actually, I did. But I didn't say what I knew. The info-noise I swam in told me more about this overstuffed mushroom of a man than any sentient being should ever have to know. Most of the busy was busy-work, shell processes requiring null-decisions, all designed to keep his fat pork-stained fingers out of the real business of war, where real people would die if he were in charge. Loading him down with briefing books was one of the ways of keeping him preoccupied, except—like too many others—he didn't read.

"Give me the short version," he said.

"There is no short version," I said.

"Explain it anyway," Barksdale insisted.

Anderson nodded encouragement. He was enjoying this too much. He looked across to the pilot's station. "We're in a headwind. You've got at least fifteen minutes."

"Do I have to make it an order?" Barksdale said.

There were so many places I could have gone with that particular piece of nonsense. I could see that on Danny Anderson's face as well. But why bother? I decided to answer the question anyway. "It's not a creature, it's a convention."

Barksdale's expression puckered as he tried to sort that out. He couldn't find the sense in the sentence. Anderson gave me the look. "A little more than that, McCarthy?"

I finished taking a drink from my canteen and put the cap back on. "The Chtorran infestation isn't deliberate," I explained. "It isn't even conscious. Some people have said it's an ecology looking for a place to happen, but even that's not accurate. It's the *possibility* of an ecology. It's the potential for an ecology. Still with me?" Barksdale nodded, smiling vacuously. Behind all that blood-infused fat it was hard (even for me) to tell if he was actually hearing what I was saying or just listening because he was happy for the attention.

"You drop seeds from space. Lots of different ways to do it. The most common, the seed heats up on entry, pops like popcorn, continues to pop like popcorn all the way down, each time releasing great webs of nano-silk. With micro-seeds embedded in the webs. Some of the webs work like parachutes, slowing the seeds down, some rip away and drift off. It doesn't matter. As long as the DNA survives the trip down. The seeds, the popcorn, the webs, the stuff embedded in them, everything is message—the goal is to deliver genetic material to a viable domain. So everything that happens on the way down is another possibility.

"The problem is...none of this stuff has any way of knowing where it will land. Polar, temperate, equatorial. It has no idea whether it's going to land on savannah or desert, fresh water lake or salt water ocean; arctic wasteland or tropical jungle. How many different ecological domains do we have on this planet? The seeds can't be customized for any of them. They have to be adaptable to *all* of them. Okay, the webs that rip away from the falling seeds have some advantage; they'll drift wherever the winds take them, and the winds usually drop their burdens on mountainsides, which are often fertile specifically because the winds drop rain on them. But the truth is, most of this stuff comes down wherever it comes down. Most people know about the stuff that's running amuck in the Rockies and in the Amazon and in the Congo. Giant red and purple worms, shambler trees, swarms of stingflies, and great pink dust clouds. But more than two-thirds of this planet is ocean. Assuming an equal distribution of genetic material More than two-thirds of the Chtorran seeds fell into the ocean. That's the point."

I could see it in Barksdale's eyes. He didn't get it. He was still waiting for more. He was waiting to have it explained. Spelled out.

"And...?"

I took a breath. "And...wherever the seeds fall, you get a *different* set of Chtorran organisms. A convention. Each one is a different expression of the possibilities inherent in the Chtorran ecology. And even that's an inaccurate statement because it doesn't even begin to address the multiplex dimensions of relationships and opportunities and possibilities. There are so many different genetic relationships, so many different environmental opportunities, so many different developmental possibilities, so many occasions for random chance to stir the mix, that each creature that arises isn't a specifically designed response of the ecology to its circumstances as much as it is an emergent recombination of elements that arise in response to the opportunities around it."

"Uh—" Barksdale faltered. Barksdale wasn't quite as stupid as he looked. He obviously understood words with more than one syllable. Whether or not he understood nuance, intended meaning, natural results, and consequences—that was another whole discussion.

Anderson tried to clarify. "He's saying that if you drop identical seeds into dissimilar environments, you get dissimilar ecologies. Right?" He looked to me for agreement.

I shook my head. "Sorry, no. I'm saying that even if you dropped identical seeds into identical environments, you'd still get dissimilar ecologies. There is no Chtorran ecology, there never was. It isn't structured and its pieces don't behave predictably. It's an opportunistic synergistic recombinant multiplex confluence of biological processes that *randomly* adapt and express themselves according to the circumstances of the moment. The Chtorr takes advantage of whatever opportunities it encounters in whatever way pops up when the genetic lotto balls start percolating. The so-called 'Enterprise Fish' is only one of those expressions. It could just as easily have been anything else. And probably will be. We don't have a very clear picture of what's happening in the depths beyond our submersibles."

"Oh," said Barksdale, blinking. He was having trouble sorting it out. He let go of Anderson's seat back and straightened up, pretending to understand. Normally, I don't info-dump like that. But when someone is determined to be deliberately stupid, I'll make an exception.

Anderson, obviously still annoyed at the way Barksdale's flesh had been pressing uncomfortably against him, folded his arms, satisfied. If I hadn't managed to terrify Barksdale, at least I'd rubbed his nose in how much he didn't know that he didn't know.

"We're beginning our descent," the pilot announced. I'd already noticed the slight shift in the aircraft's attitude several moments ago, but this gave Barksdale the chance to make what passed for a graceful exit from an uncomfortable confrontation with his own ignorance. He smiled weakly and said, "I'd better go sit down now."

"Good idea," Anderson added. After Barksdale had left, he looked across to me, a look that would have been mutual understanding if I were still human. There was still understanding, but it wasn't mutual. What he understood was not what I understood.

As we dropped toward sea level, the aircraft bumped and slid in the wind. The Air Force boys in the back whooped and hollered "wheee" at the bigger bumps, thinking that turbulence was an occasion for jubilation and that this particular adventure was no different than any other joyride into Colorado Springs, or even what was left of Colorado Springs. The ignorance and the enthusiasm of youth. Until— "Christ! What's that stink!"

"That's the target," I said.

Anderson was used to the smell. Points to him for that. He nodded to the brat and pointed out the forward bubble. "Directly ahead."

"I don't see it. Where? Next to that shit-colored island?"

"No. Not next to it. The island."

"That—?" The brat and friends rose out of their seats, unbelieving.

"That's an Enterprise Fish." General Anderson's expression went dark. "Didn't you read your briefing book?"

"Sir, I got put on this ship ten minutes before it lifted. Berney went to sick bay, throwing up. Couldn't stop."

"Sorry to hear that."

"Not as sorry as Berney." That remark hung in silence for a moment. It was unlikely that Berney would be on any future missions. Any of a half-dozen things could have caused his symptoms, none of them optimistic. Don't start any trilogies, Berney. Oh hell, don't even start a short story.

Anderson called back to them, "You might want to put your breathers on now. That stink is only going to get worse." He pulled his headgear on, pulled the mask down over his face; he pulled the ear flaps down and fastened the padded strap under his chin. With his whole head covered, he looked like some kind of military insect. The stink of the beast didn't bother me as much as it did the humans. It had the taste of a place I'd never be able to escape. You can take the psycho out of the mandala, you can't take the mandala out of the psycho. But I didn't need to have them thinking that, so I pulled my own headgear on, trying to ignore the discomfort. The earphones whispered with industrial silence, a steady stream of dry background chatter.

I don't like wearing most human clothes. I can taste where they've been, where they grew, what they ate, who or what they rubbed up against, what they've been washed in. Even the polymers and polycarbons and nano-weaves have their own distinct flavors, vaguely medicinal and metallic. Old-fashioned nylon and microfiber knits are the least uncomfortable. Whatever I can find. Whatever is left in the warehouses from the days before the plagues. Everything from lady's underwear to skintight athletic gear. There aren't a lot of specialty tailors anymore. I wear them to mute the ceaseless noise of the world, the scouring taste of the wind, all the desperate flavors of the day—especially the tastes of the city, the smells of other humans.

When I absolutely have to deal with humans, I have to wear human clothes, so I wear the nylons and the microfibers as underliners. Today, on top of the lingerie, a self-heating undersuit and two layers of protective outergear. Multiplane polymer nanoweave. As long as I don't have to taste it.

The aircraft dipped and shuddered as the pilot slowed. We dropped steadily toward the heaving surface of the beast-thing. Great waves moved slowly across its surface, gently lifting and dropping the men and equipment already waiting there. Anderson looked to me, a question in his eyes.

"It's not dead," I said.

He looked confused. "It's been beached for seven weeks." Like this meant something.

"I told you, it's a convention. Stop expecting it to be like things you know. Don't be a Barksdale."

"Right. I keep forgetting. Thanks for reminding me again why I don't like you very much." He reached under his seat and pulled his situation-boots forward; he shoved his feet into them, first one, then the other, then pulled up the zippers in the back. I followed his example. The bottoms of the boots spread out like snow-shoes. The soles were metal honeycombs, studded with 10-centimeter cleats. The back of the Enterprise Fish wasn't just slimy, it was blubbery and greasy and it rolled like a restless sea. Even with cleats, footing would be tricky. Everything on its back had to be anchored—equipment tripods, habitats, storage sheds, landing platforms. Vehicles had studded tires or tank treads. Most of the bots were multi-legged, either spider-based or tripods, all with oversized feet and cleats.

We waited in silence until the airship plopped down onto the rolling landscape of the behemoth. The pilot tapped buttons on his screens and idled his engines. "Welcome to Hell-Stinky. Abandon help, all ye who hope to intern. Please return your flight attendants to an upright position. Gentlemen, you may start your exos. Please use the rear doors to exit. Thank you for flying Air Apparent. We hope you'll think of us for all your future air travel needs into the zone." He popped open the rear of the airship and six pallets of equipment slid noisily out into the bright cold day. They squished into the surface of the beast. A scattering of bots came rushing up to move the pallets toward the meager settlement of Hell-Stinky base. As they pushed, pulled, and dragged the machinery, they carved deep tracks through the oily pudding of the monstrous landscape.

At the back of the cabin, mobile exo-skeletons stood securely fastened to the walls. Anderson stepped backward into the first one and it quickly adjusted itself to his frame, anchoring itself to his feet, his legs, his torso, and his arms. Exos were convenient for magnifying the physical strength of a human, but here on the roll-ing back of the Enterprise Fish, humans needed them just to stay upright; the exos would adjust their balance to the tides of flesh far more accurately. I stepped into my own exo and waited while it sorted itself out.

I'd worn exos of all kinds—both before and after my transformation in the Amazon—but the equipment was always in short supply. No matter how fast they came off the assembly lines, there still weren't enough. Plug an intelligence engine into an exo and you have a bot. Useful for construction, supply, maintenance, patrol, police-work, surveillance, even combat. So the desk-warriors couldn't see the logic of wasting a perfectly good exo on a grunt, who shouldn't be out in the zone anyway. A bot can do the job just as well, with no risk to human life, so why put a grunt in an exo-skeleton when you have trained professionals in Des Moines running in virtual mode?

On the other hand, putting exo-skeletons on a grunt makes a whole lot of sense, especially if you're the grunt. You can lift, carry, and run for hours. You've got extra-sensory augmentation, and if you're injured or even unconscious, the exo can bring you home. But if it weren't for General Dale Hale Barksdale the Third, we might not have had even these. I probably didn't need it, but Anderson didn't want me showing off among the ordinaries. He said it would increase the alienation. A very peculiar observation. I didn't see how I could be any more alienated from the rest of humanity, but despite his dislike of me, he was one of the few humans who made a genuine effort to understand who I had become.

The exo-skeleton completed its process of connection and calibration. It had clamped itself to my boots, my calves, my waist, my shoulders, my arms, and my wrists. I had metal hands just beyond my own. When I walked, I should have *clomped*, but instead I moved with an unnatural grace, almost cat-like. In Manhattan, we'd seen ballet dancers performing impossible acrobatic feats in exo-skeletons; but they were using special-mods and the troops were specifically ordered not to attempt anything they had not been certified for.

The other members of the team had also fitted themselves into their exos and as a group, we glided down the loading ramp to the glutinous surface of the alien thing.

It stank. It reeked. It assaulted. It was a collection of rank and fetid odors, death and decay and decomposition, a wall of olfactory offensiveness that would have stopped us dead in our tracks and knocked us flat to the glutinous ground, had the exo-skeletons not held us up and walked us forward. It was an almost visible presence, a vomitous stench so thick you could chew it. I had the small advantage of a Chtorran sense of smell. I could separate and identify all the different components of the repellent horror. But identification was insufficient. I had just enough residual humanity to experience the attack on my senses as a detestable abomination. There were no human equivalents for what I smelled, but my imagination was inventive enough and working overtime, creating its own bizarre menagerie of possible nightmares; I had too much history with Chtorran things that smelled bad.

We paused at the bottom to get our bearings. Getting our "sea legs" meant giving the exos a chance to calibrate themselves against the slow-rippling flesh of the Enterprise Fish. While the others tested their new agilities, I *sat.* I assumed a sitting position and the exo-skeleton became a chair. Not the most comfortable chair, but comfortable enough. If I wanted to put both legs up on an invisible hassock, I could have done that too. The exo had a tripod at the base of its spine. I'd seen field-mechanics lying flat on their backs this way, sometimes pushed five or ten meters in the air to work on an underwing fitting or inspect the work of a bot. A lot of the hardcore mechanics still didn't trust bots, even though the stats said bots were more accurate. Human stubbornness. I'd given up human stubbornness a long time ago. I had something nastier. Undefinable.

Two rollagons came trundling up. We hooked ourselves onto the outside let it carry us, bucking and rocking north to the drill sites. We had to detour around several deep fissures in the creature's landscape, and at one point we even rolled off its flank onto the rocky shore and paralleled the sagging wall of flesh for half a kilometer.

At one point, the vehicle swerved up onto a cliff overlooking the shore. "Check it out. On your left," the driver said. Not very chatty, he clicked off again. He rightfully assumed we'd already seen all pertinent video.

Beneath us, we could see seven polar bears licking and chewing at the sides of the beached Enterprise Fish. Here and there were gaping holes ripped into its skin. Great gobbets of oily flesh oozed out onto the rocks, like the stuffing pushing out of a sagging broken couch. One of the bears was a large male, two were females, each with two cubs. All had pink patches in their fur. Two of the cubs were tugging at a long stringer of blubbery skin. During the summer, a polar bear needs to eat its own weight in blubber to have any chance of surviving the winter.

And then they passed behind us. "Well, see," said Barksdale, his voice coming loud over the earphones. "It's not all bad news. "The polar bears are surviving."

"If you like pink polar bears," I replied.

General Anderson glanced backwards toward me, surprised that I had responded at all. Hanging off the side of the rollagon, it wasn't possible to shrug. I just shook my head. The fact that I wasn't human didn't stop me from pretending to be one from time to time. Just to keep my hosts at ease.

We rolled back up onto the seething flesh of the Enterprise Fish and rolled out onto the expanse of its greatest width. This was the primary drill site. The surgery team had brought in a dozen industrial bots, armed with lasers and timber-saws. The machines had anchored themselves with meter-deep cleats and sliced deep into the skin of the beast, clamped onto, pulled up and peeled back flubbery layers of thick unwieldy flesh. Oily grease oozed and dripped from every cut. Steam still rose from the dark red soup beneath. Even through the breathers, it made my eyes water. It was probably worse for the humans, they didn't know what they were smelling.

The rollagon had a crane on the back. The operator unfolded its arms. They screeched against the cold. The grappling arm swung out and the grapple came down. Someone behind me pushed it into place, and it automatically grabbed onto the handles on the back of my exo-skeleton. This was why I had been brought here. Remote videos don't give you the smell and the taste and the...the song of the beast. I was the only one who could interpret that part for the humans.

Foreman's voice in my memory. "What are you feeling, Jim?"

My answer. "Too much to assimilate, conceptualize, catalog. When you ask me what I'm feeling, I stop feeling. When I think about what I'm feeling, I'm feeling my thinking, not my feeling."

Foreman's face, posture. A nod. He understood the dilemma. Nevertheless....

The machine lifted me up. *Deus ex machina.* The god of the machine. The ancient Greek theatre. The machine was a huge lever, it served as a crane. The god sat in the basket, the stagehands pushed down on their end, raising the god up in the air, swinging him out and forward, over the top of the theatre and then down again to the front of the stage. The god in the machine comes down to Earth to save the mortal humans from the disaster they have made of their lives.

A gust of cold wind came up suddenly, catching me and pushing me sideways. The crane flew me out over the smoky pit. Literary allusions rose around me. I swung like a pendulum. I waited for the movement to still. Five million years of alien biology moshed beneath me. Of course the humans were puzzled and confused. Inside the Enterprise Fish, they expected to find organs—not organisms. A convention. Wet and pulpy. Churning. Rhythmic pulses, a biological tuning fork, slow and steady. And other things—large and impenetrable, small and squirming. Things that moved between the other things, dark things and darker things. Things that slithered like snakes, winding in and out. Things that swam like ambiguous millipedes. Things that crept and crawled and pulled themselves between. Bacteria upon the backs of the mites which lived in the shells of the lice that crawled through the fur of the bats that fed on the insects that sucked out the blood of the rats and the voles—all of it roiled and boiled in biologic soup. Crabs lurked under the boulders of flesh. Flounders slipped and slid between the shelves of tissue. Tiny gnats floated in the fetid stink, silvery guppies twinkled in the blood; larger fish leapt and darted; eels wound within. And larger things as well, darker shapes, unidentifiable; things for which there were no earthy analogs. Things that snatched like sharks, with sudden vicious movements; and other things that simply moved and sifted. Everything within the flesh of the fish was its own self—and yet, all of it was interconnected by pink spiderwebs that drifted and parted and reformed with every ebb and flow of the beast's internal tides. The red and purple fur, colorless in the darkness; neurons floating, touching, attaching; then, pushed by circumstance, breaking, moving on, forming new patterns of attachment and connection, thought and awareness. A shifting consciousness, a movable identity, a transportable selfness, sliding around in and in and under and through a hundred million living things, each of which had its own feelers and antennae and ways to connect with the synapses of the web, sharing itself and being shared, contributing its fragmentary awareness and accepting as much as it could of the flood of noise and information all around it, an endless sea of noise and confusion, somehow making enough sense of itself to cooperate in a larger purpose that emerged silently from the collective urges of life. All these separate creatures and creations, all of them, they were all aware of each other, simultaneous existence for every living thing. Eat and be eaten. The eaters enjoyed not only the taste of the flesh they bit into, they experienced the intense rush of sensation that the meal felt as the eater's teeth sank in. Life lives on life. Everything eats everything else. And the only difference between humanity and the Chtorr is that the Chtorr experienced itself feeding on itself. A gigantic self-devouring meal. This was the Chtorr, in all of its astonishing *allness*.

They lowered me into the pit. The walls of rubbery flesh rose around me. Almost down to the surface of the swarming goo. A voice shouted something and the cables yanked to a stop. This was as low as someone deemed safe. They didn't want to drop me. They didn't want to lose me. If I fell in, or even if I went too deep, they feared I would be overwhelmed and relapse into a babbling psychedelic psychotic psychopath again. If I still had a sense of humor—if I still had enough humanity left inside me to have a sense of humor, I would reach down and grab one of those crawly things. I'd take a big fat bite out of it and announce that it needs salt. But I knew it didn't. The interior of the Enterprise Fish was almost twice as salty as the sea it swam in. Another indicator of the extreme age of the ocean it had evolved in, somewhere else, someplace lost in the gray memories of time. How long had it taken to find its way here?

Here, only an arm's length above the soup, I swung precariously. I shifted my position. The exoskeleton accommodated and I leaned forward, arms and legs spread wide apart, as if I was sailing over a gloppy red landscape. It bubbled and stank like a sulfurous mud pit. I closed my eyes and tasted. I listened. I floated. I shared. I went—

There is no human word.

It looks like unconsciousness, but it isn't. It feels like non-consciousness, but it isn't. You could call it all-consciousness, but it isn't. It's all of that and none of it. It's like letting go and melting, all the pieces of self flying outward, sliding out across the surfaces of awareness and identity and attaching, connecting, becoming aware of a larger selfness that moves and feels and bleeds and eats and excretes as a process that processes itself—and against that background the self rides, floats, flies, moves, contracts, expands, exists, and becomes its own small part of the allness—all in the middle of the sea of noise, the endless drone of living things shouting, "Here I am!" except there is no *here*, and there is no *I*, and most profound of all, there is no *is*. Is-ness is an illusion. There is no permanence. The verb "to be" creates the illusion that this condition exists as an inherent element of the subject. But no, there is no permanence and existence is a shared delusion that we pass onto the next set of delusionaries before we pass on ourselves. And like the endless pink webs, they form and reform the narrative in their own images, their own reformatory dormitory, and there we all are, sleeping with the wishes.

If I still had a sense of humor, I would laugh. Not because it's funny, but because it isn't. What's funny is that we think it is.

And all the while...I smelled the song of the fish. I smelled the things within and all their separate songs, as many as I could feel. I tasted the flavors of the processes of the beast and the humans left me hanging their, lost in the symphonies of infestation.

The Enterprise Fish is not a fish. It swims in the ocean and it grows. It eats and it grows. But it is not a fish, it never was. It is a Chtorran worm, a gastropede. A gastropede is a slug. It doesn't get very big. Maybe the size of a bus. When it gets too big, it can't support its own weight. It can't eat enough to feed its own volume. Its organs begin to die. And the creatures inside of it, the symbiotes, the partners, they feed on the dying organs and take over the jobs. As the heart of the slug slows down, the pump-muscle slugs around the blood vessels take over the job, feeding themselves from the bloodstream and paying for it by pulsing. When the slug's lungs are unable to extract enough oxygen from the air, they begin to die and other creatures take over the job. Eventually, there is no worm; only a partnership, a symbiotic symphony, a convention. A self-sustaining biological society. And so the slug continues to grow and expand, adding new partners to the process until the process itself outgrows its ability to expand and sustain. And then—it collapses into smaller processes, comes apart and becomes the next stage of its existence. Not death. Just the next phase of life churning life to spread more life.

In the ocean—the slug becomes an island. Its mouth becomes a maw, a collection of many mouths. It drifts, turning itself into the current and sweeping all before it, sifting the sea for sustenance. Within its flesh, countless new organisms take root and thrive and grow and take on the responsibilities of partnership. Within the flesh of the beast are nations. Life is hungry, life expands. The islands grow, they rise, they fall. Sometimes the Enterprise Fish develops deep chasms where the flesh splits apart, torn by the strains of its own internal tectonics. The beast fissions and fragments, leaving in its wake the bloody flesh of many smaller islands. But sometimes, before that happens, the current carries it to shore, beaching it on the hot sands of Baja or the glimmering rocks of Vancouver Island or snagging and catching it on the oily rigs of Prudhoe Bay.

The fish are named like storms. Albert and Betty and Chad and Debra. Edward and Fanny. Gabriel and Harriett. Isadore and June. Most of the older fish, all the way up to Fanny, had long since grown so big they couldn't survive. They'd broken up and become Karl and Lena, Max and Nora, Oscar and Patty, Quinn and Ruth. We stood on the back of Sally. Sally was beached and breaking up. Not dying, just changing. Enterprise Fish don't die; conventions end, form and reform; just like the endless webs of pink fur spiderweb silken strands that ebb and flow within the beast, within each creature in the beast, within the flesh of every living thing the Chtorr can touch. I am, therefore I think.

There were great pink whales in the sea. Humpbacks and blues and sperms. Earth-beasts with Chtorran fur. Sally had followed them northward, deep into the arctic, and beached herself on the broken shores of Norway's coldest coast, where rocks and sea and glaciers argued for supremacy, an endless battle of weather and erosion, the waves turned pink with bloody froth. The air stank with bubbling noises gurgling from the pit, the things within cried and whimpered and gibbered and sang. All their needs and desires. It rose up toward the darkening sky. The stench could be tasted a hundred klicks downwind.

And then the cables yanked and I rose away from the multitudes below. Neither relieved nor regretful. The moment was over and I detached. I floated. The senses took census. The sense of me. No sense at all. The allness collapsed with distance.

They lowered me to the icy back of the beast. General Anderson took my gloved hands in his. The illusion of intimacy. He focused his goggles on mine. The illusion of eye contact. He spoke softly. "What did you taste?"

I took a moment to assimilate, to catalog and conceptualize. "It's not dead. It's not dying. It's doing what it's supposed to do."

Anderson knew enough to wait.

I said, "It's an incubator. Just like the nests under the shambler groves are incubators—the Enterprise Fish are gigantic factories. They're a big warm safe place for all the different pieces of the ecology to assemble themselves. It swims in the ocean, it gathers nutrients, it feeds itself and all of its pieces; and inside, everything churns around, forming whatever sustainable relationships it can. And then...eventually, it bumps into a continent. It's inevitable. It's *supposed* to beach itself. That's what it's designed to do. And when it does, it doesn't die, it just falls apart. And then all the separate pieces of itself turn into whatever they turn into. Some go back into the sea. Some root themselves on the shore. Others will eventually eat their way out and go hungrily exploring. The job of the Enterprise Fish is to deliver a massive biomass to the land surface. That's its job—one of its jobs. But where there is land, it delivers itself and its passengers to shore. If there's no land, it becomes land. Imagine an ocean full of these things. The Chtorr is designed, adapted, evolved—choose your own word—to find a way to thrive no matter where its seeds land. Humans have never really appreciated the scale of this thing."

Anderson nodded. "We know that. You've said it before. A thousand different ways already. Some of us are starting to get it."

"If I don't repeat it, you forget it. It's the way your brains work. You don't know how to recognize when you don't know that you don't know. You insist on translating it, running it through your filters of what you do know, thinking that because one part of the universe works one way, so does another. Well, it doesn't. Welcome to Chtorr."

Anderson leaned in close and switched to the private channel. "McCarthy? Remember how you and I made an agreement? That I was supposed to tell you when you were acting like an arrogant jerk? More than usual, I mean? Well, this is one of those times." He poked me in the chest with the flat of his hand—more than once. He backed me away from the others. Around the corner of the rollagon. I shut up and let him dump his anger. I could wait. It wasn't my anger. To him, I must have appeared impassive.

"Yes, I know what you've been through and I know the effect it's had on you. I'm your baby-sitter. But I knew you before and you were an arrogant jerk then. So I have some sense how much of this is the Chtorr and how much is you using the Chtorr as a justification for being an ass. We put up with it because you're useful, but frankly, it's getting old. It's beyond disrespect. Now, it's just a frigging waste of time. You acting like you're some kind of superior and enlightened being is just you hiding from the real truth."

"And what truth is that?"

"You figure it out," said Anderson. "If you're so superior and enlightened, that shouldn't be a problem. You should have already seen it. Now—" He took a breath, straightened and became General Anderson again. "Just answer the question we brought you here to answer. Will it work? Can we neutralize this thing?"

I considered it. Had already been considering it since I first started tasting the stink of the beast fifty klicks downwind. "No," I said.

Anderson didn't react. "Why not?"

"I already told you. I told you before we came. I've told you repeatedly. This is not a single creature. If it were, you could kill it easily. Its size would be its vulnerability. But you'd still end up with a couple of square kilometers of dead Chtorran flesh. And that's a much bigger problem, because dead Chtorran flesh is a place where Chtorran decomposition occurs. Decomposition isn't destruction, it's simply a biological transformation of life from one state into another. A dead Chtorran—of any kind—is simply a place for a different set of Chtorran creatures to grow and in their turn become food for more Chtorran creatures and ultimately it's all just more Chtorran flesh. Stop thinking of it as a creature, or even as a set of creatures, and see it as a much larger process. The whole ecological system functions as a process for turning local biomass into Chtorran biomass, whether any specific part of it is composing or decomposing."

Anderson was clearly annoyed. Annoyed at the distraction, annoyed at the conversational tangent. Annoyed that he couldn't get a clean and simple answer. And at the same time, annoyed at his own curiosity. "So if you already knew what you would find, why did you come?"

"I came to find what I didn't know what I would find."

"And—?"

"It's not all Chtorran down there."

"Eh?"

"There are Terran creatures living in that soup. I smelled flounders, crabs, dartfish, possibly even some Atlantic cod."

"Are you sure?"

"You've sunk cameras into the beast. You have thousands of hours of video. But you and your boffins have assumed that everything you see is Chtorran. It isn't. The Chtorran ecology is opportunistic. It assimilates everything it touches. Like polar bears. Like me. What you're seeing in that soup—that's the Chtorran ecology learning how to use what's already here. Life on Earth is already adapted to survival on Earth. The Chtorr is willing to adopt and adapt and take on new tenants, new partners. The convention is open to anything that can contribute something. When you finish analyzing all the video, it'll be obvious. The Chtorr is caretaking as much Terran biomass as it can manage. We saw that in the Amazon. It's just the fastest and easiest way for it to grow."

I could tell by his posture. He understood. This was another way to lose the war.

"Stop thinking of this as a war," I said. "That's why you're losing."

He shook it off. It wasn't that he didn't hear it. He didn't want to hear it. Not yet. He still wasn't ready to understand.

"All right." He came back to the present. "Can we neutralize it?" He nodded past the rollagon toward the drill site. He already knew the answer. But he needed to hear it from me. He'd appointed me the expert. I was the justification that took him off the hook.

I spoke slowly. Not for him. For the microphones. For the log. "Pumping poison into this thing, pumping radioactives into it—that will disrupt the process locally.

For a while. But you'll also end up poisoning the local environment, both land and sea, for most Earth species as well. So you don't gain anything. The Chtorran species will re-seed the area faster than Terran ones."

"What about fire?"

"You already know the answer. You don't have enough men or machines, and you don't have enough phosphorus or a reliable way to deliver it. And even if you could pump this thing full of inflammables, you'd have to keep burning it for a month or two, and even then, at least ten percent of its biomass would escape into the air or back into the sea. The cost-per-payoff ratio doesn't work."

"So we're back to the nuclear option?"

I nodded agreement. "The spread of devices your men are planting in this thing will certainly vaporize the beast." I waited for him to ask the next question.

"Will it work?"

I raised my gaze beyond. I looked outward. Past the edges of the grayish-pink landscape that we stood upon were endless fields of broken ice. I thought about the furies he wanted to unleash, how far the nuclear fires would scour down to the bedrock. It wasn't a rational analysis as much as it was a visceral one. He already had the projections. Turning back to him, I gave him half the answer he wanted to hear. "Considering this circumstance—yes, it will work. It will buy you time. But only here. This is a local solution, not a general one."

"That's good enough for the moment," he muttered unhappily. He looked across at me. Even through the goggles, I could read his bitter expression. "The folks at home need something to feel good about. If nothing else—" He trailed off. "Well, if nothing else, this will be good for morale."

"Yes," I repeated. "If nothing else." We both knew it was insufficient.

We came back around the rear of the rollagon, back to the drilling site, where Dale Hale Barksdale the Third was just rising up into the air. He saw us and waved. The motion caused him to swing in the wind.

"What the hell are you doing?" Anderson shouted angrily.

"What I came out here to do—get a first-hand look." He waved to the crane operator, motioning himself forward.

"Belay that!" ordered Anderson.

"Sorry, General," came the reply. "I'm a civilian contractor. I work for Barksdale Industrials." The crane turned and Barksdale swung out over the gaping hole in the Chtorran landscape. Barksdale motioned downward and the cables screeched. He sank down into the steaming wound.

Anderson's posture shifted, stiffened. This was not going to have a happy outcome. He touched the keypad on the back of his forearm, cycling through camera angles until his goggles showed him the close-up view of Barksdale's descent. I clicked up two separate angles myself—a close-up view to my left-eye, a wider angle through my right.

"It stinks down here," Barksdale called up.

"Don't touch anything," Anderson ordered.

"Why not?" Barksdale was already reaching as far down as he could, as if he wanted to palpate the Chtorran flesh. Perhaps he wanted to brag when he got back home. "Yes, I've touched the inside of an Enterprise Fish."

Before Anderson could answer Barksdale's question, his fingers brushed the dark purple skin of something that looked like a giant liver. Wet and pulpy. It rippled. Barksdale giggled. And touched it again. This time it shuddered. He touched it a third time; this time, he punched it. That was Barksdale's mistake.

The dark purple thing, whatever it was, it whipped around faster than it should have been able to—it opened itself as if it were all mouth, rose up and up and up, faster than the cables could turn, faster than the crane could lift—it came up high and higher, stretching and reaching to swallow Barksdale like a great white shark coming up beneath a hapless seal. It enveloped him completely. He was gone. For a moment, the liver-beast hung there on the cables, a purple pulpy shapeless mass, dripping ooze and gore down its sides, a bloody black rain of bile and skittering little things that had been pulled up with it. And then, with a terrible wet gurgling sound, it slid back down the cable, all the way back down into the churning squirming soup of things below the skin. The cable swung back and forth, empty. The grapples hung broken and apart.

"Well," I said, finally. "He was right. It's not *all* bad news."

General Anderson ignored the growing uproar in front of us and stared at me, astonished. "Now that's the McCarthy we used to know and love—"

THE PATIENT DRAGON

The dragon exploded.

Sitting on my shoulder, clucking to itself, it started to say something, and then flashed into fragments—

—a hot spray of spray of needle bits shattering against my right cheek, but before I could feel burning flesh, something grabbed me from behind, one arm around my neck, across my wind, pulling back so fast I couldn't breathe, a knee pushing up in my back, so hard my spine stretched until it cracked and then cracked again and then I couldn't feel anything and then—

—*noise*—

The light came up bright in my eyes, hiding the disembodied voices from me, I didn't care, was beyond caring, and the voices weren't speaking to me. They talked around me for a while, then floated away into the bright—

Came up again. Voices. One voice. Light, not too bright. "Can you hear me?" Open. Look around. Can't find voice. Blur out. Blur in. Again. Later? Voice again, "Squeeze my hand." Somebody's hand in somebody else's. Thought about squeezing. Couldn't feel any difference. Somebody crying? Me?

Came awake. Stared at ceiling. Soft music somewhere. The voice again. I turned my head. "Who are you?"

The woman's hair was close-cropped. She wasn't wearing any make-up. Blue scrubs. Stethoscope. "How are you feeling?"

"Not feeling anything," I said hoarsely.

She put a plastic straw between my lips. I sucked. Water. Cool. Wet. Swallowed. Still dry.

"How long—?"

"Three weeks. You were hurt pretty bad. They cracked your spine. You're in a body cast. We're going to begin regenerating as soon as we finish calibrating your matrix. We'll need you awake for that. Do you remember anything—?"

I tried to shake my head. Couldn't. "No."

"That's all right. I didn't think you would. Considering the head trauma. You may have lost some of your memories—when was your last upload?"

"I don't remember."

"You were attacked by a gang. A sniper took out your dragon, two or more baggers grabbed you. You're lucky to be alive. Your dragon got out half a distress call before it was shot, so it must have sensed the laser sight. There were police in the vicinity, all the alarms went off. The baggers dropped you and ran."

"Did they catch them?"

"No. I'm sorry."

Passed out—

Four and a half months of rehabilitation later ...

Whoever they were, they were good. Most people wear prosumer dragons. Professionals wear industrial dragons, those are a lot more expensive. Then there are the military-grade dragons, but those aren't available without the right kind of clearance. And then there are the special-purpose dragons that no one can buy. Mine was one of them. Had been one of them.

The new dragon? Samsung 9007-R model, with Balthazaar-2 modifications and synchronous integration. I'd lost a lot of wet memory. But the insurance company had my backups and had been restoring me concurrent with full brain regrowth. The new dragon impressed itself with my ID, linked to the insurance-backup, and did a data-suck. Backup Inc. had a complete record of everything the splattered dragon had been thinking right up to the moment it flashed out of existence. Nothing lost.

Nothing lost. Only wetware, and that was being phased out anyway. I'd been on the slow track to immortality. Regretted that I hadn't paid the higher premium and tracked faster. No matter, past that now. Emotional core damage had been charted and software reconstruction would proceed with tissue regeneration.

Fiber optic spine installed, polytanium wrapped. Info-flex flow, five hundred and twenty-five times faster than unaugmented nervous system. Polymer-carbon spine installed. Nine hundred times harder than bone. Nanotech sensors impregnated. Twelve hundred times more sensitive than surface neurons. Not quite military-issue, but durable enough.

Couldn't give it a lot of thought while reassembling. Didn't have the data-suck and rehab held me in a healing mode. But after the legs were certified, I was jogging again, twelve miles every morning, riding the endurance model. That gave me an hour a day to think. Oxygenated blood working the meat.

Balthazaar-2 whispered in my ear. Analyzing. The questions had been chugging for half a year. What were the baggers after? Me? The previous dragon? Something else? Did they get it—or not?

There's no profit in meat-bagging. It's cheaper to grow organs. And safer. More profit in bagging plug-ins. Except mine weren't all that fresh. I was slow-tracking, waiting for the investments to trigger before the next upgrades. Besides, if you're going to bag, you go after the body with Sony parts, you don't target the Wal-Mark line. Some of my parts had been broken—deliberately so—but nothing was missing. So the baggers weren't legging.

Obviously, not the dragon. They splattered it first. And even if they could have netted, foamed, and immobilized the drac, it would have burnt its ram in the first

0.05 seconds of capture, leaving only a useless wad of carbolyne-polymer, bio-plastic, and trace metals.

Analysis of the attack and wound patterns showed these boylettes were pros. Not a gang. Gangs are sloppy. A gang wouldn't have splattered the lizard; they'd have taken me out with a head-shot; that's assuming they wanted the meat or the parts. So, no—this was something else.

So, if meat and parts were accounted for, what else was missing? Approximately twelve hours of short-term meat-memories. Probably less. What happened in the twelve hours prior to the bagging? Except ... anything I would have seen, heard, or spoken aloud, the dragon would have monitored, filed, uploaded. So taking out short-term doesn't destroy any records. The worst it can do is erase any private cogitations, and even those were relayed and uploaded through the drac.

Not a lot of possibilities here. Balthazaar politely reviewed the possibilities. I studied the proferred menu. The wine list—the baggers hadn't had time to get what they wanted—which didn't make sense, pros know how to slash and grab. Item two, appetizers—they didn't want anything at all. They were just practicing. Statistically unlikely. Item three, entrees—somebody wanted/needed to put me out of action. Possible, but no candidates on the radar. I'd been keeping my nose and most other parts of my rented body clean for at least 18 months since my last round of upgrades. And if that was the case, then why bag and run? Why leave me repairable? A personal mortar shot would have been just as easy and would have terminated the corporeal expression permanently. And finally, dessert and after-dinner coffee—the goal was to have me in repair, so persons unknown could stinker my upgrades. Best guess. Except that all my upgrades tested pure. And I'm not talking about vanilla testing either.

Enforcement Authority had sifted the facts, come up with no useful heuristic, then moved on to other issues. But EA never takes it personal, that's the blind spot—that's why people like me exist.

So? Who? Why? What was changed?

If anything, everything. All new and improved. And a lot less meat than before. Still female—approximately. Mostly. These and that. Never got around to switching back. Turned female for a case, enjoyed the ride well enough to stay curious, left the package in place and practiced a new set of skills. Whored around for a while, rode a few men, killed two, and collected the bounties. Some people still believed in gender, I didn't. Whatever worked. But I still thought like a male. Not a handicap in my line.

Being in repair and rehab for the better part of a year put me ten years behind on the learning curve. Even with data-pumps, channeling, and pre-paid upgrades, even with Balthazaar, I'd still spend years playing catch-up. A mad caucus race— you can't catch up, the tech evolves faster than your ability to assimilate. An endless game. Not cost-effective. I had a six-month bubble in my pipeline. I was off the A-Team. So the company paid my medicals and handed me an early retirement. I'd still list as a reserve unit, but the effect was the same. Maybe that was the object of the exercise—somebody didn't want me employed. It worked. Whatever else was pending, I wasn't.

Leaving me to freelance.

Which might have been the point of the whole exercise anyway. Somebody needed hands. The job was probably dirty. They'd find me when they thought I was hungry enough.

I disappeared.

Out of the box, off the rails, over the hill and through the woods—stealth-retrofit took me off the grid. I caromed off three continents and ended up in Morocco, sitting on an old wooden chair under a drooping awning of faded yellow silk, a sweltering afternoon street café, sipping that hard bitter coffee that roasts itself in the burlap as it works its way up the scorched African coast on camelback, watching the table-top laser zap flies out of the air and listening to the news-buzz. Balthazaar 2 proxied around the edges, chuckling to himself as he constructed a model of the lockboxes we'd left behind. Someday, maybe, the investments would climb out of their graves, but not this week. If I had bothered to check my feelings, I would have felt like I looked—leathery and hard, used up. Not a good look for any female, and in this place, suspicious as well. It was time to move. So when Balth whispered it had a job offer, I said, "Tell me."

The drac angled its wings to catch the shifting sunlight. Feeding on photons. Its voice was dispassionate. Take the train south. Get off at K-station. Thought about it for a while, considered options—there were none to consider. They were paying for the ticket, what the hell, nothing was happening here and I needed a change of scenery.

I got off at the base of Kilamanjaro. Ordered beignets and cocoa at the café. Excellent view of the catapult. Great shuddering booms every time a cargo-pod launched, slicing up the side of the mountain and hurling east into the upper reaches of the atmosphere, sometimes firing course-correcting rockets on the way up. When the window was good, launches came every thirty seconds; as fast as the batacitors could recharge. But now that the Ecuador beanstalk was operational, sending slow-pods up the cables night and day, the business model here was shifting to shock-resistant cargos and harder launches, mostly nitrogen and water for Lunar expansion. Later on, industrial machinery. All those folks who'd believed that the beanstalk would put the catapults out of business were wrong. Every oxygen-user who bought a one-way up the line needed at least a dozen catapult pods of CHON-maintenance to precede him.

From time to time, K-station still did slow-launches—when the windows were open. Some folks didn't trust the beanstalk, especially the old-timers, others didn't want to take a 24-hour elevator ride. Most of the local emigres didn't want to pay the cost of traveling halfway around the equator, not when there was a convenient facility on their own continent. And there were those who just didn't want to leave a paper trail. While the catapult had a much more limited set of orbital options than the beanstalk, the company made up for it by asking a lot less questions about cargoes and destinations. Pick an orbit, pick a trajectory, we'll launch you, no questions asked. Once you achieve insertion, our job is done, you're on your own.

Asked Balth for a menu. He'd picked up the personality of his predecessor—hard not to—and showed me a list of possibilities, all of them low-confidence. Local contract? Possibly, but lots of local contractors could pick up the work, no need to import someone with my talents. Off-world? More likely, but most of the off-world employers had their own onsite skillage. Unless this was an old-fashioned, "Call our friends in Detroit" operation. Except, I'd never been from Detroit.

At the bottom of the menu, one item, flashing red—a no-confidence hunch. *This whole thing is too convenient.* **B-2**'s built-in paranoia processor. Conviction without evidence.

The fat man, it's always a fat man, sat down opposite me. The chair groaned with his weight. He could have rented an office, but it would be a waste. All of his business is done in cafes. The fat man waggled a finger at the waiter, pointed at my order, then at himself, the universal gesture, I'll have what she's having. "You like the launches?" he asked.

I answered with a shrug. "I've turned off my ears. They're too loud. Painful."

He nodded. "How's your health?"

"You already know the answer to that or you wouldn't have offered the job."

"Ever been to Luna?"

"You know that too."

"Want to go back?"

Another shrug. Luna has its disadvantages. But if the money is right....

The waiter brought his beignets and chocolate. He dipped and bit. Around a mouthful, he asked, "Can you take a five-gee launch?"

Thought about it. Five gees for thirty seconds, including scramjet boost to orbital velocities. Painful. **B-2** wasn't keen on the idea, the meat parts might bruise, but the risk of permanent injury could be minimized. At that speed, we weren't talking passenger launch—someone wanted to ship me as cargo. I would not be getting my passport stamped.

"How long in transit?"

"68 hours, with bounce down on farside, pickup within six hours. Hypothermic sedation will reduce your fuel and oxy consumption to less than 20%. We'll provide margin up to 33. You'll reanimate in a Class-3 medical facility. Minor risk, but manageable."

"And—?"

"You'll receive further instructions from the client."

"That's it?"

"I'm a headhunter," he said. "Nothing more." **B-2** rang a bell in my brain. "Liar, liar, pants on fire." Yeah, I'd already figured that out. But whatever else he was, whoever else he was working for, he'd never say. Couldn't say. He only knew the information he needed when he needed to know it, the rest of the time it didn't exist. I'd been there, I knew how that worked.

"What about return?"

"The client will guarantee passage back to Earth—or to any other destination you choose. Mars, the belt, the rings, how far away do you want to go?"

"How much?"

"The client guarantees 18 months of maintenance, plus 500% on completion. The guarantee is already on file with your public account. You can transfer it to any private account you choose. In the event of your death, contract is immediately terminated."

"How about the client's death?"

"Irrelevant. The money is in escrow." He finished stuffing his face, wiped himself with a napkin. "I need your answer. We've got a window in three hours." He slapped a bill on the table, enough to cover both of us. "If you accept, follow me." He levered himself to his feet, the chair sighed in relief. I watched skeptically as he waddled off in the general direction of the loading district. Of course. Overhead, a steady stream of sealed pods, already bearing inspection stickers, rolled on white steel tracks toward the launch arrays.

B-2 whispered. "It's a standard contract. Protected mode. Hazardous duty allotment. Off-world bonuses. Insured. Registered. Encrypted. Validated. Anonymous, of course." Of course. Dirty. Very dirty. Just how very dirty, I wouldn't know until it was too late. The contract guaranteed right of refusal of course, with a kill-fee attached—but if the work was dirty enough the kill-fee would be paid with prejudice. The extreme kind.

I asked Balth, "Am I bored, desperate, or curious?"

"Yes."

None of those were good enough reasons to take the job, but those weren't the reasons I decided to take it.

I stood up, arranged myself. Wide-brimmed hat, sunglasses. Long red hair—attached to the hat, not my head. Loose-fitting top and tits that would come off with my bra. Knee-length skirt revealing legs that went all the way up—those were real. I could walk in one door looking like a wet dream, drop three articles of clothing, reverse the skirt, flatten the shoes, and walk out the other door looking like the teenage boy who'd had that dream. All the important musculature was metallized and trimmed. I could take down a trooper in power armor if I had to, but it would be painful and expensive. The important thing is not to look powerful. You want the other guy to underestimate the package.

I followed the fat man's scent trail. After-shave so cloying and thick it showed up visible. **B-2** ran background checks. Not a high-risk district, security cams everywhere. Deep analysis results pending further processing. This was a political job. Possible assassination. Target unknown. Lunar politics a gray area. Most likely target, person or persons invisible. Invisible Luna, off the Lunar network. Most likely client, Lunar Authority. Or just as likely, the reverse. Most likely reason—who knows?

Followed the cheap after-shave down a narrow side street. One-story industrials, no signs. Everything whitewashed and sun-faded. The street cornered, revealing a narrow space between two shabby buildings, barely wide enough for me, let alone the fat man. Nevertheless.

The passage was deeply shadowed, the overhang made it a corridor. Halfway through, on the left, a widening. Step into and beyond, a small gloomy cube. A single overhead panel for light, very dim and so old its color temp has slid visibly into the red. The fat man was nowhere to be seen. A wooden table and a faceless bot.

"Do you agree to the contract?"

"I agree."

Balth notarized and filed the paperwork.

The bot waited for confirmation. Half a second. "Take off your clothes."

Balth jumped down to the table. I tossed hat and hair aside, also sunglasses. Shrugged off the blouse and khaki skirt. Kicked off the sandals. The bra unsnapped in the front. I stepped out of my panties. Hairless and naked, I turned slowly while the bot angled scanners on the ends of a half-dozen arms, all the way down and all the way up again. "Spread your legs wide. Hold your arms away from your body. Bend over. Open your mouth." Everything but turn your head and cough.

"Deactivate your dragon now."

"Balth, go to sleep." I thought about Fred, the orange cat, and Balth knew I was serious. But Fred always slept with one ear open and so would Balth.

The bot put a shielded carry-bag on the table. "Put the dragon in the box." Not a surprise. But Balth had listened from inside shielded boxes before.

"Now lie down on the table. Disconnect all non-biological processes."

I hesitated half a second. Intentionally. That hesitation was my last upload to the repository. Encrypted. If they were paranoid enough, they could have stopped me, but if they were that paranoid, I wouldn't have taken the job.

The table was old. Its surface was cool.

"Thank you—"

—came awake, my body screaming. Arms and legs and back still sore and aching from the launch, stomach still queasy from the weightlessness, neck hurting from the bounce-down. I recognized the pain; they'd dropped the pod in a blueberry, a bubble of inflatables. It had probably caromed across the surface for a half-dozen kilometers, and when it stopped bouncing, if it was still green, it called for pickup.

I was on the floor. A padded floor. I don't mind being on my back if I'm having a good time, but this was not my idea of a good time. I didn't have the strength to sit up yet, so I rolled over onto my side. It would have been a mistake in Earth-gee, just a nuisance here, but I'd already turned off the pain. Nothing was broken, I knew what was stiff and sore, I didn't need any more information.

This was an inflatable. I'd seen enough of them. Portable and transparent, a two-person bubble, sitting in the shadow of a Lunar sunset. Or sunrise. I'd need an hour or two to see which way the shadows were going. Monochrome scenery. Dry airless slopes. A sharp horizon close enough to jump over.

Someone had left me here to recover while they decided. If they decided one way, someone or something would come and get me. If they decided the other way, they wouldn't bother. And after a long-enough while, it wouldn't matter. Convenient.

Ration packets. Water. Protein-bars. The usual life-support modules—heater, recycler, humidifier, etc. And a very passive first-aid bot. But no Balth. Not unexpected. I thought *louder*. Nope. No Balth. I was working naked. Literally.

A quick internal status check—I was green all over, some yellow spots where muscles and organs were still recovering from the journey, but nothing red. I was mostly optimal and confidence was high. But I was very much on my own.

I stood up. Stretched. Went through the whole cycle of exercises. Twice. Three times. Watched my internals and thought about going for four. I wasn't in any hurry. It was thinking time. But without B-2 there were things I couldn't think. On the other hand, perhaps the me-time was a good thing. Time to learn how to be *me* again. Too much time on the dragon, sometimes I forget which one of us I am.

I read somewhere—if Balth were here, he'd tell me exactly where—that most people stay connected all the time simply because they can't stand being alone with themselves. That's a cruel assertion, but possibly true. Being alone—? Well, Sartre was wrong. Hell isn't other people. It's yourself. Nobody can torture you as good as you can.

—stopped that vicious little thought before it chewed any deeper. I knew what was at the bottom and I didn't want to go there. Checked my blood sugar, aha, and opened a water bottle and unwrapped a ration bar. Ate very slowly. Concentrated only on the physical act of biting, chewing, swallowing, breathing. Three bites, four, five, another sip of water, and I put it aside. Now I knew.

My timing was off and it wasn't the launch and the weightlessness and the bounce-down, it wasn't the Lunar gravity, and it wasn't the absence of B-2. It was *me*.

This was good news as much as it was bad news. The bad news was that I was off-center. Even worse, I'd been off-center a long time, possibly even before B-1 was splattered. Balth had been compensating. The good news was that I was aware of it now. Being aware is the first step.

I sat down, full-lotus, closed my eyes, open palms resting on knees, and focused on my breathing. Breathing is good. Deep breaths. Listen to the air, inspire, expire, those are the options. Compose or decompose. Listened to my heartbeat, listened to the blood rushing through my veins. Listened to myself. Listened to the thoughts scrambling and clamoring and scuttling around. Listened myself to awareness.

Then—finally. Conversation. What do I want? Who am I? What do I need? What next? The answer to all of them was the same. Nothing. This is it. The now is now until it stops being now. The need to be more than now isn't me, it belongs to the story that lives in me.

Okay.

One more conversation. This one, with my personal god, name of Ghu. The church of Ghu is very clear on this. Ghu isn't there. Ghu is never there. Ghu is the smartest of all the gods. He respects us so much, he has chosen not to exist. He doesn't interfere, he doesn't make demands. You have full responsibility for yourself.

Ghu, give me strength. No. You already have all the strength you're ever going to have. Learn how to use it.

Ghu, give me peace. You want peace? Create it yourself. If you're not strong enough to create peace, you don't deserve it.

See how it works? You can ask Ghu for anything. Because he doesn't exist, the answer is always no. There are no holidays to celebrate, no sins to atone for, no rituals to perform. Thank Ghu for that. Try and figure out the sabbath when sunset only comes once a month? No thanks.

Ghu, thanks for not being there. Thanks for not listening. Thanks for giving me the chance to figure it out for myself. Thanks for respecting my personal climb toward sentience.

When the smile returned to my face, I was centered again. The question is never *who am I?* The question is always *who am I creating?*

I knew the answer to that question. That's why I was here.

You don't hear sounds on Luna. But you can feel vibrations—if you listen hard enough. If your butt is sensitive enough. Hit the moon hard enough and the whole thing rings like a bell. The vibrations in my butt weren't big but they were close and getting closer. I opened my eyes, looked to the right.

There, on the close horizon, a strider. An airless pillbug, tall and spindly—a cargo-pod, riding vertical, slow-motioning across the gray. Spotlights bright enough to dazzle. No distinctive markings, no identifying colors or signs.

The strider arrived, stopped, squatted. The pillbug's legs bent out and back, lowering the pod almost to the ground. The pilot studied me, perched behind the controls. Young, dark, close-cropped hair. Shaded eyes. No expression. Speaking to a headset, listening to a reply. Nods an affirmative and bends to the controls. Right. Somebody was about to do something stupid. I stood up in readiness. The pilot glanced up, then bent back to his controls. Something *very* stupid.

One of the pillbug's upper arms unfolded. The tool-set on the wrist rotated. The blade flashed bright in the scalding sunlight. The arm came down and forward and the blade came upward through the plastic of the portable. I whooshed out with the exploding air, leapt and caught the rising arm—bounced hand-over-hand up to the shoulder, grabbed the handle to the airlock and wrenched it open, all this even before the last air exploded out of my lungs—didn't wait for the machinery to cycle, ripped open the inner door and yanked the idiot pilot from his perch. He went flying backward out through the airlock, a surprised expression on his face—

I hadn't lost my touch. The hatches were undamaged. They sealed and shone green. While the atmosphere rebuilt, I took inventory. Aside from some cosmetic damage, I was still operational. But now I had more questions than before. And less time than ever to consider them.

A quick check of the systems boards; the pillbug had to have monitors through-out, but if there was a kill-switch it wasn't in any of the usual places, or even the unusual places. I didn't waste much time looking for it. Whoever had sent this idiot errand-boy must have seen what happened to him. They could have launched a missile by now. Depending on how far over the horizon they were, I had maybe three minutes to evacuate. First thing, strip the comms. Less than thirty seconds to pop the panel, pull the module, and disappear from the web.

I slid into the harness and put the damn thing into gear, I still remembered how to moonwalk, and even if I'd forgotten, the software would correct—but could I run? Better than that, could I bounce? Yes, I could. Not fast enough to outrun a missile, but far enough that it wouldn't find me where it was looking.

I found a rhythm and fell into it. A hundred klicks should be enough, I could do that in two hours, ninety minutes if the terrain was right. But there were other options too. Plugging into the system board gave me a god-view of the terrain and I found what I wanted almost immediately, a rill deep enough to hide in. This was good. I veered right and watched the horizon. The cliff came up quickly and I leapt— used short bursts to soften the touchdown, caught myself, whirled and scrambled backward up the broken rocks into the darkness beneath an overhang. Powered the damn pillbug down as fast as I could. Even the life-support. I was probably good for 30 minutes, maybe an hour. Would the air get stuffy first or chilly? Interesting question. Worry about it some other time. I'd already proven I could go without air, if I needed to. The meat was hardened. I'd paid extra for that.

First things first. They had not dropped me here by accident. So...who sent the pillbug?

If it were my employers, they wouldn't have. They'd have known from the pre-launch scan how thoroughly I was hardened. Even the meat was resistant. Slashing open the bubble was an idiot's mistake. The advantage was mine from the moment the idiot made the assumption that I could be killed so easily.

So if it hadn't been my employers, then the pillbug had come from someone else—someone who knew that my employers were importing a package and who had the tools to keep that package from arriving. Big boys.

Another possibility. Slim one. My employers were testing me—to see if I was as good as represented. But they would have already known what I was when they scanned me. So was it likely they'd sacrifice a stooge just to find out what they already knew? No.

A third possibility. My employers had decided they didn't want me after all. But they couldn't afford the possibility that I might survive the bubble, they needed to verify my termination. But their headhunter hadn't fully informed them on the capabilities of the package they were renting, so they'd underestimated me. No. That assumed stupidity on the part of my employers. Not very likely. On the gameboard stupidity gets cured quickly. As one unlucky young man had already discovered.

So the pillbug belonged to the enemy. 85% probability. Balthazaar might disagree on the accuracy of my number, but he wouldn't have argued the estimation.

Time to search the bug. Found tools, supplies, food, water, medi-kit, but not a lot of information. Very annoying. Information leaks everywhere—except the information you need never leaks when or where you want it. Only when and where you don't. Even worse, it's almost always your information that leaks, never the other guy's.

I couldn't stay here long. Sooner or later, they'd track the bug. Luna's skies are wide open. Satellites scanning all up and down the spectrum would track the heat and electromagnetic signatures of the walker. And eventually its trail of footprints. `All it needed was someone to ask the right question of the right database. Even the best-shielded technology leaves ripples if you know where to look. I had to get somewhere I could abandon the bug and disappear into the crowd.

And from there, find out if I still had a contract. I didn't care that someone had tried to kill me, that's part of the business—I cared that they might try it again. Strictly from a tactical position, I would prefer to neutralize that possibility as soon as possible.

The vehicle was clean. Even its memories had been wiped. It was as if it had come into existence only thirty seconds before it appeared over my horizon. But there were other ways to track it back to its source. Backtrack its footprints in the Lunar dust, that would be easiest—but it was likely this machine had erased its own tracks. I could scan for residual heat trails or search the satellite maps myself—but that might expose me to net-sniffing agents. That left me with probabilities and logic.

Assume the idiot pilot had traveled the shortest course, a straight line. Follow that line backward to...? Yes, that's what an idiot would do.

I allowed myself a power-snooze, forty-five minutes of recovery time. Refocus the beast. Consider the possibilities. Yes, I had to move fast—but not stupid. I waited until the temp inside hit fifty and the meat was asking for sugar to burn so it could shiver. Just this side of hypothermia, I powered up and hit the ground running. South for fifteen minutes, to where the rill widened out onto the plain of the mare. Set a wide course back, not quite paralleling my outward trek. If anything, angling farther from the origin point. I'd circle around and come at them from behind. If it bought me thirty seconds, it was worth the effort.

It did. And it was. I came up through a shallow crater, striding low, came over the rim and the station was laid out before me. Six inflatables, three of them habitats; and a scattering of low humps—burrows. I kicked the strider forward. Thirty-three seconds across the dead gray plain and then the machine went dead. Not unexpected. A remote shutdown.

Plan B. I popped the hatches and bounced out naked, brandishing a cold blade in each hand. If I'd still had my long red hair, and if I could have screamed like a banshee, the effect would have been even more terrifying—but nobody expects to see a nearly-bald, sword-wielding valkyrie bounding naked across the Lunar landscape either. I had two minutes to terminate the meat. The machines would be another problem. I saw some suited figures scrambling, but they weren't an immediate concern. They were more vulnerable than I was.

I slashed all three of the habitat inflatables, then punched holes in the roofs of every burrow I saw. Air and moisture geysered in high quick fountains. The suits were bouncing toward the last inflatables. I wanted to preserve at least one of them. Two of them were farms. If I could avoid killing the animals, I would. I bounced for the last one.

The insight hit me as I pushed into the valve and grabbed oxygen. Long deep gasps. Painful. I can handle vacuum without exploding, that doesn't mean it doesn't hurt. Air rasped down the tubes like acid. This wasn't accidental. Nothing is. Especially not in this biz. I'm the bullet, locked and loaded, aimed and fired. Target neutralized.

This wasn't about the dragon or the upgrades or what I knew or when I knew it. It was never personal. It was just somebody grabbing and firing a particularly useful piece of artillery on a specifically calculated long-range trajectory. Me. And I never had a choice in the matter. Once fired, the bullet is going to do its job no matter what it thinks.

Or I could lay down and die. That would show them.

Forty seconds and I'm in a wrap-me suit. Slapping seals, reading green, and bouncing out the lock on the other side. Scan for heat-signatures, two already over the horizon, a third rolling away in a wheelie, carving a line of dust behind him like an arrow.

Okay, these boylettes were not expecting a war, weren't prepped for this. So why did the pillbug pilot want to kill me—? Without **B-2**, the menu wasn't on the table. Fuggit. I'd have to do this the old-fashioned way, inside my own head. Click-click. This wasn't the farm it pretended to be.

Crap. The top was only a nipple. The rest of the teat was buried. Probably deep. And probably already in lockdown. Which wouldn't be a problem if I had **B-2**, but I didn't, and that was a clue as well. Whatever might be under, I wasn't getting in. I was supposed to fail. And die.

I decided to dislike my employer. There are rules. Sometimes you make them, sometimes you break them. But mostly, you don't. Otherwise, you get kicked out of the game. I decided to do some kicking.

First, find out where I am.

LPS put me south of the equator. No Earth in the sky put me on the far side. A wheelie has a range of a hundred klicks, and the boylette had headed off to the east, maybe looking for line of sight to the marble. But not necessarily. He could also have been retreating to another settlement. Farside was pocked with invisibles, some of them heavily armed.

I could follow his tracks for about thirty klicks, that was my range. Anything beyond that, I was dead. Or I could start digging and discover the hard way what defenses were hidden under the farm.

Or...I could bounce.

Risky, but not impossible.

I liked that better. I didn't like the way this game was played. But I had to move fast.

Every settlement has racks of tanks. Liquid O, Liquid N. Some of those tanks were big enough to keep a settlement going for a month, if necessary. I chose the largest full tank of N. Waldoed it from the rack, outside again, and pointed the business end down. Hooked myself to a handle, and opened the bottom valve all the way. Liftoff. Did the math in my head, counted the seconds, then shut the valve and coasted east. Not quite orbital, but I had at least a couple revolutions. LPS showed my course on the heads-up. I could drop at Armstrong, Gagarin, or Clarke.

Never got the chance.

One and a half times around, Lunar Authority tried to intercept. Corvette class drone, ultra-maneuverable, came up from below, curious about the flying gas tank with a suit attached. But you can't catch a target that doesn't want to be caught. They read the IDs on the tank, the suit as well, and told me to surrender. Not on my menu, sorry, no thanks. Aimed for the ground and fired. They'd track me, of course. It's a lot harder to disappear on Luna than on the marble, but it's doable. You just have to move fast and be smart about how you move. By the time they caught up, I wouldn't be me anymore.

Put the gas tank down at the Triple-Cross—appropriately named. Three cable-lines cross. Traffic to and from six compass points, with another crossing only sixty klicks west—that would be the first place they'd look. Burned through three identities faster than the locals could track, came up as an unlicensed boy, hustling for tricks, picked up a lonely tourist and caught the second train southeast with him. Industrial stations all the way to the pole. Back around to farside and I could grab a ride on the beanstalk, cargo drop back home. That was what I wanted them to think anyway.

Left the tourist at the second stop, burned two more IDs, and caught a ride on an outbound truck to the eastern solar array in Mare Humorum, this time as a female security manager, an octogenarian. The real one had died in a tube blowout two days before, but her body was still unrecovered so she was not yet officially deceased. What I needed was an access to a dragon—one that wouldn't set off alarms from here to Punjab. I could grab an industrial. It wouldn't have all the bells and whistles of **B-2**, but I could grab a bootstrap.

The trucker didn't ask questions, I didn't answer any. I'd spotted him as a part-time invisible, he'd made me as an illegal. We chatted in Black Spanglish. He liked Luna, but missed the peppered chorizos of Arizona, grilled over mesquite. I pretended to miss them too. We passed a bottle of Tequila back and forth and let the truck drive itself.

By the time Lunar Authority had figured out where to look for me, I was already under the roof of the solar array, ten thousand cones rotating slowly, turning the avalanche of photons into an alternating current of electrons. The installation was nearly self-maintaining, monitored by drones, bots, dragons, and the occasional dirt-goblin. A scattering of habitats and maintenance burrows pocked the naked gray slope overlooking. I avoided those and headed for an equipment locker under the closest edge.

Guessed right. Racks of spares. Including a dozen dragons. Wonderful. I activated all of them, gave each one a handle to a different ID and turned them loose to travel randomly across the surface of Luna. They were cheap units, but I transferred cash from a dummy account anyway. Whatever else I might be, I'm not a thief. Kept three of the dragons for myself, in case I needed to burn one. Or two.

Stashed all three in a duffel and grabbed a ride on a cargo-bot. The other dragons were doing the research I needed, they'd bounce it off a couple thousand relays, and put it in a place where I could find it later. There was nothing I could do that couldn't be traced, but I could make whoever was tracing work a very long time navigating the maze. By the time they found the cheese, the rat would be long gone. I had to assume pursuit.

Came up for air the underside of Turtledome, or what was left of it after the war. Most of the burrows had survived, of course, and a good deal of the gridwork that had once supported the sky still arched overhead. But when the dome collapsed, it had dropped a thick layer of lunar-crete across the basin, giving the undercity serious protection from micro-meteorites. Instead of rebuilding the sky, Turtledome burrowed deeper. Ten, twenty levels—no one knew how deep anymore. Invisible Luna wanted it that way and Authority didn't have the resources to go digging for answers.

Checked into a no-questions-asked hole in the ground, plugged into the net, proxied around for a bit, tunneled through various anonymizers, until I finally got to my own VPN, and took a long hot soak in the raw data.

My employer did not exist. There was no record of the contract. There was cash in the escrow account, but that was set to evaporate soon. Nicely done. I had to admit that was a respectable piece of work. **B-2** did not exist anymore either. Okay, I had assumed that from the moment I'd awakened after bounce-down. Checking his status, he'd disappeared shortly after deactivation, probably destructed.

Pinged **Balthazar 3**. Wake up.

He should have arrived on Luna only a few hours after me. And at a dropbox half a bounce away. Ponged back almost instantly. Confidence highest. Lotsa good stuff to share.

What happened to **B-2**?

Not immediately obvious, but not too hard to guess—they scavenged the little guy. Despite being boxed, he'd transmitted anyway. Think quantum entanglement dots. No time-lag, everything goes. The whole enchirito. GPS-tracking, datadumping, brave little warrior right up to the moment they pulled his plug. But he'd offloaded everything the moment they'd boxed him, so there was nothing for the black hats to rummage. But that wasn't what they wanted anyway—not the data, just a **B-2** unit. An untraceable one. For no good purposes. Invisible Luna? Maybe. Lunar Authority trying to crack Invisible Luna? More likely. This went deep and I had fragments only.

Someone had splatted **B-1**—fragging me was merely a cover. Waited until I was back on the grid with **B-2**, made me an offer I wouldn't refuse, separated us and dropped me on Luna far away from anywhere. No planned pickup. I was supposed to die out there, forgotten.

Except they dropped me too near some innocents with a secret. Or maybe they weren't so innocent. Why did the guy in the strider try to kill me? Maybe that was the point—to drop me someplace they don't like trespassers.

None of it made sense.

And that explained everything.

Based on the evidence, these were paladins. Corporate blackhats. Mercenaries on a mission of their own design. Incompetents.

Somebody had hired somebody who had hired somebody else who—as it worked its way down the chain of deniability, finally a dozen somebodies later—had hired some testosterone-infused bluffoons who had no idea who had really hired them or even what it was they were supposed to accomplish anymore, so they went off and did what they wanted to do anyway, regardless of any original objective.

Me? I was just a bump in the road. A thing to be used as part of the larger plan. Whatever that was.

Like I said. Incompetents.

Didn't matter one way or the other. Whoever they were, they shot first. Waived all right to courtesy.

B-3 pinged. Someone is scanning for unusual travel patterns. They're searching for anomalies. Trying a track-back. Will report shortly.

Ahh.

If they're looking for me, they know I'm not dead.

Which means they know they underestimated me.

Which also means, things are going to get ugly. Uglier than that. Real fast.

Told **B-3** to put a message in the system where they were sure to find it: "I might be a bitch, but I'm not your bitch."

Once they scrambled, the rest was easy. The last surviving piece of **B-2** woke up and reported—

First, I collected the kill fee.

Then—

I won't say who and I won't say how, I don't want anyone to know, and I might need to do it again someday. Most of all, I don't want to give anyone else ideas. The new crater is impressive and that should be warning enough.

You don't mess with a girl's dragon.

Writing this story was intense. I surprised myself, several times over. But I couldn't have done it without Ctein's input and insight.

BUBBLE AND SQUEAK
BY DAVID GERROLD & CTEIN

Hu Son ran.

He ran for the joy of it, for the exhilaration—for that moment of hitting the wall and breaking through into the zone, that personal nirvana of physical delight. What others called "runner's high." A sensation like flight—Hu's feet didn't pound the ground, they tapped it as he soared through the early morning air.

A bright blue cloudless sky foretold a beautiful day. A sky so clear and deep you could fall into it and never come back. Later, the day would heat up, glowing with a summery yellow haze, but right now—at this special moment—the beachfront basked in its own perfect promise.

Hu usually started early, when Venice Beach was mostly deserted, all sand and palm trees and stone benches, all the store fronts sleeping behind steel shutters. It was the best time to run. Hu liked the crisp air of dawn, the solitude of the moment, the feeling that the day was still clean, still waiting to be invented—before the owners could ruin it with their displays of tacky, tasteless, and vulgar kitsch.

Some of the cafes were open early though, and by the time Hu reached the Santa Monica pier, run its length and then headed back toward home, the morning air was flavored with the smells of a dozen different kinds of breakfast, the spices of all the various cuisines that flourished here.

Heading home, Hu passed other morning joggers. This was a favorite track. Nods were exchanged, or not—some of the runners were lost in hidden music, others in their personal reveries. He recognized most, he'd been running this track for more than a year. He was probably regarded as a regular by now.

The final leg now. He trotted past the last of the brash touristy areas. Later this strand would teem with summer crowds, exploring the brash souvenir stands, the ranks of T-shirts printed with single entendres, the displays of dreadful art, all the different fortune tellers and street performers, but right now, this community was still lazily awakening, coming back to life at its own pace. There were still the occasional shapeless lumps on the stone benches—the homeless, wrapped up against the chill of the night, waiting for the heat of the day to revive them. Even in July, the morning air still had a bite, with a salty flavor from the grumbling sea.

Hu turned and jogged up the narrow way that pretended to be a street, a block and a half, slowing down only in the last few meters. He hated to stop, hated to drop back into that other pace of life—the faster more frenetic life, where you weren't allowed to run, you had to walk, walk, walk everywhere.

He glanced at his wristband, looking to see where his numbers were today. Not bad. Not his personal best, but good enough. "Probably still stuck on the plateau," he muttered. "Gonna have to push to get off. Just not today."

Hu pushed through the back gate and started peeling off his T-shirt. He liked the feeling of the cold morning air cooling the sweat off his skin. He took a moment to slow down, to let himself ease down into this world, then finally stepped through the door and called affectionately, "Honey, I'm homo—" then headed straight for the shower.

Hu Son didn't just appreciate hot water, he loved the luxury of it. In eighteen months, he'd have his master's degree in cultural anthropology, and after that, he'd go for his doctorate, but already his studies had given him a clear sense of how lucky he was to be living in an age where clean water was taken for granted—and hot water available on demand.

California's drought had officially ended some years before, but Hu rarely lingered in the shower. Even at this remove, he could still hear his mother banging on the door, shouting, "Leave some for the rest of us!" Old habits endured. Today, however—today was special. So he took his time, soaping up and rinsing, three times over. He closed his eyes, paced his breathing, and allowed himself to sink into his personal contract with himself.

"I am powerful," he whispered. "I am vulnerable," he continued. And smiling, he concluded, "And I am loving." He repeated it a few times, a personal mantra, until it was no longer a declaration, only his renewed experience of himself. And then, one more phrase. "Especially today!" Opening his eyes, Hu nearly shouted that last. "Because today, I am getting married!"

An electric screech interrupted him—alarm sirens outside. It sounded like the whole city was howling. Like any other Angeleno, anyone who'd lived in the city more than six months, Hu ignored it. It was meaningless noise. Everything was noise, from the daily growl of motorcycles and Asian "rice-rockets" to the nightly screams of drunks and junkies.

Hu turned off the water, and heard James calling from the kitchen. "Hu, you need to get in here!" Something was wrong, James only called him Hu when he was upset. He grabbed a fresh towel and wrapped it around himself. A second towel for his hair and he headed toward the kitchen where James was standing, leaning with his back against the counter, a mug of tea in his hand—but focusing intensely on a small television on the end of the kitchen table. Without looking up, James held out the usual mug of tea for Hu.

Hu took it and pecked his fiancé on the cheek. "What's up, Bubble? What are all the sirens for? Some kind of test?" He didn't wait for an answer, he took his first sip. Chai.... "Ahh." He glanced toward the television. The president was talking.

"Now what? Are we at war?"

"It's Hawaii," said James.

"We're at war with Hawaii?"

"There's been a quake—"

Hu's buoyant mood evaporated. "Oh no. How bad?"

"Both Honolulu and Hilo were hit by tsunamis. Really big—the biggest ever." James turned to Hu. "When did your folks fly out?"

"They didn't. Dad needed an extra day. So they're flying out this evening, they'll catch up with us tomorrow at the hotel."

"No, they won't. And we won't be there either. Honolulu airport is gone."

"Wait. What?" At first, Hu didn't understand. How could an airport be gone? Then he realized what James was telling him. "That's not possible. A whole airport—?"

"And half the city—"

"Oh, shit," Hu said, his mug of tea suddenly forgotten in his hand. "That's—just bad."

On the TV, the president was still talking, a row of grim-faced people stood behind him. Or maybe it was a repeat. The scroll-bar across the bottom of the screen was filled with incomprehensible words. They moved too fast for him to make sense of them. And outside, the sirens still screamed.

"Shit!" said Hu. "All I wanted was one little honeymoon—" He became aware of the sirens again. "And what's all that noise about—? We're not— Shit! What's going on?"

James put down his coffee. He turned to Hu. He took Hu's mug from him. "Squeak. Sweetheart—" His expression was grim. "It's not just Hawaii. It's the whole California coast. The tsunami is headed for us now. We've got maybe three hours before it hits—"

"A tsunami? Here—?"

"A tsunami. Here. A mega-tsunami. Just like the movie, only bigger—"

"But that was only a movie—" Hu stopped in mid-sentence, remembering that movie, that scene.

James Liddle had been SCUBA diving since his teens. After college, he'd set up his own small company, specializing in SCUBA services to local studios. "Underwater? Let it be a Liddle thing. Call us!" Because of his skill, his professionalism, his dependability, and his charming good looks, he was on speed dial for several stunt coordinators.

More than once, James had been called in to teach various film and television actors how to dive safely—or at least look like they knew how to dive safely. More than once, he'd doubled for actors who were too valuable to the studios to be allowed to do their own diving, but he couldn't say who. Most of the bigger shoots involved non-disclosure agreements.

Hu's family had moved from Hong Kong to Vancouver when he was eight, where his father opened a consulting service/business school, where he taught westerners how to do business in China and occasionally set up deals himself.

When Hu was twelve, an aunt he'd never met died of cancer, so his mother came south to Los Angeles to manage her brother's large unruly family, she brought Hu with. As the new kid, as the Chinese kid, and also as the smallest and the smartest in his class, Hu was a target for bullies of all sizes—so his uncle enrolled him into a series of physical activities to build up not only his body, not only his ability to defend himself, but also his self-esteem. Eventually Hu studied karate, judo, Tae Kwan Do, and modern dance. By the time he was nineteen, Hu was earning extra money doing stunts in occasional action films. Though he never doubled for any of the major actors, he was often somewhere in the background—and in one particular picture, a comedy, he'd been featured as one of the dancing ninjas.

James and Hu had met at Culver studios. A massive team of stunt doubles had been assembled for a disaster picture, another overblown disaster picture, a fantasy of multiple simultaneous disasters—hurricanes, tornadoes, earthquakes, volcanoes, tidal waves, and the return of disco. Everyone knew the picture was going to be awful, it was assumed (though never spoken aloud) that nobody upstairs knew how bad it was—either that, or it was actually intended from the beginning to be a flop, a tax write-off, or perhaps even some bizarre kind of money-laundering. Who knew? The only people who understood Hollywood financing were alchemists, and few of them were ever allowed out of their dungeon laboratories into the light of day.

But on the ground, the money was good. A lot of people had a profitable summer working on the film. As with any big effort, there were sexual relationships, babies started, babies stopped, babies born, and of course, a few divorces and emotional breakdowns, plus a number of lifelong feuds begun and exercised, some in private, others in public.

James had worked for seven weeks on various underwater sequences. Hu had come aboard in the last week as a stunt-player, running from the onrushing water. The first few days, there was no actual water. All that was to be added later by a team of talented CGI artists in Hong Kong or New Delhi. Anyone whose name came before the credits would be taking home seven figures and points on the gross, but domestic jobs were shipped overseas in cost-cutting acts of dubious economy. But there was still work to be done locally.

They had to shoot one key scene on a stretch of Wilshire Blvd—from Rodeo Drive to the Beverly Wilshire Hotel—and they had exactly seven minutes out of every thirty when the Beverly Hills Police Department would block off traffic for the director to capture his carefully orchestrated panic, a frenzied evacuation from unseen waves.

Hu's job was to be part of the crowd, running down the street, running through the cars, until he finally hit a specific mark, where he would fall to the ground as if he was being swept under the killing wave—except one of the assistant directors liked his look and gave him a different role, he'd get to be a featured kill.

The camera would start at a high angle, looking up the row of stopped cars, with the distant wave roaring toward the foreground. Hu would come running toward the camera, running between the line of vehicles. The camera would lower, promising a closeup, but just as Hu would arrive at that spot, a panicky driver—another stunt player—would open his driver-side door and Hu would slam into it—and then the wave would inundate them both. The unseen side of the car door was carefully padded, so Hu could hit it hard without injuring himself.

The director liked the shot so much that he decided to add a follow up bit, giving Hu two additional days of work. Finished with the devastation of Wilshire Blvd., the film moved to a Hollywood backlot for specific closeups of death and destruction.

For these shots, the director needed real water, not virtual, and the production relocated to the Paramount lot, the site of the city's second-largest outdoor tank—the Blue Sky Tank, so called because its towering back wall, could be painted to represent any kind of sky, stormy to cloudless, that a director might need. Although the Falls Lake tank at Universal was noticeably larger, it was also more expensive to fill, filter, and heat.

The filmmakers needed a variety of shots with Asian men and women as background players. This was so their Chinese co-financers could edit a somewhat different version of the film for the Asian markets. The Chinese version would include several characters and subplots not in the American version. The joke had initially been whispered in the front office, but of course it eventually filtered down to the production crew as well—the picture would do well on that side of the Pacific, because Asian audiences like to see white people die. But to be fair, a few Chinese extras had to go down too.

Hu didn't care, he was just happy to work. Because of his marvelously startled expression when he'd slammed into the car door, the American director wanted to follow up by showing Hu struggling for a while in real waves before finally (fake) drowning. So Hu spent a hot August morning in the tank, pretending to die—"On this next take, could you look a little more terrified, please?" Dutifully, Hu struggled, gasped, and waved his arms for help that would never come, until finally, disappearing obediently beneath the surface of the foaming water.

The tank was barely four feet at the center, the waves were machine-produced and the foam was a specific detergent. Floating across the entire surface of the water was an assortment of Styrofoam flotsam, representing the debris stirred up by the tsunami. The shot didn't seem very dangerous—at least that's what Hu believed until he was caught unprepared by a sudden sideways push of prop debris, hard enough to punch the air out of his lungs and leave him gasping for air, involuntarily sucking in a mouthful of water, coughing, and choking desperately as he flailed.

James was one of the safety coordinators. He'd dived into the water, swam under the crapberg, grabbed Hu, and pulled him off to the side of the tank, hanging him on the sloping surface and staying with him until he regained his breath. Neither noticed when the director shouted, "Cut! That's the best one yet, we'll use that one! All right, let's get the camera in the water for the dead body shot—"

The director hadn't noticed what had happened, but one of the assistant directors had seen and on James' direct recommendation, quietly added an additional stunt-fee to Hu's paycheck. No one said anything to the film's director—a man notorious for arguing with stunt players about the cost of each gag. He had a bad reputation in the stunt players' community.

After that, James kept an eye on Hu. In the last shot of the morning, Hu had to pretend to be dead, floating face down in the water while a camera crew in dive gear photographed him from beneath. James had been there to coach the camera crew, showing them how to keep their bubbles out of the shot. And that was when Hu, not knowing James' name, had jokingly called him the bubble-wrangler.

Later on, at lunch, they sat opposite each other—the group shared a table under a large craft-service tent that dominated the parking lot next to the commissary.

Hu had a smile. James had a grumpy charm—it was enough.

The two began that long careful dance of curiosity that would eventually, though not immediately, lead to James' little house in Venice Beach. Hu had gotten his nickname—Squeak—from the sound his running shoes made on James' tile floor.

It began as a physical thing, but eventually grew into a relationship. Bed-buddies became roommates. Roommates became lovers. And lovers became—

One strange stormy night, while the two of them were lying side-by-side, staring at the ceiling and listening to the rain, the usually taciturn James had said, "What do you think—"

"About what?"

"About *us*, about stuff—"

Hu was still learning how to listen to James, but this time he heard more than the words. He heard the intention.

"I think..." he began. He rolled onto his side to face James. "I think yes."

"Yes?"

"Yes, you big bubble-wrangler. Yes, I will marry you."

"Oh," said James. "I was going to ask you if we should get a cat."

"Huh—?"

James grinned. "But getting married—that's a good idea too." He pulled Hu close, and kissed him intensely.

The rest was details.

After a few weeks of dithering about plans and schedules, and how much neither of them wanted the gaudy circus of an actual wedding ceremony they decided to just go down to City Hall, do the deed, and then fly to Hawaii for a week. Hu's parents, now together again, were initially more concerned about Hu marrying a Caucasian than a man—but finally decided to show their acceptance by joining them on the island.

The plane tickets were sitting on the kitchen table—and the president's voice was still droning on—now repeating the original broadcast. Outside, the sirens abruptly fell silent. "I suppose—" said Hu, staring at the travel folder, "I suppose—we can get a refund."

And then, it hit him.

The grim expression on James' face said it all.

"Shit! We're going to lose the house, aren't we? Jimmy—?"

"We're gonna lose everything. Everything we can't carry on our backs."

◇◇◇◇◇◇◇◇◇◇◇◇◇

There were only three people in the world who had ever called James Liddle "Jimmy."

The first had been his mother, right up until the day he came out to her. From that moment on, to express her disappointment, he was "James." The second had been Nate Lem, his arrogant overweight fraternity brother—he'd called him "Liddle Jimmy" once too often and gotten a bloody nose for it. After that, he didn't call James anything at all, he left the room whenever James entered.

The third was Hu Son. When he said "Jimmy" it was either affectionate—or important.

James said, "They don't know how big it's going to be, but we've only got three hours to get out of here." He took a breath, his mind racing. "Let's not panic. Let's take a moment and think. It's all about the prep. We gotta get all our cash, all our IDs, all our cards. Um, I have a go-bag, you'll have to pack one. We'll need bottled water and protein bars and—and whatever else is important. Tablets, laptops. All our legal paperwork, especially the insurance stuff—"

Hu Son stood frozen for a moment, his heart racing. "You're serious—oh my god, you are. Oh, god, Jimmy—"

James grabbed him, held him close. "It's okay, it's okay,—we're going to be okay. Let's just take it one step at a time. First step, think—what's important? What are we going to need? What can we leave behind. What do we absolutely need—?"

Hu said, "Um—I don't know. Um—" He looked around the kitchen, mentally sorting through everything, his favorite mug, the pictures on the wall, the beautifully sculpted merman figurine they'd bought on a trip to New Orleans. None of that really mattered. He realized he was naked. He headed toward the room they had christened as "the badroom"—the place where it was good to be bad.

"Um, clothes. I'll grab clothes—"

"Not the big suitcase," James called after him. The one they had packed last night for Hawaii. "Only what can fit in the carry-on. Jeans, hoodies, T-shirts, underwear, socks—"

Hu was already pulling things out of drawers. "Toothbrushes, deodorant, first-aid kit—"

"Right, good." James realized he was still holding a mug of hot tea. He took one last swallow, poured the rest into the sink, and opened the dishwasher to put the mug on the rack. It didn't matter now, did it? But he put the mug on the rack anyway.

"Okay, Jimmy-boy," he said, talking aloud to himself. "What else? The camera, for sure. Eight thousand dollars for an underwater camera rig—I'm not leaving that behind. And the memory cards and batteries. Oh—" He turned to the shelf, grabbed a nearly full box of Zip-Loc plastic bags and followed Hu into the badroom. "Here. Triple bag everything that isn't waterproof."

"You think—?"

"I think we're going to plan for the worst, hope for the best, and prepare for anything. We'll stuff it into dry bags at the office." While Hu pulled on shorts and shirt, James continued sorting through drawers, throwing stuff onto the bed. "Fuck—"

"What?"

"The motorcycle is in the shop—"

"No prob. We'll take the van—"

James had gone to the nightstand. He grabbed a large folding knife from the bottom drawer, and the travel-safe, then the travel bag from the closet shelf. He shook his head. "Bad idea."

"Huh?" Hu stopped, shirt halfway down over his head. His voice came muffled.

"Squeak, you didn't grow up in this city."

"Yes, I did—"

"Not as a driver. We are not gonna be traffic today—"

Hu finished pulling his shirt down. "Then, how—?"

"My SCUBA gear is at the office. I can't leave that behind—" James tossed the travel-safe into the carry-on. He shoved the knife into the pocket of his jeans. "I don't know how bad it's going to be, but I'm thinking there's gonna be a big need for divers after this thing hits. I don't know, but I'll need to be prepared. We can bike to the office, grab whatever gear, and from there, we can head inland. Are you ready—?"

"Half a minute—" Hu stopped, looked around. "Last minute check—"

"I don't want to scare you, but we need to get moving."

Hu debated with himself, finally lost the argument, grabbed his running shoes and shoved them into the carry-on. "I paid too much for these shoes. They're coming." He stopped, looked uncertainly to James. "You think it's gonna be that bad—"

James' looked grim. "You know all those safety courses I had to take, the fire and rescue courses, the Red Cross courses, lifeguard, all the paramedic stuff?"

"Yeah. You did that for the licenses, so you'd be more valuable to the studios—"

"It was part of the job. Stunt safety. Water safety. Everything." He gave the badroom one last check of his own, still talking. "We had to learn about disasters, all kinds, and prepping for survival too. That's why I keep a go-bag under the bed, and why I'm always nagging you to keep one too." He stopped, he took a breath. "I got to see the pictures from the Christmas Tsunami and Fukushima as well, the ones they didn't show on TV. I never told you—but it was...ugly. So we are walking out of here right now and we are heading for the highest ground we can get to the fastest way we can. Is that it? You got everything?" James moved to close the carry-on—

Hu stopped him long enough to toss in two more items, a fist-sized bronze Buddha that he grabbed from the top of the dresser, a wooden cross with a naked Jesus pulled from the wall—and one more, a small resin replica of Mickey Mouse in red robe and blue sorcerer's hat. "Gotta take the household gods, Bubble. Bad luck to leave 'em."

The television was no longer replaying the President. Now, the Mayor of Los Angeles, backed up by a phalanx of City Councilmen and Police, and confronted by a forest of microphones, stood behind a podium, trying to look calm as he laid out the first attempts at emergency evacuation plans. His voice was shaking.

James and Hu stopped long enough to listen, long enough to realize that whatever the Mayor was saying, none of it was going to help them. "Wait," asked James, "Have you eaten? Grab those boxes of protein bars. Eat two of them now. And the water bottles, drink one now. Don't scarf, don't guzzle, bring it along. Come on, let's go."

They almost made it to the door, James with the knapsack holding his expensive new underwater camera, and his go-bag in his left hand—Hu with a knapsack holding water and travel-rations, his carry-on in his right hand.

Hu stopped abruptly. "No! Wait!"

"Now what?"

Hu dropped the carry-on, ran back to the badroom, came out a moment later, carrying a small black box. "I almost forgot the rings! The wedding rings!" He held the jewelry box high for James to see, then shoved it into his pocket. "Hell or high water, we're getting married."

"Probably high water, but yeah. Hell or high water."

"Promise?"

"Promise. Now let's go—"

◇◇◇◇◇◇◇◇◇◇◇◇◇◇

James pulled the plastic tarp off the bikes and unlocked them. Despite the high wooden fence around the tiny yard, he still didn't trust the neighborhood's population of permanent transients.

"I'm gonna miss this place," Hu said.

James didn't answer. He just shook his head and led them out to the bike path. They took a moment to pull on their helmets and double-check the bungee cords around their bags, holding them firmly to the racks on the back of the bikes.

"You ready?"

"No. But let's go anyway."

It wasn't a long ride to the office. The beachfront had gone curiously empty—few of the stores were open, several looked abandoned. There were still people here, but not the usual slurry of ambling shoppers and tourists. They saw a few speed skaters with backpacks, several people puffing and pulling oversized wheeled luggage, a scramble of surfers running for their van, and more bicyclists than usual. Most had backpacks and other luggage strapped to their bikes and handlebars. But everyone was moving with purpose. Most were walking fast, trotting, a few were even running. It wasn't a panic—not yet, but the clock was running.

James' company, their company now—Liddle Things—was set in a small white building, three blocks up from the beach. James didn't rent to casual tourists, too

much risk, so there was little need to be on the beachfront where rents were noticeably higher. He unlocked the heavy front door, they wheeled their bikes inside and
locked the door behind them. James went behind the desk and unlocked the back
room where he kept the tanks and masks, the diving rigs, tool belts, and assorted
other paraphernalia.

"Shit!" he said, looking around, taking stock, realizing how little he could save.
He blew out his cheeks. "We're gonna lose it all, Squeak. More than fifty thousand
dollars invested in this stuff—all gone."

Hu wasn't sure if he should say anything. He recognized the mood—the same
growling darkness that always came over James when dealing with money, especially
a shortage of it. "The insurance—?"

"Won't cover the half of it—" James shook his head. "No—there's just no way to
save, no fucking way." He sighed in resignation. "All right, let's get the bike trailers.
You take the new one, it's lighter. You attach, I'll do triage." He began pulling things
off the wall and out of lockers.

Hu knew the drill. The bike trailers were convenient ways for cyclists to carry surfboards, SCUBA gear, camping gear, or even a few bags of groceries. They
attached easily. He and James used them a lot, for almost any trip less than three
miles. Hu didn't mind driving, he could listen to his music, but James hated getting
behind the wheel, because he found urban traffic frustrating—the poor behavior of
other drivers made even the shortest outing feel like a death-defying exercise.

James talked as he worked, annotating every decision with a justification. "I'm
gonna want my wet suit and my new dive computer—$1500 that thing cost, it does
everything but make coffee, and I still haven't had a chance to use it. I'm gonna need
it if there's rescue work. You grab those spare tanks and put them on your trailer.
And the camping bag. I'm afraid we're gonna need it. I'll take the main tanks and the
portable compressor. I might have to wear the rig. Hmm, harness, backplate, maybe I
should wear a couple tanks too? What else? A pro-grade mask—no the one with the
dual lamps, fins, tool belt—I can hang the belt on the handlebars, anything that isn't
waterproof goes into the dry bags, we can put those in our knapsacks, everything else
in the travel case, that'll go on the trailer. Oh, and grab those new headlamps too—"

Hu laughed. "We're gonna look like a couple of underwater bag ladies—and
you with the SCUBA gear on your back—"

"Not gonna leave it—"

"Jimmy—? Isn't it all too much to carry? All this weight?"

"If it is, then we've both wasted a fortune at the gym. And all that damn healthy
eating." James paused, got serious. "Squeak, this is my career. Just like your new
expensive laptop. I need this."

"You don't have to convince me, Bubble. Give me whatever you need me to
carry. We'll do it."

They finished quickly. Less than fifteen minutes.

"Is that it?"

"It's gonna have to be." James looked to his partner, his tone abruptly thoughtful. "We'll take the bikeway—that'll be the fastest. The only traffic will be other cyclists. But only to 26th street, or Bundy if we can, then we'll turn north. I think if we can get to Sunset, we can go up one of the canyons to Mulholland, maybe take it to Topanga, get down into the valley that way—"

"And from there?"

"I dunno. Who do we know in the valley with a guest house? Or a backyard big enough for the tent?"

"Whatsisname—that writer who's always calling you?"

"Mr. Source Material? Maybe. What about your cousin?"

"Maybe. If you're willing to put up with my uncle—"

"Yeah, there's that."

"Maybe if we can get to Pasadena, there's Chris and Mark—"

"Melinda has a guest house—"

"So does—never mind. We have options. First thing, let's get out of here." James pointed to the bikes. "Okay, safety check on the bikes. Is everything secure?"

Three minutes to double-check all the tie-downs and bungee cords, and they were ready to leave, but at the door, they paused. James put his hand on Hu's arm. "Okay, Squeak, we've got two and a half hours. We can do this. Ten miles an hour, easy-peasy. We could get all the way to Union Station if we had to. All we have to do is pace ourselves. The idiots are going to ride like crazy and exhaust themselves before they even get to the 405. Just keep thinking of Mike Sloan's teddy bear—"

"Huh?"

"Don't you remember? Sloan's teddy wins the race—"

"Oof. Remind me again why I agreed to marry you?"

"Because I'm the daddy, that's why." James grinned.

"Except when it's my turn."

They pushed the bikes outside, first Hu, then James behind him. Hu started to plug in his headphones, but James stopped him. "You don't want to do that—"

"Shouldn't we listen to the news—?"

"Aren't you scared enough already?"

"Oh." Hu shoved the earphones back into his knapsack, glanced at his wristband, looked west toward the beach. Beyond a lonely palm tree, the horizon looked peaceful and bright. Hard to believe a disaster was rising somewhere beyond. "It's gonna be hot today," he said. "Especially inland."

"Yeah," James agreed, behind him. "Gonna need the extra water."

Hu turned back to him. "All right. I'm ready."

With the trailer attached, his bike was loaded heavier than he expected. He had to take a running start to catch up to James, but they were on their way, heading east.

It wasn't far to the bikeway, less than a mile, but they weren't the only ones who'd had this idea. The bikeway wasn't crowded, not at first, but the farther they rode, the more cyclists joined them—a steady stream of riders peddling inland with a grim determination. Every few minutes, a light-rail train passed them, howling east on elevated tracks that paralleled the bikeway. Despite himself, Hu looked up—the railcars were already crowded. James had guessed right.

"Sloan's teddy," called James. "Just like one of your marathons."

"Ha ha," said Hu. He focused on his pace, using the same steady counting exercise he used when he ran in the morning. Occasionally, other cyclists passed them at a furious pace, almost panicky. Not wise—but their choice.

Two miles in and the bikeway was filled. Most of the traffic was other cyclists in professional gear, helmets and backpacks, but sometimes just ordinary people on bicycles—sometimes whole families pedaling in a group. Most were wearing knapsacks, or had cases strapped to the back of their bikes or hanging from their handlebars. A few, like James and Hu, had well-loaded bike trailers.

Occasionally people passed them, a few speed-skaters, and motorized skateboards as well. Once a couple of assholes on motorcycles came roaring past. Hu stood up on his pedals to look ahead. If the bikeway kept filling up, kept getting more and more crowded, those motorcyclists weren't going to have much of an advantage.

By the time they reached 26th street, traffic on the bikeway had slowed to a sluggish crawl—and east of the avenue, there were so many cyclists ahead of them, riding was impossible. People had to dismount and walk their bikes. A few groaned in annoyance, a couple others shouted angrily, some muttered to themselves, but most just kept pushing along. Hu and James dismounted and walked their loaded bikes side-by-side.

More frustrated riders piled up behind them, but no fights had broken out. There was still plenty of time. Most people were helping each other. One woman was holding another's bike while the first one changed her baby's diaper. Elsewhere, a professional-looking rider had stopped to patch a flat tire for a crying teenage girl. Another was helping an uncertain middle-aged man put a loose chain back on his bicycle's gears.

It wasn't a panic, not yet. It was still an exodus. Not disorderly, but it wasn't moving fast enough. At this pace...James looked to Hu, shook his head, leaned over and whispered, "Time for an alternate route."

It took them nearly ten minutes to work their way to the next opportunity to exit the bikeway, Cloverfield Avenue. They weren't the only ones abandoning the narrow route. Some of the cyclists were turning south, most were turning north.

James and Hu went north. Just on the other side of Colorado Blvd., there was a good-sized parking lot. The lot was already emptying of cars, the last few people driving away frantically. James pointed and Hu followed.

They pulled themselves out of the steady stream of people remounting their bikes. Hu pulled out the first water bottle, took two swallows and passed it to James, who did the same, then passed it back. A familiar ritual. Having done that, they both pulled out their phones. Hu checked The Weather Channel—the temperature was already above 80 and still rising. Okay, not unexpected.

James went to Google Maps, then he tapped for Waze. Both were bad news. Red lines showing heavy traffic everywhere, some routes already painted with stretches of black Absolute gridlock was beginning. But at least the bikes were moving here—in the bike lanes and on the sidewalks, and even between the long rows of cars. The automobile lanes were barely inching forward.

"It's crowding up faster than I expected. Apparently people are taking this thing serious. All right, we'll head north here—" James started to push his bike forward again.

Hu said, "Wait."

"What?"

"I've got a text."

"Forget it—"

"It's from Karen—" A series of messages rolled up the screen. Hu looked to James. "She's at work. She needs someone to pick up Pearl."

"Can't she do it?"

"She's doing triage in the E.R. She couldn't get out, even if she wanted to. The streets there are gridlocked."

"Pearl can't get a ride?"

"The neighbor who promised left without her." Hu read the next text. "What an asshole. Apparently, her cats were more important."

"There's no one else."

Hu kept scrolling through Karen's frantic notes, his expression darkening. "Doesn't look like it. Karen says it's desperate. Pearl is trapped. She can't get an Uber or a Lyft, Ride-Share is down, Access isn't picking up. The Fire Department is moving all their equipment eastward. She tried calling for an ambulance, but—" Hu lowered his phone. "James, we can't leave her there. We gotta get her."

James made a razzberry of disgust. "Fuck. The problem is...that damn wheelchair."

"Can we pull her—?"

"I'm thinking—" A heartbeat. "The wheelchair is light enough—it's Pearl. She's not exactly a spring potato. Fuck."

"James—"

"I know, I know—" He puffed his cheeks, blew out his breath, exasperated. "Yeah, we have to try. Uh...all right, lemme think." He went to scratch his head, fingers fumbling across his helmet instead. "Fastest way there—"

James made a decision. "Okay. Forget Sunset. Forget the mountains. We'll go up to Santa Monica, it's the next one after Broadway. Then..." His voice tailed off as he plotted a route. He turned to Hu. "It's a long slog. If Pearl can get herself down to the street, we'll figure something out. We might have to lose one of the trailers, I dunno, I'll do the math in my head while we ride."

"Can we make it in time?"

James looked at his watch. "Yeah, I think so."

"Can we get her to high ground? Can we get us to high ground—?"

"Straight north up Fairfax would take us to Laurel Canyon. Might be high enough. I don't know. That's not a great route, but...fuck, I don't know." James shook his head. "Worse comes to worse, I don't know, we might be far enough inland. Even a ten story building might be tall enough. Maybe. I don't know. This is fucked. Let's just do it. Come on, we've been through worse—"

"No we haven't," said Hu. "*This* is the worst." But he was already tapping a message into his phone. "We're on our way." He sent it to both Karen and Pearl, shoved his phone back into his pocket and grabbed his handlebars. "Okay, let's go."

James and Hu pedaled east on Santa Monica Blvd., weaving their way through a slow-moving mass of cars and people. But at least it was moving. Both sides of the avenue were headed inland. There was no westbound traffic. It helped—a little.

It was a business district here, but none of the stores were open. There were a few broken windows, but not many. People were determinedly walking east, most of them turning north at suitable intersections. Some of the cyclists were walking their bikes because there wasn't enough room to ride. James and Hu had dismounted as well and were now walking their bikes side-by-side.

The exodus was serious now. Even the motorcyclists were having trouble maneuvering through the impatient lines of automobiles. It was turning into a crush. The inevitable speed-skaters darted everywhere, sometimes nearly colliding with unwary pedestrians. Occasionally, they saw an ambulatory bundle of rags doggedly pushing an overloaded shopping cart. Even the homeless were leaving. And once, a pair of hipsters rode by on hoverboards.

A woman behind them started complaining loudly—making pointed remarks about their overloaded bikes and bike trailers. James muttered a curse under his breath, but shook his head and kept pushing forward. Hu looked over to him. "Are you okay?"

"I will be. Are you?"

"I'm … not complaining," said Hu. He had a thought. "I'm wondering. Do you think maybe Pearl's building might be tall enough? If we could get her to the roof—"

James went silent, thinking about it. Finally, "I wouldn't want to risk it, would you? It's an old building, wood frame, it might not survive the impact. It's not just the water, it's all the crap being pushed by the water. It'll hit like a horizontal avalanche. And even if the building survives the impact, she could be stuck up there for days before anyone could get to her. And the damn wheelchair is another problem. So, no."

"It was just a thought. I was worried about the time."

James looked at his watch. "We're okay." He pointed. "We're almost to the freeway. Once we get to the other side, it should be easier going. Well, could be. We'll burn that bridge when we get to it." James pushed his bike ahead, effectively ending the conversation.

The 405 freeway divides the LA Basin. It separates the western and southern communities from the rest of the megalopolis, as it winds south, vaguely paralleling the coast. Parts are elevated highway, parts are sunken, but all of it is a ten-laned barrier to traffic trying to move to and from the coast. The inadequate and infrequent underpasses and bridges that cross the 405, its on- and off-ramps, are bottlenecks that can backup traffic for blocks even on a good day.

This was not a good day. Gridlock spread outward from every crowded access ramp and crossover. In a few hours the entire length of freeway—from the Sepulveda pass all the way to the Mexican border would be gone. But right now it was a major obstacle.

Where Santa Monica Blvd. crossed under the 405, several LAPD motorcycle officers were calmly working to unravel the chaos at the underpass. Surrounded by frantic and desperate drivers, they were doing their best. They were scheduled to withdraw at least twenty minutes before impact—if they could get out. That wasn't certain anymore.

At the mayor's desperate orders, both sides of all major surface streets were now mandated for eastbound and northbound vehicles, especially through the underpasses and across the bridges. Both sides of the 110 and the 405 were now handling northbound traffic.

It wasn't enough.

Police and news helicopters circled overhead. Other choppers, all kinds, were shuttling east and west, their own small contributions to the evacuation. The apocalypse was being televised. Further south, at LAX, every plane that could get off the ground was heading inland, some with passengers sitting in the aisles.

James and Hu came to a stop on the sidewalk just past the Nu-Art theater—an ancient movie house that had survived for more than nine decades. For most of its history, it had been a cinematic sanctuary, unspooling an assortment of independent films, obscure foreign dramas, various cult classics, assorted Hollywood treasures, a variety of otherwise forgotten and questionable efforts, occasional themed festivals, and the inevitable midnight screenings of crowd-pleasers like The Rocky Horror Picture Show and other film-fads of the moment. In a few hours, it would be closed forever.

James pointed ahead—the underpass was gridlocked. The officers had blocked off the northbound onramps with their motorcycles, and were now directing traffic to use the southbound offramp instead, their only remaining access to a northbound escape, but even that was moving slowly. Too slowly. Even with cars crawling along the shoulders of the freeway, the 405 just couldn't accept any more traffic.

Los Angeles had not been designed for an evacuation—not on this scale. No city had ever been designed for such a massive torrent of people, an exodus of unprecedented size, a titanic crush of desperate humanity.

And yet, somehow, it moved.

Not fast enough. Not nearly fast enough. But it moved.

Some of these people would survive—if they could just get over the hill into the San Fernando Valley, or even halfway up the Sepulveda pass. There was time.

Except—

—except for the angry shouting.

Which was why James had stopped.

An old green van, a decrepit-looking Ford Windstar, hastily overloaded, had collided with a silver Lexus, a fairly new model. Both vehicles were in the middle of the road, blocking three separate lanes. A frightened woman sat in the passenger seat of the Lexus.

Two desperate drivers had left their vehicles to confront each other—neither had given way, both had tried to force their way forward, only to demonstrate that specific law of physics that two objects cannot occupy the same space—so now they were screaming at each other in near-incoherent rage.

A crowd of other drivers surrounded them, also screaming, demanding that they move their fender-crunched vehicles out of the way. Snippets of conversation echoed off the underpass walls—

"Get your fucking cars out of the way—"

"Not until I get this asshole's insurance—"

"It's your goddamn fault, I want your insurance—"

"There's no time for that, you assholes—"

"Will both you idiots move your goddamn cars—"

"Daddy, I wanna go home—"

"The police are right there—"

"Good! They can arrest this jerk—"

"Just please move it to the side, so the rest of us can get by—"

"Move it where?! We're boxed in by the rest of you—"

"I don't back up for assholes—"

"It's okay, I do—"

"I'm not moving till he gives me his insurance information—"

"We don't have time for that, and your piece of shit Ford isn't worth it anyway. You're just trying to hold me up, and I won't stand for it—"

"That's just the attitude I'd expect from a spoiled brat manbaby—"

"Guys, please! This isn't helping anyone—"

"Daddy, I gotta pee—"

"If you won't move it, I will—"

"Touch my car and you'll regret it—"

"Why don't the police do something—"

"Okay, enough is enough. You're gonna move this shit outta the way now—"

That last was a burly member of the sasquatch family—red-faced, long-haired, scruffy-beard, flannel shirt, and the kind of expression that usually stopped all conversation.

"You gonna make me—?"

"Officer, over here! Please!" That was a woman shouting.

Two of the officers were busy trying to stop impatient drivers from backing up onto the south-bound onramp, intending to join the northbound exodus that way. Two more were struggling to keep the evacuation orderly—one had to dodge sideways as an impatient driver forced his way around the sluggish line of cars ahead of him. They had more immediate priorities than the argument in the underpass. But the backup of cars was growing, and so was the angry crowd.

From his position, at the ramp, one of the officers waved furiously at the drivers of the two vehicles, urging them to get back into their vehicles and move, but the two men were too angry, each so focused on winning this argument they couldn't see past their own rage. It looked like violence was inevitable.

"Can we get past that?" asked Hu.

"I don't know," said James. "I'm wondering if we should try to go around it." He pulled out his phone to study the map again. Where was the next closest underpass? Half a block north. Ohio Avenue.

The immediate problem would be just getting across the street. Santa Monica Blvd. was gridlocked. The closest cross street was Sawtelle, just on the other side of the Nu-Art theatre. Maybe they could thread their way around the stalled cars—

A sudden shift in sound, a scream of incoherent rage, both James and Hu whirled to see—

Sasquatch was now waving an aluminum baseball bat. "You gonna move it—?" This was followed by a well-aimed blow. The right-front headlight of the Lexus shattered in the impact. "You gonna move it now—?"

"What the fuck are you doing—?"

"Giving you a reason to move it—"

"Fuck you! You're gonna pay for that—"

"Let's make it two—" Another swing of the bat, it bounced off the left headlight. A second swing shattered it. "And three—" The windshield shattered next. The woman inside flinched and tried to scramble across the seat.

"Stop it, goddammit! Stop it!"

"Move it and I will!"

The driver of the Lexus scrambled into the car, but instead of starting the engine, he came out waving a—

"Gun! He's got a gun—!" The crowd scattered. The panic rippled outward. At its spreading edges, people ran or ducked, hiding behind the most convenient cars.

And just as quickly, three of the police positioned themselves, flattened across the hoods of several stalled vehicles, guns drawn, and pointed, held steady in both hands, red laser dots wavering on the Lexus driver. The lead officer shouted, his voice electrically amplified—"Drop it! Drop the gun! Now!"

Confused, the Lexus driver turned, staring from one officer to the next. "But he... he smashed my car." He waved the gun around, as if to point it, but Sasquatch had conveniently disappeared.

"Drop the fucking gun! Now, goddammit!" Not exactly standard LAPD procedure, but the pressures of the situation were getting out of hand.

"I just want to get out of here!" the Lexus driver wailed.

"Drop the gun and move your car!"

"No, no, no!" The man insisted. "I didn't do anything! He hit me! He has to move!" Sensing that he was blocked in, he turned around and around, pointing the gun from one driver to the next. "Everybody get out of my way! Let me out of here—" He looked desperate, he was shredding into incoherency—

"Last warning! Drop the gun. Drop it. Now."

"Please! Just let me out of here—"

"Oh fuck," said James, quietly. "They're gonna shoot him."

Hu put his hand on James' shoulder and pushed. The two of them flattened to the sidewalk together, their bikes falling beside them.

Three quick gunshots, followed by a beat of silence—and then the screaming started. "Oh my god, my god!" And: "You didn't have to do that—!" Followed by orders from the cops. "You, move that Lexus. Move it now! You, back up! You, follow him!"

But there was no organization. There were too many voices. There was too much screaming, and too many people pulling in too many directions at once—

And a couple more gunshots, coming from another direction—

James half rose up to look, then quickly lowered himself back to the sidewalk. Once, a long time ago, he's seen a riot start. It was ugly.

This was worse.

James looked to Hu. "Let's go back."

Tentatively, they levered themselves back to their feet, both a little shaken. Hu touched James' arm and pointed. The building behind them had a fresh hole in one of its windows.

James smiled weakly, nodded, pointed west.

Hu hesitated. "Shouldn't we see if anyone needs help?"

"Pearl needs us more. Let's get out of here."

Hu hesitated, uncertain.

James touched his elbow and said quietly, "Triage."

Hu didn't like the thought. But James was right. He followed.

Somehow, despite the narrow sidewalk, despite the people around them, they got their bikes turned around and headed a half block west to Sawtelle.

They weren't the only ones. Drivers who had gotten out of their cars to see what the blockage was at the underpass were now climbing back into their vehicles and turning north onto Sawtelle. James and Hu threaded their way across the intersection and remounted. There was just enough room on the sidewalk to pedal north.

It wasn't far to Ohio Ave, a block and a half. But when they reached the intersection and looked right, they came to a stop, both at the same time.

This underpass was blocked even worse. It was narrower and too many cars were trying to get through it. The avenue was backed up with cars arriving from the west, but adding to the gridlock, traffic from Sawtelle was also trying to merge into the sluggish flow.

"Can we get through there?" asked Hu.

James considered it. There was a cluster of motorcyclists blocking the sidewalk that went through the underpass. It didn't look like they were getting through. Something blocking them on the other side, maybe—?

"No," said James. "Too narrow." That was the most convenient excuse, but he was still thinking about the violence they'd just escaped. This was another potential disaster—another riot looking for a place to happen. He pointed north instead. "Let's see if we can get across. We'll take Wilshire." There weren't any other options.

They pushed their bikes forward. Most of the going was single-file, but there was still room to make it through. Despite their urgency, most of the drivers here were leaving almost enough space for the two cyclists to navigate carefully across the intersection. Their bike trailers bumped a few fenders where they had to push between the lanes, but aside from one red-faced future stroke victim who shouted at them for blocking his nonexistent way forward, most drivers pretended to ignore them.

And then they were on Sawtelle again, pedaling into the Veterans Administration Healthcare Center. Where Sawtelle dead-ended inside the campus, before a cluster of shining white buildings, there was a concrete path cutting directly north, and it was wide enough for them to pedal. They weren't the only cyclists with this idea, a few others raced past them. But James and Hu stopped to walk their bikes because of the foot traffic—the old men in bathrobes and pajamas and shapeless sagging trousers.

In the rising heat of the July day, these ancient men trudged steadily north. They were clusters of fragile age, old but determined. Most of them were using canes or struggling with walkers, a few pushed others in wheel chairs, a few were coming with their IV stands, but all of them were heading slowly and deliberately toward Wilshire. They smelled of old age and soap.

These were the leftovers, the forgotten warriors, the heroes of yesterday—the abandoned ones, abandoned one more time. No one had remembered they were here. There was no evacuation plan for them. The buses had never arrived, they'd been commandeered for the schoolchildren and for anyone else who could scramble aboard.

Maybe, when they reached the boulevard, someone would give them a ride. Or maybe they would just end up as a few more bodies in the long line of hopeful old men gathering along the side of the road, more zombies for the frightened drivers to ignore.

James and Hu passed them as quickly as they could—they tried hard not to meet their eyes, tried hard not to see their frail bodies and watery expressions. But one of the men stopped James with an outstretched hand. "You go. You go on, get out of here. Go and live. Find someone to love and live a glorious life." Another added, "But tell them about us. Tell them to remember. Please—" And a third, "Tell them how we were forgotten, betrayed, abandoned—" And a fourth, "And tell them to go fuck themselves too—"

Both James and Hu nodded and promised. "We will, we will."

They nodded and said yes to everything, they shook the trembling hands of those who reached out to them—and then they pushed on, a hard lump in their throats. They wanted to do more, but what could they do?

And then one of the old men called, "Jimmy, is that you?" Hearing his name, James stopped. Force of habit. He turned and looked.

A frail spectre, dragging an IV stand, came wobbling, hobbling across the grass. "Jimmy, it's grampa."

No, it wasn't. All of James' grandparents had passed a decade earlier. But still, he was startled enough to stop and stare.

Another old soldier came shuffling up. "It's all right, pay him no mind. He's—he doesn't know who anyone is anymore. "

But grampa had grabbed Jimmy's arm. "I knew you'd come," he said. "I told them, I told them you would come to see me—"

The other man shook his head. "Jimmy died. A long time ago. But he doesn't believe it. Or he forgets."

James said, "Hu, hold my bike." He dismounted, put his arms around the self-appointed grampa. "I love you, grampa. I'm sorry I waited so long to come and see you. I missed you so much. I have to go now. Your friends will take care of you. But I have to go. They need me at the... at the station, okay?"

The old man didn't want to let go. His frail hands trembled as he tried to hang onto his long-lost grandson, but Jimmy pulled away anyway, and finally grampa said, "Okay, Jimmy. Okay. You be a good boy now. You tell your ma you saw me, okay?"

"Okay, grampa." Jimmy gave the old man a quick hug, then pulled away just as quickly. He took hold of his bike again—

James mounted and they pedaled on.

"That was... that was a good thing you did."

"Triage," said James. "Goddammit."

Hu didn't answer.

They traveled past the line of old men, castoffs in a younger world, all of them struggling in the rising heat. As they turned right to go up the ramp to Wilshire boulevard, even more old and frail men were gathering in a crowd. Some of them were weeping. Others were stepping into the traffic lanes, knocking on the windows of slow-moving vehicles. Others stood silently on the sidewalk, sunken in despair, gaunt and resigned in the heat of the day. Two looked like they were unconscious on the sidewalk. Here and there, car doors were opened for them—but not enough.

It was a nightmare.

They pushed past. Most of the old men ignored them. They were just two more bodies in the passing parade of people who couldn't or wouldn't help them.

A couple of the old men were shouting obscenities—mostly at the cars, but a few directed their streams of abuse at James and Hu. One hollered at Hu, "That's right, you dirty Jap, run away, run away—or we'll get you again like we did at Pearl Harbor—"

"I'm Chinese," said Hu, but the old man didn't care, or didn't hear. Hu followed James, they pushed on.

There were officers working the underpass here too, but without the same frustration and confusion that they had seen a mile further south at Santa Monica Blvd.

The officers here were also directing traffic up onto the southbound lanes of the 405, pointing cars up the offramp, shouting and waving them forward, even demanding they use that side of the highway as an additional northbound escape. Some drivers looked reluctant, this felt *wrong*, but they followed the officers' directions and headed up the offramp anyway

The traffic inched along slowly, jerking spasmodically, filling every spare foot of space—but it moved—only a little at a time, but it *moved* with a single-minded purpose. If these vehicles could get far enough north, far enough up the Sepulveda pass, these drivers would likely survive.

James and Hu lowered their heads and pushed themselves forward as quickly as they could. They blinded themselves to the naked desperation and pushed east, somehow getting through the traffic at the ramps and into the cooling shadow of the underpass. They didn't linger, the place smelled of fumes. Finally, they were out to the other side and across Sepulveda.. They threaded their way through the cars on this side.

When they came to the giant Federal building on the south side of the boulevard, a massive white monolith Hu looked to James, an unspoken question in his glance. They looked to the crowds gathering at the structure, surrounding its entrances, including another legion of old men. James shook his head, an unspoken reply. Bad idea. Not gonna be enough room for everyone... and still too close to the shoreline.

They pushed on.

A long row of tall buildings lay ahead of them, not quite skyscrapers in the modern sense, but tall enough to be imposing—tall enough to look like safety. Already, the foot traffic was getting thick, businessmen, residents, students from the UCLA campus, a mile north—the buildings were filling up. The top floors would be crowded.

When James and Hu finally got to the intersection of Westwood and Wilshire Blvds, they hit a new obstacle—a huge gaping hole in the ground that was the excavation for the Westwood terminus of the Purple Line, the latest extension to the Los Angeles subway system.

If it had been completed, if the tracks had been laid and energized, the city could have evacuated another half-million people. But today, it was a gaping promise. Unfinished. Empty. And shortly to be flooded, inundated, and scraped away by a bulldozer of debris—

James stopped himself.

Don't go there. Just don't.

He checked Google Maps, nodded, pointed to the right. "We'll take the side streets."

A block south, along Wellworth Avenue, they could easily pedal east again. It was a residential area, mostly one or two-story houses. Traffic was thick here, but not impossible—just a steady stream of cars, pushing slowly east. James and Hu kept to the sidewalks, there weren't many other riders here and they made the best progress since leaving Venice.

James glanced at his watch. They were behind schedule, but there was still time. They were going to make it.

If there were no more shootings.

∞∞∞∞∞∞∞∞∞∞∞∞∞

They followed the side streets —Wellworth, Warner, Ashton, Holmby — past the worst of the jams, and then they were back on Wilshire. It cut easily through the golf courses, but it was an uphill slog and the bikes and trailers were heavily loaded.

Halfway up the hill, Hu called for a stop. He opened a fresh water bottle, drank half of it, and passed it to James, who finished it... and tossed the bottle over the fence onto the green. "Always wanted to do that."

"Jimmy—?"

"Yeah?"

"It's awfully hot."

"Yeah—" But he knew that wasn't what Hu meant. Their shirts were sweat-stained, they were both damp with the effort of pedaling with the extra weight. The uphill part was just an excuse to stop.

"The bike-trailers," said Hu. "The tanks—"

"I know—"

"They're holding us back—"

James fell silent. He took a deep breath, then another, tried to compose himself. Hu was frustrated. And when Hu was frustrated, then James got frustrated, because he had to talk Hu down. But this was different.

"I think we can make it."

"I don't think I can."

"We have to try." James pointed. "This part is all uphill. Once we get to the top, it'll be an easy ride down the other side."

Hu looked past James, up toward the crest. It really wasn't that far. He knew he could make it—but it wasn't the top of the hill he was worried about. It was the rest of the distance, to Pearl's house and then to safety. He felt overwhelmed, almost to the point of tears.

"Jimmy, you know I'd never ask you to—"

James leaned his bike against the fence, went quickly back to Hu. "Squeak, I know, you wouldn't ask unless there was no other way. And it's the same for me. I wouldn't ask you if I could see any other way. But I don't think we can leave any of this behind." He stopped himself. "Wait—"

Beside them, the traffic chugged slowly past. James ignored the curious stares of several small children leaning out the open windows of a passing SUV.

"Okay, look," James said. "Let's put only our must-haves into our backpacks, okay? All our paperwork, money, phones, your computer, all the stuff we can't leave behind. The stuff in the dry bags, right? And then let's see how much farther we can get with the rest. Is that okay?"

Hu nodded reluctantly. It was a concession. Not the one he wanted, but he had to trust James—James was the better planner. He started thinking what he could repack. It wasn't much. He'd already put the most important things in his knapsack. Some of the weight was water bottles. He felt damp and sweaty all over. For a moment, he dreamt of the long luxurious shower he could take when they got back home.

Then he realized he would never see that shower again. Abruptly he realized he had to pee.

Hu looked around, they were at least a mile from anything that might serve as a rest stop—the hell with it—he turned to the chain-link fence, lifted up the left side of his shorts and let loose a personal torrent, splashing at the fence. James joined him, yanked down his own shorts, and for a moment, their two streams arced toward the silent green of the golf course.

Hu giggled.

"What?"

"Don't cross the streams—"

"You see too many movies."

"You watch 'em with me."

"Hey!" a distant voice called. "Stop that!"

They looked through the fence. Three middle-aged men in bright-colored shirts and pants were playing golf, totally oblivious to the evacuation. One of them was waving his golf club angrily at them.

"Didn't you hear the news?" James called. "There's a tsunami coming in."

"Don't you believe it," one of them called back. "Just another drill."

"Fake news," muttered the second.

The third said, "I'd rather die golfing than running—"

"Have it your way," said James, zipping up his pants, and suddenly doubting. What if they were right—?

No. They were wrong, he wished he could believe them, but they were wrong—and in a couple hours, they'd find out how wrong. He wondered if they'd make it to the 18th hole in time, shook his head in disbelief, turned back to Hu. "Idiots."

Hu smiled weakly. "Suddenly, I don't feel so stupid."

"Yeah. Let's get out of here."

Refreshed by their rest, rehydrated by the water, they made it to the crest of the hill, then half-coasted, half-pedaled down the other side.

They continued east on Wilshire Blvd., past the Beverly Hilton Hotel to where it criss-crossed Santa Monica Blvd. Navigating the wide diagonal intersection with Santa Monica wasn't as hard as James feared. Traffic was inching along here, but there was still room to thread the bikes between the ranks of cars.

Wilshire was a straight line east from there, a gilded belt around the waist of Beverly Hills, lined with elegant palm trees. Much of the traffic here was turning north at every opportunity, aiming for Benedict Canyon, Coldwater Canyon, any higher ground at all. A lesser but steady stream of vehicles pushed eastward and inland. At an average speed of ten miles per hour, there was still a chance for most of them to survive.

Overhead, the sky was filled with more helicopters than either James or Hu had ever seen. Police, news, rescue, fire, military, and private services as well. Some were monitoring, others were evacuating.

Here, the sidewalks were wide enough, they had room to ride—they werean incongruous sight pedaling through the most elegant district in Los Angeles. Elegant—and doomed. All the surrounding communities that kept these businesses thriving would be gone in less than two hours.

∞∞∞∞∞∞∞∞∞∞∞∞

As James and Hu pedaled steadily east, they heard a steady drone of chattering voices leaking from the radios of the vehicles they passed, bits of audio flotsam that refused to assemble into any kind of coherent narrative.

Here, the pedestrian traffic was lighter. There were other cyclists on the road and on the sidewalk, but not a lot. Motorcycles growled between the rows of cars. Three people on Segways rolled past them. And surprisingly—for this neighborhood anyway—they even saw a pair of homeless women, determinedly pushing their overloaded shopping carts eastward. There were buses too, all kinds, packed and overloaded, some with people even riding on the roofs, something Hu had never expected to see in America.

If anyone had expected last-minute desperate looting of Wilshire Blvd.'s elegant storefronts, they would have been disappointed. Even those who might have been tempted were seeing survival as a much more useful priority.

The day was growing hotter, and this far inland, the hot yellow sun was shaded by a smoggy brown haze—a rising cloud of dust, stirred up by a million vehicles.

For some reason, James was reminded of a scene from Disney's *Fantasia*. The "Rite of Spring" segment. All those thirsty dinosaurs, plodding slowly east across an orange desert, toward a sanctuary that didn't exist, eventually dropping to the dirt and dying, leaving only their whitened bones as evidence they had ever existed. He wondered what future archaeologists would be digging up here, a thousand, ten thousand years in some unimaginable future.

"James?"

"Huh?"

"Are you all right?"

"Uh, yeah. I'm fine."

"It's time to stop. Drink some more water."

James shook his head to clear it. He rolled to a stop. Hu was right.

But they'd made it down the hill, past the golf course, past the Hilton, past the intersection, even past the Beverly Wilshire Hotel. What was that—two miles? Three? Whatever. He was starting to feel the exertion—not tired, not exhausted, but definitely, his muscles were tightening. He hoped Hu wouldn't mention the trailers again. He might be tempted to give in.

But Hu said nothing. He passed James a water bottle. James had to resist the temptation to gulp it all down. Instead, he sipped carefully, once, twice, a third time. "Where are we?" he asked, looking around.

"We just passed Robertson. We've still got another couple miles." Hu burrowed into his pack. "Do you want a protein bar?"

James nodded, held out his hand. He unwrapped the little granola brick and hesitated with the wrapper—then he realized how little difference it would make if he found a trash can here in Beverly Hills or not and let it fall to the sidewalk. He chewed and swallowed slowly.

Hu grabbed a water bottle and a protein bar for himself as well. "Do you think the tsunami is going to get this far?"

James didn't answer immediately. He chewed thoughtfully. "Well...if this wave is as big as the president said, a hundred feet high, it'll certainly get as far as the 405, but how much farther, I dunno, that's a lot of water. If it was less, then the 405 would be a pretty good breakwater—except around LAX, of course. The airport's just gonna disappear. But—" James frowned, picturing the geographical layout of the basin in his head. "But I don't think the 405 will stop it. Might slow it down a bit, but a lot of water is still going to get over it, under it, through it." He took another bite, still thinking. "Y'know, those underpasses are bottlenecks, they're going to generate a lot of pressure, all that water trying to force through. Anything directly east of any of them is probably gonna take a hit, and if the pressure is strong enough, the overpasses will certainly blow off. So yeah—it's gonna get this far. A hundred feet—it's just too much water."

Hu looked west, toward the beach, as if he could already see the onrushing catastrophe. He looked at his watch. "How far east do we have to get?"

James shrugged. "It's not just one wave. It could be several waves. You haven't seen the footage I've seen, from Sumatra and Fukushima. It's not what you think. It's not like a wave at the seashore, just bigger. It's like the whole ocean rises up in a flash flood that comes in for... I don't know, an hour? Maybe more? All that water pushing in behind. It has to go someplace, the path of least resistance."

"It's gonna hit hard, really hard. It's gonna knock loose, knock down, knock out everything it hits, pushing it all forward, like a horizontal avalanche. Everything loose, cars, boats, buses, everything that breaks free, trees and billboards and lamp posts, everything that collapses, houses, stores, buildings. All that water, it's going to drive that in like the front end of a bulldozer. "

"It's gonna be bad. Real bad. Maybe those golfers had the right idea. Do what you love doing, right up to the end." He took another bite and waited for Hu's response.

Hu looked nervously to his watch, then back to James. "We're not gonna make it, are we? I mean, with Pearl. Where she is, she's awfully far from any hills—and we're running out of time."

"I know—" James said. He took another thoughtful bite, chewed for a moment, then spoke with his mouth half full. "But I've been thinking. There's that big black building, less than two blocks from Pearl's house. It's what?—ten stories high. We can get there, easy-peasy. The top two floors should be high enough."

"What about the bulldozer—?"

"There's a big building just to the west of it that should catch the brunt of the wave and most of the crap it's pushing."

"It'll be crowded—"

"Probably. But it's our best hope." James took another drink of water. Despite the grim conversation, he was still concentrating on energy and hydration. "Squeak. There has never been a mess like this before. It's gonna be—well, a challenge."

"We're gonna be on our own for a bit, won't we?"

"Yeah," said James sourly. "It's gonna be an adventure all right." He looked to the street, at the desperate stream of cars filling the boulevard. A terrible thought was finally becoming real.

"That bad, huh?" Hu asked.

"Worse than that," James said. "Worse than anyone can imagine. Hate to say it, but a lot of people are gonna die—"

And even as he said the words, he realized just how impossible an idea it was. He couldn't comprehend that all this—the cars, the buildings, the people, everything—was about to be wiped away. And yet, he couldn't deny it any longer. The magnitude of this thing—James couldn't speak it, but he realized that somehow he was still hoping that this was somehow all just a colossal mistake, a false alarm, and that maybe somehow—

He finished the last bite of his protein bar, took a last swallow of water and tossed the empty bottle at a darkened storefront. It bounced harmlessly to the street.

"—But not us. Not today. Come on, let's go."

✧✧✧✧✧✧✧✧✧✧✧✧✧✧✧✧

Two blocks west of La Cienega, James and Hu turned right on South Stanley Drive. Halfway down the second block stood a white two-story building. Once, it had once been a private residence, but now it was subdivided into three Tetris-shaped apartments, with a handicapped access ramp cutting through what had once been a lush front lawn.

At the bottom of the ramp, underneath the inevitable palm tree, Pearl sat waiting in a lightweight folding wheelchair. She had a carpet bag on her lap and she held the leash of a large, sloppy-looking beast that might have had some pit-bull in its parentage, but probably dumpster dog as well. She waved happily when she saw "the boys," James and Hu. They pedaled to a stop in front of her. Several cars passed them in the street, drivers looking for alternate routes.

James looked unhappily at the dog.

"Oh, don't mind Fluffy—he's just a big friendly goofball."

"Fluffy?" Hu raised an eyebrow.

"That's what we call him. His real name is—never mind. He's Joey's dog, but Joey's off in Bakersfield or somewhere, so we keep Fluffy when he's traveling. Mrs. Petersen hates it, but she's afraid to complain or we'll tell the city about her cats."

"Some people—"

"Tell me. She went screaming out of here with a dozen cat carriers the moment the president said tsunami. But the old bitch wouldn't take us. Didn't want to be in the same car with Fluffy. Selfish old bitch. And I just couldn't leave Fluffy behind. He's family."

James sighed. "I admire your gumption, Pearl, but sometimes—"

Pearl's expression changed then. "Honey, where's your car?"

"We didn't bring it," said Hu. He waved his hand to include the bicycles and the trailers. "This was faster."

"Are we in trouble—?" Pearl asked.

"I don't think so—" James pointed. The top of the LFP building was visible even from here. "We'll go up there. It's high enough. If the wave is only a hundred feet high when it hits the shore, by the time it gets this far inland, it'll have lost most of its power—"

"James! What are you talking about?" Pearl half-rose out of her chair. "Not a hundred feet! Three hundred!"

Both James and Hu stopped in mid-word. "What—?"

"*Three hundred feet!* It's what the guy on the internet is saying! The one in Hawaii—the one who measured it!"

"Oh, fuck—" That was Hu.

James didn't say anything. His expression went ashen. When he finally did speak, it was almost automatic. "No, no, it can't be, the president—"

"Honey, that sumbitch is just plain wrong. Or stupid. The guy on the Internet is an actual geologist. He's the director of the Volcano Lab. Now, who ya gonna believe? The politician or the scientist?"

Hu touched James' arm. "What are we going to do?"

James ignored it, he leaned in, grabbed Pearl's arms, stared into her face, and almost shouted, "Are you certain? There are a lot of cranks on the Internet."

She met his stare, unflinching. "James, honey—what do I do for a living? I do research, remember? For the studios. For that stupid movie where you two met. I didn't just google him. I did the whole data-dive. This isn't bullshit. He's for real. *Three hundred feet.*"

James released her, whirled away, furious. "Fuck," he said. "Fuck, fuck, fuck, fuckity-fuck, fuck, fuck." He turned to Hu. "Remember that map I hung in the office? The one that showed the effects of global warming—what the coast line would look like if all the ice caps melted and the sea level rose two hundred and sixty feet?"

Hu nodded. "Yeah. Everything up to Boyle Heights would be underwater."

"Yeah. Well, if this guys's right, this is gonna be worse."

Hu said, "Okay, okay, okay—but we're not dead yet. I've got an idea."

"It's too late—"

"No, it isn't. Hu pointed east. "The subway! The La Cienega station. It's across the street from the tower. Remember how excited Pearl got when it opened? If we can get onto a train, we can get all the way downtown in ten minutes, fifteen."

"And then what? We're still in the disaster zone."

"We'll do what you said. We'll figure something out." Hu rubbed his chin. "I dunno, maybe the Gold line out to Pasadena. Maybe Chris and Mark can put us up. They're always having those big sprawling house parties. If not—I dunno. Maybe Amtrak to my cousin in New Mexico? If we have to pitch the tent in some park, we can do that. But let's go."

"Oh, hell—if I'd known you boys didn't know, I'd have wheeled myself over—" Pearl's face crumpled. "Oh, boys, I'm so sorry. I'm so stupid, you could have gotten up into the hills by now—"

"Stop it, Pearl." That was James. "You're family. Shut up and let us rescue you!"

Just out of her field of vision, Hu tapped his watch meaningfully.

"Right," said James, as if the matter was finally settled. "So let's get out of here. Um—" He fumbled with one of the ropes on his bike trailer. "Here, tie this to—um, loop it around yourself—and we'll pull you."

In reply, Pearl handed him Fluffy's leash. "Here. Tie this around your handle-bars. The monster-dog will help pull."

"Really?"

"Really. Let him lead. Don't worry, people will get out of his way. Real fast."

"We're gonna be a whole circus parade," said James, but he took the leash.

Fluffy led the way. He pulled pulled his own weight, and half of Pearl's too—up the side streets back to Wilshire, a block east and the subway station was directly ahead. The station had only been open a few months, a promise for the future, but this would be its last day of operation. Even if the system survived, there would be nothing left above ground for anyone to come to.

James was right, they did look like a parade. But Pearl was right too. People saw them coming, saw Fluffy grunting and slobbering in the lead, and they moved fast to get out of the way.

They had to wait a few minutes to cross the street. James kept glancing at his watch. Hu put his hand on James' arm. "It's okay. We're gonna make it. We will."

"Cutting it close, too close," James muttered.

"Sloan's teddy..."

"Sloan looks terrible in a teddy," James said, then added. "Halloween. Before your time."

"Oh. Dear."

"Let's go. Light or no light—" They pushed their way into the street. The huge garbage truck waiting to turn north had left enough room for them to squeeze through. The next driver, a frightened-looking woman, had opened her car door and was standing in the street, still clutching the handle, looking confused and desperate. "There's not enough time, is there?"

"Come with us. The subway's still running—"

"The subway?" Her confusion increased. "Los Angeles has a subway—?"

Hu pointed past her. "It's right there—"

The woman grabbed her purse and hurried after them. A few others followed, a black woman dragging two small children, a portly man with his arms full of file folders, the driver of the garbage truck as well.

The elevator to the lower level wasn't working and even if it had been, neither James nor Hu wanted to risk getting stuck in it. The station's turnstiles were frozen open for the evacuation.

The escalators weren't working either, but there was a wide staircase and most of the travelers with baggage were hurrying down it. Hu waited with the bikes while James maneuvered Pearl's chair down the stairs, Pearl held Fluffy's leash, his stub of a tail wagged in excitement, he was having a great time. He looked around the platform eagerly—all these great new playmates—but even the nearest people were keeping a careful distance.

James came trotting back up the stairs and he and Hu began working the bikes and the trailers down. A couple of people grumbled at them as they passed—but they were dragging their own bags down the steps, so James and Hu ignored the comments.

The bottom level was crowded, but not packed, not insane, not panicky. Most of the people who had thought to escape by subway had already gone. These were stragglers, people who had finally abandoned their vehicles. Many were carrying backpacks or dragging suitcases on rollers.

The overhead signs were promising trains arriving at this terminus every four minutes. Hu pointed. "See, we'll have time."

James started to say something, thought better of it, and shut up instead. He scanned the faces of the crowd, looking for signs of desperation or panic. He could still hear the screams and the gun shots from the Santa Monica underpass.

<hr>

UNION STATION

The Red Line and Purple Line trains were arriving so fast, one after the other, that sometimes as many as three trains would have to wait in the tunnel while the first in line unloaded. As fast as each train unloaded, it was sent out again.

The outbound Red Line trains went directly to the Hollywood and Highland station, picking up passengers there and taking them out to the North Hollywood station on Lankershim Blvd. The area surrounding the Universal City station had already reached overload capacity.

Inbound, all the trains were staggered to pick up passengers from the most overloaded stations. As soon as any train was packed to capacity, it went straight to Union Station. It was a frustrating experience for those waiting on the platforms, watching the densely packed trains screech by without stopping, but every available train was running and most people were able to board a train in less than twenty minutes.

The Purple Line trains were on a similar schedule, with most going directly to the Wilshire/La Cienega station, picking up passengers from the most desperate locations first.

Several trains were running direct shuttle service to the Seventh Street station, the terminus of both the Expo Line and the Blue Line from Long Beach. While many evacuees assumed they would be relatively safe this far inland, most were taking advantage of the train service departing from Union Station.

At Union Station, every available train—both passenger and freight—was loaded to capacity. Most were heading north through Glendale and Burbank, all the way to the Burbank airport, where a tent city was being set up on the top level of the parking structure. Others were heading west with stops in the San Fernando Valley and Simi Valley. Ventura County was an uncertain risk. Although parts of it were sheltered by the Santa Monica mountains, there wasn't a convenient train service. Other trains headed north to Santa Clarita, or as far east as Ontario. The closest returned for another trip as soon as they were unloaded.

Additional relocations would be necessary after the initial evacuation. Las Vegas, Phoenix, Tucson, Salt Lake City, Albuquerque, and other cities were already making plans to receive refugees. But the initial goal was to get as many people as possible out of the disaster zone as fast as possible.

In the last half-hour before impact, police and fire rescue would withdraw their personnel and any vehicles still not evacuated. When further evacuation operations became too risky, the subway trains would also be removed to their safest locations.

The last train from Union Station was being held for emergency workers. As soon as the tsunami reached San Clemente Island, a five-minute alarm would sound and the train would pull out before the onrushing water overwhelmed the coastline. It would not wait for stragglers,

That was the plan anyway.

Just one little glitch.

Roy Jeffers.

He did not look like a hero. He did not intend to be a hero.

He was a skinny little bastard (accident of birth), stuck behind thick glasses and a scowl. He was also a stubborn son of a bitch. He had issues with authority, and the surest way to get him to do anything was to tell him, "No, you can't."

Roy Jeffers had another bad habit as well. He was a rescuer.

He had a long history of opening his house in south-central Los Angeles to anyone needing a place to crash—cousins, friends, stray dogs, the occasional feral cat, and once in a while, even a girl friend. (And once, as an experiment, a boy friend.)

At the moment, however, he was single, about to be made homeless by the tsunami, and genuinely resentful that the evacuation was going to take a horrendous toll on those who could least afford it, his entire demographic. People of Color was the current euphemism. Among friends, he'd occasionally rant, "First we were Colored People. Then we were Negro, then we were Black, then African-American. Now we're People of Color. Progress my black ass!" But he didn't have a lot of friends, so it wasn't a rant that many had heard.

Adding to his annoyance was his realization that as a driver for the Purple Line, he was servicing many of the wealthier neighborhoods along Wilshire Blvd., where if he had been working the Blue Line, he would have been rescuing his own neighbors. Even the knowledge that the Crenshaw connection directly served part of his community did not alleviate his smoldering anger.

But—

The knowledge that the Crenshaw connection directly served part of his community had somehow transformed his annoyance into a specific commitment. He wasn't going to abandon anybody and he didn't care what color they were. He was going to do the job anyway.

So when he unloaded at Union Station and his supervisor, Molly Cantway waved to him and said, "Okay, that's it, Roy. Take your train out to the service yard," Roy Jeffers said no.

"There are still people out there. My people—" he insisted. "*Our* people."

Cantway shook her head. "Roy, I am not sending any more trains out. There's no time."

"Then let's not waste it arguing," Roy said. "I'm going."

"You do and I'll fire you."

"Ain't gonna be no job after today anyway—"

Jeffers pushed the control lever forward. His train rolled west into the tube. Cantway didn't know whether to be annoyed at the inevitable loss of a Purple Line train—or admire Jeffers' for his stupidity.

On the other hand, there probably wasn't going to be much of a subway system after this. After Hurricane Sandy, parts of the New York system were down for five years. This was going to be worse than that. Maybe Los Aneles would never have a subway again.

Cantway watched as the last car of Jeffers' train disappeared into the dark tunnel. If that damn fool was able to outrun the incoming flood, he'd be a hero. If not—well, he'd get a nice obituary. And maybe even a funeral, if they ever recovered a body.

Somebody called for her attention and she turned back to the more immediate problem—getting the last of these people upstairs and onto a train out of the city.

And very shortly, herself as well.

She crossed herself and went back to work.

◇◇◇◇◇◇◇◇◇◇◇◇◇◇

The subway platform was filling up. More and more people were realizing that an eastbound train might be their only remaining hope of escape.

A steady stream of future refugees came down the stairs, or walking down the frozen escalator. As the crowd became ever more dense, people jostled for position, all wanting to make sure they'd be able to board the next train.

Most kept checking the overhead arrival signs, but even before the sign flashed, "Arriving now," they could feel the breeze of its approach, as it forced the air from the tunnel ahead of it, then a distant howl echoing out of the tube, a glimmer of light that ballooned into a glare, and finally the train came screeching into the station.

As soon as the doors slid open, the crowd pushed in. Hu held the bikes and James pushed Pearl forward. Fluffy grumbled at the people pushing past him. Abruptly, a female police officer blocked their way. She was short, all muscle, and she wore don't-fuck-with-me expression. Her name tag identified her as Officer Reese.

"You can't take that dog on the train," she said.

Almost immediately Pearl began wailing loudly. James recognized the performance, he'd seen it before, an award-worthy rendition of Frightened Old Crippled Lady. It usually worked. "Oh no, no," cried Pearl, clutching her heart. "I can't leave him. He's my service dog. He doesn't bite. He's big and friendly. I don't know what I'd do without him!" She was loud, very loud, and people already aboard the train, or still trying to board, turned to look. Pearl was playing to the court of public opinion.

Reese was immovable. "Sorry, ma'am. That animal looks dangerous. We can't take any chances—"

James started to object. "You want to leave him here to die?"

But Pearl spoke first. "No, no, James, we must obey the officer. Officer—" She peered forward. "—Officer Reese." She shifted her performance from Frightened-Old-Lady to Frightened-Old-And-Confused-Lady. She held up the end of the leash, offering it to the officer. "Officer Reese, will you hold him till we get back?" Pearl patted the dog's head. "Here, Slobberchops, go with the nice lady."

Fluffy's posture changed dramatically. He was suddenly alert, suddenly eager—he curled back his upper lip, revealing enough teeth for a piano keyboard. He grunted and drooled and pulled at the leash as if someone had just announced fresh peasant for dinner.

Officer Reese put her hand on the hilt of her gun.

"No, no, don't do that! He's just being friendly. Honest. He just wants to play."

Officer Reese must have been painfully aware that all eyes were on her. And the clock was ticking. Fluffy grumpled impatiently. Reese blinked—and took a step back and aside. "Oh, the hell with it. Just keep a tight leash on him."

As James pushed Pearl into the already jammed subway car, those nearest squeezed back to make room, especially room for Fluffy. James bent to her ear and whispered, "Slobberchops?"

Pearl whispered back. "That's his real name. When you say it, he gets ready to play. That was his smile. Works every time."

"Nice." James let go of the wheelchair, turned back to Hu. "Come on—"

Hu gestured. The bikes? "There's no room—"

"Leave them. Grab your case. Come on—"

"You sure, James—?"

"Just do it!"

Hu let go of the bikes, grabbed his most important bag, and started to board, but Officer Reese stepped in ahead of him, into the last available space, blocking his way. "Sorry. This one's full."

James started to object. "But he's my—"

She half-turned, "You got the dog, don't push your luck. There's one more train coming, he can get on that one."

James made a decision. He leaned quickly down to Pearl. "Give 'em hell, sweetheart." Then, "If he stays, I stay." He pushed past Reese and stepped off the train.

As the subway doors closed, Officer Reese glared at them both. James didn't care. He grabbed Hu. "Wedding or not, you're my husband and I'm not going anywhere without you." Then he kissed Hu passionately.

Which surprised them both—because James had never kissed Hu in public anywhere before.

◇◇◇◇◇◇◇◇◇◇◇◇◇◇◇◇◇

They weren't alone on the subway platform. There were at least thirty or forty others, the last few stragglers. Several of them were screaming at the departing train they'd been unable to board A couple had even been pushed out as the doors closed in front of them.

"You selfish bastards!" Somebody else yelled, "That was the last train." Followed by, "Come on, upstairs. The roof of the—"

His words were drowned out, running for the stairs. There was still time to get to the roof of the tallest nearby buildings. It might be enough. But if Pearl was right—and Pearl was rarely wrong—it probably wouldn't be.

James looked to Hu. "You want to follow them?"

"She said there was one more train coming."

"Do you believe her?"

"She wasn't Miss Congeniality, was she?"

"More like, I dunno, Miss Convenience Store." James looked to the stairs, looked down the track, looked to the stairs again.

Hu said, "Are we fucked?"

James didn't need to consider the question. The answer was obvious. "Well... yes. Probably."

Hu looked at his watch. "The water is probably pulling away from the shore by now."

"Uh, no," James said. "It's not gonna work like that. Not this one. That's what they were explaining while you were in the shower. A big part of the island fell into the sea, it pushed an equivalent volume of water outward. The first thing that hits is the wave. Afterward, more waves. Like the whole Pacific is sloshing."

"Should we wait here? Or...?"

Before James could answer, a Korean woman came dragging a little girl, five or six, maybe seven, running down the stairs. "She was out playing, I couldn't find her! Are we too late? Are the trains still running—?"

And as if in answer, they both felt a rising breeze.

"One more," Hu said to the woman. "The last one."

"Oh, thank God, thank God."

Down the tunnel, the distant light became an onrushing glare. The train's horn howled like an electric banshee. It came screeching into the station, the doors sliding open almost immediately.

James and Hu let the woman rush past them, the little girl almost flying like a rag doll, then they pushed their bikes into the subway car. The bikes and the attached trailers filled the space at the end of the car designed for bikes and wheelchairs and luggage on wheels. As soon as the doors slid closed and the train lurched into motion, James looked to Hu and smiled. For the first time today, since walking out of their small house in Venice Beach, James allowed himself the smallest bit of confidence. Finally, they were on their way. If they could beat the onrushing wave to Union Station, maybe.

Would there be a train waiting there? Maybe. Maybe. Otherwise...

Without stopping, the subway could get downtown in seven minutes, probably less. If they stopped for passengers, if there were people still waiting at each station, and there probably would be, then you'd have to add a minute for each station, maybe even two or three for braking, loading, accelerating again—okay, so figure maybe fifteen minutes at worst.

James wasn't certain about the speed of the onrushing water, somewhere between ten or twenty miles per hour, but that was an ordinary tsunami. A mega-tsunami? That was a whole different kettle of physics, but he had to believe they had a chance.

Union Station was sixteen miles inland from Santa Monica. The waters should be slowing that far inland, but—again, the physics on this were unknown. Okay, doing the math in his head, fifteen minutes to get downtown, maybe there's another ten or fifteen minutes margin at Union Station. If Pearl was right, there would be that one last train for evacuees and emergency workers. They'd probably have to abandon the bikes and take only what they could carry. James studied what they'd brought, already sorting it in his head.

The train stopped at the Fairfax station, there was a larger crowd here, everyone who couldn't fit into the previous train. But there was room. At least a dozen more people pushed into the car. James and Hu pulled themselves back against one side. The woman and her little girl stood across from them, the little girl staring curiously at their bicycles. The doors closed and the train lurched forward, quickly gaining speed and rushing eastward toward La Brea.

"What's that?" The little girl asked, pointing at the air tank on James' bike-trailer.

"It's my rocket-pack," said James. "For when I'm being rocket-man. Like in the song. Do you know the song?"

"No it isn't," the girl said. "It's an air tank. And you're being silly."

"Well, if you knew it was an air tank, why did you ask?" James pointed at her, as if catching her in a game of tag. She giggled and buried her face in her mother's side.

"What's your name, sweetheart?"

That was enough. She stopped hiding and turned back. It was all a game. "Julia. What's yours?"

"I'm James." And then, for no reason he could understand, maybe because he just didn't care anymore, he added, "And this is my boy friend. We're going to get married. His name is Hu."

Julia looked at Hu curiously. "Who?" she asked. "Like Doctor Who?"

"No," Hu said. "Just Hu. Like boo-hoo without the boo."

"Oh, okay." And then she said, "Could I be your flower girl? I did it for my cousin's wedding."

That's when Julia's mother put her hand on the little girl's shoulder, pulled her back. "That's enough, Julia. Don't bother those men."

Something about the way the woman said "those men"—James sensed her disapproval. Her expression had hardened.

"It's okay, ma'am. Just being friendly. We're all in this together." But he turned away anyway. Maybe another time, another place, he might have said something more. But not here, not now. There was still the problem of this time and this place.

Hu put his hand on James' arm. "What's the matter?"

"Nothing—"

"You should tell that to your face."

"I was just...doing the math in my head."

"Are we all right?"

"Should be."

Hu knew James too well. He recognized the lie. But he said nothing. Neither of them said anything until they reached the La Brea station.

This platform wasn't as crowded as the platforms had been at Fairfax and La Cienega stations. Fewer people here believed they were in danger. Maybe they were right. Or maybe they'd believed that they would find safety on their roofs.

The train was momentarily delayed in pulling out—there was a last minute rush, someone up ahead was holding a door and calling something to the motorman. The reason was quickly apparent. Nearly a dozen people, including several police officers, came charging down the stairs and across the platform—they pushed into the forward cars.

As the train pulled out again, Hu looked to his watch. "The wave, the first one. It just hit." He held up his phone for James to see. "No wi-fi down here, but I downloaded the sim while we were getting Pearl to the subway."

James studied the screen, a blue stain spreading inland. "You think it's accurate?"

"It's the one all the links pointed to. It's that scientist in Hawaii. It's supposed to be the most accurate geographic model. If his timeline is correct, our house is gone, the Third Street Mall—" Hu looked at the map. "Everything up to Bundy. Do you think the 405 might slow it down?"

James shook his head. "Not a chance, not if the wave is as high as that guy said."

"Well, Pearl said he passed the sniff test. And she is the research queen." Hu frowned at his phone. "I wish we had wi-fi down here."

"I don't."

"We could see what the news choppers are broadcasting—"

"I don't need to see it." James said. "I don't want those pictures in my head. Do you? Give me your phone—"

"Huh?"

"Give me your phone."

Hu handed it over. "Why?"

James didn't bother to answer. He pulled out his own phone and shoved both into a water-tight bag, then slipped it into his backpack.

"Really?"

"Just a precaution."

"Uh-uh. You're thinking of something."

James lowered his voice. "When the wave hits, if it reaches the Purple Line before we're in the safe zone, that water's gonna go down into the stations and flood the tunnel. We may not be safe down here."

"How long till it catches up with us?"

James stopped. He hadn't considered the question. He'd been so focused on just getting to Pearl, just getting her to the subway, just getting everyone aboard a train, just outrunning the wave front—he hadn't thought much beyond that. He frowned in thought, trying to decide what he could say—and whether or not he should say it.

"James. Answer me. Can this train outrun it?"

James didn't reply immediately. He took a deep breath. Finally, he reached across and put his hand on Hu's arm, sliding all the way up to his partner's shoulder. "We're making good time, Squeak. A mile a minute. We're moving faster than the wave front—"

Hu reached over and put his hand on James's. Quietly he said, "I looked at the video—the simulation. It looks like the water comes in awfully fast. 50 miles an hour, maybe even faster—"

James thought hard. Finally, he admitted, " It's plumbing. It's physics. It's everything. It's the depth of the water, how much volume on the surface, how big the tunnel is, and how much pressure—" He trailed off, trying to visualize the problem.

"If there's a hundred feet of water above us—" He was thinking aloud now. "I don't dive usually that deep. A hundred feet, maybe a hundred thirty, that's pretty much the limit. At a hundred feet, that's 3 atmospheres, 4 counting the weight of the air above the water, 44 PSI—pounds per square inch. That's a lot of pressure. If there's that much water, it'll be coming in fast, over the streets and through the tunnel. And if the water's higher, there'll be even more pressure. It'll move even faster." Seeing the look on Hu's face, James stopped himself.

"We're gonna get hosed, aren't we?" Hu said. He kept his voice soft, trying not to attract the attention of the other passengers.

James realized his mistake then. He tried to cover quickly. "Only if it hits, only if it hits—" It wasn't enough.

Hu closed his eyes against the mental picture, against the rising turmoil of emotions that were suddenly flooding up inside him, fear and anger and something unidentifiable. His expression collapsed and suddenly, he was sobbing. "I'm sorry, Bubble."

"What for—?"

"For...everything. For the subway. It was a stupid idea—"

"No, sweetheart, no. It was a good idea. A really good idea. You'll see. We'll be okay."

But Hu refused to be reassured. The moment was reawakening his panic—that same panic he'd felt that day in the tank at Paramount. And this time, there wouldn't be anybody who could save either of them.

James slid his hand up Hu's shoulder, putting his palm on the back of Hu's neck—their own private gesture of reassurance. He pulled him into a hug and whispered, "Hell or high water, Squeak. I promise."

Hu pulled back, just enough to smile at him.

The train screeched and rocketed through the dark tunnel, but James and Hu didn't notice, didn't care. They had retreated into a private space between their shining eyes, their own special world of connection.

After a moment, Hu pulled away, recovering enough to reach into the pocket of his jeans. He pulled out the small velvet-covered box, opened it, withdrew the larger ring and slid it onto James' finger. "This is not the way I wanted to do it, this is awful, but...I take thee, James D. Liddle as my awfully wedded husband, forever and ever, and for all the days of my life."

James took the box from Hu, took the second ring and likewise slid it onto Hu's finger. "I take thee, Hu Son, to be my husband, to be my lawfully bedded husband, forever and ever, and for all the days of my life."

They looked into each other's eyes again, trying to make the moment last forever. Finally James leaned forward and gently kissed Hu. He wanted to kiss him more passionately, but it wasn't necessary, not here—not with so many strangers watching. He hadn't realized they had attracted an audience. Several people applauded and cheered, but not the uncertain Korean woman still clutching the little girl close to her.

There were tears forming in Hu's eyes. He said, "This is the real one, Bubble, but I still want a ceremony." He whispered, "After all, we've already got a flower girl. I mean, if her mother will let her."

It was too much, all too much. James finally laughed. "We're about to lose the house, the car, the motorcycle, our business—we still don't know if we're going to survive—" He couldn't help himself, the words came fumbling out. "—And here we are, this is the happiest day of my life."

"It's certainly going to be one to remember—"

And that's when the subway train lurched.

The train lurched as if it had gone over a speed bump. Someone gasped, someone else screamed. Then the train roared on, faster than before.

"What was that—?" Hu had to raise his voice to be heard.

James shook his head. "Dunno. Felt like a power-glitch to me."

"Do you think they're shutting down the grid?"

"Makes sense they would—"

"But not the subway—"

"We're still rolling—"

Hu opened his mouth, not quite a yawn, something else. "James—?"

"What?"

"My ears just popped."

"Yeah." James forced his own yawn as well. "Mine too."

"What would—?" But Hu already knew the answer.

"Air pressure," said James. "The water is definitely in the tunnel. It's coming in fast, compressing the air—"

"It's gonna hit us, isn't it—"

James didn't answer. He looked down to the rear end of the car, but there was no view out the back. Even if there had been, there were too many people in the way. He turned around to his bike, pulled his divebelt off the trailer, made sure his knife was in its sheath. He pulled Hu to his side. "Face your bike, now. If you have to, throw yourself over the tank. Hide it from view."

"What? Why—?" And then understanding. "Oh." And then, "Oh, shit—"

"Yeah," James finished buckling his divebelt around his waist. "It's gonna get ugly."

"James—"

"There's nothing we can do—"

Hu grabbed his arm. "We can do something. We've got two regulators on each rig. We can save Julia and her mom."

James wanted to argue, but Hu was right. He stepped over to the Korean woman, looked directly into her terrified eyes. "Come stand next to us. Both of you. Please." He reached out and touched her elbow. It was enough. Still clutching her daughter, she moved closer to the bikes.

"Listen to me," said James. He lowered his voice, almost to a whisper. "I'm a SCUBA professional. The wave is coming, it's going to flood this car. When the water hits, it's going to get panicky in here, but each of the tanks has two mouthpieces and there's enough air here for four people, Hu and myself—and both of you. You'll be okay if you do what I say. Here's what you need to know. Are you listening, Julia?"

The little girl nodded, her eyes wide.

"Okay, when it's time, Hu's going to give you a mouthpiece. We don't have a mask for you, so you're gonna want to close your eyes and just concentrate on breathing as slowly as you can. Take really long, really slow, breaths, in and out, only through the mouthpiece, really slow—okay?"

Julia nodded solemnly.

"Now, remember, I want you to keep your eyes closed and just concentrate on breathing—" Julia looked confused. James leaned down and whispered in her ear, "Okay, here's how to do it. You count a hundred breaths to yourself, because that's how long it takes. And if the water still hasn't gone down, then you start over and count to a hundred again. You might have to do that more than once, but that's how Hu and I are gonna do it—" He straightened and turned to the mother. "Did you get all that? You and I will share the other tank—"

The woman started to say something, an objection—?

James held up his hand. "Don't say anything. Just stand here. Turn away from anyone else. Both of you. Keep your backs to them. And—"

The subway lurched again. This time, the car bumped as if something had struck it from behind. Someone at the other end of the car screamed, several people screamed, both men and women—

Something lifted the rear of the car off the tracks, tilting them forward. Outside there were sparks—the train was slowing, there was no more power to the wheels—and then there was light outside, flickering light—the subway train was careening into the Wilshire/Western station and angry brown water flooded up onto the platform from the tracks. More water poured down the stairways and escalators, battering the walls and the train with debris, all of it rising rapidly and rocking the car with its force. The air smelled suddenly *wet*.

The other passengers, mostly men began shouting and pushing scrambling at and over each other. Muddy water was already flooding into the car from Underneath. Men were shouting, several were trying to force open the doors, trying to escape. Others were demanding they stop, terrified because the darkness outside the train was already rising past the windows—

And then someone finally pushed the doors open and the flood—cold, salty, and gritty—came roaring in, pummeling and pounding, an inescapable torrent. People screamed and floundered, pushing at each other, climbing over each other, trampling anyone smaller, fighting their way through the current, desperate to get up the station stairs toward the air they imagined was waiting for them.

And then the last of the lights went out.

Green emergency lights flickered on, self-powered, but they weren't enough. And they didn't last. They were extinguished one by one by the rising muddy water.

James and Hu were already pulling the bungee cords off the bikes, off the tanks. They fumbled in the gloom, depending on experience and muscle-memory.

Hu pushed the first regulator at Julia, the water was up to her chest. She grabbed the mouthpiece with both hands, pushed it into her mouth. James had already pulled Julia's mother to the other bike—yanking the whole rig off the bike trailer, he shoved a regulator toward the terrified woman, then helped her get it into her mouth as the water rose to her neck. He looked to Hu, who gave him a quick thumbs-up, pushing his own regulator into his mouth.

Hu rummaged in his case, triumphantly pulled out two headlamps, and pulled one over his head. Right, James thought, we're going to need those! His own face-mask had a headlamp built in, but he felt around in his case for the other lamps. He slipped one of them over Julia's mother's head, started to hand her the second one for Julia—

"Please, sir—me too, please—"

James grabbed his face mask and pulled it down over his eyes just as the water came rising up over his chin. He turned and saw a frightened young teen, a black boy in a red T-shirt. The boy bobbed up desperately, his hand out for help. "Please—"

"We'll have to share—"

"Okay, yes, okay—"

James held his mouthpiece to the boy, they were bumping up against the top of car. "Long slow breaths, okay. Two, three breaths—into the mouthpiece, both in and out. Then it's my turn. Okay?"

"Okay." The boy took the mouthpiece just as the water forced the last of the air out of the subway car. James put the last headlamp on him. It switched on automatically when the water hit it. Then he turned to his left, looking to make sure Hu was all right.

He wasn't.

There was a struggle going on. James couldn't see far in the murky water, but one thing was clear. Someone was fighting Hu for the regulator. Someone else was trying to get to Julia. She was curled up in a ball, holding her regulator tightly in both hands.

James kicked off, directly head-butting into Julia's attacker, pushing him backward toward the open subway door. Outside the rushing water surged past the train, filling the station and pushing into the next bore. James head-butted the man again, forcing him into one side of the open door. The current grabbed him, yanked him away and he went flailing into the turbulence, disappearing into the dark and muddy gloom. James had to grab a pole to keep from being pulled after him. Desperately, he grabbed the overhead bar and worked his way back to Hu.

Hu's eyes were wide, his mouth bubbling open. The stranger had gotten the regulator away from him. Hu was grabbing futilely for it—it was his drowning nightmare all over again, but there was no James at his side.

The stranger was holding Hu at arm's length, while sucking greedily for air. Hu saw the man pulling away into darkness—until one arm came reaching around the stranger's chest and another hand sliced across his throat, releasing a cloud of red-brown darkness, expanding outward like inky smoke. The man stiffened, choked, gasped, struggled, and thrashed away in the dark, pummeled by the rushing water, but still held by the regulator tube.

James came around from behind the thrashing man, pulled the regulator from his mouth and as the body turned away into darkness, he pushed the regulator into his own mouth, grabbing a quick suck of air for himself—rule number one, take care of yourself first—but he was already swimming back to Hu. He met Hu's terrified eyes, then passed the regulator over, watching to make sure that Hu had it safely back in his mouth. James held firmly onto Hu, watching to see if all his careful training was paying off. Hu was scared, but somehow he remembered what to do. He choked past his panic—James watched to make sure that Hu was finally breathing again, breathing slowly and deliberately, before he gestured for the regulator. He'd waited almost too long—his own lungs were feeling tight.

Hu passed the regulator back to James, who took three hasty breaths, then turned headed back to his own tank. He had to take a moment to steady himself. This was all happening too fast. He was still feeling his own adrenaline-panic as he swam back to the teenager, still holding his knife—

He had vision—of a sort. The new headlamps he'd grabbed back at the office had switched on automatically when the water hit them. Each had a pair of matching LED arrays, so he could see where Hu and the Julia were by the illusion of bright eyes in the darkness. Paired fingers of light probed at the gloom, illuminating almost nothing.

The black boy and the Korean woman were equally visible, another small circle of brightness. James swam back to the teenager, still holding his knife, and turned the boy to face him. The water was cold and it was pounding at them, shoving them this way and that. The boy could barely focus in the dark, he didn't have a facemask, but he saw the lamps on James' mask and he could see enough to recognize the man who'd saved him. He gave James a thumbs-up and passed the mouthpiece over—

James was glad. One murder was already one murder too many. He knew that Hu had seen it, but he couldn't tell what Hu was thinking, how he was reacting. Probably he was still trying to calm himself. James hoped that both Julia and her mother had kept their eyes closed as instructed. This was going to be a long afternoon.

Now it was James' turn to manage his breathing—and his fear. If he didn't manage himself, he couldn't manage anyone. He took three long breaths, then passed the mouthpiece back to the boy. Then, finally, he remembered to slide his knife back into its sheath.

The thrashing of the water was lessening. They were still being pummeled by surges of uneven pressure, why was that? Something up the tunnel must be blocking the flow of water, alternately blocking and opening. James imagined a giant pink heart valve, but it was probably a humongus piece of debris being pushed back and forth by the torrent. If it could settle, if it could block the worst of the flow, then maybe—but no, they shouldn't depend on it.

He had to convince himself that they could do this. He wasn't sure for how long. It depended on how much water they had above them, on how much pressure they could stand, on how long their air would hold out, and on how long they could last in the cold. Maybe the incoming coastal waters were warm enough they wouldn't be plunged into hypothermia. Maybe, just maybe, they had enough air to hold out for an hour, but probably less because they were sharing? He had to figure this out—

Then he remembered. His $1500 dive computer. He'd packed it, hadn't he? For a moment, he felt embarrassed, but then he realized, he'd hadn't had a chance to use it, so it wasn't part of his muscle-memory. What bag was it in?

He went back to the boy, shared his three breaths, steadied his breathing, and visualized the morning. He usually talked to himself when he worked. Saying things out loud imprinted them in his memory. Ah, there—

He passed the regulator back, went straight to the case he'd almost left behind, and it was right where he remembered, right where he'd said when he packed it. It would have been easy to find anyway. It had switched itself on when the water hit it—its display was bright, even in this darkness, and now it was beeping an alarm. He slid it onto his left wrist and tried to focus on the dials.

The numbers flickered with confusing speed. The device kept beeping contradictory warnings. James was an expert in with sport diving. At a hundred feet deep, a diver would use his air four times faster, but right now the dive computer was telling him that his current rate of air consumption might be ten times faster, might be twenty, might be five—the numbers kept changing, up and down, too fast to make any sense. They were either five hundred feet underwater or fifty. It was the fluctuating pressure of the water still pounding through the tunnel. The damn thing couldn't calibrate.

James tried to visualize what was happening. How much water? Too much and they wouldn't be able to stay down for long. If they needed to decompress, then the longer they spent under pressure, the longer decompression would take, and if they had limited air that would be a problem. They'd have to start up as soon as the flow of water ebbed. But how long could they wait for the current to slow? He had to balance time at this depth against time needed to ascend.

The tsunami was still pushing inland, what were the physics of that? Here in the tunnel, the rushing water was still battering at the car and stirring debris throughout the station. And all the things that should never have been debris—

Unless and until things equalized, they could be stuck here. How long until the water stopped flooding eastward? How long till it settled? How long till it started receding back into the sea? And how fast would it retreat? When would the next wave arrive? James had no idea.

He wondered if Pearl's train had made it safely to Union Station. Maybe. Probably. It had been packed full, so it wouldn't have made any stops. They would have gained a few minutes. And maybe ith this train blocking part of the tunnel, maybe the flow would have been less, and maybe Pearl's train could have made it all the way downtown—?

And maybe that was all wishful thinking.

And maybe, despite everything they weren't going to make it after all.

∞∞∞∞∞∞∞∞∞∞∞∞

The churning slowed.

It didn't stop, but it slowed.

And they were still alive.

How did he know that?

Because they were still alive.

It didn't make sense.

They hadn't outrun the tsunami.

And they were under how many feet of water—

And yet...here they were, still alive, still breathing.

Still alive.

The water was brown and murky where the headlamp beams pierced it for a few feet it looked like as much mud (and who knew what else) as water. If they hadn't had the headlamps...

Maybe that was what had attracted the attackers, maybe they saw the light as a beacon. He wasn't sure. It had all happened too fast, the subway car had flooded so quickly. James was wearing a professional-grade mask, it had extra-bright lamps, but down here, the advantage was minimal. He had only a small tunnel of vision, a gloom just a bit lighter than the darker gloom surrounding. He hung in place, thoughts trying to race, circling in confusion. He was a frozen moment of awareness in a shadowy underwater coffin.

He looked to the others. Julia was holding onto the regulator with both hands, her eyes were closed. She was fine, almost relaxed. Her mother too, though not as calm—she understood how precarious their situation was. Hu was floating close to Julia, watching her carefully. And the teenager—he was watching James as warily as a feral cat. He must have seen what James had done. James took his three breaths, then turned to look toward the raised end of the car. There were dark shapes floating in the water, he didn't look long, he didn't want to see them clearly. He already knew and his gut churned.

He turned his attention to the dials on the tanks. They had air—just not enough. Nowhere near as much as he had hoped. The chaos, the exertion, they were sucking air faster than he had planned. And the pressure, more pressure meant each lungful sucked in more air. He had to assume they were under at least a hundred feet of water.

But how deep were they, really? How much water was pressing down on them?

It didn't matter. They were in trouble. They had to move.

James wanted to stay nice and safe. Underwater was always nice and safe—if you knew what you were doing. But if you knew what you were doing, then you'd also know, you can't stay underwater. It's not just how much air—it's the *other* reason. At any serious pressure, they'd get wonky.

James knew what it felt like. It's a little like being drunk or stoned—except it isn't. It's the rapture of the deep. And if you succumb to it, you become a statistic of the deep. No, you have to focus. You have to concentrate on every single task. Each specific task, one careful moment after the next.

James focused. He took his next three breaths and passed the mouthpiece back to the boy. Options. He had to consider the options. They weren't good. But they were options. That was more than most people had—especially the ones now floating limp in the darkness. There were so many of them, and they couldn't escape them, could they? They were a silent gauntlet, guarding any exit.

In the chaos of the moment, James hadn't considered the panic, the terror, of those caught in the water, unable to escape, those last few desperate moments of grasping for possibility, gasping for air, choking on their own last screams of denial and rage.

James knew what it was like to drown. It had been one of the worst parts of his training. He'd never understood the necessity of the exercise—being pushed into that near-death moment—at least, not until afterward when he'd been painfully pulled out of the tank, choking and gasping and coughing up water, not until the medic checked his heart and listened to his lungs and nodded to the trainer. Not until the trainer had looked him straight in the eyes and said, "Now do you understand what you'll be dealing with when you try to rescue a drowning man?"

And James had somehow managed to get the words out, "Was that fucking necessary?"

"I hope to fucking God it never is. But if it saves one life—yours—then, yeah." The trainer added, "Given a choice, I'd rather lose the idiot. His funeral I don't have to go to."

James had made up his mind, there and then, never to repeat the experience. Not voluntarily. And definitely not involuntarily!

That had a lot to do with his relationship with Hu, as well. That first day, in the tank at Paramount, he'd been watching this beautiful young man with multiple overlays of awareness. At first, he'd thought him just a gangling teenager, then he realized not only was Hu older than he looked, but also how inexperienced he himself was at gauging ages, especially the ages of Asian men. He just didn't have enough history.

For a moment, he'd wondered if Hu were...what's a good word? Accessible? An interesting question, not one he usually considered, and not one he intended to pursue here. It was only a passing thought, quickly pushed aside by the necessities of the job.

Once in the tank, once the plastic and Styrofoam flotsam had been added, once the wind machines had been turned on and the mechanically produced waves had started churning, it became obvious—to James at least—that Hu did not have a lot of experience with this particular kind of stunt work. And even though plastic and Styrofoam looks and feels lightweight—if enough of it piles up against you, or on top of you, it can rapidly become an impenetrable mass. You can drown just as easily as if it were the real thing.

So James had watched Hu. He watched all the people in the water, but he watched Hu especially—because the beautiful young man wasn't watching out for himself, not the way a more experienced stunt player would have.

James hadn't waited for anyone to call "cut!" The rule was simple. Don't worry about ruining the shot. Get out of the way of the bus. Dodge the falling rocks. Don't get bitten by the mechanical dinosaur head. Don't. Get. Injured. Especially don't get killed. That costs money. It shuts the production down for two or three days. And it pisses off producers.

Rule Number One: Getting killed can ruin your whole day.

So James had dived into the tank, swum under the prop flotsam, grabbed Hu, and pulled him off to the side. He hadn't been thinking of anything more than just getting the poor dumb schmuck out of danger. It wasn't until later, over lunch, that he'd realized what an amazing smile shone on Hu Son's face.

And even then, he hesitated. He'd been burned enough in the relationship fire. He wasn't that eager to put his hand back into the flames—or any other part of his anatomy. But one thing led to another anyway—and now he had a ring on his finger.

It was an unfamiliar sensation. Hu's life was the other half of his now. His responsibility. And not just Hu. Three other lives were depending on his expertise.

So. Options. They could head up the nearest stairwell, head for the surface. Except, where was the surface? Right now, Wilshire was under water. James didn't know exactly how much, but it had to be a lot of fast-moving water. 10 mph, 20 mph, it didn't matter. It would be like stepping into a hurricane, except they'd be weightless with no footing. The waters would carry them away like balloons in a storm.

Wait for the waters to subside? That would work. If they subsided fast enough, before the five of them ran out of air or succumbed to cold. That was another problem. The temperature of the water. It was cold—not cold enough to produce hypothermia in an adult, not right away, but Julia's smaller body put her at increased risk. And perhaps the skinny teenager as well. They had to get above the water.

The subway car lurched, distracting James. Not quite unseen, the drifting bodies lurched too.

James took an extra deep breath, then passed the mouthpiece back to the young man. He swam deeper into the car to investigate. His headlamp gave him some sense of the mess—one of the subway doors was jammed open—by a body. His internal conversation was deafening. *Please, God, no children. No children, please—*

God did not comply.

His beam illuminated an infant, blanket still unraveling around its lifeless body. *Oh, fuck, fuck, fuck—fuck you, God—*

James retreated, his mind already postulating what must have happened. A mother rushing home from work, finding the baby-sitter gone, grabbing the baby, rushing for the subway, but somehow getting to the station just a few minutes too late, getting on the last car, hoping to escape. Dying in cold dark terror.

He bumped into a floating cat carrier, a furry body within, the handle still gripped by an elderly woman, her white hair floating around her head like a cloud.

Another body, this one in a dark uniform, the garbage truck driver? James didn't want to know. It was too much. He was starting to feel the horror—and painful pressure in his chest.

The subway lurched again—and all the separate bodies echoed the movement, a synchronized ballet, all the different dancers bumping sideways to the same unheard music. The moment passed and they resumed their slow deliberate gavotte. No longer panicked, in death they had become patient observers, the staring jetsam of disaster, their faces now relaxed and lifeless, they hung almost motionless, a silent jury—their fatal judgment dark and unspoken.

The dive computer was certain now, it beeped in alarm—they were too deep. They had to start ascending now. And as quickly as possible. Too much water, too little air—the bends would be inevitable.

James swam back to the others, back to the air tanks, still struggling with the math of their survival. He couldn't sort it out, it was the pressure, the paralyzing effects of it. His thoughts wandered in a drunken haze—and if he was having trouble, then the others were probably faring worse.

He had to focus. He hadn't expected to do this, not this soon, but there wasn't any alternative. He had to switch the tanks now, before he got fuzzier.

Switching tanks underwater wasn't hard. He'd done it before, but he hadn't done it a lot, so—after the necessary three breaths—he took his time to make sure he was doing it right. He had to focus carefully on each part of the process. As soon as the connections were secure, as soon as the pressure gauges were good, he relaxed a little. Hu and Julia had a little more time. He'd switch their tanks in fifteen minutes, maybe ten.

What had he been thinking about? He concentrated—oh yeah, options. Can't swim for the surface, can't wait for the waters to subside. Could they get higher?

Maybe! The Wiltern—wasn't there something? He tried to remember. There was a subway entrance in the building, wasn't there? Part of some expansion project? A pedestrian tunnel under the street, from the lobby to the platform. That would get them up a couple floors—that is, if the building was still there and if it was tall enough to stick out of the water, then maybe they could get to one of the upper floors before they ran out of air. So many ifs—

But, the numbers didn't leave any room for negotiation nor delays. They were too deep and they had too many bodies breathing too little air. But maybe—

Everything was maybe. James shared another three breaths, passed the mouthpiece back, then fumbled in his bag of gear until he found what he was looking for—a plastic panel and a grease pencil on a leash. Another three breaths of air, then he wrote frantically. "Get out now. Tunnel to Wiltern."

He didn't have time to write more. He wouldn't have anyway. But when the waters started to recede, when worst of the flood finally started to flow back to the sea, he worried that the pressure in the station would also reverse and the subway train would be sucked back into the tunnel, where no escape would be possible. He wasn't sure about the physics, his mind wasn't focusing that far, but he couldn't chance it.

Three breaths, then he held the panel in the teen's headlamp beam. The boy's eyes were wide, bright in the gloom, he gave a thumbs-up response. James maneuvered himself over to Hu, held up the sign. Hu gave a thumbs-up too, then reached for the panel. He touched the Julia's shoulder. She opened her eyes and then squinted them almost shut—this muck hurt! Hu tapped her shoulder again, holding the sign in front of her, his lights pointed at it. She nodded. She was tired, she was scared, but she was determined. James admired her spirit. She gave him hope.

James took the sign back, turned back to his own tank for another three breaths, then to hold the sign for Julia's mother to see. She was too frightened to respond with anything more than a half-nod of acknowledgment.

Another three breaths.

Stay focused, James told himself. One thing at a time.

Another tough decision. They were going to have to leave the bikes behind—and everything they'd so carefully packed. Abandoned. For a moment, he considered the impossible—could they carry any of this? None of them were wearing weight-belts, they had a buoyancy problem, they were all bobbing toward the roof of the subway car, the bikes might serve as ballast, and keep them from rising too fast—

No, it was too much to ask, too much effort. Not enough air. But at least, he and Hu had already transferred their most important belongings to their backpacks, they could take that much at least.

Three more breaths. He waved to Hu, caught his attention, and pointed to his backpack. Hu nodded. He gave a double thumbs up and checked his straps. At least they could save what they could wear.

James turned back to the bikes and pulled the air tanks off the trailers, the ones they were using, and the last set of spares. Another three breaths and he gave the signal. He was in a small circle of light, fingers of illumination surrounded him. He gave a thumbs-up signal and the entire group began to move—Hu and Juilia, the teen and Julia's mother.

They worked their way to the jammed-open door of the subway and somehow he managed to push the bodies out of the way. Two? Three? He wasn't sure and it didn't matter. The doors stayed open, one small piece of good luck.

Three more breaths.

The subway car was tilted. A wedge of debris had been thrust under its rear wheels, raising at a lopsided angle—it leaned away from the platform, its upper frame jammed against the outer wall of the tunnel. The end of the car was more than a foot above the platform, wheels caught on the edge of it. Their door at the front of the car was almost a foot above the platform, and angled upward. Without the water, it would have been a hard leap. Here, this deep, under this much pressure, gravity was almost irrelevant. If anything, they were going to have a hard time staying down.

Three more breaths.

James swam to Julia's mom, patted her on the shoulder reassuringly, gave her a thumbs-up, then to the boy to reassure him as well—three more breaths—and then back to look at the pressure gauge on Hu's tank.

Two and a half adults had drained his own tank, but Hu's tank, with only one and a half bodies draining it, still had a useful margin. James gestured to Hu, pointing at the mouthpiece. Hu understood, he passed it over, sharing his air.

James took four breaths, a luxury, but a necessary one, then passed the mouthpiece back. James went through the door first. Hu brought up the rear. He had learned from James, they'd spent time together underwater. Be slow. Be methodical. Keep the beginners between you. Do one thing only, then the next. There's no rush. Impatience kills. Panic kills. Count to three. Or four.

Once out the door, they bobbed upward, bumping into the ceiling. Hu shared his air with James again. He looked worried, but James refused to acknowledge it. He'd already made up his mind. They were going to live. They hadn't come this far to die.

Another few breaths from Hu's tank and James swam away for a quick reconnaissance of the flooded station. He had to find the pedestrian tunnel.

There were bodies here. Too many, most of them floating up toward the ceiling, bobbing there like dreadful balloons. He tried not to think about them, but some of them turned toward him as he passed, he couldn't ignore their faces.

And fish, there were fish here too! Not a lot, and nothing James could identify, but some struggled feebly in the muddy currents. They wouldn't survive.

It gave him pause. Maybe later he would think about it. Maybe later someone would be able to explain how they got there. Maybe there'd be "later." Too many maybes.

At the front of the train, where it had shuddered to a stop, James pulled himself down to look into the first car. His headlights found the motorman's booth, the driver still behind the controls, his face an angry expression of disbelief and rage. James' beams illuminated the badge on his chest. It said "Jeffers."

You stupid schmuck, thought James. *Stupid, stupid, stupid. You should have just run for home, we could have made it. But no! You had to stop, didn't you. One more station, one more heroic pickup. Instead of saving a few, you killed us all.*

That last thought startled James. He hadn't realized it, but he'd been identifying with the dead. Down among the dead men, he had no choice. Despite his conviction, he still had no certainty.

It didn't matter what he thought. He kept going. He pushed a little further into the gloom, now exploring along the walls—no, nothing here, nothing here, nothing here. The darkness refused to give up its secrets. The tunnel had to be in the other direction.

Feeling the pressure rising in his lungs, James headed back to Hu and sucked eagerly, much too eagerly, at the regulator. He had to take a minute to recalibrate himself. Slowly, dammit, slowly.

This time he headed around the escalator, feeling along the walls—but carefully. If he bobbed up that diagonal shaft he might not be able to get back—but there it was. The pedestrian tunnel, a darker dark in the dark. Maybe it was his brain playing tricks with his eyes, the way he could "see" the furniture at home when he got up in the middle of the night to pee. And maybe it was a hallucination from nitrogen narcosis. Too many maybes. But no—a little closer and he was sure. It was the tunnel. He turned around, and just as carefully, he worked his way back to the others.

Three more breaths.

Time to switch out the tank that Hu and Julia were using. It didn't take long, but he had to concentrate, had to be careful. He had to focus.

When he finished, all the headlights were pointed at him. He existed as an oasis of light in a dark universe. He passed his mouthpiece back to the boy and pointed. Time to go.

Everybody but Julia had to carry a tank. They had the two they were still breathing from—and the last two spares.

As a group, they moved, all five of them—James and Hu, Julia and her mother, and the unnamed black teen. It was a tough swim, they bounced along the roof of the station, James herding them carefully away from the escalator shaft. Their headlights weaving in the dark.

They made their way slowly toward the promise of escape.

James didn't know what was at the end of the tunnel. He hoped it wasn't blocked by debris. Or worse—

◇◇◇◇◇◇◇◇◇◇◇◇◇◇◇

There were bodies floating in the pedestrian tunnel. Their headlamps revealed a gauntlet of bobbing shapes. James tried not to think about the panic that must have happened in here, the water flooding in so fast, it would have been like trying to swim up a waterfall. Dark shapes bobbed everywhere. And the floor of the tunnel was littered with everything they'd tried to carry with them.

They paused several times for James to suck air. This was not what he had expected. Or hoped for. They had to push their way through a nightmare, faces coming out of the dark—all too close. It was a bumping gauntlet of horror, a gallery of silent accusations, each body turning in its own final orbit. James tried not to look, tried not to illuminate them, but he had no choice. They were passing through a tunnel of horror—a silent community, patiently waiting for James and the others to join them.

Three more breaths—

And at last, the end. Another set of steps. They half-swam, half bobbed up the diagonal shaft. At the top—only darkness. James made them wait. He took three breaths and entered first, turning around slowly, looking to see if it was safe.

He could barely make out any details. It was still way too dark in here. But they were definitely in the foyer of the Wiltern tower, the part that had been carved out for a pedestrian entrance to the subway. That much he could recognize, but he was otherwise unfamiliar with the building. The lobby ceiling was high. He didn't want to get caught up there with no weight-belt to bring him down. There was a railing here, he held onto it against the eddies of current. He could feel himself being pushed this way and that—not a lot, but enough to make him uncomfortable. Outside, the water must still be moving, but he couldn't tell which way. The gloom was that complete.

James swam back into the tunnel. He took breaths from Hu, then from the boy. He didn't want to be selfish, but he didn't want to lose himself to the rapture either.

He steadied his breathing and aimed his light around the group. He wasn't familiar with the layout of the building. This was the lobby of the theater. He grabbed his grease pencil and scrawled on the plastic slate. "Stairwell?"

Hu shrugged. He didn't know either.

But Julia's mother reached out and grabbed his arm. She pointed outward and then toward the left. Over there—

 But they couldn't just swim over. The problem was buoyancy. They needed to get across the lobby without rising so high they couldn't get to the door.

James looked back into the tunnel. A weird though—

Three more breaths.

He swam back into the pedestrian tunnel, searching. The bottom was littered with the abandoned belongings of the dead. James was looking for suitcases—the canvas ones with one handle on top and another on the side. Whoever these poor fools had been, they weren't smart enough to leave their lives behind. James tested several of the cases for weight, then pulled the two heaviest back to the end.

Three more breaths.

Hu understood immediately. He'd take one suitcase, holding it by the top handle. James would take the other. Julia's mom and the teen would hold on to the side handles. Hu would hold Julia's hand. They should be able to make it.

Three more breaths—and James gave the thumbs-up signal.

As a group, they moved, a curious underwater tableau, a cluster of bobbing lights that revealed air tanks and baggage and faces tight against any further horrors in the dark. The Korean woman kept pointing and gesturing. James kept checking back to her, but in the darkness, it was impossible to know if they were actually heading in the right direction. He had to stop for breath again—and even a second time, until he realized they were paralleling a wall. But he wasn't sure if it was the outer wall of the lobby or the one they had been swimming toward. He didn't know this building, but maybe the lobby wasn't rectangular.

Left or right? James had to guess. He could make out vague shapes in the distance, but those could have been hallucinations. He took three breaths from the teen, then make a decision—the fire stairwell would be against an outer wall of the lobby. Okay, he'd lead them to the left and hope it wasn't a dead-end.

It wasn't. Left was right. He realized with a start that he shouldn't be thinking word games now. That was dangerous.

But they were at the door. It had a wide emergency bar, the kind that pushed to open. For a moment, James felt fear. Without leverage, how could he push it?

Hu was already there, he batted the door with the heavy case he was holding. It bumped open enough for James to wedge his shoulder in. He pushed it further open, revealing only darkness.

James let go of the case he was dragging and entered the stairwell. He grabbed a railing and turned around slowly, looking to see if it was safe. Above, far above, did something glimmer? The surface?

It looked doable.

He gestured, a slow-motion wave.

Hu and the others pushed their way in. James shared three breaths and considered their circumstance. The stairwell was a silent column of dark water, but it was clearer water. They could actually see something. Their headlight beams penetrated for several yards. There wasn't a lot of debris here, and nowhere near as much mud and murk. The water must have filtered in instead of flooding, rising at its own rate.

James looked back. Hu had dropped his case to push the door closed. His own abandoned suitcase—the teen boy was pulling at its zipper, curious to see what was inside. James swam over and touched the boy's shoulder. The boy looked to him and he waggled his finger no. We're not grave-robbers. Out of the water, the boy's gesture would have been a puzzled shrug, but he let go of the zipper anyway.

Here inside the stairwell, with the fire door closed behind them, they should be safe from any rough currents. Even better, if all the fire doors above were closed, then this column of water would be a convenient chimney. They could ascend at their safest rate. Maybe... If the building hadn't been weakened, if it didn't collapse around them.

The dive computer was still beeping in annoyance. It said the water's surface was less than 100 feet above them. It wanted to know how much air they had—but James couldn't tell it, he didn't know.

The surface might be reachable. If their air held out. If hypothermia didn't get them first.

If a second wave didn't arrive and destroy everything the first wave had already weakened.

James calculated in his head, it was still hard to focus down here, but the math wasn't impossible. One floor every five minutes. Maybe two—? No, they didn't have enough air. They had to get as high as they could as fast as they could. They might manage an extra ten or twenty minutes of decompression nearer the surface. Maybe they could make it.

He took his three breaths, passed the regulator back, and pointed upward.

The light at the end of the tunnel was still a hundred feet above them, and it was still invisible.

◇◇◇◇◇◇◇◇◇◇◇◇◇◇◇

It is not a good idea to laugh underwater.

You could drown.

But as James did the math in his head, as he computed the safest rate of ascent through the stairwell measured against his estimate of the amount of air they had left, he ended up reminding himself—

Sloan's teddy....

For a few dangerous seconds, he splurted bubbles. The more he tried to stop himself from laughing, the funnier it got. Hu looked at him, curious, then worried. James finally somehow managed to control himself. He held up a hand, he grabbed his board and wrote on it. "I'm fine. I'll tell you later."

Three breaths and he pointed upward. A single flight of stairs. Then another. Thirty feet. Sloan's teddy indeed.

Five minutes max, then they bobbed up a flight of stairs Except the dive computer on his wrist beeped to let him know that they were still ascending anyway, even as they waited. The waters were receding and somewhere, the chimney must be leaking. Not good. If it leaked too fast and too much. If they "ascended" too rapidly, they were in serious trouble.

James had had the bends. Twice. Once was bad planning, once was stupidity—not his, the diver he'd had to rescue—but either way, it was not something he wanted to do a third time. Rashes, joint pain, headaches, even paralysis. But the bends are survivable—most of the time. Symptoms of decompression sickness can show up in the first hour, almost certainly in the first six hours, and if not in the first 24 hours, then probably not at all.

But if it was a choice between the bends and death?

Another joke occurred to him. "Death? Good choice. But first, Oompah!" He had to suppress a giggle. And then he wondered, what the fuck? Am I getting giddy? Nitrogen narcosis was playing at the edge of his brain.

Three breaths from Hu, then three breaths from the boy. He was going to have to start watching himself. All these people were depending on him. It was time. He pointed. Up the next flight of stairs. And the next. And the next.

The higher they rose, the brighter the stairwell, the brighter the promise above. The water here wasn't as murky as it was below, but now there was debris floating in their way—a lot of paper, and a large rubber trash can, someone's jacket, and when James looked up, he thought he saw a body caught under a railing.

He checked his goddamn beeping dive computer and frowned. There was nothing he could do. Maybe they should wait an extra two minutes here? He took three breaths from Hu, three from the boy, gestured for them to wait and swam halfway up to look.

Yes, a body. A woman, stocky, possibly in her fifties, hard to tell. Her hair floated like a cloud around her head, but her dress had floated up revealing thick legs and pale underpants, they had become translucent, revealing her nakedness before his light—one last embarrassment. The tsunami had not only taken her life, it had taken her dignity as well.

James came back down again, grabbed another six breaths, then gestured for the others to follow him—but he waved his hand down past his eyes to show Julia and her mother to close theirs. Up the stairwell and James tried to push the woman's body into a corner while the others rose past. Her name badge identified her as Mrs. Hayes. She was entitled to this much consideration—he didn't want the others to see her shame. Poor Mrs. Hayes.

Another flight up, another rubber trash can. And here was the cause of the decreasing pressure. The fire door was jammed open by another body, this one a janitor in a dark uniform. James could feel the current here—the water was being sucked away. Outside the broken tower, the current must have become too strong to resist. James felt himself being pulled—it was strong enough to be a challenge.

He pulled on the fire door, pushing it open enough for the poor man's body to be sucked through and away. He let go and the current pushed the door shut again, cutting off the water's escape.

He was surprised that he'd been able to pull the door open at all. The force of the water was less than he'd expected. This was both good news and bad news.

They were closer to the surface—but they were also more at risk of decompression sickness. He swam back down to the others. Three breaths from Hu, three breaths from the boy, and three more breaths from Hu. They were going to have to wait here ten minutes at least. Maybe more.

And they were already on their last tanks. He didn't remember when they had switched over, but apparently he had done so at some point up the chimney of the stairwell. Maybe at the bottom, before they started up? Not a good sign that he didn't remember. He studied the dials on the last two tanks.

Good—

—Just not good enough.

He floated on his back so he could peer upward through the gap between the stairs. There was light up there, brighter than before. He watched his bubbles rise up through his headlamp beam toward it.

He did the numbers in his head. The math was not negotiable. The bends were no longer a risk, no longer a possibility. Now they were simply inevitable. The only question was how to manage the ascent to make them survivable.

They had maybe twenty minutes of air left in the tanks, maybe thirty. They had at least fifty feet still to ascend. That is, if the dive computer was correct. James sorted through his memories—his research, his training, and the experiences of other divers.

His instinct was to ascend slowly and safely. That was what his training demanded. But the math said no—not gonna make it. The alternative was to rise to a point maybe ten or fifteen feet just below the surface and wait there. At that depth, their air would last much longer, giving them more time to decompress before it ran out. From there, they could safely ascend the last short distance to the surface.

James would have preferred to stick with the advice of the nagging, beeping dive computer, but that wasn't his best option. The water was still receding, draining out of the building around them. Even if they waited here, they were still ascending—or rather, the surface was descending to meet them.

And in addition to everything else, he was starting to feel the cold as a painful presence. He was starting to shiver. That was okay. If he stopped shivering, that would be very not okay. It would mean his body was shutting down. He wasn't worried about that, he knew his tolerances. But what about the others?

He was reaching that point where he really wanted to get out of the water—he wanted to get out *now*. And if he was feeling this way, then it was probably a lot worse for the others. He turned his headlamps toward Julia and her mom, who was holding Julia close to her body, trying to share warmth. In this water, it was a futile effort.

James took his three breaths. He looked across at Hu, who looked back at him hopefully.

It was enough.

Fuck it. We are not going to die today.

He swam from one to the other, Julia, her mom, the boy, and finally Hu, checking once again to make sure that each was all right. Later on, perhaps, he might be able to marvel at their endurance—but right now, they had no choice. Either they hung on, or they became like all those others they had passed below. Like poor Mrs. Hayes.

More breaths. And another flight of stairs. Another and another.

The surface was a lot closer than he realized. The stairwell must be leaking somewhere. Had they closed the door at the bottom? He didn't remember. Or maybe the fire doors weren't all that water-tight. Or maybe there was enough structural damage that the whole building was as secure as a screen door.

The good news, the afternoon light flickered brightly above. He could see rippling light through the water's surface now, a promise of survival, and even though he still swam in a dirty murky world, filled with little floating things, the walls of the stairwell were no longer hidden behind a fog of gloom. But he wasn't ready to feel confident. Not yet. Overconfidence is just another way to die.

They had to wait here as long as possible. James took his three breaths and studied the dive computer. It had finally given up and stopped beeping, but it still insisted that the surface of the water was steadily descending to meet them.

A large rubber trash can drifted by. Was this the fourth or fifth? Why so many? Something else to wonder about. He began to imagine the episode of Nova that would examine these events.

Three breaths. Three breaths. Three more breaths.

He checked the gauges again. He studied the dive computer, blinking. It didn't make sense. No, it made sense. *He* wasn't making sense. It didn't matter what the gauges said, they were running out of air. There was no more time.

Not today. We didn't come all this way to die here.

James fumbled for the plastic slate, felt along the leash for the grease pen, wrote on it frantically. "Drop tanks. Go up. My signal." He turned to the others, holding the slate so that each of them could see the words. He took three quick breaths, then pointed up. Waving his arm in a broad "Let's go, now!" motion.

He didn't have to push them. They were eager to go. They each took a last long suck of air, then dropped the regulators and scrambled up. Hu grabbed Julia by the waist and they half-swam, half-walked up the last flight of stairs. James pushed Julia's mom and the black boy after them. He followed, the pressure in his lungs growing. He should have taken a last breath himself.

He looked back. The tanks were tumbling away. bouncing in slow-motion irretrievably down the stairwell, a lost opportunity. He pushed himself upward.

He couldn't see. His vision was blurry, closing in, he needed one more breath, he couldn't hold it—

The top of the stairwell was open to the sky. The walls were broken here. A twisted doorframe remained where a fire door had been. James struggled to reach for it, he felt himself sinking back—

—and a pair of hands reached down and yanked him roughly out of the water.

A confusion of words, an unfamiliar voice, "Are there any more—?"

"No, no. Just the five of us—" That was Hu. His voice sounded strange, garbled by water. Someone else was choking, a small high voice. Julia?

He couldn't see. Everything was a glare. He was on his back, gasping, choking, coughing up water—how had that happened? His last strangled ascent? Everything here was blue, incongruously bright. Two faces abruptly blocked his view, dark silhouettes, he didn't know them. Where had they come from?

"Don't try to talk. Just concentrate on breathing, okay?"

There were hands all over him, pulling away the last of the rig on his back, pulling his mask away, loosening his shirt. Someone had their head to his chest, trying to listen to his heartbeat. James coughed, choked up more water, and the person pulled away. His lungs hurt badly.

"Hu—?" he called. "Hu?"

"I'm here. I'm okay." A hasty answer.

James concentrated on breathing now. A deep breath. Another. Stop to cough, spit up, cough, then breathe again.

Three deep breaths. Three more. Three more. Don't hyperventilate. Hold your breath a moment and appreciate that you can.

He was almost back when he suddenly remembered an old movie, a favorite. He called out, "Are we dead, mon?"

Hu called back, falsetto. "I'm not dead yet, I'm not."

James laughed. He laughed until he coughed and choked up even more water. His throat hurt, but he laughed anyway. He rolled over on his side and looked across at Hu. His husband was half up on his knees, also laughing.

James flailed, helplessly, trying to sit up. Hands grabbed him from behind, someone helped him to a sitting position. James looked around. They were on a wide empty floor, slightly tilted, very broken. But his vision was still blurry, partly from the glare of the day, partly from the painful tears filling his eyes, an involuntary reaction to the overwhelming dazzle. The whole world looked overexposed, the people here were silhouettes, vague shapes in the glare. Maybe a dozen, he wasn't sure.

Hu scooted over to him, looked at him carefully, then scooted around to sit beside him. He bumped him affectionately with his shoulder. James looked at Hu, a weak grin on his face. Hu looked tired. But alive. Even smiling.

After a moment of silent acceptance, a moment of just surviving, James looked around at their rescuers. "Who are you people? How did you get up here? How did you get through?"

"We should ask you the same question," said one of the men. "I'm Scott Copeland. Who are you?"

"James Liddle. And that's Hu Son. And the little girl is Julia. I don't know her mother's name. Are they all right?"

"They will be, yes. Sophie's looking after them. And the teenager too. Looks like you had a rough ride."

James nodded. "The subway. The last train. Didn't make it."

"Yeah, we heard—" The man pointed. "We've been following the news. The cellphone towers are down, but Jack's Walkman has FM. Three trains were lost."

"Three—?"

"Yeah. Real bad scene at Union Station."

James didn't say anything then, didn't want to say what he was thinking, didn't want to make the fear real. He realized he was weak. Exhausted. He looked around. They were on a sloping tile surface. The stairwell was a square opening with a few broken steps rising out of the water. "Is this the top floor?"

"No. This was the tenth floor. The top three floors were ripped away." Copeland's expression went grim. "That's where most of the people went. I suppose it seemed like a good idea. It was wall-to-wall crowded. Probably exceeded the structural limits. But, see, the top floors of a building are never the strongest. The lower floors are built to hold the weight of the floors above."

"You're a builder—?"

"Architect. I know this building. It's a good one. Well, it was. We started on the seventh floor, that's where our offices were. When the water started rising, we moved up to the eighth, eventually the ninth. Had to stop there. The people above wouldn't let us keep going, said there was no more room." Copeland sighed and shrugged—a gesture of both sadness and grim irony.

"We'd been shredding old blueprints. We had thirty or forty bins of paper we still hadn't emptied. When the water broke the windows and started rising inside the building, we emptied all the biggest trash cans, turned them upside down and stuck our heads in to breathe. It was a gamble, but it worked. Each bin had enough air to last ten minutes, twenty if we were careful. And we had, I dunno, thirty bins. I saved my people. Most of them."

"But you lost a couple..." James glanced toward the broken stairwell, wondering if the bloated cadaver of poor Mrs. Hayes might suddenly bob up in the surface of the trapped water.

Copeland followed his glance. "Yeah. We had some panic. It was pretty bad. We did everything we could." Copeland was reluctant to explain. "What about you? Down in the subway—?"

James remembered the man who'd tried to take Hu's regulator. He could still see the man's startled expression, the sudden horrified realization that he was dying—dying twice, once by drowning, once by knife—and the crushing certainty that this was truly death. James shook his head, he didn't want to talk about it.

Copeland recognized the expression. "Yeah. Bad day all around." He straightened. "Let me see if there's any water left." He disappeared from James' field of view.

James concentrated on his breathing for a while. Open air. There was a delicious luxury. How had he ever taken breathing for granted? Finally, he looked around, searching for Julia and her mother. Spotting then, he crawled over on his hands and knees. He still didn't feel like standing. Julia was clutching her mother, her face buried in her mother's side, her shoulders rising and falling as if she was sobbing.

"Are you okay?"

"I prayed to God, and he sent you to save us."

"Well, I don't know about God, but—"

"No, it was God—"

"Okay. It was God. I'm just glad that you and Julia made it. You must have been scared."

"No. I knew that God sent you. So I wasn't scared. I just kept praying and thanking God for sending you to us."

"Ahh. Well, I guess it worked."

"Yes. And God will bless you for what you did."

"Not gonna argue that—I can use all the blessings I can get. I'm just glad you both made it." James patted her shoulder, patted Julia's shoulder, but the little girl didn't look up. James had seen this behavior before, Julia was going to have nightmares. She was going to have some serious post-traumatic-stress. And she was going to need some serious therapy. Oh, hell—they all would.

He turned away, crawled back to Hu. The unnamed black boy was sitting next to him, sucking at a bottle of water. He passed the water bottle to Hu, the two of them had been talking, sharing, debriefing each other.

Hu looked to James. "This is Jesse. He's a student at LACC."

James held out his hand. "I'm James. I'm glad you made it."

"So am I, man! That was intense! I am never riding that subway again!"

"I don't think anybody will," James agreed.

Jesse waved his arm, indicating the world around them. "How long we gonna be up here, you know?"

James hadn't even considered the question. He put one hand against a fragment of wall. He raised himself half-up onto his knees—

The hot July sun blazed above. The landscape rippled and foamed below. Everything was too bright. It took a moment for James' vision to clear, for his eyes to focus all the way to the horizon. And then it took another moment for him to make sense of what he was seeing—all the devastation that surrounded them.

James levered himself to his feet, holding onto the spur of the broken wall. He turned slowly, slowly, shaking his head, saying only, "Fuck. Oh, fuck. Oh, fuck." And then, even more sadly, "Oh, fuck."

They were alone in the middle of a vast brown sea. The water was receding—slowly. But more water was still trying to push in—uneven ripples of the reverberating shockwaves. Everywhere, the water foamed and surged, churning the debris.

Things tumbled in the water, all kinds of things, broken signs, buses, cars, trees, the inevitable palm fronds, pieces of buildings, roofs and walls—and bodies. Too many bodies.

The sea of desolation extended north, all the way to the Hollywood hills. A few buildings stuck their tops out of the water—but not many. To the west and the south, the view was much the same. There was a rise in the southern distance. Baldwin Hills was now Baldwin Island, probably nothing more than a naked lump. The ferocious power of the waves would have scraped everything away.

The rest was mud.

James saw the past as if it were still the present. The riot at the Santa Monica underpass, the old men at the VA Health center, the carefree golfers, and all the people in all the cars they'd passed, the little boy staring from a car window on Wilshire Blvd...

How many of them had escaped and how many more had been caught in the overwhelming wrath of the tsunami? It was all unknowable, all washed away too quickly to comprehend.

James tried to imagine—something, anything—a future.

He couldn't.

It would take months just to catalog the devastation. The scale of this thing—there was nothing left. Nothing to rebuild. The city was gone.

"Fuck," said James.

It was going to be a long uncomfortable afternoon.

Hu pulled him back down, pulled him next to him. "You okay?"

"No."

Hu didn't respond to that. He waited a bit before saying anything else.

Finally, "You kept your promise."

"I did?"

"You said we weren't going to die today."

"The day's not over."

"Shut up." Hu said it gently, affectionately. He took James' left hand and held it up to admire the gold band on the third finger. He traced it with his own fingers. "But I will say this." He paused.

"What?"

"This is the worst honeymoon I've ever been on—"

"Oh, really? How many others have you had—?

"This is the first."

"Then it's also the *best* honeymoon you've ever been on."

"Yeah, I guess so." Hu leaned his head on James' shoulder. They were silent for a while. Just being together.

"Hey—" said Jesse, interrupting their silence.

"Yeah?"

"You guys are fags, aren't you?"

James hadn't heard that word in years. He was more surprised than offended. "Yeah, I am. I'm not so sure about my husband though. Is that a problem?"

Jesse pointed to James' discarded facemask, as if looking for the lost regulator. "Yeah, man—! I had your—your thing in my mouth. Yuck—" He got up and moved away.

Hu and James looked at each other. Both started laughing.

"What an ungrateful little prick," Hu said. "Why did you save him, anyway?"

James shrugged. "It seemed like a good idea at the time."

⬦⬦⬦⬦⬦⬦⬦⬦⬦⬦⬦⬦⬦⬦⬦⬦

Swarms of helicopters filled the air over the seething brown water that used to be Los Angeles. They were clattering dragonflies, darting here and there, exploring, recording, reporting. The afternoon was bright, but ugly.

Some of the newer buildings, the ones designed to resist a massive earthquake, had survived. They stuck up out of the water like broken stumps.

Where there had been neighborhoods, there was now only mud and water and debris, occasionally patterned by the gridwork of streets that had survived. Mostly the terrain below was a vast sea of desolation. What remained of the 405 was a scar. The Federal building looked like a fractured tooth. The Veterans' Health Care Center was gone, only a broken steel outline remained to mark its location.

Nevertheless, the choppers swarmed, relentlessly searching—and occasionally, improbably, also triumphantly rescuing. Here and there, despite impossible odds, some people had survived the onslaught of the tsunami. Soon or eventually, whenever they could get to safety, they would have the opportunity to tell their stories to the hungry cameras. Every survival was an improbable adventure—a delusion of luck and prayer, sometimes even a bit of good judgment and courage.

Several Air Force communications planes circled patiently overhead, coordinating the fleets of choppers. The Army, the Navy, the Air Force, the Coast Guard, and several civilian companies were patrolling, each in their assigned area. All other air traffic was forbidden. Even the news choppers were under military guidance now. The Goodyear and Fuji blimps as well.

Three Navy choppers were assigned to an area formerly known as Little Korea. There were few landmarks left on the ground, they had to depend on GPS mapping to locate themselves.

"There—" said the co-pilot. "Two O'clock."

"What am I looking for?"

"Over there. It's a light, hard to see in the glare—"

The chopper pilot brought the machine around. "That green stump sticking out of the water—?"

"Yeah? See that flicker?"

"I see it." As they approached, the pilot said, "Holy shit. That used to be the Wiltern!"

"You recognize it?"

"My grandmother used to live in this area." He added, "Actually, it's the Pellissier building, but everyone calls it the Wiltern."

They came in lower for a closer view. The tsunami had ripped the top off the building. But it had left enough for several stories to remain sticking up out of the water. Open floor space was visible, enough for several people to gather. One was waving a light of some kind.

The co-pilot called to the divers in the back of the machine. "We've got survivors. More than a dozen."

"Any injuries?"

"Maybe. Some of them are down."

"We'll take the worst. Blue Team can pick up the rest."

"Copy that."

The chopper came in low and the people on the top of the building stood up to wave at them. One of them was aiming the headlamps of a diver's mask. He switched it off as the aircraft approached.

The heli hovered over the building, stirring up the waves in great rippling circles. Four lines dropped from the machine. Two figures in wetsuits came down two of the lines, two rescue stretchers came down the others.

"Who's the worst injured?" asked Seal Team Commander Wright.

The survivors looked around, uncertain, but a young Chinese man pointed. "Take the little girl. She's got hypothermia and maybe the bends."

"The bends?"

"Long story," said the man next to him. "And her mom too."

The other Seal was already pulling the rescue stretchers over to Julia and her mother. "Anyone else with the bends?" asked Wright.

The Chinese man pointed to an African-American teenager, held his own hand up, then pointed to the man next to himself, who tried to wave them away. "I'm okay—" But his hand trembled.

"Bullshit, you are." Commander Wright peered from one to the other. He spoke to his microphone. "Gonna need two more stretchers. No, make it three." He turned to the other survivors. "We've got another bird coming in behind us. We'll have you all out of here as quickly as we can." Back to the microphone. "We'll need water and blankets. And maybe some protein."

The first two stretchers lifted away, one after the other, Julia and her mother wrapped in heating blankets. Three more stretchers, all tied together, hanging in a cluster, came down another line—and another Seal Team member as well.

When they came for James, dragging a rescue stretcher with them, he shook his head. "No," he said, pointing. "Hu Son first."

"What?" asked Wright?"

"He's on second," said James. But they were already wrapping him, lifting him into the stretcher, fastening the Velcro straps.

As they secured Hu into his own rescue stretcher, he looked over to James a bemused expression on his face. "I can't believe you just said that."

James said, "It's been a long day—" and passed out.

Wright signaled the chopper, the first stretcher with James lifted away. A moment later, Hu followed. Then Jesse. Wright followed them up, leaving two Seals behind with the remaining survivors. Even as they clattered away, the second chopper was moving in for the pickup.

"Where we taking them?" Wright asked.

"Wait a minute—" Co-pilot called back. He was talking to someone on one of the communication planes. "Getty isn't taking anymore. And Dodger Stadium is full. The parking lot is tent city now." Abruptly, he paused, listening. "Okay, Copy that." To the pilot, he said. "Griffith Observatory."

Pilot nodded. The co-pilot turned back Wright. "Did you hear that? Griffith Observatory. They've got an aid station there—and they're running shuttles down into Burbank. They want to shorten our turnaround time." Turning back to the pilot, he added, "They're bringing a fuel truck up too."

Pilot nodded, his only acknowledgment.

The Hollywood Hills were directly ahead. But below them, muddy water still churned across the flooded city.

The center of Los Angeles was gone —and so was its heart.

∞∞∞∞∞∞∞∞∞∞∞

Griffith Observatory stands on one of the highest hills on the southern edge of the basin. It overlooks the entire city. It is a familiar landmark for both tourists and filmmakers.

Today, its wide lawn and parking lot served as a rescue station, a place for helicopters to bring survivors and refuel, a place for ambulances and buses to take survivors down the northern side of the hills to Burbank and North Hollywood, and other places safely beyond the reach of the churning ocean.

James and Hu stood at a western railing, one of the better viewing positions, and looked out over what was now called The Bay of LA. Or Bayla for short. On the hills to their right, the Hollywood sign survived untouched. It still declared the fabled town, but of Hollywood there was nothing left. Only a sea of mud. Already a smell of wet decay was rising from below. Despite the lingering heat of the day, they were both wrapped in blankets.

They held hands, but neither had anything to say. Despite their mutual joint pains, their headaches, and their blotchy patches of red skin, they had not been considered at severe risk. They'd been given oxygen, it had helped, but Julia's condition was much more serious, so was her mother's, so they were taken for immediate treatment. James and Hu would have to wait awhile for further attention. If at all.

"Triage," someone had explained, not understanding why Hu and James had exchanged a look.

But it was obvious now. Sooner or later, everybody is triage.

They both hurt all over. Hu had thought to dump the contents of their medicine cabinet into his backpack. They had Ibuprofen and it helped—a little. Just not enough. They were going to have to walk this off and wait it out.

The wide lawns in front of the observatory were filled with tents, tables, and bustling emergency workers. The parking lot in front of that was filled with more tents and more crowds of people. The only open area was a space set aside for helicopters to land and take off. A fuel truck waited nearby. Several television vans were parked on the grass.

A Red Cross tent had been set up where people could get coffee and donuts and even some packaged meals, but despite their growing hunger, neither James nor Hu felt like eating. They were still too uncomfortable.

A young black woman came up to them, carrying a tablet. Her badge identified her as some kind of city official, James couldn't read it. He was still having trouble seeing clearly.

"Have you been logged in?" she asked, holding up the tablet.

James shook his head.

"We're trying to assemble a roster of survivors. You were in the Wiltern building?"

"No. We were in the subway. We came up the fire stairs of the Wiltern building—"

She looked puzzled. "How did you do that?"

"SCUBA," said James. He was still holding his facemask. He held it up as if that was the only explanation he needed.

"Um, okay," she said, not quite sure what he meant, but it didn't matter anyway. "Your names?"

"James Liddle. Hu Son."

The young woman was wearing a headset, she repeated their answers to her headset, checking that the tablet properly translated her speech to text.

"Address?"

"Nowhere," said James.

"Venice Beach," said Hu. He told her their address, but it was meaningless now.

The woman asked a few more questions: Email addresses, cellphone numbers, Social Security numbers, birth dates, and preferred gender identification. Finally, "We're going to try to find you a place to stay. I can't promise that you'll be together—"

James held up Hu's hand in his own. "He's my husband. We stay together."

She didn't blink. She referred to her tablet. Apparently it was connected to some master database somewhere. She looked up. "Do you have any documentation?"

James held up his left hand, showing the ring. "Is this good enough?"

"Um, I'm sorry. No. We've had people trying to lie to us."

"Does it matter?"

"Yes, it does." She looked annoyed. "The relief benefits are different for married couples—"

Hu interrupted. He was already fumbling in his backpack, pulling out a dry bag. "Does a marriage license count?" He had a sheaf of papers, all safe inside three concentric Zip-Lok bags. He sorted through the papers, passed one over.

She took it, looked at it, shook her head, and passed it back. "It's not signed—"

"We were supposed to get married today. We would have been on our way to—to our honeymoon."

James said, "Is there a judge up here? Or a minister? Someone who can sign this?"

"Uh—" She looked confused. "Let me check." She walked away, already pulling her phone out of her pocket.

Hu said, "Well, that's—"

"— fucked." finished James.

It was all too much.

James turned away, leaned on the stone railing, not wanting to look at anyone or anything anymore. But there it was—the muddy sea of Bayla and its broken towers. He tried hard not to give in to his rage. But—it was all too much. Everything was gone. Everything. He had nothing. No words. No feeling. He was numb.

He had the clothes on his back, whatever was still attached to his tool belt, a diving watch that had stopped, an expensive dive computer he never wanted to see again, a half-empty backpack, and for some reason, he was still holding onto his facemask, afraid to be let it go, even up here.

And Hu.

He still had Hu.

But ... he had nothing else. Nothing left to give. Nothing for Hu. Nothing for anyone. He was empty. Scraped raw. Numb.

He had finally hit bottom.

Hu stood next to him, silent. He put his hand on James' shoulder, but James didn't react, didn't even acknowledge the touch. Finally, Hu reached out to take the facemask from him, but James pulled it back.

"Jimmy—? Talk to me. Please?"

James didn't respond. He looked at the mask—as if seeing it for the first time, an ugly reminder of everything he would never see again. It was a useless appendage. He might as well throw it away and have nothing left at all. Without thinking, he lifted his arm, poised to throw it over the edge of the railing and down to the rough hillside below.

But Hu grabbed his wrist and stopped him—

"Jimmy, no—"

As if startled awake, James looked to Hu. "What—?"

Hu took the mask, turned it around and held it up to show something to James. "Did you know your camera was on?"

"It's automatic," James said. He took the facemask from Hu. A pair of fisheye lenses were mounted above the glass, one on each side of the two headlamps—they were designed for capturing virtual-reality 3D video. James frowned at the readout on the left side of mask. "Hmp," he said. "Looks like it recorded everything from the moment the water hit—"

"Really?"

"I'd have to pull the card, but yeah—"

Hu cut him off. "Jimmy, maybe we could sell that footage to someone? Some news channel? Or maybe even Nova? Someone? It might be worth something—"

James shook his head. "I doubt it. Everybody will have footage. Every survivor with a phone. And probably a few thousand amateur drones as well. There's going to be more video than anybody will have time to review."

"But nobody has underwater footage of the subway—"

James stopped in mid-sentence. Hu was right. He started to agree, then stopped abruptly. "No. We can't."

"Huh? Why not?"

James put his hand to his belt, touched his knife.

Hu's eyes followed. "Oh," he said, realizing what James meant.

"Squeak—I killed a man—"

"It was self-defense—"

"No. It wasn't. It was deliberate—"

"We could talk to a lawyer—"

"Christine retired, remember the party—"

"She could recommend someone. Maybe Suzanne? Or Cindy?"

James didn't answer immediately. "Yeah, maybe. But—"

"But—?"

"But that's not the point."

"What is?"

"I killed a man, Hu. That's murder. I committed a murder—"

"Jimmy—"

"And I did it without thinking. I did it so easy—"

"You didn't have a choice. You did it to save me—"

"—and I'd do it again. In a heartbeat. But—"

Hu understood it—James was in pain. A lot of pain, and most of it wasn't physical. Hu wanted to say something, but he didn't know what. "Bubble—?"

"I don't know who he was. I don't want to know. What if he had a family? People waiting for him? Oh, God. What if they recover his body someday. They'll see his throat. And someone will figure it out—"

"Jimmy! Stop it. Look out there. Look at that mess—nobody's going to recover anything."

"Squeak, you stop it! I know what I did! I have to live with it."

Hu put his hand on James' arm. "Bubble—listen to me. What we went through—it was horrible. It was all my worst fears, everything, all at once—but I made it because you were there—you. Just like the first time."

James started to protest, but Hu grabbed him by both shoulders and poured out the rest of his words in a frantic rush. "Out of all the millions of people who died today—God knows how many, but we survived, you and I—and Julia and her mother, and that little prick, Jesse too. We survived because survival is what you do. It's who you are."

"Who I am—?" James couldn't stand it. "I know who I am now. I don't want to be who I am—I couldn't save him! I had to—had to—"

"No, listen! Listen to me—as much as I hate to say this, because it's so fucking cruel and selfish to even think this way, but it's still true anyway—that man was already dead when he boarded the subway. Every single one of them. We all were. We just didn't know it. And if you and I had left the bike trailers behind, if we'd abandoned the tanks when we thought they were too heavy, we'd be dead too. All five of us. And your last thoughts would have been rage at yourself for listening to my whining—this is better! Isn't it?"

But James was adamant in his pain. "I know what you're trying to do, Squeak. And I love you for it. But—I know what I did—and it hurts me so much inside to know that I did it—that I'm even capable of it. This hurts like you can't imagine—"

"Excuse me, guys—?" An interruption. A voice from behind them. They turned to see Seal Team Commander Wright. He was holding Jesse by the upper arm. "You the guys from the subway?"

"Yeah?"

Wright let go of Jesse, but not before saying to him. "Stay." Then he held out his hand to James. "I heard what you did down there, heard it from the kid. It must have been rough, but I wanted you to know, it's one of the best things I've heard today. I mean, you done good." Wright shook James' hand, then Hu's. He nodded back toward the chopper. "We're refueling, going back out in thirty, but I wanted to make sure you were good. And uh, the kid here has something to say to you too." He poked Jesse. "Go ahead, mister."

Jesse looked embarrassed. He swallowed hard and looked at his feet. When he looked up, his eyes were wet. "I'm sorry for what I said. I don't know why I said it. It just fell out. But I wouldn't have made it if it wasn't for you guys. So ... um, I guess, I want to say thank you, I owe you my life, and I hope you'll forgive me for being such a dick."

Hu's smile came easier than James'. He said, "It's okay."

"No, it's not. I mean, why'd you do it? You didn't have to. I mean, I saw what you did to that other guy and   "

James interrupted quickly, "You said please."

"Huh? That's it?"

"Yeah, that was it."

"Whoa," said Jesse. "Whoa."

"Yeah, whoa."

Jesse looked confused. "I don't get it."

James smiled sourly. "Neither do I, kid. Neither do I."

Wright had watched the whole exchange. He spoke up now. "There's nothing to get. You did what was in front of you." To Jesse, he said, "He gave you a second chance. Now you gotta make the most of it. Make a difference." He pushed the teen gently.

Jesse held out his hand. James took it, shook it. So did Hu.

"We're good then?"

James and Hu nodded. Wright seemed satisfied. He lifted his hand in a salute of respect, and headed back to his chopper.

Jesse stood there, still looking embarrassed, shifting from one foot to the other. Finally, he gave a nervous smile. "I'm gonna go get in line for the phone. Okay? Gotta call my gramma and let her know I made it. I hope you guys land on your feet." And then he was gone too.

"Well," said Hu. "That was something."

"Yeah," agreed James. "He said please."

But he was still in a funk so deep it was no longer blue, it had gone to indigo. He turned back to the railing and stared across at the Hollywood sign without really seeing it.

"Excuse me—?" Another interruption.

This time it was a man in a clerical collar. He looked like some casting director's idea of the perfect priest—but one who is falsely accused of molesting little boys until exonerated in the third act denouement. "Are you the ones looking for a minister? I'm Father Feigenberg—"

"*Father* Feigenberg? Really? You're kidding me."

"I get that a lot, yes. Someone said you needed a priest." He looked at them with puzzled curiosity. "Do you want me to pray with you?"

James and Hu looked at each other, then back to Father Feigenberg. Hu spoke first. "We need you to make us legal. We want you to say some nice words and then sign this—" He passed over the marriage license.

Father Feigenberg looked at their marriage license, looked from one to the other, back to the license, then back to the two of them again. "Um, I'm afraid I can't—my faith doesn't recognize same-sex unions."

"Oh, hell!" said James, frustrated. It was just too much. He said it loud enough that a few nearby people turned around to look. James turned angrily to the railing, glowered out at the landscape of mud and desolation and everything buried under it—then, just as abruptly, he whirled back. "Father? Will you hear my confession?"

Hu's eyes widened. "I didn't know you were Catholic—"

"Recovering," admitted James. "Father—?"

Father Feigenberg nodded. He led James a short distance away, to the best privacy they could find—a quiet space behind a pedestal with a bronze bust of James Dean. It had been installed as a commemoration of the famous observatory scenes in Rebel Without A Cause.

Hu watched from a distance as both James and the priest knelt together. First James crossed himself, then bent his head to whisper to Father Feigenberg's ear. He took a long time, and halfway through, the priest reached over to put his hand on James' shoulder, a gesture of solidarity and comfort. James kept talking—and then a little after that, he started weeping. Father Feigenberg pulled him close and let him cry into his shoulder.

Finally, James pulled back and Father Feigenberg made the sign of the cross over him, and said some words in Latin, some words that James so desperately needed to hear. His whole body relaxed. And even from a distance, Hu could see that James' pain had been lessened. Not released, not yet—but lessened. It was a start.

Finally, after a few more minutes, Father Feigenberg led James back to Hu—the two shared a look.

"Are you all right?"

"A little better. Yeah."

Feigenberg looked from one to the other. He hadn't met many same-sex couples, a side-effect of his particular calling. But he felt there was something else he needed to say before this moment could be considered complete.

"The two of you—" He looked from James to Hu and back again. "You didn't get here by accident. You got here because...yes, I know it sounds presumptuous, and you don't have to believe me, but I'm certain that the two of you are here because you're supposed to be here. Together."

That last word from Father Feigenberg surprised both James and Hu. It wasn't the word so much as the man saying it.

Hu managed to speak first. "Thank you."

Feigenberg nodded an acknowledgment. "So how long have you two been together?"

"Three years."

Feigenberg was impressed. "Mm-hm. That's a commitment, isn't it?"

"Commitment, hell," said James. "It's a privilege." He put his arm around Hu's shoulder and pulled him close. "He's the one."

"Yep," agreed Hu, smiling. "Today was gonna be the day." He held up his hand to show his ring.

James held up his hand to show a matching ring. "We made a promise. Hell or high water, we're saying our vows today. It was high water. Really high water. So we said 'em. In the subway. Just before the water hit."

Hu said, "It was really romantic. And terrifying too. I spent the whole day afraid I was going to lose him—"

Feigenberg nodded gently. It seemed a polite acknowledgment, but then he said, "Listen to me. As a priest ordained in the Catholic church, I cannot formally bless your union in the eyes of God. But...as a legally established authority in the state of California, empowered to recognize the union of two consenting adults—" He paused to clear his throat. "—I now pronounce you...married. Congratulations. Mazel Tov. Now, let me sign your document." He held out his hand for the marriage license.

And now it was Hu's turn to cry—but this time for joy.

BURNING BLUE

My knee hurt worse than usual, but there was nothing to eat and my son wouldn't be here until Saturday, so I had to go out. My cane was by the door in its usual place. I don't like to use the cane, it makes me look old, but I don't like falling down a lot more than I don't like looking old. Besides, I am old.

I pulled a sweater on, I fumbled with my coat. That should be enough. The day would warm up as soon as the sun was high enough. If there had been frost on the lawn, it was gone by the time I was up and stumbling around.

I get by. I suppose I'm lucky. Not everybody survives this long. People ask me how I did it, as if there's some secret they're desperate to know. I just shrug and say, "I forgot to die." If there's a secret, nobody told me. I get out of bed in the morning and that's about it.

Outside, the sidewalk was covered with drifts of dirty brown leaves. The wind had been busy overnight and the air still had a crisp bite to it. The day burned white in the morning, it would burn blue in the afternoon and orange in the evening. At night it would smolder with pinpoints until it burned again.

I hadn't yet decided where to go. Used to be, I would have breakfast at the local diner, around the corner half a block away. It had been owned by the same family for nearly a hundred years, passed through three generations, but the great-grand-children decided they wanted something else and last year they sold the place to new people. The new people were friendly enough but they changed the menu and nudged the prices upward. It wasn't the same. I missed my friends.

I trudged past it, heading toward the main street of what some of us used to call "the village." Now it was just another neighborhood in the sprawl, not even big enough to call a suburb. I could have coffee and something at the little place next to the supermarket. I could pick up some bread and cheese for lunch, and a small meat loaf for dinner. I'd have enough leftovers for tomorrow's lunch. Maybe a little bag of salad and a small piece of chocolate cake too, but no more than that. Not too much to carry.

I wasn't hungry yet. It takes me a while to get my body awake. I need to walk for a while. Today maybe I could walk off the pain in my knee. Sometimes it helps, sometimes it makes the pain worse, especially in the cold weather. But I had the cane and if I took my time and paced myself, and if I stopped to browse in some of the old stores, the ones that hadn't closed or been bought out, I'd probably be all right. I had to get out of the house a little bit every day.

Half of main street had been replaced by strip malls and lookalike franchises. I tried not to shop at them but sometimes I had no choice, like the pharmacy, and that was only because Nathan's Drugs had finally closed. The people who worked in the big place were strangers, they didn't know me and they didn't care about me. They couldn't have been more sour if they had been chained to iron bars under the counter. Maybe they were, I never looked.

But down the side streets there were still a few remnants of the old town, scattered fragments of the past. Like me, they were too stubborn to die. There was the Lavanderia for those who couldn't afford washers and dryers, the do-it-yourself car wash so you could use up the quarters you'd stashed in the ash tray, the little office of real estate managers, the cluttered office supply place next to it where you could get copies made and notarized, and passport photos too. The shuttered veterinarian as well, the reason I couldn't have a cat anymore, the new vet was too far away.

But Terry's Used Books was still there. I should stop in. I hadn't visited in a while. Maybe I could pick up an Agatha Christie or an old Heinlein. I'd certainly browse through the shelves of used CDs and DVDs. Maybe I could find a symphony or a movie for tonight.

Terry's wife, Alice still hobbled around in the dust of literature. The children in the neighborhood liked to say she was a witch, that she had a big oven in the back of the store, and that whenever anyone's cat went missing, she was making stew.

When Terry died, Alice sold the house they'd lived in and turned the back of the store into a little apartment where she puttered around, making salves and oils, ointments and potions for her various ailments, real and imagined. Gassy? Take this. Dry skin? Rub this on your elbows. Unhappy? Have some tea.

Alice didn't sell her tinctures, she was strict that way, she'd only give them away. She said they only had power if they were gifts. Money tainted magic. That was her conviction. But she wouldn't object if you bought a book. She always had interesting suggestions.

She smiled when I came in. "I knew I would have a visitor today, I had a sensing. I'm glad it's you. Come, sit. I made tea. I'll give you a reading."

"Oh no, it's all right, I'm good—"

"No, you're not. Sit down."

Ordinarily, Alice's readings were mostly an excuse to sit and drink tea. Some people believed her readings were magic, but they were the kind of people who believed in magic. I didn't know if I believed or not. The tea was good and Alice always had good stories. Sometimes her stories were about people we both knew, sometimes about people neither of us knew, but the stories were always interesting, funny or tragic or romantic.

She peered at me. "You haven't eaten yet today. And you didn't eat much yesterday. Are you taking care of yourself?"

"I'm still standing," I said.

"So is the oak tree in front of the high school and it's been dead for three years."

"I thought they were going to take it down."

"They're still arguing. It'll fall down before they ever make a decision." She led me to the back of the store where she had a scattering of comfortable chairs circling a small round table, what passed for her living room these days. "Sit." She pointed.

I sat. The chair crackled. Or maybe it was just me crackling. Or both of us.

In past years, visitors could sit quietly here, leafing through books they couldn't afford to buy. I'd spent more than a few hours here myself, but that custom had evaporated like so many other things. People read off screens now, everything they wanted. Those luxurious old books, only collectors might want them now, but there weren't that many collectors anymore. The store was usually deserted now.

Alice had installed an overwrought iron stand next to her chair. That's where she had her tea kettle steaming on an electric hot plate. She took it now and began pouring tea. "I don't mind the quiet," she said, as if she had been reading my mind. "I miss people, I miss the conversations. We'd talk about our favorite books, the old ones and the new. Every book was an adventure, remember? But..." She sighed. "People today ... so many of them seem so anxious and stressed. They're so unhappy. Especially the ones with small children. Maybe it's just me, but I remember when we used to teach the little ones better. 'Touch with your eyes, dear, not with your fingers.' Nobody does that anymore. And you can't say anything. They give you that angry look, you know. I'm sorry, I shouldn't rant. But do you know how hard it is to clean grape jelly off an old leather binding? Not that hard, actually, not the leather, but the pages get ruined. Terry knew how to charm the children so they'd just stand and stare at him, so amazed they forgot where they were. How's the tea?"

That was her way of prompting me. I hadn't tasted it yet.

I leaned my cane against the chair and took up the cup in both hands. My trembling wasn't bad this morning, not as noticeable. I sniffed the tea carefully. "What is this. I don't recognize it."

"My own little blend. A little of this, a little of that. Try it."

I took a small sip. The tea was hot, but not uncomfortable. Another sip. I frowned. "It tastes like wine. How did you do that?"

"Magic," she said.

"Yes, that's you say whenever you don't want to explain anything. Magic."

"Magic is explanation enough, isn't it? Give me your hands. I'll give you a reading." I put the cup down and placed both my hands on the table. She put her own cup down, reached across and took my hands in hers. She turned them face up and studied my palms. "Ah ha!" she said.

"What?"

"You're still using the same soap. I can smell it."

"My son brings it."

"I'm not criticizing. It gets you clean." She squinted, frowned, and bent her head to her study the lines and creases of age. "Well," she said. "I guess that's it."

"What is."

"You're still alive." She let go of my hands. She picked up her cup and slurped noisily.

"Uh-huh. What is it you're not saying?"

"Oh, please. You and I both know it's just a game. I tell people what they want to hear, they're amused. They leave happy. They have something to talk about. Sometimes they come back. Sometimes they bring friends. And sometimes they buy something. I don't care. It's something to do. I know, I could sell this place, but then what? Where would I go? And who wants a dusty old store on a side street anyway? Except maybe some of those people selling medical marijuana now. But they're all in the strip malls now, so they don't need an out-of-the-way location, do they? But this is perfect for me. Look around. I have all these books, more than enough for a hundred lifetimes. I have music, so much music—most of it is crap, but I have Mahler and Mozart and Bruckner and Brahms. And tea, I have my wonderful tea. Do you like it? It's my own special blend. I can sit and sip. I can read without interruption, because nobody visits anymore. I have all my hours to myself. One day, they'll find my body sitting in this old chair, a book in my lap, a smile on my face. That's how it's going to be. Because I say so." She busied herself with the tea kettle, refilling her cup. "Do you want some more?"

I pushed my cup forward, mostly out of politeness. She poured, then put the kettle back on the hot plate. The fragrance of the tea had changed. It smelled deeper now. It tasted darker too, because it had been brewing longer. I put my cup down on the saucer.

"Yes, it's all a game," I said. "Unless you believe in it. And sometimes, even if you don't. Sometimes you say things, Alice, like you know more than you're saying."

She shook her head, mildly annoyed. She pushed the words away with a quick wave of her hand.

"See? That. right there. There's something you don't want to say."

Alice frowned at me. "You're old. You live alone. And your knee hurts. There. Now you're happy?"

"I already knew that."

"We're all old and alone," she said. She sipped at her tea, as if hiding behind her cup. But no, she wasn't hiding. She lowered it and looked across at me. "It's how life works. You get born, you live, you die. If you live too long, you get old and things fall apart. Then you die. So what?"

"You say that like it's not a bad thing."

"It's neither good nor bad. It just is. It's what you do with life that's good or bad."

I had a lump in my throat. It wasn't hunger. It wasn't anger either. "Well, it still feels bad," I admitted. "It hurts."

"Of course, it hurts. That's how you know you're alive. If it stops hurting, you're dying."

"Well, if pain is the only the measure of life, then I'm—"

"No. It isn't." She cut me off. "You have a son. How often does he visit you? Twice a week? Three times? He brings you groceries. Sometimes he takes you out to dinner. On most Tuesdays, he takes you to the movies. He takes time off to drive you to the doctor. And when his kids come home from college, don't they always visit and help you with things? Your granddaughter bakes cookies for you and helps you with your laundry. So please, don't tell me you're alone. You're not alone. You have things to be happy about. Happiness is the other measure of life."

"And you saw all that in my hands?"

She made a face. "I don't need to look at your hands. They're clean. You have a life."

"Don't you?" I looked around. "You have the store. You own the building. You have money to live on. You have your health. You have your books and your music—"

She cut me off. "That right. I have no complaints. No complaints at all. I have nothing to complain about, do I?"

I didn't answer.

"Do you know what I have here? Silence. Look around. It's peaceful, right? It's peaceful because it's empty. There's no one. I can live with that. If I need people, I can open the door and then what? Where do I go? Who do I talk to? Do you know what's out there? A world of more silence—a different kind of silence. Silence of the soul. No, I don't want to go out. It's not good. Everywhere I go, it's unhappy. Everybody's lost inside their screens, texting across the world to someone else who's also lost inside their screen. And when they do look up, it's like they've been poked awake, annoyed at being interrupted. I can understand that. Okay, they're busy, everybody's busy, so busy everywhere, too busy to be real. Too busy to be kind. But I'm here, right here. Don't people deserve even a pretense of courtesy? I smile at people. I say please and thank you and have a nice day. Do you know what I get in return? I get their annoyance. Like I'm an idiot. Out there, outside, it's not good. It's like the whole world is sick and tired and empty. Like there aren't any souls anymore. That's what it feels like and—and I'm tired of pretending that this is normal. So I stay here because at least in here I be away from all that. I can sit with a book and a symphony, I can drink tea until I have to pee. And I don't have to deal with all that crap out there. That's my life. Terry's gone. The village is gone. And I haven't heard a kind word from anybody in so long I can't remember. And do you know what's the worst of all? I haven't been hugged since the funeral—" She stopped abruptly. "Never mind," she said.

Maybe it was the tea. Maybe it was just me. But I was feeling warm inside. I reached for my cane, decided I didn't need it, braced one hand on the table and stood up. I crossed to her and pulled her carefully to her feet.

And held her.

For the longest time.

Until she stopped trembling.

Until she relaxed and finally hugged back.

Until the warmth filled both of us.

And then we just stood there.

For the longest time.

Until she finally said, "I really do have to pee."

When she came back, I was sitting again. She sat down opposite me. "So," she began. "Your hands. I see good things for you. Your son is coming to surprise you tonight. It's the anniversary of his adoption. You thought he forgot. He didn't." She hesitated. "Oh, maybe I shouldn't tell you this part—"

"No, go ahead."

"There's a new dog at the shelter."

Before I could protest, Alice said, "She just became available this morning. She's a senior dog. Her owner died and she has no one. She's confused and afraid. The adoption fees are already paid for, so she's free to a loving home."

"I haven't had a dog since—"

"Yes, I know. You should go meet her. You're not doing anything else today. Go take a look."

"Okay, I will."

"You're not just saying that?"

"I'll go. I promise."

"All right." She looked satisfied.

I finished my tea. I reached for my cane. When I stood up, my knee wasn't hurting anymore.

Outside, the world had gotten brighter. A young couple came walking by, holding hands. They smiled and waved at me. "Have a wonderful day," they said.

I smiled back. "Yes, you too."

Some people say Alice is a witch. Maybe she is, maybe she isn't.

I don't know.

But I do know this.

Not all magic requires spells or potions.

CPSIA information can be obtained
at www.ICGtesting.com
Printed in the USA
BVHW051358260522
638205BV00017B/499

9 781958 482011